Also available from Allie Therin and Carina Press

Magic in Manhattan

Spellbound
Starcrossed
Wonderstruck

Roaring Twenties Magic

Proper Scoundrels
Once a Rogue
Viscounts & Villainy

Sugar & Vice

Liar City
Twisted Shadows

VISCOUNTS & VILLAINY

ALLIE THERIN

carina press

If you purchased this book without a cover you should be aware that this book is stolen property. It was reported as "unsold and destroyed" to the publisher, and neither the author nor the publisher has received any payment for this "stripped book."

Recycling programs for this product may not exist in your area.

ISBN-13: 978-1-335-47792-7

Viscounts & Villainy

Copyright © 2025 by Allie Therin

All rights reserved. No part of this book may be used or reproduced in any manner whatsoever without written permission.

Without limiting the author's and publisher's exclusive rights, any unauthorized use of this publication to train generative artificial intelligence (AI) technologies is expressly prohibited.

This is a work of fiction. Names, characters, places and incidents are either the product of the author's imagination or are used fictitiously. Any resemblance to actual persons, living or dead, businesses, companies, events or locales is entirely coincidental.

For questions and comments about the quality of this book, please contact us at CustomerService@Harlequin.com.

® is a trademark of Harlequin Enterprises ULC.

Carina Press
22 Adelaide St. West, 41st Floor
Toronto, Ontario M5H 4E3, Canada
www.Harlequin.com

Printed in U.S.A.

For those who inspire hope,
especially when it's hard to find

Chapter One

November 1925
New York

Angels were far more aggravating than devils.

Wesley stood at the curb, arms folded, as he watched Sebastian's taxi finally make its way down Broadway. It was raining, the kind that bordered on frozen and fell in freezing, stinging droplets on one's neck. Around him, the industrial neighborhood was stained with soot, the pedestrians loud, and it smelled like car exhaust and stale sweat had been layered onto the buildings like another coat of paint.

He waited impatiently as Sebastian paid his fare and finally stepped out of the cab to join him.

"You do realize," Wesley said, as the taxi pulled back into the thick traffic, "that if someone had told me two months ago that in my own near future, I would willingly traverse the icy pavement in Yonkers to rendezvous with Arthur's angry infant simply because Miss Robbins had requested it, I would have had them committed."

"Hello to you too." Sebastian was adjusting his thick plaid scarf, which matched his brown coat and wool cap. The cold November evening was aggressively gray, from the concrete to the clouds to the patch of filthy snow persisting on a square of dead grass. Sebastian's warm olive skin, brown waves, and gold-brown eyes shone bright as a new penny in a handful of dingy nickels, and if Wesley was thinking of nickels, then he'd been in America too damn long. "And Rory is not an *infant*. He's twenty-one."

"The only person who thinks twenty-one is grown is a twenty-seven-year-old who's gotten too big for his breeches," Wesley said, as they fell into step together, heading toward the river. "The actual adults like myself know better than to trust children playing at being grown-ups."

"You are only thirty-two—"

"Nearly thirty-three—"

"Still thirty-two," Sebastian interrupted. "And Rory might be twenty-one, but he's brave and tough and you admire him for it."

You're just being an arsehole because you haven't had a smoke in three days and you're climbing the walls. Sebastian, of course, was far too kind to say something like that out loud. But Wesley knew who he was.

Even now, his hand wanted to stray toward his jacket, where he still kept a pack of cheap cigarettes in his pocket. He forced it to stay at his side. "Regardless of what I think of Brodigan's relative maturity, or lack thereof, the actual issue here is that an English viscount is somehow *bootlegging*. In *Yonkers*."

"Yonkers is nice." Sebastian gestured around them. "I can hear the river, and see a lady walking a cute dog, and smell a bakery."

Bloody typical. Where Wesley went looking for

thorns, Sebastian gave his attention to the roses. "But we're not here for bakeries, are we?"

"Rory can see the history of the liquor, but he needs someone to keep watch while he scries," Sebastian said, as they crossed the street. "Arthur is with his family, and Zhang is with Jade at the hospital with Alasdair."

Alasdair Findlay, a paranormal who had previously been able to hear magic and had nearly murdered a mansion of New York's elite at a Halloween masquerade. October had been an entire mess, discovering Wesley's own former commanding officer and a baronet he knew from London had been involved in a plot attempting to get rid of magic. Now Major Langford and Sir Ellery were both dead, and Alasdair had been unconscious in a mental hospital since then.

"Surely the time someone needed to deal with Alasdair was three weeks ago?" Wesley said. "When he helped kidnap all of us and was willing to murder his way through an entire party to unlock the pomander relic."

"Yes, but we think he might not have any magic anymore," Sebastian said.

It hung between them for just a hair longer than it should have, because the reason Alasdair no longer had magic was because *Sebastian* no longer had magic—because Alasdair had been swept along with it when Sebastian had sacrificed every bit of magic he had to destroy the pomander relic that would have killed Wesley.

Sebastian had said many times now that he believed his magic was never coming back. He had one of the softest hearts Wesley had ever encountered, able to somehow still see roses in a world full of thorns, but he never seemed to have any of that optimism for himself. The Wesley of a few months ago would have agreed that was a sensible choice, because that Wesley had believed that hope and faith were for the naïve.

But the Wesley of months ago hadn't known that magic existed—and, more importantly, hadn't known that a person like Sebastian existed. And now, it was Wesley's cynical, jaded heart of stone that couldn't seem to shake the feeling that Sebastian's magic was still with them.

But Sebastian didn't mention himself now, already soldiering on. "You and Jade both believe that Alasdair and the others did not mastermind a plot to destroy magic by themselves. The mental hospital called this morning and said someone needed to come urgently. Hopefully that means Alasdair is awake; it would be our first chance to question him since the masquerade."

They did need to question Alasdair. A plot to destroy magic through combining deadly fifteenth-century relics spoke of someone with deep knowledge of the magic world, a true mastermind still out there, possibly licking their wounds and ready to try again.

"I am able to appreciate that questioning needs to happen," Wesley said. "I'm less able to appreciate that I am not the one doing it. What if Mr. Findlay is still dangerous?"

"That's why Jade took Sasha with her," Sebastian said. "Alasdair wouldn't stand a chance against telekinesis and superstrength. Don't underestimate Jade and Sasha because they're women."

"I'm not underestimating them because they're *women*. I'm underestimating them because they're not *me*," Wesley said, which drew a huffed laugh from Sebastian. "I still don't understand why I'm here and not there."

"Because I said *please*. And you said *yes*."

Wesley rolled his eyes, mostly at himself, because that was, in fact, what had happened, and it was exactly why angels were a bigger nuisance than devils. A devil one could simply tell to go to Hell; an angel would smile sweetly and one would scramble to wrap one's self around their little finger.

Wesley stole another glance at Sebastian.

Hell if it wasn't fucking worth it, though.

They crossed another street and picked their way over the train tracks, heading for a run-down structure on the edge of the Hudson River that must have been a factory at one time. At present, it was deserted, the windows broken and the door boarded shut.

"We could be at the hotel right now," Wesley pointed out, both of them picking up the pace as the rain continued to needle them. "I could be watching you strip off most of your clothes."

"Wesley. *Priorities*."

"What could possibly take priority over that?" Wesley said, without apology, as they reached the dilapidated structure. "Do you have any idea how good you look at twilight, as the glow of city lights starts to dance along your skin?"

Sebastian side-eyed him. "That's very romantic."

"Particularly when I finally get your trousers off and your legs over my—"

"What happened to the romance?" Sebastian said, as they ducked beneath the arch that sheltered the building's front door, tucked away out of sight and away from the rain.

"Please, I'm a fucking poet," Wesley said. "Miss Robbins should have me on her speakeasy stage at the Magnolia, not acting as errand boy."

Sebastian grinned. "I could listen to you for hours," he said, gaze on the empty street. "And you agreed to run this errand because no matter how grouchy you pretend to be, you're a very good friend who would do anything for Jade. It's a short list of people she trusts to help her with bootlegging."

And in the hidden shadows of their shelter, he tilted his head up and brushed his lips against Wesley's cheek, light and soft.

Wesley stilled. The kiss had been over in an instant. Subtle enough that it might have been missed even if they'd been standing in a crowded room, innocent enough that Sebastian could have gotten away with telling Americans that he'd absentmindedly slipped into a Spanish cultural habit. Sebastian had even checked the street for prying eyes before he'd done it. Wesley had been blown by a stranger in a public park on no less than three occasions, all of which had brought a far greater risk of discovery than that tiny kiss.

They hadn't been seen and Wesley wasn't afraid that they had. He was hyperaware of the action for a more aggravating reason.

Sebastian had gone back to watching the street. Wesley surreptitiously touched his cheek. The kiss had been subtle, sweet, and innocent. An affectionate gesture to go with affectionate words, and Sebastian had given it without a second thought. Meanwhile, Wesley was already giving it third, fourth, possibly infinite thoughts.

Casual affection was, of course, a thing. He obviously knew that. It was a thing some couples did, and more to the point, a thing Sebastian sometimes did, and a thing Wesley secretly appreciated; he craved Sebastian's touch the way he craved nicotine and was quite on board with having as much of it as possible.

But if more touch was an option, Wesley also wanted to give it, to get his hands and lips on Sebastian even when they weren't having sex.

And he didn't have the first fucking clue what to do with that feeling, or how to go about it.

"Wes, look." Sebastian pointed. "I think I see Rory."

Wesley raised his eyes heavenward. Christ, how very Sebastian, to send Wesley spiraling into the insensible world of emotion and not have the decency to even know he'd done it.

Rory was crossing the street, shoulders hunched and hands shoved deep in his coat pockets. His houndstooth newsboy cap was pulled low over blond curls and he was eying their building suspiciously from behind round black glasses.

Yes, he was short and young, and that was how he physically appeared. It had been all Wesley had seen, when they first met. But Rory had been aged emotionally by a hard life and his volatile magic. His psychometry let him see the past of objects—and he'd become stuck in those pasts more than once, Wesley had learned from Arthur, Wesley's ex-lover-turned-friend and Rory's current beau.

It wasn't fair or nice for Wesley to harp on his youth, especially considering Rory had once saved Wesley's life. But then, Wesley had never claimed to be a fair or nice man.

Sebastian ducked out from under their shelter, waving tentatively. He was getting more confident of his new status as friend, but he'd once kidnapped Rory. It never seemed to matter that Sebastian had been under the control of blood magic at the time and that everyone else had forgiven him; he still struggled to let go and forgive himself.

But Rory genuinely brightened. "Hey Seb," he called to Sebastian, waving back, which made Sebastian break into a real smile.

And yes, Wesley was going to call Rory an infant, likely forever, but at the end of the day he'd also do anything for someone who could make Sebastian smile like that. Maybe friendship was complicated; Wesley was, admittedly, still fairly new to the concept.

A moment later, Rory had joined them, squeezing into their tiny shelter under the roof. "Look at you, out of Arthur's sight," Wesley said. "How is he coping? Should we telegram and assure him that you haven't been mugged or, I don't know, unacceptably jostled by passersby?"

Rory gave him a disgruntled look, which seemed to be his default expression around Wesley. "I can handle myself."

"I'm well aware," Wesley said. "Arthur is the one who needs constant reminding. I can't believe he's letting you bootleg unsupervised; it seems very out of character for him."

"Well," Rory said grudgingly, "he didn't want to. But that's why you two are here. I told him to stop worrying and stick with his brother; John needs his help and the three of us are gonna be fine."

"Yes, we are," Sebastian said. "Rory, you can call in an actual tornado if there's trouble. We will be—what is that word you say?—copacetic."

"Thank you, Seb," Rory said, looking a lot less disgruntled. "Bootleggers still aren't here, then?"

"No." Wesley pursed his lips. "But then, I don't supposed criminals put much stake in punctuality."

"Depends on the criminal," Sebastian said, and it wasn't light but it also wasn't as heavy as it could have been. *Was* Sebastian finally getting to a point where he wasn't blaming himself constantly for everything he'd done under blood magic? Wesley was, frankly, going to be damn proud of him.

"I can wait as long as the bulls don't show." Rory blew into his hands to warm them. "Did Jade say what kind of hooch we're grabbing?"

He had one ring on his right hand, around his fourth finger. Not the so-called Tempest Ring, the fifteenth-century relic which let Rory control the wind, but a plain gold band, like a wedding ring. Wesley hadn't commented on it, but he could guess who'd put it there and what it meant. And obviously it didn't do anything as ridiculous as *warm his heart* to see evidence that sometimes, against all odds, good people did find each other and the love they deserved. No, Wesley was just happy that Arthur and Rory were occupied with each other and out of his hair.

"We're picking up rum," Wesley said. "It's Latin night at the Magnolia."

"It is?" Sebastian perked up. "How did you already know that?"

"Miss Robbins mentioned it yesterday, when I picked up the record for your brother." Wesley added, for Rory, "Mateo's last letter mentioned they've already had snow at Oberlin." He gestured at Sebastian. "I already know how this Caribbean boy feels about cold weather; one assumes the other Caribbean boy will also appreciate listening to a tango to warm an Ohio winter."

Sebastian brushed his fingers against Wesley's, like he sometimes did when he thought Wesley was being sweet. An absurd thought, of course; Wesley appreciated corresponding with Sebastian's younger brother because Mateo was a man of exceptional intellect and refreshing cynicism. It had nothing to do with Wesley missing his own brother, who'd been lost in the war.

"Is Mateo's magic still controlled?" Rory asked. "After— Well. The masquerade and everything."

Rory would understand, and empathize deeply, with Sebastian's brother, who was telegnostic and had been overwhelmed by his own ability to see the future of magic. Or *had* been overwhelmed, before Sebastian had bound his magic. Credit to Rory now, for trying to be sensitive, and not bluntly asking *did the binding on Mateo's magic survive when you lost your magic the night of the masquerade?*

"Seems to be," Wesley answered. "He mentioned he has the occasional odd dream, but he spent more of his letter grouching that he wasn't in Havana with Miss de Leon and Miss Finnegan."

"We could also have some of Stella's records shipped to Spain, for when Isabel and Molly come home," Sebastian said. "And what about to England?"

"Already sent," Wesley said. "Ostensibly for myself, but I'm fairly certain my footman and my cook's daughter will wear them out before I make it back."

That made Sebastian smile. "What about your family?"

"Well," Wesley said, "the cable from Lady Tabitha three days ago informed me she'd once again met the perfect potential Viscountess Fine, while yesterday's cable from Geoffrey was checking whether I was returning to England for the Christmas social season or if I was dead and the title was his now. Perhaps unsurprisingly, I prefer to correspond with your family."

Rory glanced unsubtly at Sebastian. "Viscountess Fine, huh."

Sebastian cleared his throat. "I think I see them," he said, pointing to the Hudson River.

A boat was coming downriver from the north, turning in and making its way toward the dock.

"Here we go," Rory muttered, as the three of them stepped back out into the rain.

Wesley led the way across a paved lot, in the shadow of the run-down building with its boarded windows rising up on their left. At the edge of the lot, they stepped through mud and onto the long dock extending into the wide Hudson River. The wind was colder and stronger on the dock, enough to make the waves choppy, and the river was a dark slate gray, the shallows at the shoreline quickly giving way to deep waters that could accommodate industrial shipping.

The wood was rickety and hollow-sounding under Wesley's feet as they moved farther out into the river, to where the boat was puttering closer. It was more of a skiff, really, not even big enough to have a proper deck, but the front of the boat was enclosed by some cheap wood and tarp. Nothing was visible to the naked eye, but there would have been room for a stash hidden from sight.

Two men in dark overcoats and fedoras stood in the body of the boat. One of them was moving around, pulling up the rope into his hands as the boat approached the pier. Wesley caught the outline of a gun through the overcoat.

"They're armed," he said under his breath, for Sebastian's and Rory's ears alone.

"Good to know," Rory muttered, his hand stealing into his pocket.

Sebastian's face had shuttered, impossible to read. He stepped forward, as if to go ahead of Wesley and Rory.

Wesley's hand darted out and snagged his coat sleeve. "What the fuck do you think you're doing?" he hissed, under his breath, pulling Sebastian back toward his side.

"I'm talking to them," Sebastian said back, shooting Wesley a frown. "What are *you* doing?"

"Stopping you from taking on two armed men when you don't have a weapon yourself," Wesley snapped, and then bit his tongue so hard he almost broke skin.

Up until three weeks ago, Sebastian's weapon had been his magic—a literal part of him. And now Wesley couldn't even match *Rory's* level of tact; Sebastian had given up that magic to save Wesley's life, apparently so Wesley could be here to throw it right back in his face.

Sure enough, a flash of hurt crossed Sebastian's face, unmistakable even if he buried it so fast Wesley could have imagined it. "I'm only going to talk to them, Wesley," Sebastian said lightly. "I think even I can handle that, yes?"

He didn't wait for Wesley to respond before stepping out in front again. Probably for the best, because what was Wesley supposed to say to that? *Perhaps you can handle that, but apparently your lover can't? Because he's a giant fucking hypocrite who mocked Arthur for not seeing that Brodigan can take care of himself only to do exactly the same to you?*

Wesley swallowed a sigh and followed.

It's fine. Wesley is still getting used to you not having magic and he also needs time to adjust, Sebastian told himself. *He doesn't actually think you're incapable of talking to people.*

Hopefully.

One of the men had leapt out of the boat onto the dock and was tying the skiff up to the pier. And Wesley was right; there was the unmistakable outline of a firearm beneath the overcoat.

Sebastian kept his eyes on the men. "Nice weather we're having," he called.

The day was gray and cold, the clouds thick with the rain that fell on Sebastian's cap and shoulders. The man on the dock straightened up. "Blue skies all around," he replied, completing the code phrase.

"Marvelous," Wesley said flatly. "Can we get a fucking move on, then?"

He was, of course, dressed with his usual disdain for current trends and preference for clothes two to three decades out of style, and had an unmistakable accent. The two bootleggers exchanged a look.

"Miss Robbins didn't tell us we were expecting a Spaniard and the crown prince," one of them said.

"You getting paid to make wisecracks or you got something to sell?" Rory said, with an edge. He was the youngest and shortest of everyone on the dock, but Sebastian caught a new flash of gold on his left hand. He'd put on the ring relic, arming himself with the power of the wind.

The bootleggers exchanged another look. But then the man in the boat pushed the tarp aside and reached under the covered bow.

A moment later, he was straightened, holding a medium-sized, round glass bottle with a narrow spout. "The name's Lenny. That's Tommy on the dock. And this here is the finest rum Nova Scotia has to offer," he said, holding it out over the edge of the boat. "This one's free, as a show of goodwill. Go on and have a sample."

"Don't mind if I do," Wesley said, reaching out for the bottle that Lenny was holding out. "After Mr. Brodigan has a first look, of course."

"You're having the kid test the rum?" said Tommy, like that was funny. "I thought Miss Robbins was a professional. Why'd she send you clowns?"

"Our young gentleman friend here is a prodigy," Wesley said, his tone icy, as he handed the rum to Rory. "And I would suggest the two of you more carefully consider your choice of words."

Rory had closed his eyes, turning the bottle around in his hands. Sebastian bent to put his head close to Rory's and caught faint muttering. *"Bought from a bartender, bottled in a factory."*

Rory abruptly opened his eyes, glancing up at Sebastian. "This one's the real McCoy, but they bought it by itself, in a bar," he said under his breath. "I need to check the ones they're trying to sell. Fine can drink this if he wants, though."

Sebastian took the bottle and straightened up. "We need to see the rest of the product."

Lenny gestured to the boat with a showman's air. "Climb aboard."

Sebastian heard Rory swallow, the deep brown eyes

behind his glasses going to the choppy river. The Hudson was probably forty feet deep at this point, their pier far enough into the river to accommodate the old factory's industrial ships. *He can't swim*, Sebastian remembered, from stories Rory and Arthur had told. *And he's had some bad luck on boats.*

Sebastian handed the rum to Wesley and stepped forward. "We'll both go."

Wesley opened his mouth. Sebastian shot him a look, and Wesley put the bottle to his lips instead of speaking—grudgingly, Sebastian was pretty sure.

Sebastian stepped into the boat first. It wasn't a big boat, and it rocked under his weight, but the Hudson River would never have waves like the ocean Sebastian had grown up with. He found his balance, then angled himself to put his shoulder where Rory could easily reach it if he needed to steady himself.

Rory's lips tightened but he didn't protest, and his spine was very straight as he stepped into the boat. It rocked again, and Rory's hand shot out to grip Sebastian's shoulder.

"You afraid of a little water, kid?" Tommy said from the dock, with an obvious jeer.

"I'm sorry, did you have something to say outside of our business?" Wesley took a step toward the man. "Perhaps you'd care to say it to me?"

Apparently Wesley could give Rory a hard time, but that didn't meant strangers could. At over six feet, he was the tallest man in the group, and while he didn't have Arthur's breadth he had his own dangerous air. Sebastian could see Tommy reassessing him.

"If anyone is gonna tell these two to go chase themselves, it oughta be me." Rory was gingerly moving forward in the boat. Lenny pulled back the corner of the tarp, revealing four crates.

Rory knelt by the closest crate and put both hands on it.

Lenny was eying him with a look Sebastian didn't like. "What's he doing?"

Sebastian stepped between Rory and Lenny. "Whatever he needs to do," Sebastian said coolly. He could hear faint muttering, mostly lost to the wind, as Rory scried the crates.

And then Rory suddenly yanked his hands off the crate. "Who the hell do you think you are?"

Oh shit. "Rory," Sebastian said, but Rory was already on his feet.

"You think you're gonna scam Jade?" Rory was pointing at the bootlegger. "Not on our watch, buddy."

"Hard to watch anything from the bottom of the Hudson." And Lenny shoved Rory off the boat and into the river.

Chapter Two

Of course everything had gone to shit.

Of *course* it had.

The moment he'd seen Rory straighten up with an all-too-familiar look of outrage and all the subtlety and good sense of an angry bull, Wesley was already pivoting. Tommy was reaching into his coat for his gun, but Wesley was faster, jabbing him in the stomach with the bottle of rum.

"Oof." Tommy grunted loudly, doubling over, and Wesley followed the blow with a hard kick to his leg. The man hit the dock just as Wesley heard a splash and Sebastian's panicked shout echoed up from the boat.

"Rory!"

Fuck. It could always get worse, because Rory might have the power of the wind but he couldn't fucking swim.

Wesley bent and snatched up the gun out of Tommy's jacket, straightening just in time to see Sebastian shoving Lenny aside. A second later, Sebastian's heavy coat was off his shoulders and he was diving headfirst into the Hudson after Rory.

Wesley didn't have time to even attempt to process the feelings that flooded him; down in the boat, Lenny was scrambling up to his feet and pulling out another gun, his gaze on the shape of Sebastian gliding under the gray river water.

Wesley was moving again without thinking. Tommy was starting to stand, so Wesley kicked him straight off the pier and into the water. He'd be able to swim to the ladder and climb out, but it bought Wesley the seconds he needed to cock the gun in his hands.

"Drop the gun," he barked at Lenny down in the boat.

Lenny ignored him. Out in the river, the surface was breaking, and Lenny was bringing the gun up.

Wesley fired a shot into the bottle of counterfeit liquor at the man's feet, which shattered, spraying the bottom of the boat with glass.

Lenny froze.

"Drop the fucking gun," Wesley said, through clenched teeth, "or the next one goes between your eyes."

Lenny held up his hands. But he hadn't dropped the weapon. Down in the water, Tommy had reached the ladder. In a moment, he'd be back on the pier.

"Tommy only had one bullet left in that gun," said Lenny. "And you just wasted it."

Wesley refused to flinch, keeping the gun steady and trained on Lenny. "Are you willing to bet your life on that?"

Lenny hesitated.

In the river, two heads surfaced: Rory in front, eyes closed and missing his glasses and hat; Sebastian behind him, arms around Rory's torso and keeping his nose and mouth above the water line. Sebastian was a strong swimmer, but Rory would be like an anvil with the weight of a soaked winter coat, in a river temperature akin to ice water. They weren't going to be dodging bullets in their state; how long could they last?

Behind him, in the parking lot, he heard more voices. Shit. Did the bootleggers have reinforcements? Was Wesley really out of bullets?

Tommy was cresting the top of the ladder onto the pier. In the boat, Lenny grinned. "I think we got friends coming."

"Not yours. Theirs."

Wesley had only a moment to register the shock of relief that Jade's voice brought before an invisible force swept across the pier. The gun flew out of Lenny's hand and into the Hudson just as Tommy appeared to be dragged by an invisible hand on his trouser leg and thrown bodily into the boat next to Lenny. A moment later, the ropes around the crates had unwrapped themselves and were twining around Lenny and Tommy like snakes.

"What the fuck is going on?" Tommy said, eyes wide.

"You shouldn't sample your wares, it'll make you see funny things." Wesley's eyes were on the figures struggling in the river. "Miss Robbins, I don't know why you're here instead of at the hospital with Mr. Findlay, but if I could beg of you—"

"I've got them." Jade's hand was up as she scrambled with impressively quick steps down the pier in her ruffled coat and dainty high heels. Sebastian and Rory were already gliding through the water as if she'd grabbed them by the scruff of their collars and bodily yanked them back toward shore. "I'll fill you in on Alasdair momentarily; let's get these two safe first."

A moment later, they were flying out of the water and landing on the pier at Wesley's feet. Wesley heard Sebastian's grunt of pain as his back hit the wooden dock, his arms still gripping tightly to Rory.

"Sorry, sorry," Jade said hastily, as she joined them. "I'm still getting the hang of how strong the magic is now with this brooch relic. Is everyone all right?"

Wesley had already dropped to a crouch next to Sebastian and Rory on the pier, reaching for Rory's wrist to check his pulse. "Brodigan, are you—"

Rory abruptly coughed, rolled off Sebastian and onto his side, and vomited river water all over Wesley's shoes.

"—alive," Wesley finished. "Yes. It would seem you are."

"Ugh." Rory made a face. "Sorry, Fine."

"Better my shoes than your lungs." Wesley's heart was still pounding too fast. Sebastian's eyes were open at least, a little hazy as he coughed himself. Down in the boat, Lenny and Tommy were securely hogtied and—hang on. "Miss Robbins, did you gag our would-be assailants with their own neckties?"

"Useful trick I picked up, a few years back." Jade was kneeling on the decrepit dock in her fashionable trousers at Rory and Sebastian's other side. "What on earth happened?"

"Assholes tried to swindle you." Rory pointed with a wavering hand. "They didn't like getting caught."

"What Brodigan means is that when he discovered their attempted subterfuge, he lost his temper and ran his mouth and we found ourselves in a fight," Wesley said, with an edge. "And one of said arseholes shoved him into the river."

Jade raised her eyebrows.

"Something like that," Rory said weakly.

"Oh, Rory." Jade bent to wrap him in a sisterly hug. "I'm so glad you're all right. You're terribly lucky Sebastian and Lord Fine were here."

And now she was leaning across to squeeze Sebastian, who gave her a tired but real smile.

"Yes, and you know, that's actually another way to say Sebastian flung himself into the river so that when he was shot, he could conveniently sink his own body to the bottom of the Hudson for our assailants," Wesley said, again too sharp. Ugh, he had feelings rattling about his chest, knocking into his hard heart. Unacceptable.

Sebastian turned his head to look up at Wesley. "But we were safe because you had our backs."

"Put the doe eyes away; they don't work on me," Wesley lied. He slid his overcoat off his shoulders. "Here—"

"Put it on Rory," Sebastian said firmly. "My coat is dry in the boat and his lips are blue."

"What color do you think yours are?" Wesley said, but he was passing the coat over to Jade, because Rory was shivering so hard his teeth were chattering and Wesley didn't actually want him suffering either.

Jade helped Rory sit up as Sebastian's coat came sailing through the air and landed in Wesley's lap. Christ, telekinesis was useful.

Jade turned to the empty air at her side. "We take them straight to the Magnolia, I think," she said, as she wrapped Wesley's coat around Rory's shoulders while Wesley mirrored her actions with Sebastian, getting him upright with the coat around him. "Ace is going to cast a kitten no matter where we take them; we've got to get them warm and the club is closest."

"Call the bulls first and have them come get these assholes," Rory said to the same empty patch of air. "I'm fine, don't make Ace worry until—" He groaned. "You're already on the phone with him?"

Ah. Mr. Zhang must have been there as well, somewhere on the astral plane.

A small movement from Sebastian caught Wesley's eyes. He was staring at Jade and Rory, his expression unreadable.

Oh. Of course. Sebastian had also figured out that Zhang was here.

And Sebastian still couldn't see him anymore.

But before Wesley could think of something to say that might be comforting—or at least not add salt to the wound—Sebastian was turning to him. "At least without my magic, I'm not blocking Zhang from finding us anymore."

He said it casually, like that was fine, or perhaps like he was determined to make it fine whether it really was or not. Wesley didn't push. "I don't care if there are twenty Mr. Zhangs with us on the astral plane right now, you caused me to nearly experience emotions and that's unforgiveable," Wesley murmured, but his hand had shot out of its own accord to touch Sebastian's, wrapping ice-cold fingers in his own and squeezing.

Rory was touching his face and bare head, the soaked blond curls that hung limply dripping. "Aw damn," he said, sounding disappointed all the way to his heart. "My hat. That's the one from Ace—"

But Jade had her eyes closed again. A moment later, two small items came whipping across the pier to fall in front of Rory: a pair of glasses, and a sopping-wet newsboy cap. "The cap's going to need a wash," Jade started. "But—"

"You're the best." Rory had snatched up the hat before even the glasses. "You too, Zhang. I don't know how you found these in the river."

"Oh my goodness." A voice much like Jade's, but even more musical, floated down from the top of the dock. "It's freezing and they're soaked."

Wesley glanced up. A stunningly lovely woman with the same russet-brown skin and bright eyes as Jade was coming down the pier in a slinky sheath dress and large fur coat, looking every inch the star she was as she picked her way down the dock in heels even higher than Jade's.

Behind Stella was a woman with a short blond bob, dressed in trousers and flat shoes. Sasha, Stella's bodyguard and girlfriend.

As she approached, Sasha was looking into the boat that held the gagged and hogtied Lenny and Tommy. "Who are these two?" she said, her voice a bit deeper than Stella's, with a noticeable Russian accent. "The knots look very skilled; this must be your work, Jade. Are we worried they are going to tell people what they saw? You want me to handle them?"

And perhaps Wesley did need to stop underestimating people who weren't himself, particularly when they were telekinetic and had superstrength.

"No one's gonna believe them, especially when they're running rum," Rory said, teeth chattering. "Let the cops have them; I just want outta here before they show."

"What were you going to tell us about Mr. Findlay?"

Wesley said to Jade, as he and the women helped Rory and Sebastian to their feet. "Why was your hospital visit cut short?"

Jade blew out a very long breath. "The whole story is going to have to wait for the Magnolia," she said. "But there was no point staying at the hospital when Alasdair is dead."

"Dead?" Sebastian said in shock.

"Yes." Jade met Wesley's gaze. "And it might be *murder*."

Even with his coat around his shoulders and Wesley pressed to his side, Sebastian shivered the entire car ride to the Magnolia. Luckily it didn't take long to get from Yonkers back to Harlem, and in short time he and Rory were being bustled through the Magnolia's alley door.

Stella was immediately pulled away by Mack the bartender while Sasha took Wesley off to see Jade's brother, Benson. Jade was the one to take Sebastian and Rory backstage.

"The band is already here and in their dressing room, and Grover is holding a staff meeting in the office," she said, as they made their way down a narrow hall with four doors. A side table was pressed up against one wall, decorated with a lace cloth and several floral arrangements, presumably from Stella's admirers. The speakeasy had previously been a tobacco shop, but this part of the hall smelled like flowers. "Which means there's only one room left, so I'm afraid you're going to have to borrow Stella's boudoir. Sasha's gone to find you dry clothes."

Jade opened the final door, painted gold with one of Stella's show posters hung on the outside. Sebastian stepped inside to a space bursting with color and even more floral scents. The molding had also been painted gold and the walls were papered with rows of pink roses, interspersed with more prints of Stella's Paris and New York shows. There was a pink-and-white-striped chaise, a giant vanity with a chair and its own lighting, and racks and racks of clothes, most of them gauzy or sequined. Every flat surface held either more vases of flowers or bottles of perfume with labels in French.

"Aw geez," Rory muttered behind him. "This place is exactly what we shoulda expected of the prettiest doll in New York." He reached for a nearby table, picking up the closest bottle and taking a sniff. "You want to smell like the Hudson or orchids?"

Sebastian scrunched his nose.

Part of the room had been set up for clothes modeling and alterations, complete with a full-length mirror and changing area behind a tall, flower-decorated screen. Sebastian let Rory have that corner and instead stood over by the vanity, where he hopefully wouldn't drip river water on any of Stella's clothes.

He'd just stripped off his coat and soaked button-up shirt when the door cracked open and Wesley poked his head in. "I am delighted to inform you that your best option for clean, dry clothes are spare tuxedos kept on hand for the band."

"Why would that delight you?" Sebastian asked, awkwardly hopping on one leg to pull off his shoe and wet sock as Wesley came fully into the dressing room.

"Because," said Wesley, as he squeezed a stack of towels and folded black-and-white clothes on the only available corner of space on the small table by the door, "every time you ought to wear a proper tailcoat, you refuse like a petulant child."

"I have a tuxedo," Sebastian protested, grabbing the back of the vanity chair for balance as he wrenched off the other shoe. "You've seen me in it."

"I said a *proper* tailcoat," Wesley said. "Not those modern dinner jackets you insist on. I'm afraid you can pout until you're blue in the face and it won't matter one whit. Tailcoat is all you've got, so you don't have a choice."

"Not true." Sebastian gestured at Stella's racks of clothes. "Look at all these dresses. I'm spoiled for choice."

"You're spoilt all right," Wesley said, the corner of his mouth turning up in a grudging smile. "Spoilt brat dodging proper clothes." His gaze was on Sebastian, more specifically on the sheer T-shirt sticking to his skin. "Are you about to take that T-shirt off, by any chance?"

"Oh yes." Sebastian pulled the T-shirt over his head, dropping it on top of his wet shirt. "I'm going to swap it for that little red number with the feathers."

"In fairness, you've got the legs for it." Wesley was watching him strip with complete attention. "And I am admittedly now speculating on the variety of outfits I could you get into when it's just the two of us."

"It's *not* just the two of you." Rory's disgruntled voice broke the spell, from behind the screen. "If you're gonna flirt, then scram already."

Wesley's eyes went heavenward. "Brodigan—"

"Give me two minutes and I'll be out," Sebastian promised.

"Fine," Wesley said, sounding even more disgruntled

than Rory. He reached for the door, his gaze going to Sebastian's bare chest one last time in a familiar look that rippled through him like Wesley had touched his skin. It was the same look Wesley used to give him right before Sebastian found himself pinned to a wall or flattened against the nearest surface for some of the best sex of his life.

Wesley slipped through the door, back into the hall. Sebastian reached for the buckle of his belt.

He hadn't been pinned or flattened to anything since the night he'd lost his magic. Suddenly finding himself powerless—truly powerless, in a way he'd only been for one terrible period of his life—had come with a lot of complicated feelings.

Wesley was bigger, heavier, and more knowledgeable about combat. None of that had mattered when Sebastian had his magic and the ability to knock Wesley down and keep him there; it had been easy to play at helpless when he knew he could turn the tables at any moment. Now, though, Sebastian didn't have magic. And if Wesley wanted, he could actually pin Sebastian down and make it very hard to escape.

Except Wesley wouldn't hurt him physically any more than Sebastian would have hurt Wesley with magic. And Wesley hadn't pushed—wouldn't ever push. The battle scars of a bad past were something Wesley deeply understood and treated with utmost care. Sebastian wasn't going to be pinned or flattened to anything unless he asked for it again.

Perhaps ironically, the unconditional gentleness was making Sebastian crave the rougher handling again—if he could just get past those complicated feelings.

He peeled the rest of his clothes off and gratefully

wrapped himself in a dry towel. He grabbed the other towel and the smaller of the two suits and carried it over to Rory's corner. "Can we have our clothes sent to be cleaned?"

"Yeah, just leave your stuff here." Rory poked his head around the screen. "Your clothes are nice ones, like Ace and Fine, right? Tailored for you and all that?"

"Well—I mean—"

"Look, it's obvious you're not wearing cheap stuff, even if you don't show off with fancy suits," Rory said dryly, as he stuck out a hand and grabbed the towel and tailcoat. "Ace has a place. We'll take it there. Just leave your stuff behind and don't bother waiting for me—Fine's waiting on you and it's gonna take me forever to get this getup on."

Sebastian went back to the vanity, rough-drying his hair with the towel before pulling on the tuxedo pants with their ribbon stripe up the side. He left the tailcoat folded on the vanity chair, along with the waistcoat and the bow tie, so that he was dressed in just trousers, suspenders and the button-up white shirt, which he rolled up the sleeves and left open at the collar.

As he stepped out of Stella's dressing room, closing the door behind him, he found Wesley waiting in the hall.

"For fuck's sake." Wesley's gaze locked straight on him. "I don't know what's more attractive, you half-dressed like this or knowing you did it just to give me a hard time."

Sebastian casually leaned against the wall, tilting his head back so he could look up at Wesley. "I don't know what you're talking about," he said innocently. "I did it to be comfortable."

"What bullshit." Wesley's gaze was now on the open collar and Sebastian's throat. "You did it so *my* trousers would be uncomfortable."

Sebastian grinned. "You keep thinking you're the bigger villain, but I'm always going to be badder than you, Wes."

Wesley moved closer, his movements slow and deliberate, giving Sebastian plenty of time and space to shift away.

Sebastian's heart was beating faster, but he didn't want to move. He kept his spot as Wesley put a hand on the wall next to Sebastian's head and leaned forward in a way that had Sebastian boxed in but not trapped.

"Truly, not a single person downstairs would believe me if I told them what an impertinent brat you actually are," Wesley said, his voice lower. "To a one, they'd say, *Sebastian is the sweetest, most polite of gentlemen; how dare you besmirch his character.* Only I know the truth—"

Their moment was cut short by the door at the other end of the hall flying open.

"Teddy, are you—ugh, no, it's just you two."

Sebastian and Wesley hastily pulled apart. "Arthur!" Sebastian cleared his throat, trying to bring his voice back down to a normal pitch. "Were you looking for—"

"Rory, yes, obviously." The door slammed shut behind Arthur as he strode down the hall. "For Christ's sake, Wes, do you have to have your mitts all over Sebastian in Jade's speakeasy? Let the poor man breathe."

Wesley sputtered. "My *what*?"

"Speaking of Jade, she wants to talk to us. But Rory and I are going to have words first."

"My *mitts*—?"

Sebastian pointed to the gold door. "Rory is in there."

"Thank you." Arthur pushed past them and shouldered open the door. "Teddy, what in ten hells were you thinking—"

The boudoir door swung shut behind Arthur. Wesley looked very sour as he turned back to face Sebastian. "Rory is a terrible influence on Arthur's language."

Muffled voices came from behind the closed door.

"Ace, I'm fine. You're being overprotective again."

"This is not overprotective; this is exactly the right amount of protective. You told me I didn't need to be there and then you fell in the fucking Hudson."

"I think it's cute Arthur is picking it up," Sebastian said. "I like how Rory talks, like when he says *are you screwy* or calls something the cat's meow."

Behind the door, Rory and Arthur had raised their voices.

"I'm letting you teach me to swim—"

"Even a strong swimmer can struggle in icy water when the current is strong. And all because you lost your temper. Thank God Sebastian was there."

Sebastian ducked his head, chest and face warming.

"Your imitation of Rory is on par with your imitation of me," Wesley told him. "Which is to say it's wretched, duck, I'm sorry. But Arthur's right; you did save Rory today. It was foolhardy and idiotic and also very brave."

Sebastian bit his lip. To go from kidnapping Rory under blood magic to actually being able to help—it felt good. The kind of thing friends did, not former enemies. "I'm glad he's okay."

"Aw geez, Ace, I'm sorry." Behind the door, Rory did sound genuinely contrite. *"'Cause you're right, I need to learn not to blow my lid just 'cause people are crooks."*

"If you're expecting me to forgive you just because you're giving me those big eyes and sad voice, you can forget it. I'm going to stay cross with you this time."

"What a filthy liar," Wesley muttered. "Arthur is about to fold like a cheap hat."

"Oh come on," Sebastian said. "Who could ever stay mad at Rory?"

"I can, and have," Wesley said unapologetically. "But I could stay angry with anyone—could write the damn text on holding grudges."

"You forgave me," Sebastian pointed out.

"Did I?" Wesley said meaningfully. "Or is this all an elaborate revenge plot where I'm taking my vengeance on you in my bed every night?"

Sebastian couldn't help tilting his head back, bringing his lips closer to Wesley's. "Maybe you should show me a little more of that vengeance." His tongue darted out to wet his lips. "If you want."

"I always want. That's never in question." Wesley's gaze had gone to his lips. "And the things you make me want are diabolical."

"I don't know what you mean," Sebastian said innocently. "I am the sweetest, most polite of gentlemen. Stop besmirching my character."

Wesley's lips curled in a smile. "You are such an arse." He was leaning down, Sebastian stretching up, then Wesley abruptly paused. "Did you hear that?"

"Hear what?" Sebastian said.

"Silence."

Sebastian paused as well. The hallway seemed strangely quiet.

"Arthur and Rory appear to have stopped talking," Wesley said.

Sebastian glanced at the closed gold door. "Rory was still changing when I left."

Wesley's eyebrow went up. "Meaning Arthur walked in there in a high fit of emotion and found Brodigan naked, and now they've gone silent?"

Sebastian's and Wesley's eyes met.

"Leaving now," Wesley said, hastily pulling away, just as Sebastian said "Vámonos" and scrambled off the wall, and the two of them made for the door out to the speakeasy.

Chapter Three

Since the night in Tarrytown, Sebastian and Wesley had spent most of their evenings at the Magnolia, a welcoming space with drinks, dancing, and world-class music that had quickly become one of Sebastian's favorite places in New York. He followed Wesley now through the main club, weaving around tightly packed round tables and skirting the edge of the dance floor. Stella wasn't onstage yet—probably waiting to get into her dressing room—but the piano player was entertaining the early arrivals. One brave couple was doing the Charleston, and judging from the tapping toes, they wouldn't be the only dancers for long.

Jade was at the bar, looking very pretty perched on a stool in her man's suit and fedora, long legs crossed and one high heel dangling from her foot. She was sipping what appeared to be ginger ale and talking to the bartender, but turned as they approached.

"There are you two, at least." Jade tilted her head. "Where are Arthur and Rory?"

"They, um," Sebastian started awkwardly, "they need a minute."

Wesley, eying the top-shelf liquors, added, "Our misadventures on the Hudson triggered Arthur's mother bear streak and now he's reading Brodigan the riot act."

Jade groaned. "In my sister's *dressing room*?" she said, in a tone that suggested she knew exactly what that implied. She sighed. "All right, well, I'm going to pretend I didn't hear that. Sebastian, did the tailcoat not fit? I'm usually quite decent at estimating size."

"Yes, Sebastian, why *are* you half-dressed?" Wesley said dryly. "Do tell."

"I thought I might dance." Sebastian shrugged innocently. "It is Latin night, yes?"

"Well, in that case," Jade said, with a glance at Wesley, "I suspect he'll have no trouble filling his dance card."

"I'm bloody certain of it," Wesley said, even more dryly. "And as you might surmise, I could use a very stiff drink."

Jade grinned. "We've got French cognac from Quebec. Mack does a very good sidecar, I'm told, and Arthur has an open tab."

"Excellent," Wesley said. "Except let's move it all to my tab."

"That's nice of you," Sebastian said.

"Hardly," said Wesley. "Arthur always wants to be the one seeing to everyone. It will drive his overprotective little heart mad if I foot tonight's bill instead." He tilted his head, gaze on Sebastian. "And for you?"

Alcohol made paranormals lose control of their magic. Only weeks ago, Sebastian had been a paranormal and would never have even considered drinking in a full speakeasy, on the chance his magic sent everyone to the floor. Now, he didn't have magic—and yet, the past weeks, he'd continued to stick to soda. Maybe the new Sebastian still didn't drink; plenty of people didn't, with or without Prohibition, and that was a perfectly valid choice.

Or maybe he was clinging to an echo of old Sebastian because he didn't know how to navigate the world as the new person he'd become.

"Just a soda," Sebastian said, pushing his thoughts away. "Cola."

If Wesley had noticed Sebastian's complicated feelings—and it was Wesley, he noticed almost everything—he'd never commented or pressured. And now, Wesley simply nodded and turned to the bartender.

They got their drinks and made their way to a table at the perimeter of the speakeasy, where Zhang and finally Arthur and Rory joined them. The club was rapidly filling up, forcing the six of them to squash together in a semicircle around one small table along the wall. There were only four chairs, so Jade took a seat on Zhang's knee, his arm slipping around her waist.

"Seb, here." Rory shifted to the edge of his chair. "You're probably lighter than the high hats, so you and me can share."

"The perks of being pint-size, I suppose, not that I would know," Wesley said, which made Rory's eyes narrow. "Though I don't see why Sebastian ought to share with you instead of me."

"Because," said Rory, "I wasn't sure you could sit at all with that giant stick up your—"

"Thank you, Rory, I appreciate it," Sebastian said hurriedly, and squeezed in next to him as Wesley took the last vacant chair with a huff.

Arthur leaned in, addressing Jade. "What is this about Alasdair at the hospital?" he said, and Sebastian had to awkwardly shift his legs to the side as Arthur's hand came to rest protectively on Rory's knee under the table. "Rory said he's dead and you suspect *murder*?"

Jade nodded grimly. "The official report says fatal reaction to medication. But Alasdair wasn't lucid yet; he didn't have access to medications other than what the doctors gave him, and they hadn't given him anything new."

"So you think—what?" Wesley said. "Poison?"

"It's unfortunately possible," Zhang said. "I went over the whole hospital from the astral plane. Plenty of security keeping patients in, very little keeping others out. Someone posing as a nurse or an orderly could have slipped into Alasdair's room under the guise of delivering food or medicine."

Sebastian's stomach turned over. "That's awful."

"I know." Jade rubbed her face. "We weren't the only ones to have the thought, either. The police were there."

Alasdair had helped to kidnap all of them; had murdered his own friend, the baronet Sir Ellery, in cold blood and been ready to murder many others in order to destroy magic. Sebastian hadn't forgotten any of that, but his heart was heavy nonetheless.

Wesley steepled his fingers. "We do have to ask the next question, then," he said. "If Mr. Findlay was, in fact, murdered, who killed him—and why?"

"But we have a good lead on the why, don't we?" Arthur said. "Someone wants to see magic destroyed— someone who knows enough about paranormal lore and history to know about the relics and think to try combining them. And I agree that Alasdair was unlikely to have been the true mastermind behind those plans, but perhaps he knew too much about the plot to be allowed to wake."

Zhang had pulled a small notebook out of his jacket. He set it now on the table. "Jade and I have been piecing together what we know." He pointed to the names on the paper. "Alasdair Findlay, a paranormal who could hear magic and was driven mad by it. Major Charles Langford, who was Lord Fine's commanding officer in the British Army. And Sir Ellery, a baronet whose cousin had stolen the pomander relic from the Earl of Blanshard. We know Sir Ellery was the one to spring Alasdair from the Hyde Garden asylum in September, because Ellery wanted Alasdair's help to claim the pomander relic for his own. But he had to have learned about the pomander, and Alasdair's existence, from someone else."

"Could it have been from the earl himself?" Arthur suggested.

"Possibly, but I don't think so," Jade said. "The pomander relic came to New York with your valet, Lord Fine, and you mentioned Major Langford knew your valet was involved in collecting and selling rare artifacts. Langford claimed the War Office was investigating Sir Ellery, but we know now they were working together. It very well could have been Langford who told Ellery about the pomander, not realizing Ellery's greed to claim the pomander would overtake any desire to stop magic."

"That does seem possible," Wesley said. "Though Langford did work for the War Office, that part is true."

"Which begs the question," said Arthur, "of who could have convinced a man like Langford to turn his attention from War Office business to the business of destroying magic?"

Wesley frowned.

Sebastian nudged him. "What?"

"Possibly nothing," Wesley said. "Only—I knew Ellery and Langford both, and there's at least one other man in those circles whose life has been touched by all this, whether he knows it or not. A marquess by the name of Thornton."

"Lord Thornton?" Now Sebastian was frowning. "I know that name—I knew his maid Olive. She lived in Kilburn—or she did, until the Earl of Blanshard drained her aura."

"Thornton lives near me in Kensington," Wesley said. "Utter arse, but that doesn't mean he knows about magic. Still, ghastly business, what happened to his maid. And if Langford had been shown what magic did to his friend Thornton's maid, he would have been convinced that magic needed to be stopped by any means."

Rory had been listening without speaking, playing with the slim gold band on his right hand. It was a nonmagical ring, not the ring relic that controlled the wind, but it still reminded Sebastian of how much magic Rory controlled—that Rory himself had once been locked in the Hyde Garden asylum, lost to his overpowering ability to see history.

"Rory, what do you think?" Sebastian asked.

Rory pursed his lips. "I'm thinking about what Ace said—that whoever is behind this knows enough about paranormal lore and history to know about the relics and think to try combining them. I never met anyone who knows that much about relics besides *you*, Seb."

"Oh come now," Wesley said, a little more sharply. "We're not looking for a de Leon."

"It's a fair point, Wes," Sebastian said ruefully. "One of my ancestors was a literal witch-hunter for the Spanish Inquisition, the one who hunted down all seven relics in the first place. He probably would have loved to destroy magic."

"But it was the Earl of Blanshard who stole the relics from your family," Arthur added. "And now Rory has the ring, Jade the brooch, and Gwen the amulet. Ellis transferred the dagger's magic into a ring, which is in the Zhangs' library, and Sebastian destroyed the pomander." He was counting them off on his fingers. "That's five of the seven. What are the final two?"

Sebastian wasn't supposed to talk about the relics to anyone outside of his family. But everyone at the table had helped find missing relics, along with the siphon that had made them. He trusted all of them. "There's a medallion that was worn as a pendant," Sebastian said, "and a cuff, for the arm. They were not among the Earl of Blanshard's collection when we were in his manor in September."

Zhang was leaning in now, curiosity on his face. "What do those two relics do?"

"The medallion has tracking magic," Sebastian said. "Or *hunting* magic, if you'd rather call it that," he added, side-eying Wesley.

"What, like a magical hound?" Wesley said.

"That's pretty accurate," Sebastian admitted. "The magic is supposed to work in a similar way: as long as you have a sample of what you're looking for—a *scent*—it can find more of the same."

"Could this relic hunt *magic*?" Rory asked, more quietly.

Sebastian's stomach dropped again. "I don't know," he admitted. "But it's a relic; it's been feeding on its own magical chains for centuries and growing more powerful. Whatever it could have done before, it's much more dangerous now. So…maybe."

"Well, that's not particularly reassuring," Arthur muttered. "How do you unlock it?"

"It's not a very nice key," Sebastian said, wincing. "But at least it's not easy. You have to murder a paranormal with three kinds of magic."

"Three?" Arthur said. "That's going to be a short list. Even Rory, Jade, and Gwen only have two types of magic, their own and their relic."

Sebastian himself used to have four. He carefully didn't mention it. "The Earl of Blanshard would have had three—his own innate ability to absorb auras, the brooch relic, and my ancestor's binding on *him*."

"The earl is at least quite dead, although I suppose there will be other paranormals in the world with three kinds of magic," Wesley said. "What about the seventh relic—the cuff? What does it do and how does one unlock it?"

Sebastian winced again. This was not his favorite relic to talk about. "It, um. It casts curses."

"Oh, I don't like that," Jade muttered. "Please tell me this one has a difficult key as well."

"I wish I could tell you that." Sebastian sighed. "But I don't know."

"You don't know?" Zhang blinked. "Don't you know all of this stuff? You just mentioned that you're descended from the Spanish witch-hunter who tracked down the seven nobles who made the relics. You told us the reason your entire family has magic that works on other magic is because you share the bloodline that he...*oh.*"

"You share the bloodline that the inquisitor *cursed*," Jade said, finishing Zhang's thought.

Sebastian nodded. "We know the inquisitor used the cuff relic to cast the blood curse on himself and all his future descendants." He shrugged helplessly. "But naturally he didn't want us to know how to unlock the cuff, in case one of us got the idea to try and remove the curse."

Fingers touched Sebastian's wrist, steady and warm. He looked up to find Wesley's gaze on him. "But you did remove the curse from yourself." Wesley's fingers skated across the black ink outline of the lion. "Mr. Findlay said the brooch relic was drawing on your blood curse. When you let it strip your magic, it took your curse too."

Wesley so rarely touched him outside of bed, and now his fingers were tracing the delicate skin of Sebastian's inner wrist, sending pleasant prickles radiating over him. "Are you implying I outsmarted my ancestor?" Sebastian said, trying to concentrate. "I didn't, though. I can't use a relic if I don't have magic."

"Are you certain?" Zhang said.

Sebastian opened his mouth, then pursed his lips. "I guess I can't say for sure," he admitted. "It seems unlikely, though, no?"

"Not at all," Zhang said firmly. "The relics were created when nobles stripped out their own magic and put it in something else. You also did the first part."

"But my magic didn't go into anything else," Sebastian said.

"We don't know that either," Wesley pointed out, moving his hand from Sebastian's wrist to his own drink. "There was a mass of magic and murder in that attic. Are you sure you didn't accidentally create a relic?"

"Shouldn't I have been able to tell if I did?" Sebastian countered. "Why would my own magic go into something but then hide from me?"

"Maybe Gwen can tell us, with her witch-sight," Arthur said. "She's in London again. We're all game for the trip over there with you and Wes, to see if she can figure out what's happened to you and make sure Wesley's aura is intact."

Sebastian gave him a small, grateful smile. "I would like to be sure Wesley's aura has healed," he said, once again dancing away from any mention of his now-gone magic the way he'd have avoided the edge of no-man's-land in the war. "But I would also like a lead on who might be behind everything that happened in October. Alasdair may have been murdered because of it."

"Maybe you can give us a lead," Zhang said. "We still have two missing relics. Who did they belong to?"

Sebastian had the first spark of hope. "That *is* a place to start," he said. "The two remaining relics belonged to a married couple. The cuff belonged to a Spanish countess, and the medallion was created by her husband—who was an English nobleman."

Jade raised her eyebrows. "Not an ancient marquess by the name of Thornton, by any chance?"

"No," Sebastian said. "He was a duke, according

to our family notes. He had a title like a mountain, or something-mount, maybe?"

Wesley pursed his lips. "Valemount?"

"Yes," Sebastian said. "How did you know?"

"Because I know him," Wesley said. "Well, not *him*, the fellow from the fifteenth century. But I know the line. I was acquainted with the past duke, Alfred Fairfield, who died two years ago in a hunting accident—perhaps a bit of irony there, if he was descended from a paranormal duke with some kind of hunting magic."

Arthur tilted his head. "So who's the duke now, then?"

"His younger brother, Louis Fairfield," Wesley said. "I've met him several times as well. We deployed to France at the same time, actually, but he got sent home from the war quite quickly—some kind of injury was the story, wasn't ever revealed what kind."

"Brother?" Rory furrowed his brow. "I thought those sorts of inherited things went to sons."

"When there is one," Wesley said. "But the previous Duke of Valemount had only daughters—five of them—and with no son, the dukedom went to the brother. Hell, my title would go to my second cousin, Geoffrey, if I die first, a fact he reminds me of with some frequency," he added dryly.

"So we have a duke descended from a paranormal duke with a relic, and he's a fairly recent duke at that." Arthur tapped his chin. "If we go to England, can you arrange a meeting with the duke, Wes?"

"Certainly," Wesley said. "Honestly, I'd hardly have to arrange a thing: we're on the same guest lists for the same parties. In fact, the very marquess who likely has no idea his maid was magically murdered, Lord Thornton, is hosting a ball at his country home and Valemount and I are both invited. But it's Friday next, and we'd have to be on a ship tomorrow to make it across the Atlantic in time."

Jade and Zhang exchanged a look. "Is that right," Jade said slowly, her eyes still locked with Zhang's.

"It's fine to miss this particular ball, truly," Wesley said hastily, and he seemed to be carefully not looking at Sebastian. "It's one I'm invited to through a club that Thornton, Valemount, and I are all in. It's a—you know what, it doesn't matter. The point is, it's nearly December and the Christmas season will mean plenty of other wretched social events to attend. Perhaps we can find a ship leaving next week?"

Wesley had been in a hunting club with Sir Ellery. What club were Wesley and Thornton and Valemount in together?

Sebastian opened his mouth, but Stella's musical voice, amplified by the carbon microphone, suddenly filled the speakeasy.

"We promised you Latin night tonight!" Up on the stage, the spotlight flashed off of Stella's red sequined dress. She clapped her hands together. "And coincidentally, we've got a brave rescuer with us tonight who gives us a fine excuse to take our music south. Who's ready?"

Sebastian felt his cheeks flush. The crowd cheered as Stella's band struck up a Cuban rumba, and couples began filling the dance floor.

"Look at you blush." Wesley's expression had turned amused. "Imagine if you were wearing a proper tailcoat right now. You'd be perfectly dressed to go up onstage for the crowd to admire."

"On*stage*?" Sebastian shuddered. "I'd rather sit here and be ignored, thank you."

"Ignored, huh." Rory's gaze darted past Sebastian, and his lips curled up. "I don't think that's gonna happen."

Before Sebastian could ask why not, a new voice, soft and feminine, sounded at his side. "Excuse me."

Sebastian startled, turning to find pretty young woman around his own age, with a brown bob and red lips, was standing next to his chair, smiling at him hopefully.

"I don't mean to interrupt," she said. "And I don't mean to be forward. But I just figured you might be one of the only fellas in this club who'd know how to dance to this with me."

"Oh," Sebastian said in surprise. *Don't look at Wesley, don't make it obvious.* "Well, I—"

"He probably is," Wesley said, just a little gruff. "So go on, then. Give the lady a dance."

Sebastian met his eyes. "It's just a dance," Wesley said, holding his gaze. "If you want to dance, you should."

Sebastian absently touched the lion tattoo, where Wesley's warm fingers had rested. He did want to dance. He wanted to dance with *Wesley*. After midnight, the Magnolia usually had couples of all kinds on the floor, but he and Wesley had never joined them; plenty of people from Fifth Avenue snuck into the Magnolia, and Wesley had been seen many times in Arthur's circles. Neither he nor Sebastian were willing to risk stories getting back to any of the Kenzie family or their political rivals, not when it could draw attention to Arthur and Rory.

So Sebastian buried the desire to pull Wesley to his feet, and instead stood and held out his arm to the young woman. She took it, and he walked her through the tables.

"What's your name?" he asked, as they stepped onto the dance floor.

"Edith."

He took her hand and experimentally spun her, and she moved easily with it, laughing. Her hand came to rest on his shoulder, her hips softly swaying into the *quick-quick-slow* glide of their steps. She was a good dancer, and they rapidly found their rhythm together among the other couples, slipping into that blissful place that came from movement and music.

As the song came to an end, he dipped her backward, and the band seamlessly transitioned from rumba to tango. As he pulled her back up, Edith grinned. "Another? If you're having fun?"

He *was* having fun, and he loved the tango. He glanced over at the table, but Wesley was deep in conversation with Arthur, paying absolutely no attention to them. Sebastian pulled Edith in closer, hand on her lower back as they crossed the dance floor together, their cheeks close.

They made a half turn with brisk steps, her movements perfectly mirroring his as they leaned into the bend. "You're very good," he said into her ear.

"I must've seen *The Four Horsemen of the Apocalypse* two dozen times." She was flushed and smiling. "I could watch Valentino for hours."

"Such a handsome man," Sebastian agreed.

"You're one to talk."

What did he say to that? He glanced over at Wesley

again, but Wesley had turned to Rory now, so Sebastian spun Edith in a half circle, lifting her all the way off the floor, so he wouldn't have to come up with an answer.

They danced four songs together, the dance floor crowded and swinging, and Sebastian was grinning and breathless himself by the end. When the band finally took a break, he and Edith headed toward the edge of the dance floor together.

"I could use a drink," Edith said.

"On me." Sebastian really had enjoyed the dancing and it was the least he could do. "Then I must go back to my friends."

"Must you?" Edith said lightly.

Sebastian offered her a sheepish smile. "I do."

"Oh." She smiled ruefully. "You got a girl already, don't you? Of course you do. I should've guessed."

"You are an excellent dancer," Sebastian said earnestly. "And it is a joy to dance with a beautiful woman. I would still very much like to buy you that drink."

She sighed, still smiling. "You even know how to turn a girl down like a gentleman. Yeah, all right, I'll take that drink."

There was a crowd at the bar, so they stood at the back. Sebastian made eye contact with Mack the bartender, who nodded at him.

"What would you like?" Sebastian started to ask Edith.

Only to have someone grab his shoulder, hard enough to bruise, and spin him around.

He was suddenly staring into the face of an angry white man of Arthur's size. "Who the fuck are you?" the man demanded. He was flushed red across his face, angry or drunk or both. "You dancing with my girl?"

"Billy, I told you, I ain't seeing you anymore," Edith snapped.

Sebastian tried to pull away, but Billy's fingers dug painfully into his shoulder. "She says she's not seeing you," Sebastian said, low and angry.

"I say she is," Billy said, through clenched teeth.

With a hard tug, Sebastian wrenched himself out of Billy's grasp. "Leave her alone," he started to say.

But Billy had already cocked his arm back.

Sebastian instinctively reached for his magic.

It was like reaching for a gun and finding only the holster. Reaching for a sword to find the scabbard bare.

Too late, Sebastian remembered his magic was gone, and he didn't have the time or coordination to duck.

Well shit was all he had time to think, and then Billy's fist was flying toward his face.

Wesley was doing an excellent job of pretending not to watch Sebastian, if he did say so himself. And it wasn't bloody easy, thank you very much, because Sebastian was graceful as a stag out on the dance floor. The girl was quite good as well, light on her feet as Sebastian spun her around. The pair of them looked like they were having fun.

And if Sebastian had effortlessly dipped the girl nearly to the floor and then pulled her into his arms, and Wesley had pulled out his first cigarette in three days, well. That was nobody's business but Wesley's.

Arthur was deep in conversation with Jade, but Rory was eying Wesley. "Sebastian keeps looking over here, you know. Trying to check in with you."

The music was changing and—oh, brilliant, a fucking *tango*, why not give Sebastian and his partner reasons to all but frot on the dance floor? Wesley forced his eyes back to his smoke.

"He oughtn't bother." Wesley struck a match. "He's a grown man. And more to the point, *I'm* a grown man, one who appreciates that dancing is an art, and whose partner is welcome to dance his way through Manhattan if he likes." He lit the end of the cigarette and inhaled deeply.

"Uh-huh," Rory said skeptically. "So you're not going to admit you're jealous?"

Wesley blew out a harsh stream of smoke. "Even if I was—which I'm *not*—that would be my problem, not Sebastian's."

"Uh-huh," Rory said again.

Sebastian had pulled the girl in very close. Because it was the tango and that was how it was danced. Wesley cleared his throat. "I have an open tab at the bar. You can put anything you like on it if you bring me back a whiskey neat."

"Deal." Rory stood and disappeared.

Wesley brooded through three cigarettes and two songs, and then Rory was back. He set a glass in front of Wesley, then sat down again with his own soda. "I started a tempest in here once 'cause I was jealous."

"In here?" Wesley raised an eyebrow. "I thought that was at Mr. Zhang's library."

Rory flushed. "Yeah, there too, but see, you gave me a *reason* to be jealous at Zhang's place," he added, pointing at him. "But before that, I was in here, and I got jealous just 'cause Ace told me he needed to bring his ex as a guest to a society event. I had the ring relic on and I lost control of the wind: shattered every bottle on the shelf, smashed the glasses, overturned the tables—I think I even broke the drum set."

Wesley brought the cigarette back to his lips. "Did you really?"

Rory nodded. "Ace never said but I know he footed the bill. I probably wrecked half this place, and all because I heard you were going with him to a wedding."

"Christ." Wesley took another drag. "You know, it's frightfully decent of you to admit all this to me and try to make me feel like less of a fool. You really need to stop being the better man of the two of us."

Rory huffed a kind of half laugh. "Not a better man. Just sympathetic about what it's like when half the world wants your fella."

"He says that as if he isn't the most adorable creature in this bar," Arthur said, turning to join their conversation as Jade and Zhang got up and disappeared in the direction of the stage.

"Shut up," Rory said fondly. "I'm sorry for Fine, all right?"

"Oh God, *Brodigan* feels sorry for me." Wesley exhaled the smoke. "I've truly hit a new low."

"I just don't blame you," said Rory. "I mean, that's one pretty doll Sebastian's dancing with."

"Not helpful," Wesley snapped, just as Arthur said, "Excuse me?"

"Well, she is," Rory said. "Pretty doll that can dance like that—who wouldn't be jealous? And now they're at the bar and he's buying her a drink."

Wesley had been leaning forward to tap his cigarette over the ashtray, but at Rory's comment, his gaze stole, without his permission, over to the bar.

Sure enough, Sebastian and his dance partner were part of the crowd waiting for the bartenders.

Wesley forced his gaze back to the ashtray. Yes, Sebastian was having several dances and now a drink with a pretty girl, but Wesley wasn't having feelings about it. Wasn't *green with envy* or *feeling blue* or any of the other hyperbolically colorful phrases coined by melodramatic poets with even less emotional control than Rory Brodigan.

"It's fine," Wesley said curtly, maybe to Rory, maybe to himself, as he tapped his cigarette. "After all, obviously *I* would never destroy half a speakeasy over a fit of emotion."

A sudden commotion made Wesley raise his head. His gaze was drawn to the side of the crowd, where a blond man Arthur's size was pushing his way toward Sebastian and the young lady. The big man's face was flushed with anger and too many drinks, like a bull about to make a bad decision.

Wesley was already on his feet when the man grabbed Sebastian by the shoulder—already halfway to the bar and had a full view when the man's fist connected with Sebastian's face.

And Wesley saw red.

"Get *off* him." He was between Sebastian and the angry man so fast he didn't remember moving. He shoved the blond man backward, hard enough he stumbled and staggered into the watching patrons.

"Who the fuck are you?" The blond man straightened up by pushing off some poor bystander, sending the unlucky fellow crashing into a third man drinking at the bar. "Edith's *my* girl."

"Hey, watch it!" the third man snarled as he sloshed

his own drink all over the bar. Dark liquid ran over the counter's edge and onto the lap of a woman, who yelped and jumped up from her stool.

"Billy, stop it," snapped Sebastian's dance partner, Edith apparently. She was bent over next to Sebastian, who had a hand on his face, smeared with red. Edith was speaking to Sebastian, but Wesley couldn't hear what she was saying over the ringing in his ears. This shit had made Sebastian bleed.

Two men had grabbed onto the blond man, Billy, in the futile attempt to restrain a giant arsehole fueled by jealousy and alcohol. Wesley shifted his weight, automatically falling into an old fighting stance from the war.

"What's it to you if I hit that guy?" Billy jeered at Wesley, as he yanked his arms free from the other patrons. "You think *he's* pretty?" And he came charging back at Wesley with a drunken bellow.

Wesley didn't bother fighting with honor. He dodged Billy's attempted blow and instead grabbed him by the arm, using Billy's own momentum to twist him around and slam his head down on the bar on top of a row of shots.

"You hit the wrong man," Wesley said into his ear, as drinks went flying, glass shattered and angry shouts went up.

"What the fuck?" someone snarled. "This was a new suit!"

Wesley had to dodge again as a different fist came flying his way. And all at once the mix of alcohol and angry men exploded in a whirl of shouts and fists. Wesley lost sight of Sebastian as the crowd closed in, shoving and swinging.

Some distant part of Wesley registered that he probably owed Rory an apology.

He needed to find Arthur, or even better, Jade with her telekinesis and Sasha with her superstrength. He pushed through the fight, twisting around a pair of men locked together like wrestlers, dodging a drunken want-to-be boxer—

Only to come face-to-face with Billy again, who had blood on his face and a knife in hand.

"Gonna hit the right man this time." Billy was already bringing the knife up—

And Wesley's knees gave out like they were suddenly made of water. He and Billy both hit the Magnolia floor, the knife tumbling out of Billy's hand and rolling off.

It couldn't be—

But before Wesley could process the sensation, or really even blink, his limbs were his own again.

"The fuck was that?" Billy started, already twisting on the floor in the direction of the knife.

Wesley leapt to his feet and kicked the knife toward the bar. Billy cursed, but as he grabbed for Wesley's foot, a different, even larger boot landed on Billy's chest and held him down.

"Don't even think about it." Arthur looked over at Wesley, holding Billy captive under his foot. "Did you just start a brawl in Jade's bar?" he demanded, as men fought around them.

Wesley huffed. "It wasn't actually my intent—"

"Someone will have called the cops by now." Arthur pointed at Wesley, then back at himself. "We are not going to let them raid the Magnolia. Wipe your face, dust off your poshest voice, and then you and I are going outside to handle the police."

"All right." There was something wet on Wesley's cheek, likely from where he'd hit the floor. Best not to think about what it might be. "But this cad under your foot," he said, as he wiped his cheek. "I want him thrown in the dock."

"Wesley."

"Drawn and quartered."

"This is not feudal England, *Lord Fine*, these are not your peasants—"

"He laid hands on Sebastian."

Arthur stilled.

"He drew blood," Wesley said, "from Sebastian, who has no way to defend himself anymore, because he gave up his magic to save my life."

Arthur frowned.

"Let me up, you fucking nancies," Billy snapped, from under Arthur's foot. "You mad I hit your *boyfriend*? Cops probably wanna hear about *that*."

Arthur's eyes narrowed. "New plan. First, I have a word with this gentleman. Then we bring him out with us to give to the police and pin this whole mess on him."

"I love a perfect plan," Wesley said.

Chapter Four

Rory was the one who pulled Sebastian out of the speakeasy. "Wait," Sebastian protested, as Rory steered him into a back hall. "I should help—"

"Nope." Rory tugged him toward the door at the end of the hall. "Between Jade and Sasha, they're gonna have the place locked down in a couple of minutes."

"But—"

"Zhang's with us right now, on the plane. If they need us, he'll tell me."

Sebastian huffed. "But—"

"You got blood all over your face and Fine's losing it; you're going outside."

Rory pushed Sebastian forward, and for someone short and skinny, he had a wiry strength that was surprisingly firm. Sebastian found himself swept out the side door and into the car-lined alley outside the Magnolia. A light snow was falling, maybe half an inch already coating the cars and bricks.

He grudgingly moved farther into the alley, toward a parked Model T. "What do you mean, Wesley's losing it?"

"I mean your fancy lord is in the middle of a New York bar brawl and he's not taking prisoners."

Sebastian winced. "Is Wes okay? Can Zhang see him?"

"Fine's fine." Rory pointed at Sebastian. "You? Not so much."

Sebastian bent to look at his reflection in one of the car windows, and cringed at his blood-streaked face. He gingerly felt his throbbing cheek, checking his cheekbone. Bruised, but not broken, at least.

"For the record," Rory said, leaning against the car door, "I'm never gonna let Fine live this down."

Sebastian winced again. "The fight is my fault—"

"Knock it off," Rory said, though not meanly. "You didn't do anything but dance. That guy was a prick who took a cheap shot at you. I don't blame Fine for being mad."

"But if I wasn't so useless, I could have dodged, and nothing would have happened for Wesley to get mad about." Sebastian's hand was unsteady where it touched his smarting cheek. "If I still had my magic, I could have neutralized him."

"Yeah," Rory said, with sympathy. "If you had your magic, you could've flattened the whole place. You don't, though, and that's okay, 'cause you got us, right? And you got Fine. Get the sense the fella who hit you is lucky Fine only put him on the floor and not in the grave."

Sebastian swallowed. His skin was clammy with cooled sweat from dancing and the outside cold was beginning to seep into him. He didn't even have a jacket on, snowflakes further dampening his thin dress shirt, and at the moment he happily would have taken a tailcoat for at least a little protection against a late November in New York.

"Billy should not be allowed around Edith." Sebastian scooped up a handful of snow off the car and held it to his bruised cheek. "I don't know if he'd hit her, but his temper—"

"No one's gonna let that dick near a doll again," Rory said. "Stella took your dancing partner into the back office and gave her some brandy. Ace and Fine are dragging the asshole out to hand over to the cops."

"The cops?" Oh no. "They're not going to shut down the Magnolia, are they?"

"You know Ace would never let that happen." Rory turned to a patch of empty air next to him, head cocked. "Yeah okay," he said to the air. "Ace and I will give Seb and Fine a ride."

Sebastian's skin was starting to sting under the uncomfortable cold of snow. "We can get a cab—"

"You've met Ace, right?" Rory said fondly. "He wants to see you two home safe and you might as well give in. Zhang says the cops are buying Ace and Fine's story; they're about to head our way."

A few minutes later, Sebastian was climbing into the backseat of the red Cadillac, Arthur behind the steering wheel and Rory in the front passenger seat.

"You want to come to our place tonight?" Arthur asked over his shoulder, as Sebastian scooted over to make room for Wesley.

"No." Wesley got in next to Sebastian, into the space behind Rory. "I'll tell the hotel we were mugged. They can get us a doctor."

"I don't need—"

"Yes you do," Wesley said, cutting off Sebastian's protest. "It's not up for debate."

Sebastian opened his mouth to argue, then sighed. "Okay," he said, in defeat.

Wesley raised an eyebrow. "The army medic is giving in that easy?"

"I'm not exactly winning any fights tonight," Sebastian muttered.

"Don't beat yourself up over it," Arthur said. "Only a complete lout throws a sucker punch like that."

"And maybe the fight went sour, but the dancing was real good," said Rory. "Where'd you learn to tango anyway?"

"Probably from some gorgeous woman in love with him," Wesley muttered. "I'm sure it's an outrageously sexy story."

"Oh yes, very sexy," Sebastian said, deadpan. "Isa made me learn."

Wesley blinked.

"My cousin Isabel," Sebastian said, for Arthur and Rory, "who is like my sister, and who only likes art—and women." He looked over at Wesley. "It was just a dance. But if you mind—"

"Of course I don't," Wesley said curtly. "Honestly I wasn't even paying attention. Did you tango? Didn't notice."

"Okay," Sebastian said uncertainly. He ran a hand over his hair and found it stiff with dried sweat. "I was just going to buy Edith the drink," he said, more quietly. "I told her I had to go back to my friends."

"It was a dance, not a fuck," Wesley said dryly. "I don't need to be reassured."

Of course he didn't, and Sebastian was probably insulting him by implying that Wesley might care if he danced with someone else. He hunched back against the seat. The ache in his cheek had seeped down to his jaw, crawled up to his temple and spread across his forehead, so that his entire head throbbed.

Wesley glanced at him, then huffed. "Here."

He shifted in the seat, awkwardly maneuvering until he'd managed to slip out of his jacket. He leaned over and wrapped it around Sebastian's shoulders. "I really should let you suffer, because you purposely underdressed just to tease me and now you're hoisted on your own petard. But you're shivering and our overcoats are back at the Magnolia."

Sebastian bit his lip. The jacket's lining was silk, and still warm from Wesley's body heat. He threaded his own arms through the sleeves, then glanced at Wesley. "Good thing it fits me."

The corner of Wesley's lips turned up in a grudging smile. "You *wish* it fit you."

And Sebastian abruptly was aware how much had happened that evening, and how very tired he was. How much would have liked to scoot across the seat to Wesley's side.

But the streets of Midtown were crowded, even on a cold night, with traffic thick enough that Arthur had to drive slow. Any passersby might see him pressed against Wesley unless he lay down on the seats. And as tempting as that was, if he lay down now, he might not be willing to get back up, so he pulled the jacket more tightly closed instead.

At the hotel, Sebastian hung back and let Wesley do the talking. As Wesley had predicted, the staff were properly horrified that an English aristocrat and his traveling companion had been mugged on their streets and injured.

A doctor was fetched immediately. Sebastian was bustled up to Wesley's parlor, where he was sat on the settee and had to submit to being poked at and prodded.

"Well, someone cleaned your clock, didn't they?" the doctor said, examining Sebastian's cheek.

Sebastian tried to keep his voice polite. "Nothing is broken," he told the doctor, smothering a wince as the man pressed on his face. "And I already put a cold compress on it."

"What Sebastian means is that he slapped some filthy alley snow on his cheek and thinks that's laudable," Wesley said dryly. "Please accept my apologies on the former army medic's behalf, doctor. He's unsurprisingly a terrible patient."

Sebastian narrowed his eyes at Wesley.

"Well, he's right enough." The doctor straightened and addressed Sebastian. "You'll have a bruise for a while but that should heal up, and there shouldn't be any scarring." He looked over at Wesley. "He doesn't seem to have had a concussion, but someone ought to stay with him tonight, just in case. I'll send for a nurse."

"No need, no need at all," Wesley said breezily. "He'll stay in my quarters tonight. For his own good, of course."

Sebastian fought back a grudging smile. Wesley was so shameless.

The doctor reached into his bag. "I have a powder you can take for the pain." He handed a small tin to Sebastian and added, kindly, "Next time, try to duck."

Sebastian was suddenly exhausted.

The doctor picked up his bag and Wesley began

walking him to the door. Sebastian seized his chance and disappeared through the bedroom and into the large adjoining private bath. He was achingly tired, but he smelled like blood from his nose, along with sweat from dancing and flowers from Stella's dressing room. The thought of lying on clean sheets made him cringe.

In the bathroom, he put some of the powder on his tongue, the bitter medicine flooding his mouth as he chased it with a few handfuls of tap water. As he started the bath, the phone rang out in the parlor, Wesley's voice a low rumble as he answered.

Sebastian stripped off the borrowed clothes, and then grabbed one of Wesley's soaps and climbed into the tub. He took a moment with the soap and running water to wash off the sweat and dried blood. When he was clean, he turned the hot water tap up even higher and put the plug in the drain.

As hot water filled the tub, he sat back against the cold marble with a sigh. Out in the parlor, Wesley was still on the phone, and Sebastian couldn't make out the words but the sound of his voice in the air was welcome. He closed his eyes.

A couple of minutes went by, and then the bathroom door opened. "That was Arthur, wanting to know what the doctor said. He's given up even pretending he's not New York's biggest mother bear." Wesley's voice was much closer. "You're having a bath? Are you a bath sort of man and I hadn't realized that yet? Not that I'm objecting to the view."

Sebastian cracked open one eye. Wesley was standing in the doorway, gaze locked on Sebastian. Despite his flirtatious words, however, his gaze was on Sebastian's face—more specifically, on his bruised cheek.

Sebastian looked away. "I'm getting warm."

Wesley gestured at his own body. "I'm not warm enough for you anymore?"

Sebastian leaned forward, turning off the taps. "Get in here with me."

Wesley snorted. "Duck," he said, slow and patronizing. "I'm not your lithe and lovely little Edith. I would not fit in there by myself, let alone with you."

Sebastian narrowed his eyes. "Get. In."

"Bossy tonight," Wesley said, in an interested tone of voice. He reached for his tie. "If you insist. But you can't say I didn't warn you."

A minute later, Wesley had stripped as well, and was settling into the other side of the tub. His long legs tangled with Sebastian's, bony feet and sharp knees pinning him against hard marble. And Sebastian would concede they didn't fit, and in a literal sense it wasn't as comfortable as it had been alone, but the water was blissfully hot, everything smelled clean like soap, and it was better with Wesley there.

Wesley settled into the water, facing Sebastian, arms along the edge of the tub. "Did you take the powder?"

"Yes." The bar of soap was floating along the water, light when Sebastian's own chest felt heavy. "You don't need to worry, you know. And you didn't need to get in a fight tonight. I can handle a hit on my own, Wes."

"Darling, really, do you have to make everything about you?" Wesley said, with a deceptive sort of lightness. "Has it occurred to you that perhaps *I* can't handle you getting hit?"

Sebastian blinked.

"You know, I actually wasn't aware I was capable of that sort of rage," Wesley went on, still with the false lightness. "I mean, obviously I've been angry many times in my life. Furious, even. But the way I felt when I saw that brute's fist strike your face—knowing you had no defense because you gave your magic up for *me*—"

He shook his head, not meeting Sebastian's gaze. "I do know I behaved like a bullheaded idiot, rushing to save you when you can take care of yourself, and starting a whole fucking bar brawl to boot. But what I'm trying to say is that you shouldn't take that as a knock to your ego. It wasn't that I thought you couldn't handle it; it was that I couldn't bear it."

"Wes." The heaviness in Sebastian's chest lightened, morphed, became something else, not embarrassment and shame at his own failure but something warm and sweet. He shifted, bringing his legs under him, because suddenly even tangled together in the tub wasn't close enough.

He leaned forward, fitting himself in between Wesley's legs as he brought his lips to Wesley's. They kissed softly, Wesley seeming to hold himself very still, maybe so he wouldn't accidentally put pressure on bruises. There was a trace of smoke in the kiss; Wesley must have lit a cigarette at some point, his nicotine addiction winning the battle tonight.

Sebastian pulled back. Wesley had struggles of his own and he was being honest; Sebastian was going to be honest about his own shortcomings in return. "My ego deserves the knock," he admitted ruefully. "Billy would have beaten me to a pulp if you hadn't stepped in."

Wesley licked the lips Sebastian had just kissed, looking into his eyes searchingly.

"I don't really know how to fight," Sebastian confessed. "Under blood magic, someone else pulled my strings, and with my own magic—" he shrugged helplessly "—I never had to learn." He swallowed. "So you weren't being a bullheaded idiot. I needed saving tonight. And I'm really lucky you were there."

Wesley raised his hand off the edge of the tub. It hovered in the air for a moment, like he was about to touch Sebastian's cheek, and then he lowered it. "Sebastian, I—" He uncharacteristically hesitated, then said, "You're certain your magic wasn't there?"

"I'm certain," Sebastian said. "Why?"

"It's just—there was a moment, in the Magnolia," Wesley said. "Billy had a knife, and I almost didn't see him in time, but before he made contact we both fell—"

Sebastian shook his head. "It was a fight, Wes. People fall. Magic has nothing to do with it."

Wesley didn't look fully satisfied by that, his gaze flitting over Sebastian's face. "But maybe—"

"Hope only makes disappointment sting harder," Sebastian said quietly. "You've always been right about that."

"Christ, don't *ever* take life lessons from me," Wesley said, more sharply. "Keep those rose-colored glasses on."

"But I've got to learn how to get through life without magic," Sebastian said.

"Why do you do this to yourself?" Wesley said, and this time his hand did come up, fingers lightly touching Sebastian's bruised cheek. "You were doing it in London, forcing yourself to move on immediately from literal blood magic. Now it's been barely a couple weeks without magic, yet you believe you're required to have already mastered a non-magic life?"

His words were sharp but his fingers gentle as they

drifted forward to twine in the damp hair at the back of Sebastian's head. "When life knocks you down, you can take a damn breath before you get back up," Wesley said gruffly. "You can even rely on others. Imagine that."

Sebastian's heart was beating faster, the warmth in his chest spreading through him. "I think you just said you're going to keep fighting speakeasies for me." It came out more serious, and less of a joke, than Sebastian had meant.

"Why wouldn't I?" Wesley said. "I mean, for fuck's sake. I think a knife fight was genuinely an easier feat than trying to fit together in this bathtub."

"We really don't fit," Sebastian said, and kissed him again anyway.

Wesley's mouth opened for his, letting his tongue slide between his lips as Sebastian's hand slipped under the water. He wrapped his hand around Wesley's cock and heard him suck in a breath.

"We don't fucking fit," Wesley said, against his lips, his cock stiffening in Sebastian's hand, "and soap in water is not nearly as slippery as one thinks it ought to be."

"It really isn't." Sebastian stroked him anyway, swallowing his groans with kisses. Earlier, outside of Jade's door, he'd been ready to pull Wesley on top of him. Now, though, he felt raw, aware of how lost he was without magic, aware that he didn't really know how to move on into a world where he didn't have it. But he had Wesley beneath him, letting him set the pace, pliant under Sebastian's hand and lips, like maybe this was what he wanted too.

Sebastian broke the kiss, moving his lips to Wesley's

neck and ear instead. "Can I take you to bed?" he whispered, gliding his hand up and down Wesley's cock.

"Christ." Wesley's eyelashes fluttered. "You can take me anywhere you like as long as it's bigger and softer than this fucking tub."

Sebastian huffed a half laugh and pulled all the way back.

They didn't manage to grab towels, stumbling out of the bathroom together with lips locked and hands on each other's skin until they fell as one onto the bed. Sebastian pushed Wesley over, and he went easily onto his back. The curtains were drawn and the bedroom lights off, but light spilled in from the bathroom, illuminating the long, strong lines of Wesley's body for Sebastian's eyes.

Sebastian crawled over him, balancing on all fours. Wesley had strength but didn't bend easily—in bed or in life—and Sebastian liked him just the way he was. "Ninguna magia podría encantarme como tú," he murmured.

Wesley's cheeks were flushed, his eyes gone half-lidded. "What are you saying?"

"Sappy things you won't want to hear in English."

"I know encantar is *enchant* and tú is *you* and I can guess magia is *magic*."

Sebastian kissed his neck, and Wesley's head fell back, giving him better access. "Then you can guess maybe something enchants me more than magic."

"No, stop, you're forbidden from saying anything so outrageously sentimental."

"There was a reason I said it in Spanish." Sebastian dipped his head to kiss Wesley's collarbone, then shifted to drop a kiss on his stomach.

Wesley arched up. "As much as I'd like you to keep going with that mouth," he said, breathless and needy, "I suspect that bruise on your face will not be pleased with what you're planning."

Sebastian kissed his stomach again, and his cheek twinged as if in agreement with Wesley. Fitting anything in his mouth would hurt. "I'm fine," he said stubbornly.

Wesley tsked. "Such a bad liar."

"You're not as big as you always think you are."

"That's not what you said the last time I fucked you."

Sebastian huffed a laugh into Wesley's skin. "I can handle a little pain, Wes. Aren't you the one who knows what to do with a flogger?"

"You're trying to distract me, but I know you're well aware that's a different game." Wesley's hand touched his hair, light and almost hesitantly gentle. "Christ, I'm still angry at that fucking degenerate who laid hands on you tonight. And I think you better fuck me before I storm that jail and demand to revive some of history's most gruesome and excruciating punishments."

Sebastian glanced up. "That's so...violently sweet?"

"You did say you wanted more romance."

Another laugh escaped Sebastian. Beneath him, Wesley's muscles were flexed and tensed, his cock hard and straining. Visibly wanting more, but he wasn't demanding it—was letting Sebastian take the lead.

"I think I understand why you liked this," Sebastian said, pushing away the twinge using the past tense, *liked*, had caused.

"What do you mean?"

"Why you liked pinning me down when I had magic." Sebastian kissed his hipbone, letting his tongue trace bath-warmed skin. "There is something about knowing you could take over but you won't, that you like this too. That it doesn't matter if you're bigger; I still get to have you however I want."

"I feel like you're fighting dirty right now," Wesley said, groaning. "Knowing how willing I am and using it to torture me. Except you *don't* get to have me however you want; you get to have me in a way that takes some damn care with your bruised face. You've got hands, duck; use them. Preferably *now*."

Wesley's authoritative tone sent pleasant shivers up Sebastian's spine. Only weeks ago, that tone of voice probably would have been accompanied by Wesley flipping him over and taking control. But even with the teasing, Wesley wasn't going to do that tonight—wouldn't do it ever again, unless Sebastian could handle it. Because even though Sebastian had lost his magic, he was completely safe with Wesley.

He kissed Wesley's stomach again.

"Sebastian de Leon," Wesley said, low and warning and gravelly with want. One of his hands was curled, the sheet balled in his fist. But he still wasn't taking over.

And yes, he really understood why Wesley had liked having him at his mercy so much when Sebastian had had his magic. But Wesley had endless patience to draw things out and Sebastian most definitely did not.

He shifted up to kiss over Wesley's heart, then grabbed the oil they'd left on the nightstand. As much as he wanted Wesley in his mouth, it *would* hurt. Wesley had his own battle scars from a bad past, and if he didn't want to be the cause of pain, Sebastian would always respect that. He slicked his palm with oil instead, working Wesley's cock and slipping fingers inside him, making him shift and shiver until they were both panting.

"Now, come on," Wesley said, a raw and needy edge to it. "Don't be gentle."

Sebastian thought he could almost hear the words Wesley wasn't saying. *My skin never stops crawling for nicotine. My mind never stills. Distract me, take me out of myself.*

Sebastian knew the feeling. The only place he could ever really escape was with Wesley.

He shifted, crawling up the bed so they could kiss again as he slid into Wesley, and the tightness of his body was enough to make Sebastian dizzy.

"Perfect," Wesley breathed, their lips so close that Sebastian felt the shape of the words more than heard them.

He rocked his hips gently, and Wesley arched, a groan of pleasure escaping him that sent answering sparks through Sebastian.

"Wes," he said softly, over the sound of their breaths. "Thank you for being there tonight."

"Oh no, you're talking, I'm never going to last now."

Sebastian laughed. He touched their foreheads together, rocking his hips again, all attention focused so he could move his body however Wesley liked best.

He needed to keep talking, though, to say it all. "When Billy swung at me, I didn't duck, because I tried reaching for my magic—but it wasn't there," he whispered. "I was falling, and reaching for a rope, but there was only empty air."

Wesley's hands tightened on his shoulders.

Sebastian swallowed. "But then *you* were there, Wesley. I needed help, and you were there."

"Sebastian," Wesley said, hoarse and rough.

And then they were kissing again.

Chapter Five

Wesley came awake to pale light cutting through the gap in the drawn curtains, falling across the bed. The air in the room was cold and the day would be gray. The Wesley of the past would have been unsurprised to wake to yet another miserable late-November morning.

He glanced down at Sebastian, curled so close that he was half on top of him, his skin soft against Wesley's own. The tropical flower's extra blankets were still piled on top of them, keeping their bed luxuriously warm.

The tiniest smile curled on Wesley's lips. November's weather could do what it liked; there was nothing cold or gray or miserable about this morning.

Sebastian's head was resting on his shoulder and his arm slung across Wesley's ribs. Despite the loss of his magic, he still treated Wesley like a personal teddy bear. Was it from the risks that sleep brought or did he just like Wesley's body heat? It seemed impossible that Sebastian could have no magic but still be at risk for the harrowing blood terrors that used to regularly imprison him in his own body.

But then magic itself was impossible, so who the fuck knew? As long as the uncertainty was there, it was simply good sense for Wesley to share his bed at night.

There were worse fates.

There was a stirring along Wesley's side as Sebastian shifted, pressing even closer into him. "Buenos días," he said into Wesley's skin.

If Wesley had been any good at affection, this would have been a moment for it. Sebastian was right here, where Wesley could have run a hand over his back or shoulder, or stretched down to press lips to his head—

His *head*? Christ. Of course Wesley wasn't going to his kiss his *head*, that was far too patronizing. Wasn't it? Or did lovers ever do that? Normal lovers, at least, not emotionally constipated curmudgeons like Wesley? Would Sebastian be fine with it, or would he think Wesley was being condescending?

Sebastian's eyelashes fluttered then, and he glanced up at Wesley with his gold-brown eyes and messy hair and maddeningly perfect ease at interacting with a lover outside of sex. "Come here."

And Wesley was suddenly pushed over, onto his side, Sebastian curling up behind him with his chest against Wesley's back.

For fuck's sake. Wesley had gotten stuck overanalyzing affection and now he was the little spoon. "What the hell do you think you're doing?"

Sebastian kissed the back of his neck, sending shivers over Wesley. "Sleeping."

"No, you're trying to *cuddle* me." Wesley was going to sit up and put an end to this outrageousness.

Except his traitorous body wasn't moving. In fact, his limbs were relaxing into Sebastian's warmth like he was some kind of hedonist. Why was Sebastian so bloody good at this?

Sebastian pressed his face into Wesley, prickly stubble against his shoulder like tiny fireworks on his skin. "But it's like you were made to be cuddled."

"How dare you."

Wesley was not going to stand for this. In one motion, he rolled over, drawing a noise of surprise from Sebastian as Wesley unceremoniously flipped him onto his other side.

Before Sebastian could move away, Wesley slung an arm over him to pin him down. "*I* do the holding," he said into Sebastian's ear. "This is the only acceptable position and I've got you trapped, so you may as well admit defeat."

Sebastian stilled.

Shit. Wesley hadn't been thinking. He needed to be careful, to never manhandle Sebastian in any way—

But then Sebastian was moving *into* him, pressing even closer and getting comfortable in Wesley's arms. "Okay," he said. "You win. Let's go back to sleep."

Wesley let out a huffed half-laugh of surprise. "We're not going back to *sleep*." He hesitated for a moment, then moved his hand to rest over Sebastian's heart. "Do you need me to release you?" he said, more quietly, more seriously.

Sebastian glanced over his shoulder, and their eyes met. "No," he said softly, with a tiny smile. "I'm good. *You're* the one who throws a fit when you're cuddled."

"Excuse me? A *fit*?"

Sebastian grinned. His eyes were lovely and warm against the gray morning, and his heartbeat was steady under Wesley's palm. "That's what I said."

Wesley tightened his arm, pulling Sebastian more firmly against him. "You're very fucking impertinent this morning."

"Maybe you shouldn't have told me you like it, then."

Wesley *did* like it. Heat was rising in his blood, the urge to push Sebastian onto his stomach, to pin him down, to bite at his shoulders as Wesley fucked him into the mattress, nice and slow, until Sebastian was breathless and whining and begging to come.

Wesley closed his eyes, took a breath through his nose, and forced his body to calm.

Maybe Sebastian used to enjoy that sort of thing, but he didn't have magic anymore and he had understandably complicated feelings about being pinned down now. And yes, Sebastian appeared to have no fear at the moment, despite being captive under Wesley's arm. He was even confident enough to give Wesley a hard time.

Wesley would enjoy it without demanding more. Sebastian deserved to have someone treat him carefully, even if he didn't treat himself with care—perhaps *especially* because of that. Wesley would not rush this.

The ringing of the phone cut through his thoughts. With an irritable huff, Wesley reluctantly got off the bed, grabbing his striped pajamas and tugging them on as he stepped into the parlor to take the call.

"Viscount Fine speaking."

"Good morning," Jade said into his ear. "I'm sorry to call so early, but I'm afraid you two must get packing."

Wesley raised his eyebrows. "Packing?"

"Immediately," Jade confirmed.

Sebastian was peering at Wesley from the tangle of sheets. Wesley curled his fingers in a beckoning motion. Sebastian frowned.

"Jianwei says to get dressed, by the way," Jade said.

"Miss Robbins, what on earth is going on?" Wesley asked, eyes on Sebastian as he grudgingly crawled out from under the covers. "Are you implying Mr. Zhang is about to join us on the astral plane?"

Sebastian's eyes widened. He grabbed Wesley's full-length green robe, pulling it on as he hurried into the parlor.

Wesley bent slightly, tilting the receiver so they could both hear Jade. "We're in the lobby," she said, voice floating up from the telephone, "and coming up to your room now."

The line disconnected. Sebastian and Wesley exchanged a look. "Why would we need to pack?" Wesley frowned. "Where are we going?"

There was a knock. Wesley went to the door, opening it to reveal Jade and Zhang. Wesley tilted his head. "No Arthur or Brodigan?"

"Not here," Jade said. "We have news."

"Clearly," Wesley said dryly, holding open the door for them to come in.

They sat in the parlor, Jade and Zhang taking the settee together while Wesley picked up the phone receiver. "Tea or coffee?"

"Neither, I'm afraid," said Jade.

"We can only stay a few minutes." Zhang's gaze had fallen on Sebastian. "Nice robe. Do those monogrammed initials stand for *Webastian de Ceon*?"

"Is that your own lipstick on your collar?" Sebastian said back, taking one of the armchairs.

Despite the tense set of his shoulders, Zhang smiled. "Flippant this morning, I like it."

"He must like *you*," Wesley said.

"That might be about to change." Jade held out two tickets to Sebastian. "The R.M.S. *Gaston* leaves this afternoon for the Port of Southampton. You two need to be on it."

Sebastian took the tickets with open confusion as Wesley dropped the phone back into the cradle. "I beg your pardon?" Wesley said.

"I kept an eye from the astral plane on that jerk from the Magnolia, Billy, at the police station," said Zhang. "He's trying to claim he took that swing at Sebastian because he's a criminal and a bootlegger."

"I mean," Sebastian said ruefully, "he's not *wrong*."

Wesley waved that away. "And the police are listening to that lout?"

"They might not have," Zhang said, "except they also picked up the two would-be bootleggers from Yonkers yesterday, and they described you, Rory and Sebastian to the police. The inspector has latched on to the two stories and thinks Sebastian might be using you as a mark. He hasn't been able to find any information on Sebastian either, thanks to a magical family that keeps themselves out of public records, and that's made the inspector more suspicious."

"And if the inspector keeps digging," Jade said, "he might discover guests who remember meeting Sebastian at a masquerade that was supplied bootlegged liquor by Alasdair Findlay—whose death is also under police investigation."

"For fuck's sake." Only a few weeks ago, they had jested about the police, because with a thought, Sebastian could have them all on the ground. Now, though, when he'd given up his defensive magic for Wesley—

"Outrageous." Wesley started forward. "I'm going straight to the station—"

"Obviously we're not going to let the police have Sebastian," Jade said firmly. "But it will mean questions. Time. And we don't have that anymore."

Zhang was getting to his feet. "Jade, love, we have to go; Gwen's cable has just arrived."

"*Why* don't we have time anymore?" Wesley said. "And just arrived *where*?"

Zhang gestured vaguely out the window. "Telegram office, a few blocks from here. I can't get a good enough look from the astral plane; we've got to pick it up in person."

Jade had also stood. "Arthur convinced his brother—the alderman—to distract the police. John has met both of you and will call the accusations ludicrous, but Ace also played a role in the bar fight at the Magnolia, and with John running for Senate, he obviously doesn't want any touches of scandal involving family members. We'll explain everything at the pier. Pack your trunks and meet us there, won't you?"

Two minutes later, Wesley and Sebastian were alone in the hotel suite again. "We're leaving for England *now*?" Wesley said. "I can't just tell the police to fuck off and leave you alone?"

Sebastian shrugged helplessly.

Wesley frowned. "I don't often see Mr. Zhang seem anxious. I wonder what that cable he just received said."

"So do I," Sebastian said quietly.

Sebastian's trunk was in his decoy room on the sixth floor. He had to sneak his clothes upstairs in stages to pack, trying not to make it obvious that he'd been more or less living with Wesley in New York. Then, when he was finally packed, he had to help Wesley, who had far more clothes than he did, and for all his wartime experience, was accustomed to having a footman pack his bags off the battlefield.

Finally, though, they had got everything loaded into a car for the trip from their hotel by Grand Central to the North River piers along the Hudson. A light rain started up as their cab made its way across Manhattan.

"I meant to send Teo a telegram before we left the hotel." Sebastian was trying not to poke at the contusion on his face. He'd taken more of the powder before they'd left, which helped the ache but didn't do anything for the red mottling his cheekbone. "Maybe I can still send it from the pier. He can tell my family where I'm going."

"Ignoring what an obnoxious older brother you're being, expecting Mateo to manage your correspondence," Wesley said, "I already sent one."

"You did?"

"Of course," Wesley said, like it was obvious he would keep up his letters with Mateo, which put a cozy sort of warmth in Sebastian's chest.

"And speaking of de Leons." Wesley glanced at the front seat, then lowered his voice, speaking so the cab driver could not have overheard. "I might know the current Valemount line, but we haven't really talked of the fifteenth-century Duke of Valemount. You said last night that he was a paranormal who married a Spanish countess, and they both made relics before they were found by your witch-hunting inquisitor ancestor, the original de Leon who cursed your blood?"

"Yes." Sebastian sighed, and then admitted, "The countess was also my ancestor."

"She was?" Wesley said in surprise.

Sebastian nodded. "She was a de Leon. The inquisitor was her brother."

Wesley's eyebrow went up. "And I thought my family had grievances."

"I imagine they didn't get along very well," Sebastian agreed ruefully. "With that much magic in his heritage, the current Duke of Valemount could be a paranormal himself."

"Seems possible," said Wesley. "And whatever else he is, the two of you may be related."

Sebastian blinked.

"Presuming the original duke had children with his Spanish countess, of course," Wesley said. "But if this inquisitor was your direct ancestor, and the present-day Valemounts are direct descendants of the inquisitor's sister, then you and the current duke would be some degree of cousins."

"It would be very distant," Sebastian said.

"Quite. But you'd be blood relations nonetheless," Wesley said, "in a world where blood magic exists."

It was a good point. Sebastian nodded grimly.

Soon their taxi was turning onto the busy street that ran along the Hudson, Manhattan's tall buildings rising up on their left and the row of piers and ocean liners along the river on their right. As the taxi pulled up to their pier, Wesley craned his neck, gaze on the crowd. "I see the others, already coming our way." He added, under his breath, "And I'm fairly certain Arthur and Brodigan's luggage is floating an inch above the dock."

As Sebastian followed Wesley out of the taxi and onto the curb, their four friends joined them, Jade and Arthur with umbrellas. "There you are," Jade said, as light drops fell on Sebastian's flat cap. "First class is already boarding."

"You lot could have gone ahead," Wesley said, as a

pair of dockhands approached. "Wait. You *are* coming, aren't you?"

Arthur and Jade exchanged a look. "We decided Rory and I would come with you," Arthur said. "But Jade and Zhang can't follow yet."

"What?" Sebastian said, furrowing his brow.

Jade motioned them over. The six of them huddled together on the sidewalk, forming a cozy knot under the two umbrellas while the dockhands began unloading Wesley's and Sebastian's trunks from the taxi.

"We weren't able to get four first-class staterooms," Jade explained, the raindrops now a gentle patter on the shared umbrellas. "We were lucky to get two—one for Lord Fine, and one for Sebastian. Arthur and Rory are sharing a cabin in second."

"But I don't want you or Rory to have the worse room," Sebastian protested.

"Oh no, I'll have to live for a few days without a marble sink and a butler up my ass, how ever will I manage," Arthur said, deadpan. "I assure you, it's quite fine. Frankly I'd choose bunking with Rory in *fourth* over being cloistered with the stuck-up pricks in first."

"Thank you, Arthur," Wesley said dryly.

"We need to question the current Duke of Valemount, now more than ever," Jade said. "Lord Fine said they're in the same circles and can attend the same parties. We want it known that Lord Fine is returning to England so he receives those invitations."

Sebastian didn't want to separate from Wesley, but he also didn't want to draw undue suspicion. "But your father is a congressman, no?" Sebastian said to Arthur. "Aren't you the most logical choice of all of us to travel with Wesley? You could go to any party with his peers and no one would think anything of it."

"True," Jade said, "but we have an even better idea."

She pointed at Sebastian.

His eyes widened. "What would I know of English high society?" Sebastian said, trying not to squirm under the others' stares.

"Well, let's see," Zhang said. "You had an aunt who was supposed to marry the Earl of Blanshard."

"And another aunt you just told me was the Spanish countess who married the original Duke of Valemount," Wesley added. "Somehow I doubt either of those men would have been eager to marry commoners."

"Wait," said Rory. "You're *related* to this Lord Valemount fella?"

"It would be very, *very* distant," Sebastian said weakly.

But the others were still staring at him. Wesley tilted his head. "Something you neglected to tell us, Sebastian?"

"No," Sebastian said firmly. "I haven't been hiding some kind of title all this time. The things you and Zhang bring up are ancient history."

"What do you think English peerage is built on?" Wesley said. "That Spanish princess you once mentioned, with superstrength. She wasn't *another* of your relatives, was she?"

Sebastian groaned. "Why is your memory so good?" He made a face. "Our world is magic. My parents had left all of that other stuff behind even before they went to Puerto Rico. The titles, high society—that's your world, Wes."

"Perhaps," Jade said. "But you still know enough to pass as a Spanish aristocrat, don't you?"

Oh no. "Please say you're joking, Jade."

"Of course I'm not joking," Jade said, with a grin. "We've booked your ticket under a pseudonym. You can infiltrate the aristocracy as the eldest son of a Spanish count—a glamorous international bachelor heading to London with his friend, the Viscount Fine."

"This way you can attend every social event with Lord Fine and be a second pair of eyes and ears," Zhang added. "It needs to be you who joins Fine to talk to the Duke of Valemount, and not Arthur or Rory. You're the most likely to recognize it if he refers to anything about the relics."

The others were nodding along with Jade and Zhang. "A count's son." Sebastian rubbed his forehead. "Dame paciencia," he muttered.

Rory snorted. "You gotta find your own patience," he said, sounding amused. "But are you gonna blow your cover walking around like that?" he said, pointing to Sebastian's cheek.

"Oh, that part's fine," Arthur said, with an unconcerned wave. "You'd be surprised how often so-called men of culture get in fights. Just look at the entire concept of dueling."

"I want to protest, but Arthur is right, we can invent any number of stories to explain a bruise," Wesley said. "Boxing, outdoorsmanship, or hell, simply tell the truth—you were defending a girl from some lout." He turned to Jade. "This covers us, but Miss Robbins, why are you and Mr. Zhang taking another ship?"

Zhang held out a piece of paper. "Our cable from Gwen."

Wesley held it flat so Sebastian could read it too.

```
HYDE MISSING STOP TRAIL POINTS TO TANGIER
STOP WE ARE EN ROUTE TO SPAIN NOW STOP
```

"I don't understand," Wesley said, as Sebastian stared at Gwen's message, stomach in knots. "Gwen Taylor is your friend in London, the one with witch-sight who controls the tide, married to the man who can turn invisible? And Hyde I assume refers to the paranormal who called himself Mr. Hyde, who has a very bad history with several of you?"

That was putting it lightly. Hyde was a paranormal with shape-shifting magic who'd been prisoner under the same blood magic as Sebastian, only Hyde hadn't needed any motivation to kill or maim. Arthur still bore scars from Hyde's claws, a remnant of an interrogation during the war.

"I understood from Gwen and Ellis that Hyde was securely locked away in a remote English asylum," Jade said. "Sebastian, she said the three of you took him there and saw that his cell was fully secured, with magic traps painted by your cousin Isabel. Hyde is terribly dangerous, yes, but last I knew, he was bound by Rory's magic, his mind trapped in the fifteenth century."

"And he can rot there," said Rory darkly. Despite their size difference, he'd moved to stand protectively close to Arthur. "My magic wouldn't have let Hyde go, not after what he did to Ace. If anyone deserves to be locked up, it's that monster."

Wesley frowned. "Then pardon my language, Miss Robbins, but who the hell would free him?"

"Hyde has three kinds of magic," Sebastian said quietly.

They all turned his way.

Sebastian looked up from Gwen's telegram. "Hyde cannot control his own shape-shifting because he was warped by a relic's magic. So he has his own magic, the relic's magic, and Rory's magic." He took a breath. "And to unlock the medallion with hunting magic, you need to murder a paranormal with at least three kinds of magic."

"The same medallion relic that was made by the original Duke of Valemount," Wesley said, in understanding. "This is why we're rushing back to England."

Zhang nodded. "We have to find where Hyde has gone. And we have to follow all our leads. We can't wait any longer to investigate the current Duke of Valemount."

Downriver, another ship blasted its horn, a deep reverberation that echoed around Manhattan's edge.

"Find a way to meet the duke but be *safe*," Jade said firmly. "Jianwei and I are leaving tomorrow on a ship to Lisbon. From there, we'll work our way to Gwen and Ellis, and then back to you."

Chapter Six

The dockhands disappeared with their trunks, which would be waiting in their cabins. After getting Sebastian's forged documents from Jade, and making promises to Arthur to find a way to check in, Wesley followed Sebastian up the ramp and onto one of the decks of the ship. Despite the cold and continuing light rain, there were several groups of people standing in tight knots against the railing, waving down to the people on the pier below. A group of suited Englishmen were boasting loudly of their American investments while a trio of exquisitely dressed French women were sharing cigarettes.

Wesley snagged Sebastian's sleeve and tugged him in the opposite direction of the women. "Pity our cabins aren't connecting," he said, as he opened one of the doors off the deck. "Though I probably should be grateful we're on the same floor, given the timing."

They stepped into the first-class reception room, which spanned the width of the ship. The carpet was patterned in brown and gold, with white walls and arched tall windows lining the sides. Several passengers were lingering in chairs and at tables, entertained by a string ensemble.

They crossed the room, heading for the arched opening at the far end. "I want to come see where your cabin is." Sebastian took off his cap and ran a hand through his hair, which was still a bit wild after Wesley had gotten his hands in it the prior night. "Then I guess I have to clean up for dinner."

"Oh duck, you can't make that sour face about wearing proper clothes," Wesley said, amused. "Not when you're the glamorous international bachelor Don Sebastian."

Sebastian groaned.

They passed the main dining saloon, filled with rows of white-clothed tables set amongst columns under a gilded ceiling, then stepped into a lobby. A chandelier hung from the dome two stories above, and a wide staircase with white steps and dark railings of oak and intricate ironwork led both up and down from the lobby. They took the stairs up, and Wesley found his stateroom on the C-deck. No private sitting room or private bathroom, but he did have a small desk and chair, a marble sink with running water, and a slim but elegantly appointed single bed set against the wall beneath a large porthole window.

"My room will be like this, I think; it's just down the hall." Sebastian leaned on the closed stateroom door. "I will go find it after we set sail."

Wesley raised an eyebrow. "Are you implying we're going to join the crowd for the ship's departure? As in, we'll watch from the deck outside, where it's three degrees above freezing and raining?"

"Yes," Sebastian said. "We're not going to see land for a week, Wes; we want to say goodbye to the skyscrapers. The tops may even be up in the rainclouds today."

Wesley sat on the edge of the bed. It was narrow enough that trying to fit in it with Sebastian would likely result in one of them tumbling to the floor, but Wesley was game to try. "Couldn't Brodigan simply use his own ring relic to blow the clouds away? Actually, *no*, tell me he wouldn't attempt to change the weather while we're at the mercy of the ocean. In fact, given how quickly I get under his skin, it's probably best if he never wears it in my vicinity at all."

"We're perfectly safe with Rory," Sebastian insisted.

"You're truly incorrigible, with your reprehensible faith in others," Wesley said. "That surly urchin controls the wind. I look forward to saying *I told you so* when he blows me overboard in a fit of pique, although at that point I suppose I'll likely be a meal for a giant squid."

Sebastian stepped closer, bumping up against Wesley's knees. "I won't let you become squid food."

"Oh, you'll protect me, will you?" Wesley said, letting Sebastian fit himself between his legs. "Does aquatic life have the same fondness for you as land animals? That would fucking figure, wouldn't it?"

Sebastian grinned. He tipped Wesley's hat back, and then leaned down to fit their lips together, both his hands cupping Wesley's jaw. The ship's horn went off as they kissed, two deep blasts that vibrated in Wesley's chest.

When Sebastian pulled back a moment later, Wesley blinked. He didn't seem to be starting anything more. "I don't know what you just tried to butter me up for, but yes, you can have it," Wesley said, to cover his discombobulation.

Sebastian laughed. "I'm not asking for anything. I just like to kiss you."

Yes, but I also like to kiss you, Wesley wanted to say, *so what the fuck is your secret for giving affection so easily and won't you bloody teach me already?*

"The ship is leaving soon," Sebastian went on, oblivious to Wesley's ruminations. "Let's say goodbye to Manhattan."

"And there it is," Wesley said, as he let Sebastian pull him to his feet. "You *are* asking for something; you're asking me to come look at the view."

"You have the best eyes," Sebastian said unapologetically. "You can tell me what birds you can see."

"I don't have to set foot outside to tell you that. There will be gulls, who are as much of a menace as pigeons."

"Pigeons aren't menaces," Sebastian predictably countered, starting to turn toward the door.

"Says the animal-loving menace himself." Wesley caught Sebastian by the belt. "And here you could have said you want your own Bentley," he said, as he pulled him closer. "Hell, after a kiss like that, I'd buy you the damn Bronx Zoo."

Wesley kept his movements careful, almost gentle, so Sebastian could have easily escaped if he'd been spooked. But he was grinning, his body pliant and at ease with being manhandled across the stateroom— or, at least, at ease when *Wesley* manhandled him, and perhaps Wesley alone. That thought went straight to the same reprehensibly atavistic part of Wesley's brain that had preened over having the tattoo's hidden lion to himself. Magic or not, Sebastian trusted him in ways he didn't trust anyone else, and magic or not, it apparently still drove Wesley wild.

"The only thing I want is you," Sebastian said, as he

let Wesley tug him exactly where he wanted him, which was right into Wesley's arms.

You already have that, and embarrassingly completely. Wesley didn't say it, instead sliding his hands lower on Sebastian's back. "Listen to you, trying to charm me. You know I'm not that easy."

"Are you sure?" Sebastian twined his own arms around Wesley's neck. "Because you just offered to buy me a zoo."

"I think you just called me a sucker," Wesley said. "It's almost like you're trying to goad me into throwing you down on this bed."

"No, no, I am the innocent, remember?" Sebastian's smile was a little wicked as he tilted his head back and chin up, so their lips were more aligned. "You besmirch my character."

"I can *besmirch* a lot more than that—"

There was a polite knock on the door. Wesley sighed and let Sebastian go, stepping over to answer the door to reveal two young men in bellhop uniforms.

"My lord," one of them said. "We have your luggage. Your hotel forwarded a cable from London. Made it just in time." He held out a sealed envelope.

Sebastian moved to look out the large porthole as the bellhops carried in luggage. Wesley opened the envelope to find a cable from his second cousin, Geoffrey.

```
THORNTON INVITED ENTIRE CLUB TO BECKLEY
BALL STOP ASKED IF YOU WILL BE HOME IN
TIME STOP ASSUMING OF COURSE YOU ARE
STILL ALIVE STOP IF YOU ARE DEAD HAVE
THE COURTESY TO LET ME KNOW STOP
```

Lord Thornton's ball at Beckley Park.

The Duke of Valemount would almost certainly be there, and now that they were unexpectedly aboard the *Gaston*, he and Sebastian would arrive in England in time to attend.

Shit.

"Lord Fine?" Sebastian was looking at him with a furrowed brow as the bellhops placed Wesley's trunk. "Everything all right?"

Wesley hastily tucked the cable back in the envelope like the craven coward he was. "Nothing important. Just Cousin Geoffrey being Geoffrey."

He'd have to tell Sebastian what kind of ball it was. Of course he'd tell him.

Eventually.

After leaving Wesley's stateroom, Sebastian followed him up the grand staircase to B-deck. Well-dressed first-class passengers, many with umbrellas, were clustered along the railings, some of them watching with impassive faces while others waved handkerchiefs at the pedestrians down below.

It *was* crowded, but they finally found a spot near a grouping of deck chairs on the ship's port side. Sebastian pulled his coat closed for warmth, leaning on the railing as the engines deepened and vibrated, taking them away from the pier.

"Can you see Arthur and Rory anywhere?" Sebastian asked, craning his neck to view the other classes' decks below.

"No." Wesley was scanning the crowd. "Though I do recognize a pair of London's top solicitors and a dowager who's great friends with my third cousin."

The ocean liner was making its way down the Hudson, passing Manhattan on the left. Sebastian was still keyed up from the rush of the day, the flurry of their unexpected departure. He took a breath of rain-tinged sea air, letting it fill his lungs. "Do you want to go talk to them?"

"Do I ever want to talk to anyone?" Wesley said dryly. "I'll remain here, thank you. I'll get more than my fill of others when we're back in England." He huffed. "One might reasonably have assumed all this paranormal lunacy would not include socializing, but apparently even magic can't spare me from people and parties."

Sebastian snorted. "Didn't you mention a party at the Magnolia? It was a ball, I think you said—one you were sure the Duke of Valemount was attending?"

"Oh," Wesley said, his voice a little higher. "You remember that?"

"Of course I remember," Sebastian said. "You said it was hosted by Lord Thornton. I told you that I knew his maid, the one who was murdered in Kensington in September. So sad; Olive was so sweet, and Lord Thornton is apparently an asshole."

"He is," Wesley agreed quickly. "You wouldn't like to meet him."

"I may have to," Sebastian said. "Jade and the others were right, I need to go to your society events, yes? Or, well. Don Sebastian needs to," he added wryly. "What day did you say that ball was going to be? Are we going to be able to make it now?"

Wesley seemed to be looking very intently at the skyline. "Well—boats, you know. At the mercy of the currents and the wind. Hard to say exactly when we'll arrive and if we'll make it in time, isn't it? Look, there's the Woolworth Building. And at least thirty squawking gulls feasting on fuck knows what down in the river. Best we don't ask, I'm sure."

Sebastian smiled, watching the seagulls. "I like the sounds they make. They're so cute."

"If you like feathered sea-rats—" Wesley sighed. "Which, of course, you do."

The boat continued its stately glide out of the Hudson River and into the bay. The daylight was waning with early evening, and the city lights were coming on, making the skyline glow against the silvery rainclouds. Finally, when the city and the gulls had been left behind, they returned down to their rooms.

Sebastian's stateroom was a mirrored version of Wesley's, several doors down the hall but on the same side. He found their deck's gentlemen's lavatory, where he shaved and took the time to style the sea-blown waves of his hair before heading back to his cabin to dress for dinner.

He pulled on the tuxedo he'd bought for the Halloween masquerade with a pair of generic cufflinks he'd bought in Paris. Some of the guests would be in tailcoats, true, and judge him for his modern tastes. He'd simply have to ignore it. When they'd needed to face the Earl of Blanshard, Wesley had entered Sebastian's world of magic as bravely as a soldier marching onto a battlefield. Now they were infiltrating Wesley's circles to find the source of Langford and Alasdair's plot to destroy magic. Sebastian didn't have magic anymore, but he couldn't let that stop him; he needed to square his shoulders and match Wesley's courage.

His gaze fell on the bed. Not big enough for two men,

especially one as tall and accustomed to space as Wesley. They'd already stepped into Wesley's world with this ship, and they'd be onboard with the same guests, in the same spaces, for nearly a week. People might want to know how Wesley had become acquainted with a Spanish count's son, and they would need to be careful to avoid rumors.

Would need to stick to their own rooms at night.

Sebastian straightened up. And that would be fine. He couldn't have blood terrors if he didn't have magic. The lingering nerves in his stomach at the thought of sleeping alone were a bright neon sign that he hadn't fully accepted that his magic was gone. He needed to move on to his new, magic-less life, and he would start tonight.

Wesley was the one to knock on his door a few minutes later, and then they descended the grand stairs with the other guests for dinner, joining the sea of men in black suits and women in vibrant dresses. They crossed the lobby, passing under the arched entrance and into the full dining saloon.

"I do realize masquerading as a count's son is not your first choice," Wesley said, after they'd been seated at a table. "But you completely look the part. I'm going to have my work cut out for me."

Sebastian furrowed his brow. "What work?"

"Not snapping at every well-bred lady sneaking glances in your direction," Wesley said ruefully. "And I assure you, all of them are looking."

Sebastian opened his mouth.

"If you say a single word about protecting my reputation, I'm going to make you pay for it," Wesley said first. "You're so handsome in that tuxedo that it's making me more intriguing and desirable by proxy. You already know I'm known as an intolerable arsehole; your presence literally improves my reputation."

Sebastian felt his shoulders lower an inch and the corner of his lips turned up. "Tell me, Lord Fine." He leaned in. "If I still care about your reputation, how would you make me pay?"

He got to see Wesley's gaze heat, but then the waiter was at their table with the night's menu.

They had just finished dinner when Sebastian saw Wesley stiffen, an uncharacteristic expression of surprise on his face. "What is it?"

Wesley cleared his throat. "Your three o'clock. By the column."

Sebastian's gaze followed his direction. Past two rows of tables full of other passengers, and standing alone by a column, was a stately woman, probably around Sebastian's age and nearly his height. She wore an elegant gold sheath dress and matching headpiece over her thick, chestnut-brown bob.

"That's Nora Fairfield," Wesley said under his breath. "One of the Duke of Valemount's nieces."

Sebastian's eyebrows went up.

The woman didn't seem to have noticed Wesley, or if she had, she wasn't looking in his direction. Her gaze was in the opposite direction, watching other tables as if waiting for someone.

"At the Magnolia, I told you the Valemount title went to a brother because the previous duke had five daughters," Wesley said, just as quietly. "Lady Nora is one of them."

Sebastian carefully stole another subtle glance at

Lady Nora. She was still waiting, her large blue eyes and reserved expression giving away none of her feelings. "This seems like a big coincidence, doesn't it?"

"It damn well fucking does," said Wesley. "She's also a direct descendant of the fifteenth-century Duke of Valemount. Perhaps she's here to spy on behalf of her uncle. Or perhaps we've had the wrong Valemount all this time, because it might interest you that Lady Nora has a well-known penchant for traveling. After she lost her father, she's been almost exclusively abroad. Mesopotamia. Egypt. *Morocco.*"

Sebastian's eyebrows went up. "Gwen and Ellis think Hyde's disappearance might lead to Tangier."

Wesley spread his hands. "Maybe it's just another coincidence," he said dryly.

Sebastian frowned, watching Lady Nora out of the corner of his eye. "You know a lot about her."

"*Know* is too strong a word, but we've met. My third cousin Lady Tabitha tried to match us once, right after the war," Wesley said wryly. "I think Lady Nora was even less interested in me than I was in her." He cleared his throat again. "And look."

A tall man with a walking stick was joining Lady Nora. He seemed older than her, perhaps, although he had a full beard and thick glasses like Rory's that made his age hard to place. He was sedately dressed in unremarkable black tie and wore a bowler hat, even indoors.

Lady Nora seemed to know the man well, conversing with him quietly as they began to walk through the corridor between tables to the arched entrance to the saloon. Sebastian kept his gaze forward as they approached in his peripheral vision, two rows of tables over. "You don't know her companion?"

"I do not," Wesley said. "There is, perhaps, something familiar about him, so I suppose it's possible we've attended the same event at some point or another. But I don't know who he is, and I'm now wondering quite fervently if either he or Lady Nora could be a paranormal."

If Sebastian had had his magic, he could have reached out with it right then. He would know instantly whether they had auras, which would weaken under his magic and send them tumbling to the ground—or if they had magic, which would be neutralized under his enervation.

Before he'd realized he was going to do it, Sebastian was reaching for his magic, anticipating the rush that had been with him for almost twenty years, the stampede of wild horses charging through him.

But there was nothing.

The stable was empty; his magic was gone.

Sebastian's shoulders dropped. It hurt more this time, like reaching for a lover and finding an empty bed because they'd left you in your sleep.

He reached for his water with an unsteady hand, trying to keep the loss off his face as Lady Nora and her companion continued past their table without pause.

Wesley's gaze was on Lady Nora and the man. "He's got a pipe pouch in his jacket pocket; you can see the outline." He touched his own jacket, right over his heart, rubbing his hand across his chest distractedly. "The first-class smoking room is on A-deck. A man with a pipe might reasonably be found in there after dinner."

Sebastian nodded.

This was also a British ship, not an American one, which meant the smoking room would have drinks.

Sebastian wasn't a paranormal anymore—there was nothing stopping him from matching Wesley's whiskeys, if he wanted. It was time to stop believing there could still be a chance of his magic activating. Time to stop lying to himself.

"Guess that's where we should go next," Sebastian said, and tried to pretend his heart didn't hurt.

Chapter Seven

The smoking room was paneled in dark mahogany, the wall's carvings accented with mother-of-pearl under an intricate ceiling. There were several card tables, and club chairs upholstered in burgundy leather. Attendants in black tie flitted about the space, serving drinks and bringing cigars.

Wesley picked a pair of chairs in a deep corner, where they could watch the room and the door. Sebastian had seemed a bit subdued during dinner, even declining dessert despite his fondness for sweets. Being off food might have been expected if Wesley's dining companion had been Rory Brodigan, but the seas were calm and Sebastian didn't suffer from seasickness. Wesley thought they had put the issue of reputation to rest; maybe once they were alone again, he could tease out whatever was eating at Sebastian.

An attendant came by with a box of cigars. "Drinks, gentleman?" he said, offering Wesley the box.

Wesley grabbed a cigar at random. "Whiskey neat."

"Same," Sebastian said, shaking his head at the cigars.

Wesley carefully kept his face blank. No one ever owed him or anyone else an explanation for why they were or weren't drinking. But Sebastian's abstention had seemed like it might be due to a lingering hope that his magic was still around.

Maybe Sebastian had given up even that.

Wesley didn't comment on it. Nor did he comment on the second whiskey, as they chatted together in the corner of the smoking room and watched for Lady Nora or her male companion to enter. The whiskey was strong and the pours generous; Wesley would need to pace himself if he wanted to keep his head.

So when Sebastian not only ordered a third, but made his a double, Wesley cleared his throat. "You're sure that's what you want?"

"Why?" The smoking room was dim, but Sebastian's eyes were shiny enough already to reflect the low lights, and there was more color in his cheeks than usual.

"Just thinking of the last time you drank two whiskies," Wesley said nonchalantly. "Perhaps you don't recall? You passed out on the floor of Shepherd Hall and I had to put you to bed."

"I was a different person then," Sebastian said, more quietly.

"Yes, but duck," Wesley said, slow and patronizing, "there are plenty of lightweights without magic."

"Why would I be one?"

"Because *you're* not as big as you always think you are?" Wesley gestured at his own second whiskey, which was still half-full. "At the very least, are you sure you want to outdrink me? I've had years more experience with my own alcohol tolerance and I'm bigger than you to boot."

Sebastian rolled his eyes. "Barely bigger."

"It's not *barely*," Wesley said. "And if I get you under

me, you're going to see our size difference is more than you think."

Oops. Damn, it *was* strong whiskey. Wesley needed to watch his tongue.

Though the comment didn't seem to have made Sebastian nervous. His gaze was on Wesley, sweeping over him before coming back up to his shoulders, his lips. Sebastian wet his own lips. "All talk, no action," he said lightly.

Heat rolled through Wesley. "Your efforts are impressive, I'll give you that," he said, pushing his desire down. "But you're trying to change the subject, and that doesn't work on me. I assure you, no action of any kind will be taking place if you get yourself drunk." He leaned in. "Talk to me," he said, in a whisper that wouldn't reach beyond Sebastian. "What's going on tonight?"

Sebastian's shoulders dropped. He was silent a long moment, staring into the smoking room but not seeming to see anything.

"Sebastian," Wesley said, still quiet, "you don't have to pretend with me."

Sebastian let out a sigh. "I tried to use my magic again," he finally said. "But nothing happened. It's gone, Wes. It's really gone."

"Oh, duck," Wesley said, and this time there was nothing patronizing about the endearment.

"I don't regret it," Sebastian said, with feeling. "I don't ever want you to think I regret it. I'm so grateful I was able to save you. I'd do it every time."

"I know," Wesley said truthfully, because he did know, and it was still humbling, the knowledge that

Sebastian had chosen him over magic and would do it again.

"And I don't blame you," Sebastian said, with just as much feeling. "You were only in that attic because you had come to save *me*."

"I know that too," Wesley promised. "The fault was Langford's, and Alasdair's, and whoever might have been masterminding their actions."

He leaned even closer. "But it's all right if you wish you could have me *and* magic. You're allowed to miss it." His gaze softened. "How difficult this all must be for you, missing your magic but thinking you have to conceal those feelings lest you hurt *my* feelings. I can't bring your magic back, but I can promise you don't have to hide your heart too."

Sebastian looked at him with a kind of helpless gratitude. "Thank you, Wes," he whispered.

The waiter was approaching with Sebastian's drink. "We will find out who was behind this," Wesley promised. "Lady Nora's mysterious man doesn't seem to be showing up, but we're on a ship—he can't conceal himself all week." A rueful smile curled on his lips. "And for tonight, if you're determined not to listen to my better judgment, you can find out for yourself what happens if you keep drinking those whiskies."

He pointed at Sebastian. "But I'm not going to carry you back to your stateroom. I am not actually a sucker and I do draw the line somewhere."

"I'll be fine," Sebastian said loftily.

Wesley picked his glass back up. "Sure you will."

"Wesley. Wes. Wes, I think the floor is moving."

Wesley tried not to smile as he watched Sebastian

inch across the smoking room as tentatively as if he was walking on a tight rope. "Christ, I love saying *I told you so*."

"It's not whiskey, it's waves." Sebastian gingerly stepped through the lounge doorway and into the ship's carpeted hall, one hand braced on the wall. "Las olas del océano. You know? The ocean waves are making the inside of the boat move."

"You think so?" Wesley said. "And here I'm walking just fine."

"Well, maybe I'm just not as good as you at…walking."

"I bet that sounded like a really clever retort in your head."

"Hush." Sebastian frowned at the stairs in front of him. "Is the cabin up or down?"

"You are so lucky I'm here," Wesley said, with a pitying shake of his head. "Otherwise, I'd probably find you wandering the boat deck. Down the stairs."

Sebastian's brow furrowed. He carefully wrapped his hand around the railing and stepped down onto the first stair. Wesley quickly moved closer. It was nearly midnight and the few other passengers about were paying them no attention. He might be teasing, but he wasn't going to let Sebastian tumble down a flight of stairs.

Sure enough, when Sebastian tried the third step, he stumbled. Wesley caught him before he pitched face-first into the stairs. "Steady there, duck."

"Me encantan los patitos." Sebastian made a walking motion with his fingers. "Tan lindo pajaritos, como siguen a su mama."

"A first-class education in Latin, and I'm using it to try to decipher your drunken rambling." Wesley shifted but kept a firm hold on Sebastian's bicep. They'd been to enough parks that he recognized *pato* and *patito*, by now, at least. "I said I wasn't going to carry you, and yet here I am, keeping you upright while I'm pretty sure you're babbling about ducklings following their mother. How unacceptably soft I've become. At least Arthur and Brodigan aren't here to see this."

"They're not?" Sebastian said, with sincere confusion. "Where did Arthur and Rory go?"

"They're in second class, which you've apparently forgotten. I'm sorry, but you truly have no head for whiskey." Wesley kept his secure hold as they walked down the stairs. "That's one flight down, steady on, one more deck to go."

They made it to C-deck and Wesley guided Sebastian down the hall. No one was about, so he fished Sebastian's key out of his jacket pocket and unlocked the stateroom, gently pushing him inside. "Into your room, there's a good boy."

Sebastian grabbed Wesley by the lapels and tugged him into the stateroom with him. "Call me that again. But take my clothes off first."

Wesley laughed even as heat surged through him. "You're drunk, sweetheart," he said, the endearment slipping out through his own whiskey-loosened lips. "There will be no clothes coming off."

Sebastian's arms were twining around his neck. "You want to do it with our clothes on?"

Wesley tsked, trying to push the desire down even as he let Sebastian pull him against him. "Don't tempt me. That's not going to get you called a good boy."

"Call me a bad one then."

An intoxicating mix of lust and laughter surged

through Wesley again, something he'd only ever shared with Sebastian. "You really are a scoundrel."

"This is our tale of viscounts and villainy." Sebastian tilted his head back, arms still around Wesley's neck as he stretched up to meet his lips. "Que hombre tan guapo, listo y dulce eres," he murmured, as he kissed Wesley far more gracefully than any drunk should be able to kiss. "Todavía no sé cómo tuve la suerte de llamarte mío."

Christ. Wesley only understood a handful of words—*handsome, clever, sweet, mine*—but he didn't need a translation for the warmth in Sebastian's voice or the caress in his touch. What a magic of its own it was, to be in the arms of this man.

"This is fighting dirty," Wesley said, against Sebastian's lips, trying to keep his head, "switching to Spanish so you can get away with saying soft things. And you're still drunk, so it doesn't matter how sweet your words in any tongue; nothing is happening but sleep."

He gently pushed Sebastian down to sit on the edge of the bed under the porthole. Sebastian let him slide the jacket from his shoulders, but he'd furrowed his brow, looking up at Wesley like he'd just remembered something. "I was going to tell you: you don't have to sleep with me."

Wesley frowned, setting the jacket to the side and reaching for Sebastian's bow tie. "Why are you saying that?"

"Wes, the bed is this big." Sebastian awkwardly held up his hands as Wesley worked at his bow tie, maybe trying to illustrate the narrow mattress. "Es una cama corta y estrecha, is what I'm trying to say, a short, skinny bed. You will get no sleep if I'm in it with you."

"You won't get any sleep if you have a blood terror," Wesley said flatly, as he unbuttoned Sebastian's shirt.

"They won't come," Sebastian said quietly. "They are magic. I'm not. Not anymore."

Oh please. It wasn't going to be that simple; Wesley might have known about magic for only months, but it was *never* simple.

"I appreciate you," Sebastian said, touching Wesley's cheek with aching gentleness. "But you know people on this ship, and you shouldn't be seen in my room. And if the Duke of Valemount's niece is involved in this in any way—if she's here to spy on us—she will be watching."

Wesley sighed. "If that's what you wish."

He helped Sebastian out of his dress shirt to just the T-shirt beneath, then removed his shoes and trousers. As soon as his clothes were off, Sebastian rolled over, facing the porthole, his eyes closing almost instantly.

Such a lightweight. Still, though Sebastian might be drunk, his point was well-taken: Wesley did know people aboard this ship who would be curious why he was in Sebastian's stateroom. And if they were being spied on, it would certainly be noticed if they slept in each other's rooms.

Sebastian had tried to use his magic twice and it hadn't come. It did seem unlikely the blood terrors could reach him now. And the beds *were* quite narrow; two grown men would never fit.

The sensible thing to do would be for Wesley to return to his own room and have a good night's sleep alone.

No matter how temptingly touchable Sebastian looked in that bed.

Wesley straightened up. As he did, he caught his

own reflection in the mirror above the marble sink. The man staring back at him was unexpected, and almost startling—color on his cheeks, lips flushed, eyes more blue than gray. In their short, stolen minute, Sebastian had even managed to muss his hair.

Wesley was used to the man in the mirror looking cold and severe. Untouchable and undesirable.

But this man in the reflection was none of those things.

He looked like someone's lover.

Wesley looked at himself for another moment, then stood all the way up. The hell with it: he had never done what other people wanted him to and he wasn't starting now.

He stripped off his own tailcoat and hung it along with Sebastian's tuxedo jacket in the closet. Then he turned off the light, slipping into the bed behind Sebastian and pulling the covers over both of them. Sebastian made a soft noise, shifting into him as Wesley wrapped his arm over his waist and pulled him against him. There was nowhere near enough space for them both, but this was bliss all the same: Sebastian's closeness finally satiating Wesley's relentless cravings, bringing elusive peace to his mind and body.

He rested his head on the same pillow as Sebastian and let himself enjoy it.

Chapter Eight

Sebastian woke to the gray dawn coming through the porthole and Wesley's whisper in his ear.

"I'm sneaking back to my room to dress and then breakfasting in the verandah. Take some of that powder and drink a lot of water when you wake. Trust me."

He heard the stateroom door ease open, then close. Sebastian's head was thick and achy already, but he buried his face under the pillow and closed his eyes again anyway, body languid from Wesley's lingering warmth.

He woke a fuzzy amount of time later to a cold bed and a throbbing head. With a groan, he rolled over. Why had he ever thought outdrinking Wesley was a good idea?

It was only the thought of hot coffee that finally got him to leave the bed. He took Wesley's advice and swallowed the last of the doctor's powder with three glasses of water. He might have felt like a hungover reprobate, but he did need to appear to be a count's son, so he pulled on a three-piece suit, smoothed his hair, grabbed a hat, and went to find coffee.

The verandah on A-deck was a bright winter garden, with ample greenery against white wicker furniture. Wesley was already at a table, his gaze on the large windows that framed the promenade and then the open sea beyond.

The large windows letting in lots and lots of light.

Sebastian squinted as he approached. "Good morning, Lord Fine."

Wesley glanced his way, gaze flicking from Sebastian's tie, which was snug in his collar, not loose as he preferred, then to his hat, which he'd pulled as low over his eyes as he could get away with. A tiny smile flitted across Wesley's face. "Don Sebastian," he said innocently. "I suspect you'd like some coffee."

"Please."

Wesley signaled for a waiter, and in short order Sebastian had a china cup of coffee that was weaker than he preferred, but sweet and milky, at least. Manners could wait; he drank half of it in one long sip. "I'm surprised you picked here for breakfast."

"Because it's bright and cheerful with beautiful views, and you're more likely to find me haunting dark, windowless spaces full of smoke?" Wesley said wryly. "You're not wrong. I'm watching for Lady Nora. She seems like the type for a brisk morning stroll."

Wesley ordered tea and a full breakfast, while Sebastian drank a second cup of coffee and managed to stomach some toast. He was contemplating whether to try some melon when Wesley cleared his throat.

"There."

Passing by the stern windows on the promenade was Lady Nora, dressed in an overcoat with a cloche hat. "She seems to be alone right now." Sebastian watched her for a moment. "Should we approach her?"

"I say yes." Wesley was getting to his feet. "She and I have met, after all. There's no reason I shouldn't stroll on up and say hello, and introduce my exceedingly sexy and intriguing Spanish friend."

Sebastian rolled his eyes but followed Wesley across the tiled garden and out onto the promenade. They picked a spot to lean against the railing, as if watching the sea. As Lady Nora came down the ship's starboard side, Wesley stepped into her path.

"Lady Nora?" he said, in an affected society tone Sebastian wasn't used to. "By Jove, it *is* you. I thought I saw you last night."

He held out a hand.

Lady Nora stopped her walk in surprise. A small furrow appeared between her brows, then smoothed away in recognition. "Lord Fine." She took his hand. "My word. What a surprise."

"Is it?" Wesley said smoothly, and really, that was the question, wasn't it? "Last I heard, your itinerary was the Mediterranean. What brought you to America?"

"I've been in Canada, actually, visiting one of my sisters." Nora's gaze had gone to Sebastian and was lingering.

"Forgive me, I haven't introduced my friend," Wesley said. "Don Sebastian's father is the nineteenth Count of Animales. And this is Lady Nora," he continued. "Her father was the late Duke of Valemount."

"Enchanted to meet you—is that the English expression?" Sebastian said.

"It certainly is." Lady Nora's eyes were still on Sebastian as she let him take her hand. "Spanish, then?"

"Yes, he's kindly indulging me in a visit to London," Wesley said. "But where's your companion? I thought I saw you with someone last night."

"Oh." Lady Nora's expression went instantly vacant. "Perhaps you mean Dr. Wright?"

She was traveling with a doctor? Was she sick? "I hope everything is all right," Sebastian said, before he'd meant to.

"Thank you for your concern, but I haven't taken ill," she said wryly. "Dr. Wright is a doctor of nerves, and Uncle Louis has been snookered into believing that a woman who likes to travel alone must need one. Do you know my uncle well, Lord Fine?"

That wasn't much of answer, and she'd changed the subject back to Wesley. Had her companion actually been sent by the duke himself to accompany her, then?

"Well enough, I'd say," Wesley answered. "We're in a club together."

"I know the one," Lady Nora said, her face still unreadable. "I heard Lord Thornton is throwing quite the ball for all of you on Friday, isn't he? Uncle Louis unsurprisingly asked me to attend as well."

She didn't seem particularly thrilled at the idea. "I'm sure any party would be lucky to have you," Sebastian said.

Lady Nora's gaze flitted to him, slightly thawed. "And you'll come too of course, won't you?" she said. "I think you would make the ball quite a bit more interesting. I don't particularly see anything to celebrate myself, you understand; I'd just as soon leave animals be. But perhaps the club is to your taste."

Sebastian frowned. "What do you mean—"

"You know, I've had terrible seasickness this voyage," Wesley said quickly, over him. "You mentioned your companion is a doctor? Perhaps he has something that might help. Do you know where I might find him?"

"I think he was planning to indulge in some trap shooting this afternoon. But no need to find him." Lady Nora had already opened her purse, and a moment later withdrew a small box. "Here. I always keep some on hand for other passengers."

That obviously hadn't been Wesley's intent—Sebastian had never seen him get so much as queasy—but he said appropriate thank-yous to Lady Nora nonetheless.

As Lady Nora resumed her walk, Wesley and Sebastian stepped out of the path of the promenade to lean on the railing next to each other. "Her companion is a doctor of nerves," Wesley said quietly. "And here Mr. Findlay was likely murdered in his mental hospital. A doctor might have been able to sneak inside without raising alarms and slip Mr. Findlay something deadly under cover of medicine."

That was a good point. "Lady Nora said her uncle had sent Dr. Wright with her."

"Yes," Wesley said, a little more grimly. "Perhaps the new Duke of Valemount used his niece as an excuse to send a doctor to New York. Or perhaps Lady Nora would prefer us to think her uncle is behind this."

Sebastian pursed his lips, gaze on the ocean waves far below. "Why would the duke want Lady Nora to attend the ball on Friday?"

"It could be for nefarious reasons, I suppose, but it's also quite possible he's trying to find her a suitor. If Valemount is looking for eligible bachelors to marry his niece, we're obviously going to have several in our—" Wesley cut himself off. "That's probably what it is."

Sebastian glanced to the side, looking at him suspiciously. "You're going to have bachelors in your what?"

"Ah." Wesley was now staring intently at the ocean, not meeting Sebastian's gaze. "Circles."

Sebastian's eyes narrowed a fraction. "Lady Nora mentioned your *club*."

"Did she?" Wesley said weakly.

"And would this happen to be the same *club* you were in with your other friend, Sir Ellery?"

"Well—these circles I'm in, they're not large, you understand—"

"You knew Sir Ellery because he was in your *hunting* club."

Wesley rubbed his forehead. "Christ, of course you remember that part."

"So Lord Valemount is also a member at this club where you shoot things," Sebastian said. "Why is a marquess inviting a *hunting* club to a *ball*?"

Wesley cleared his throat. "Because it's, ah. The, um. The Beckley Hunt Ball."

There was a loud moment of silence.

Sebastian stared at him. "A *fox hunt*?"

"*No*," Wesley said, immediately and firmly. "It's a hunt *ball*, not an actual hunt."

"But you're celebrating fox hunting."

"Well—yes. Because it's tradition—"

"Traditions can still be *barbaric*." There were several walkers out on the promenade, strolling briskly behind them. Sebastian gritted his teeth, leaning on the ship's railing and trying to keep his voice down. "Were you ever planning to tell me what kind of ball this is?"

"Truthfully? No, I wasn't, not unless I absolutely had to," Wesley said, lifting his chin. "I was hoping we would arrive too late and wouldn't have to attend.

Clearly foolish of me, to do anything so out of character as *hope*."

"I told you hope only makes disappointment sting harder," Sebastian muttered.

"Oh no," Wesley said, pointing at him. "No, no, no. You are not allowed to become cynical; I will turn my entire Yorkshire estate into a bloody fox sanctuary before I let that happen."

"What foxes will even be left if men and dogs are hunting them at *balls*?" Sebastian said.

"You have my word that this hunt ball will not involve any actual hunting," Wesley said. "Drinks, dancing, games, and gambling, yes, and it will be perfectly miserable as all parties are, but no one will be picking up arms and heading for the hills. Men will bring their daughters, not their dogs."

"But everyone will be celebrating hunting," Sebastian said quietly.

Wesley sighed. "Yes, they will," he admitted. "We have thus far spent all our time in your world of magic. But now we are looking for someone with a vendetta against magic who may be from *my* world, and many of my peers consider hunting the height of sport."

And Sebastian would have to blend in with those peers, pretending to be an aristocrat himself. There was no way they could miss this Beckley Hunt Ball, not now that they knew Valemount would certainly attend. Sebastian had to go, because this was how he could help—because Sebastian wasn't part of the world of magic anymore. "Fine," he said abruptly. "Then we can look for this doctor doing trap shooting. And you can also teach me how."

Wesley blinked. "I beg your pardon?"

"I've fired a gun before," Sebastian said, trying to seem casual even when his stomach was in knots, "but not since I was under blood magic. It's obviously very different now."

"Do you *want* to learn to shoot?"

"It doesn't matter what I *want*," Sebastian said. "How am I supposed to talk to guests at a hunt ball if I don't know anything myself?" He wrapped his arms around himself. "I couldn't even hold my own in a bar fight, Wes. What am I supposed to do if someone has a gun?"

Wesley pursed his lips. "But if you don't want to learn—"

"My life isn't going to get easier," Sebastian said, his throat gone slightly tighter. "I have no regrets, but I also can't wait around and hope my magic comes back. I can't wear the rose-colored glasses, as you like to say; I have to be able to hold my own in both of our worlds."

Wesley frowned. "Countless men know how to shoot. The ones who wear rose-colored glasses are the rare ones."

"Probably because they learn the truth about life and become wiser," Sebastian said, swallowing, "and they have to take them off."

When early afternoon came around, Sebastian and Wesley made their way to the recreation area of the ship to pick up supplies. The crewman who gave them shotguns offered to throw the traps, but Wesley turned him down.

The stern on B-deck was open to the wide skies above, making it cold, and very windy. On the promenade of the deck above, the occasional passenger could be seen at the railing, but around them, every deck chair was empty, Lady Nora's companion nowhere to be seen.

"This is really more of a summer activity, but I suppose this Dr. Wright may still show," Wesley said, but he sounded dubious to Sebastian's ears.

He watched as Wesley found a spot to secure the trap thrower and then picked up one of the guns, hefting it in his hand. Sebastian kept his face neutral, but Wesley was right: he didn't have any real desire to learn more firearms skills. There was nothing Sebastian wanted to shoot, not animals and certainly not people.

But they were rooting out a plot to destroy magic. Hyde had disappeared from his secure prison. And the bruise on Sebastian's cheek still smarted. He was going to have to get used to the idea of fighting without magic; that was his reality now.

Wesley stepped up to the railing across the stern, gun steady and aimed out into the open ocean. "All right. Let it go."

Sebastian released the lever on the trap thrower, and the coil launched the clay disk into the air off the back of the ship. Wesley tracked it for a moment, then fired, the sharp crack echoing over the wind and ship's engines.

The clay disk shattered midair.

Sebastian's eyebrows went up. "Wow."

"Flattering, I'm sure, but we're not here for me to indulge." Wesley stepped back, holding the shotgun out to Sebastian. "Here."

Sebastian took the gun and stood where Wesley had been. He watched the white-tipped waves for a moment, not feeling a fraction as easy as Wesley had looked. "The clay isn't bad for the fishies, is it?"

"Sebastian de Leon—"

"It was just a *question*. I still want to learn." Sebastian raised the gun and nodded once.

Wesley released the trap, which launched into the air. Sebastian followed its path, then pulled the trigger.

The clay disk spun on, untouched, falling out of sight.

Sebastian sighed.

Wesley cleared his throat. "You, er. Had your knees locked. Perhaps if you eased your stance before you tried again?"

Sebastian *was* standing very stiffly. He tried to relax, loosening his shoulders as he brought the gun up again. Wesley launched a second trap, and Sebastian fired a second time.

Yet again he missed, the disk spinning away into the ship's wake.

"That was—better?" Wesley said cautiously.

Sebastian huffed. "No. It wasn't."

"It's possible you're holding your breath—"

"*Wesley.*" Sebastian turned around, careful to keep the gun lowered. "Stop handling me with the baby gloves."

"*Kid* gloves," said Wesley. "And I'm not—"

"You are," Sebastian said. "You need to be honest. You can't—what is that word you say—you can't *coddle* me."

Wesley frowned. "I've never coddled anyone in my life."

"You're doing it now." Sebastian set the gun down on the closest deck chair. "You know I can't rely on you and Arthur and everyone else for protection forever. I need to know how to defend myself without magic."

Wesley sighed. "I won't argue with you about that," he said. "But I'm afraid I'm not a very good teacher."

Sebastian shook his head. "I don't believe that."

"It's true," Wesley said. "I haven't the faintest idea how to offer gentle correction; I only know how to teach by being harsh."

So be harsh. I won't break. Sebastian didn't say it. Wesley's sharp edges were a defense he'd built against life's cruelties and too many people were willing to use him as a villain. Sebastian wouldn't have ever wanted to be harsh with Wesley either.

But he'd bet Wesley was actually a very good teacher, if they could figure out a way Wesley would be in his element. "Did you ever teach your soldiers to shoot?"

Wesley raised an eyebrow. "Where are you going with this?"

"What if this was wartime?" Sebastian said. "You are Captain Fine again—"

"Collins."

"Collins," Sebastian corrected. "You are Captain Collins again and you've just had the terrible misfortune to have a useless medic transferred to your company."

"Oh no, not another medic," Wesley said, deadpan. "Said no captain ever in the entire history of war."

"It's *pretend*," Sebastian said. "You're pretending to be a captain again, taking charge of everything, and you've suddenly got a medic who doesn't know how to shoot. And so you've got to teach him, yes?"

Wesley folded his arms. "I don't know how things worked in the American army, but you would have been forbidden from even carrying a weapon in *my* army."

"Yes, I know," Sebastian said impatiently, "but—"

"More to the point, do you actually believe I ever would have allowed one of my medics to be armed and sent to battle?"

A flash of hurt went through Sebastian. "You don't think we can learn?"

"Not *that*." Wesley shook his head. "I don't think you should ever have to. And don't ask me to explain myself or talk about feelings; you know I don't."

Sebastian stifled a sigh.

"That said." Wesley's gaze flitted over him appraisingly. "It's possible I could *pretend* Captain Collins is being forced to teach a medic to shoot for defense—for the medic's own protection and safety, you understand."

"Yes," Sebastian said, straightening up. "You have an idiot medic in your company who's going to get himself killed unless you step in."

"That I'm willing to work with." Wesley tilted his head. "But I should warn you that Captain Collins wasn't very nice."

"Who's asking you to be *nice*?" Sebastian said. "Not me. I'm asking you to be strict and bossy."

"Oh *are* you?" The corner of Wesley's lips turned up. His gaze swept over Sebastian a second time, slower than before, lingering in a way that sent pleasant prickles over his skin.

"Well. Since you're asking for it." Wesley stepped closer and cleared his throat. "Then straighten the *fuck* up, corporal."

Sebastian's spine snapped to attention before he'd consciously decided to move.

"Shoulders back." Wesley's voice had gone sharper and deeper. "Chin up, eyes forward. Maybe your last captain let you get away with this reprehensible slouching, but it's not going to fly with me."

Jesus. Sebastian might have underestimated how good Wesley was going to be at this.

Wesley pointed toward the range. "Turn around, face the ocean, and if you know what's good for you you'll keep that spine straight. We're not in a fucking saloon, soldier."

Heat curled in Sebastian's stomach. *This is a shooting lesson on a ship's deck, not the bedroom*, he reminded himself. *Wesley is teaching you the way he knows how to teach—stop finding it sexy.*

He licked his dry lips. "Shouldn't I pick up the gun first?"

"Did I say to pick up the gun?"

"Well—"

"And why are you speaking when I haven't asked you a question? Turn the bloody hell around."

"Sir yes *sir*," Sebastian muttered under his breath, as he turned around.

The ocean stretched out in front of him, endless dark gray to the horizon line where it met the paler gray of the cloudy sky. Wesley was out of sight behind him now, but Sebastian felt the awareness of his body, just that small bit taller, as he stepped in close behind him.

Wesley's voice was distractingly close to his ear as he said, "Square your shoulders."

Sebastian straightened up.

"You're still slouching," Wesley said curtly.

"I'm *not*."

"You are," Wesley said. "How do you expect to aim properly if you don't even stand straight?"

"How do *you* expect me to aim at all when I don't even have a gun?"

"You really are asking for it."

Sebastian had to bite back a startled yelp as Wesley's hand landed on his ass, and not gently either. He turned over his shoulder and gave Wesley a dirty look. "We're on a boat."

"And we're still quite alone. Believe me, I'm watching."

"But you didn't do *that* to your soldiers."

"I thought this was *pretend*." Wesley had just a hint of a smile again, sly around the edge. "And I promise, if I had ever found myself in charge of a medic as gorgeous but impertinent as you, I would have been so bloody tempted."

He gestured at the ocean. "Now face forward and square your fucking shoulders, or I'll do it again."

Sebastian inhaled, the heat in his stomach spreading out into his limbs and under his collar. He pushed away the urge to test Wesley's threat, forcing himself to turn to the ocean and look forward.

"There is no point picking up your weapon until you get the posture right." Wesley tapped his right shoulder, the touch feather-light. "Shift here."

Sebastian took another breath. It would have been faster and easier for Wesley to push him into position. But he wasn't pushing, wasn't forcing Sebastian to move. Maybe because more than anyone else, Wesley understood that Sebastian still had echoes of someone else's control in his blood, and he wanted Sebastian to be fully in control of his own body—was willing to wait however long it took for Sebastian to move himself.

Sebastian tried shifting toward Wesley's hand, just slightly, and all at once felt his body align like the watch hand reaching noon, or a compass needle finding north.

"*There*," Wesley said approvingly. "Feel the difference?" He was shifting behind Sebastian, studying him. "Your posture isn't terrible now, but you need to breathe."

"You make me forget how," Sebastian muttered.

He felt the air move as Wesley startled, felt more than heard the quietly exhaled swear. "Don't you dare be romantic when I'm trying to focus on instructing you."

"But it's true," Sebastian said, barely more than a whisper. "You've always made me breathless."

"Corporal, you are going to hush right now or find yourself bent over this convenient deck chair right here, and then where are you going to learn to shoot?"

Sebastian swallowed. Wesley was joking, but the idea was tempting. The thought of being manhandled over a deck chair wasn't raising his nerves. He wanted Wesley to do it, trusted Wesley would let him up if it ever got to be too much.

He forced his thoughts back to the moment, his focus on the ocean.

"Breathe," Wesley instructed, "then raise your arm and pretend to aim."

Sebastian did. Wesley's hand skated across his bicep and forearm, making only the lightest taps so that again all adjustments had to be made by Sebastian himself.

"Keep this arm an inch higher." Wesley shifted fully behind him. "And bring your other hand up as you would to brace the gun, with steady breaths the whole time."

He continued the butterfly-faint touches of guidance on Sebastian's bicep, his shoulder, his hip. "Like this. I've seen you dance; I know you can learn what to do with your body."

"When did you see me dance?" Sebastian said. "You weren't watching at the Magnolia."

"Of course I fucking was." Wesley's breath was a tiny spot of warmth in the cold, ghosting over the back of Sebastian's neck. "I couldn't take my eyes off you."

"But you said you didn't—"

"I lied, because I'm a coward, and a brooding, jealous prick." Wesley's hand touched his hip. "And even when you so sweetly tried to reassure me that you had told your lady friend you were taken, my ego wouldn't let me admit I appreciated hearing that."

Sebastian swallowed. "I really wouldn't have—"

"I know." Wesley's mouth was very close to his ear. "It's an ugly thing, jealousy. I would like to claim I'm above it, but I'm afraid I'm still reprehensibly territorial when it comes to you."

Words tumbled out before Sebastian realized he was going to say them. "I thought that was just when I had magic in the tattoo. Because the lion used to be yours alone, but now everyone can see him."

"How convenient that would be for me, wouldn't it? If I could pretend all this pesky possessiveness was just the magic's influence, and without it I'm actually quite a reasonable chap." Wesley's hand lingered on Sebastian's hip a few seconds longer than was appropriate for public. "But no, I'm a bastard through and through. Do you imagine the streets are full of men willing to sacrifice the literal magic in their veins to save my life? You're irreplaceable, Sebastian. And your lion is mine more than ever now."

Sebastian swallowed again, his throat suddenly tight.

Wesley pulled a little ways back. "Anyway, all of this is exactly why emotions are terrible and ought to be abolished," he said softly. "But you should never doubt that you have my complete trust. And you're a gorgeous dancer who's going to teach me to tango someday so I can toss you around."

Sebastian huffed a laugh. "I'm too big for that."

"You *wish* you were too big for that." Wesley took a full step back. "All right, you can pick up the gun now. But return to this exact position again, holding it with both hands and aiming off the stern."

Once Sebastian was armed and facing the sea, Wesley stepped forward to help with tiny adjustments, and Sebastian focused on learning the scant centimeters that made up the difference between what he'd thought was right versus Wesley's expertise.

Finally, Wesley stepped to the side. "I'm not launching quite yet. Look down the barrel. Keep your gaze open and alert so you're ready for wherever the trap goes."

Sebastian focused on the sky, on the churning white waves of the wake disappearing behind the ship.

"Good," Wesley said. "When you're ready, take one more breath. Then I'll throw the trap."

Sebastian took a breath, taking in the scents of the sea and the ship and gunpowder, and let it out.

Wesley pulled the level, and the clay disk flew up into the sky. Sebastian tracked it, then fired.

And this time, he clipped it—and no, it wasn't a perfect shot, but he'd hit the damn thing.

"*Yes.*" Sebastian looked over his shoulder, grinning. "Did you see that?"

"I did." Wesley had a small smile of his own.

"Would Captain Collins have been happy with that?"

"Captain Collins would have been completely distracted by that smile of yours and thoughts of how he could have gotten you into his tent," Wesley said bluntly. "Now do it again until we run out of traps."

Chapter Nine

Hot under the collar was another expression Wesley had known with certainty was hyperbole—until he'd met Sebastian.

"I clipped the trap three times in a row, at the end." Sebastian was smiling at him over their poached sole. "Maybe next time I'll hit it dead on."

Once again, other passengers were sneaking glances at their table, or more accurately, at Sebastian, who was criminally attractive in his dinner jacket and black bow tie high around his collar. Meanwhile, Wesley's own collar felt near to melting from the heat that rose every time Sebastian smiled in his direction. "You improved," he allowed.

"Because you are such a good teacher." Sebastian's smile turned a little more playful. "Very good at being strict and bossy when someone is asking for it."

Wesley *had* been strict and bossy, and despite not having his magic, Sebastian had stayed comfortable with it the entire time.

"You're kind of asking for it now," Wesley said meaningfully.

Sebastian grinned. Wesley would have found this kind of flirting heady enough on its own, but seeing

Sebastian look like he was enjoying it, knowing how much trust that took—a deeply hard-won trust that Sebastian didn't give to anyone but Wesley—

Christ, if only they didn't have to worry about a plot to destroy magic, and two missing relics, and possibly Lady Nora. Wesley and Sebastian had spent most of the afternoon on the deck, joined by six or seven other hardy souls at different points, but Lady Nora's companion, Dr. Wright, never showed. Now there was no sign of either of them in the dining lounge. It almost felt like they didn't want to be seen.

"Excuse me, Lord Fine?" An attendant in black tie had approached their table politely. He had an envelope in one hand. "We've had a message for you from another passenger on the ship, in second class. Would you like to take it?"

Wesley took the envelope from the attendant as Sebastian leaned in. "Is it from Arthur and Rory?"

Wesley nodded, scanning Arthur's message. "Ace says he and Brodigan are going to be in the second-class smoking lounge this evening, if we can sneak in."

"I bet we can." Sebastian had a thoughtful expression. "Do you still have the seasickness pills Lady Nora gave you?"

"In my room," said Wesley. "I can certainly offer them to Brodigan, but I think it's a fairly safe bet that Arthur bought him twenty packs already."

"They're not for Rory to take," Sebastian said. "They're for Rory to *scry*."

"Oh." Wesley sat back in his chair. "Can he really?"

"I think he may want to try," Sebastian said. "Lady Nora said she always keeps them on hand. Maybe Rory can find out where she's been traveling—and who she's been traveling with."

"Now we're finally getting somewhere," Wesley said.

After a dessert of peach melba, they took the elevator down to E-deck and wove their way toward the stern of the ship until they found a heavy door labeled *Second Class*. From there, they followed stairs and carpeted halls until they found the second-class smoking lounge, a dark space with oak furniture upholstered in green leather. It lacked the opulence of first but was perfectly comfortable, and Wesley liked it better, the way he preferred cigarettes to cigars.

Arthur and Rory had a table at the back, by an open window. Arthur waved, and Wesley and Sebastian crossed the room to join them.

They waited for the attendant to take their order and bring their drinks—Wesley tactfully not commenting on Sebastian's decision to go back to soda. Once they were in relative privacy again, Wesley pulled Lady Nora's seasickness pills from his jacket, and stretched across the table to set them in front of Rory.

"Considerate," Arthur said, sounding unflatteringly surprised. "But I did bring Rory's pills."

Wesley shook his head. "Can you scry this?" he said to Rory.

Rory looked to Sebastian, who nodded. "We got them from the Duke of Valemount's niece."

They filled Arthur and Rory in on their encounters with Lady Nora. Rory's eyebrows were up as he picked up the pills consideringly. "You two, lean in," Arthur said. He pointed to a deck of cards on the table. "We can pretend we're playing cards while he scries."

"Not a chance," Wesley said. "We're waiting until Brodigan's done, and then we're not pretending anything. I'll enjoy watching all of you lose at poker."

Rory snorted. "Even woozy on seasickness pills, I'll still take you to the cleaners again."

"*Again*." Wesley tilted his head back, considering Rory and recalling the rounds they'd played in London in spring. "Oh, I see," he said, as that night fell into place. "When we played before, I didn't know about magic. Did you use your psychometry to win?"

"I gave you back your money," Rory said defensively.

"Yes, but now you've given me back my *pride*," Wesley said. "We most certainly must play tonight."

Rory looked at him suspiciously. "Look, if you're still sore—"

"You misunderstand," Wesley said. "I welcome a worthy opponent. I want another match, and I want you to use every trick you have. It will mean I can be ten times as smug when I beat you."

"You can try," Rory said meaningfully.

Sebastian made a face. "Poker is not really my game."

Wesley tsked. "Do you need me to fund your bets?"

"No," Sebastian said, giving him a look. "I can pay to lose, it's fine."

Rory tilted his head. "Guess money's not a big deal when your family's been connected to magic for more than four hundred years, huh? Or when you're distantly related to dukes."

"It's very distant," Sebastian said, looking self-conscious. "And money's just not something I think a lot about."

"That's how you know you have it." Rory tapped the table. "All right. Deal the cards while I scry. Fine says magic's allowed, so I'm not gonna feel bad for robbing any of you."

"We should really just hand him our money," Arthur muttered.

"Nonsense," Wesley said testily. "I'm going to win."

"If you say so," Arthur said, picking up his drink.

Rory closed his eyes. The room was dim and no one was watching the four of them in the corner, but Wesley still leaned forward, along with Arthur and Sebastian, and began to deal the cards.

"Conveyor belt, in the factory," Rory muttered. "The woman stacks pills in a box. And then—and then—argh." His eyes popped open. "Nothing."

"What do you mean, *nothing*?" Wesley said.

"I mean I can't see the history of these pills." Rory nodded at Sebastian. "It's like how it used to be with him. I can see the pills being manufactured. And I can see them way back on a store shelf. But everything else? Blank."

Arthur, Wesley, and Sebastian exchanged glances. "But you can see them with Wesley and I, bringing them here, yes?" Sebastian said.

"No," said Rory. "Nothing since they left the store."

"Well," Arthur said, "I think that at least answers the question of whether Lady Nora is mixed up with anything magical."

"Unless it's her companion," Wesley said. "The man we haven't seen again. He's a doctor; perhaps Lady Nora got the pills from him, and he's the one with magic blocking Brodigan's magic?"

Sebastian frowned. "It's not very common magic."

"Perhaps not," said Wesley. "But it seems it may be present, all the same."

"Whatever's going on, you and Seb need to be careful." Rory set the box back in front of Wesley. "*Real* careful."

Wesley looked to his side to find Sebastian looking at him as well. "We'll look out for each other," Sebastian promised.

"Should we go back now?" Wesley said.

"Jade was going to try to send a marconigram before their ship departed," Arthur said. "Stick around for a few hands and see if it comes in."

They played several rounds of poker, and Sebastian lost track of how much money he lost to Rory. However much it was, Wesley lost more, with Arthur delightedly driving up every bet.

"For fuck's sake," Wesley finally said to Arthur, as Rory laid down yet another winning hand. "Brodigan's going to be able to buy you Buckingham Palace after this."

Sebastian smiled. He'd be lying if he claimed he hadn't been rooting for Rory against all of them. "I thought you were going to win," he teased.

"So did I." Wesley shook his head. "Laughable hubris on my part."

"I'll give you your money back this time too," Rory started.

"Don't you dare," Wesley said. "I knew exactly what I was getting into."

"You might even say he was asking for it," Sebastian added innocently.

Wesley side-eyed him. "You would know all about that, wouldn't you?" he said, with a hint of heat, which sent a pleasant shiver over Sebastian.

Wesley looked back at Rory. "My ego is my problem, not yours. You deserve to keep every cent."

Rory's lips turned up in a grudging smile. "You're all right sometimes, Fine."

"Sometimes, he says." Wesley stood up. "I don't think Miss Robbins's message is going to find us tonight. Let's go back, while I still own my clothes."

"If you're losing your clothes, maybe we should stay," Sebastian said, with a tiny grin.

"And you call me shameless," Wesley said, grabbing Sebastian's sleeve and pulling him up to his feet.

They snuck back into first class via one of the staff staircases, and then made their way through the social areas of the ship. The windows were speckled with raindrops as they climbed the grand staircase up to C-deck.

When they passed Wesley's stateroom without Wesley slowing, Sebastian hid a smile. "Are you walking me back to my room? Very chivalrous of you."

"I wouldn't call my intentions *chivalrous*," Wesley said lightly, which made Sebastian shiver again.

The long hall was mostly empty, only a couple at the far end deeply engaged in their own discussion. Sebastian unlocked his stateroom and held the door so Wesley could go in ahead of him.

As soon as the door closed, Sebastian was pulling Wesley against him. "Oh, I like this," Wesley said, sliding his hands under Sebastian's unbuttoned jacket and over his dress shirt. "Though I have to ask, how much of this is wanting me, and how much of it is wanting my body heat after sitting by an open window in the middle of the Atlantic in winter?"

"The fresh air is good for Rory's seasickness." Sebastian had Wesley's bow tie undone and his tailcoat off, and was now working on his shirt buttons. "Who says I even noticed the cold?"

"You're a truly terrible liar," Wesley said, even as his hands found Sebastian's trousers.

Sebastian got the dress shirt open, getting his hands on the warmth which radiated even through the long-sleeved silk undershirt Wesley wore. "I've never asked why you don't wear the union suit."

"You mean, why have I eschewed traditional undergarments when the rest of my clothes are outrageously old-fashioned?" Wesley said sardonically.

"I wasn't going to say that," protested Sebastian.

"Oh please, I know who I am." Wesley seemed amused, not offended, as he pushed the dinner jacket off Sebastian's shoulders. "It's not about comfort, if that's what you were about to ask. I am shameless enough to admit that a separate shirt and shorts means much easier access if you're having a liaison somewhere you shouldn't be. Say, in a park."

"Or a tent?" Sebastian said slyly.

He caught Wesley's inhale. "I wouldn't know," Wesley said, his voice lowering in both volume and pitch.

Sebastian shifted closer, so they were pressed together in their half-dressed states. He'd wanted Wesley since the shooting lesson and he had no resistance left. "Captain Collins never shared a tent with anyone?"

"Never." Wesley's hands had gone under Sebastian's army T-shirt, warm against chilled skin. "Not in the sleeping sense nor in the sense you're so brazenly implying. It simply couldn't be risked."

"Maybe not." Sebastian slid his hand between them, under the hem of Wesley's silk shirt to rest on his stomach. "But maybe Corporal de Leon would not have let it stay empty if he'd been there."

Wesley's hands stilled on his lower back. "You think *you* would have snuck into *my* tent? That is a daring bit of insubordination."

"Why would it have been?" Sebastian said. "I was a medic. I could have found all kinds of excuses to visit you."

"Now that is a thought." Wesley's hand slipped another inch lower on Sebastian's back, toward his arse. "Having you in my tent would have been diabolical teasing. I would have gone mad."

Sebastian leaned in, tilting his head back so his lips were nearly against Wesley's. "Or you could have done something about it."

Wesley's arms tightened around him. "Is that what Corporal de Leon would have wanted?"

"If I'd really been in your company and you'd taught me to shoot like you did today, I wouldn't have been able to stop thinking about getting your hands on me again," Sebastian said softly. "I *haven't* been able to stop thinking about it. I've wanted your hands back on me since we left the deck, Wes."

Wesley stilled again, muscles tensed. "For the record," he whispered, "this is also diabolical teasing."

Sebastian's heart was beating faster, but in a good way. Wesley had a firm hold on him, but not so firm he couldn't move. The arms tight around his waist were sending sparks through him, not nerves. "Who's *teasing*?" He spread his hand out along Wesley's stomach, feeling muscle flex beneath his fingers. "Not me."

Wesley's gaze was still locked on Sebastian's face.

"Then what are you doing?" he said, his whisper more gravelly, dancing over Sebastian's lips.

Sebastian brushed his lips over Wesley's, feather-light. "Asking for it."

"Fuck." Wesley kissed him deeply, tongue slipping between Sebastian's lips as his hand moved even lower, to cup his ass over his shorts and pull him close.

Sebastian ran his hand down Wesley's stomach, going for his cock, but Wesley pulled him tight against him, trapping his hand between their bodies.

"Not me. Not yet."

"Wes—"

"I want to work you over first, savor it."

A jolt of arousal went through Sebastian, and he had to catch his whine in his throat. "You better not *coddle* me—"

"I'm going to do whatever I like with you." The corner of Wesley's mouth curled up in a sly smile as Sebastian shivered. "I will move as slow as I want with you, so you can stop me if you need to, but also because I'm a bastard, and while you *asking* for it is all very well and good, it's nowhere near as lovely as you *begging*."

Wesley pushed him across the small space of the stateroom in two easy steps and then they were tumbling down on the bed. Sebastian wasn't on his back, though; Wesley had turned them on their sides, facing each other, his arm wonderfully heavy over Sebastian as his hand slid down the back of his open trousers.

Wesley squeezed his ass, and Sebastian had to fight back a groan. "Oh, you're going to have to keep quieter than that," Wesley chided. "You don't want the other passengers to hear you, do you?"

"I can be quiet," Sebastian promised.

"I'm sure you can." Wesley's hand slid up and then back down beneath the waistband of his shorts. Sebastian shifted into the warmth against his bare skin. "You had too much practice."

"What do you mean?" Sebastian said, barely a whisper.

"In other tents, during the war. With men who didn't deserve you." Wesley's hand squeezed again. "If I'd had you, I would have kissed you for hours. I would have told you how much I wished we could be loud."

His hand slid around Sebastian's hip, finding his cock. Sebastian's breath left him in a rush, his eyelashes fluttering. With the new space, he reached for Wesley's dick again, but Wesley caught his hand with his free one.

"No, duck, you're just going to take it right now. Just going to let me enjoy myself by making you as desperate as you make me."

Sebastian jammed his teeth into his lower lip, catching his groan before it escaped. His head fell forward so his forehead rested against Wesley's collarbone. They were still on their sides facing each other, and it was perfect: Sebastian hemmed in cozily between Wesley and the wall, under Wesley's arm but not trapped under his body weight where he couldn't move.

Wesley began to stroke him leisurely, like they had all the time in the world. "I owe you the truth about our lesson on the deck, and why I was angry at the thought of arming a medic," he whispered, as his hand slid over Sebastian's cock. "Medics are too precious to be used as weapons. If more people had the compassion to care for others, we wouldn't have war. I would have valued you, even then, and never have treated you so carelessly as to put a gun in your hands."

"Wes," Sebastian said, voice breaking.

"If I'd had you back then, in my company or my tent, it would have changed so much," Wesley said quietly. "But I have you here now. And it's changed—well. Everything."

He kissed Sebastian then, deeply, and Sebastian returned his kiss with a desperate edge, Wesley's words sending his thoughts tumbling over each other.

Wesley pulled back and meaningfully scooted down the bed. "Stay silent now," he cautioned, as he kissed Sebastian's stomach.

And then Sebastian couldn't think anymore.

Chapter Ten

The ship made good time, with arrival in Southampton forecasted for Thursday night. Wesley had given Sebastian more trap shooting lessons on the deck and self-defense lessons in the men's gymnasium. They'd gone swimming several times in the inside pool and practiced the English dances he'd need to know for Lord Thornton's hunt ball, even if that led to more bickering about the purpose of the ball. They sent messages back and forth with Arthur, who confirmed Jade's marconigram had arrived but it was only two words: no news. Given it was in Morse code, the brevity was understandable, but it didn't tell them much.

And they hadn't seen Lady Nora or her mysterious doctor companion again.

"Are they hiding from us?" Wesley said, after lunch on Wednesday, as they stood by the windows in the drawing room. The weather had turned colder, enough that Sebastian was bringing his overcoat even to the indoor rooms of the ship. "Or are they following us around the ship with some kind of magic, like invisibility?"

"Rory would have seen them, though," Sebastian said.

"Not necessarily," Wesley said. "Brodigan couldn't

scry those pills. Maybe one of the two of them is blocking his magic."

"I have been thinking," Sebastian said, more quietly. "About Hyde. We took a lot of precautions. Getting him out of his asylum would have been difficult." He frowned. "But a doctor could have made it happen."

That was an excellent point. Wesley pursed his lips. "I say we search again. They could be hiding in their staterooms, having staff bring their meals, but surely at some point they're going to want fresh air."

They wandered through every part of first class, eventually ending up in the verandah. It was markedly more chilled than it had been even that morning, enough that even Wesley was feeling it. There was a layer of frost on the large garden windows, and no one was out on the promenade. "A front must have come in from the north," Wesley observed. "Is this Brodigan's fault?"

"I don't think so." Sebastian pulled his overcoat closed. "But I also don't think the ship's heaters have caught up." He sighed. "I guess we can see if Lady Nora or her friend are at dinner."

But as they were heading toward the grand staircase, Wesley caught a flash of movement at the end of A-deck's hall. "There."

A tall man with a dark beard and a bowler hat pulled low was standing outside one of the staterooms. He was leaning on his walking stick as he opened the door and disappeared into the room.

"That's the doctor," Wesley said. "Come on."

They hurried down the hall to the door. "What should we—" Sebastian started.

Wesley knocked on the door. Hard. "Dr. Wright?" he called, in a loud voice.

"I suppose this works," Sebastian said weakly.

Other passengers were looking their way. "It's the Viscount Fine," Wesley said, still loud, knocking again. "May I have a word?"

There was a sound from behind the door. And then, finally, it opened perhaps eight inches.

"May I help you, Lord Fine?" Dr. Wright said, his tone as chilled as the weather. He was still wearing his hat, pulled so low it hid his hair. His beard seemed even thicker up close, his glasses even larger than Rory's.

"Dr. Wright, finally," Wesley said, in his best entitled-arsehole voice. "I simply must speak with you. Lady Nora said you're a doctor of nerves?"

"I'm not taking new patients at this time."

"Wait—you think I want to speak with you about *myself*?" Wesley said, with real affront. "I haven't had nerves a day in my life."

Behind the glasses, blue eyes narrowed. "Your attitude is exactly why my patients struggle." Dr. Wright began closing the door.

"Wait," Sebastian said. "We wanted to talk to you about a patient you may have treated—"

"I'm afraid I can't help you. Good day, gentlemen." Dr. Wright firmly shut the door.

Wesley and Sebastian looked at each other. "I don't think he wants to talk to us," Sebastian said.

"We were just summarily told to fuck off, yes." Wesley turned and began to knock on the door again. "Dr. Wright?"

The door cracked open again. "Gentlemen," Dr. Wright started, "I've already told you—"

Wesley shouldered past him and strode right into the room.

"Lord Fine," Dr. Wright sputtered. "This is most irregular—"

"Were you the one who gave the seasickness pills to Lady Nora?" Wesley was already scanning the room. It had a similar layout to his own: a small space with a sink, a desk, and a single bed. There was a trunk on the floor and a large leather bag on the writing desk. "They were exactly what I needed; have you got any more?"

"What?" Dr. Wright said blankly. "I didn't give her any pills—"

"You must forgive Lord Fine, he's been ill," Sebastian said, behind Wesley. "He's not quite himself; I think he may have a fever. Do you have aspirin?"

"Obviously, in my medical bag." Dr. Wright's voice was quite sharp. "But you should call the ship's doctor—"

"I'm sure I won't stand for that." Wesley strode forward to the desk and opened the leather bag. Inside was an assortment of medical supplies, gauze and scissors, headache powders and tonics, American brands one would find on the shelves of American pharmacies.

He grabbed the aspirin and a handful of other things out of the bag. "Thank you, Doctor," he said, tucking the items in his jacket pocket as he crossed back across the room. "Don Sebastian, I wish to return to my stateroom."

"I'll take him to the ship's doctor," he heard Sebastian promise. "Right now. Thank you for your patience, Dr. Wright."

"Just go," Dr. Wright said, sounding dark and disgruntled.

They strode into the hall, and Dr. Wright all but slammed the door behind them.

"That was bold," Sebastian said to Wesley, in an admiring tone.

"He hardly left us much choice," Wesley said. "He was quite curt for a doctor, did you notice? You'll likely think me insufferably entitled, but I don't expect the Harley Street lot to address me in that tone."

"Do you usually barge in and raid their medical bags?"

Wesley's lips twitched. "Fair enough. I'll say again that something about him feels familiar, although I'll be damned if I can think where I might have seen him." He held out what he'd grabbed from Dr. Wright's bag—aspirin, gauze, and a bottle of vitamin tonic. "Come on. Let's see if Brodigan can scry anything from these."

Wesley and Sebastian skipped the first-class dinner, instead joining Arthur and Rory in the second-class dining hall. Wesley gave Rory the items, and they kept guard while he scried, running his hands over each item in turn.

But it was as before.

"Nothing." Rory opened his eyes, looking frustrated. "I mean, not *nothing* nothing. I can see them leave the factory. I can see the pharmacist put them out on a shelf. But I can't see who bought them."

Wesley leaned in. "Can you tell anything about the pharmacy where they were purchased?"

"I'd bet New York, or close by, maybe even recently." Rory held up the tonic. "This was displayed in the front window. There was a tree outside with leaves in fall colors."

"Is it Dr. Wright that's blocking Rory's magic, then?" Arthur said, frowning.

"He said he hadn't given Lady Nora any pills," Sebastian said. "He could be lying, of course, but…"

"But his confusion did seem genuine," Wesley agreed. "Perhaps he's being used, whether by the Duke of Valemount or the niece."

"Lady Nora said she'd be at the ball on Friday, yes?" Arthur said. "It still sounds like you'll need to investigate there."

Wesley heard Sebastian's sigh.

After making plans to meet in the terminal building the next day after Arthur and Rory finished with customs, they parted ways. Wesley and Sebastian quietly stole down the second-class promenade and used the same staff staircase to sneak back to first class and D-deck.

But as they came up the grand stairs to C-deck, there, in the small lobby area under the chandelier, was Dr. Wright, sitting in one of the wingback chairs. He had a book in his hands and his walking stick set on his lap, and he was staring straight at them with a very flat look.

"Don Sebastian, wasn't it?" He closed the book. "And Lord Fine, of course. How's your *fever*?"

Wesley had the distinct sense he and Sebastian had just been called liars.

Wesley cleared his throat. "Still feeling a bit ill, actually," he said easily. "Don Sebastian was kind enough to accompany me to get some broth."

"Mmm," Dr. Wright said noncommittally. He still wore his hat and glasses, and with his thick beard it was nearly impossible to read his true expression in the dim lighting of the landing. "Well, I'm sure you're headed to your rooms now for your rest. Don't let me keep you."

He opened his book, sitting back in his chair with

an air of someone settling in. Wesley and Sebastian exchanged a look and began to make their way down the hall. "Why is he reading *there*?" Sebastian said under his breath, as they walked. "Why not the drawing room, or the lounge?"

"He has a perfect view of C-deck's halls from that spot," Wesley said, just as quietly. "Was he watching for us? Did he decide that if we're going to barge into his room, he's going to watch us back?"

They were at the door to Wesley's stateroom now. Sebastian glanced over his shoulder. "He's still there. You better go into your own room alone. But lock your door and don't let anyone in, Wes."

Wesley wanted to argue. But there was still a possibility that the doctor was an unknowing accomplice, to either the duke or Lady Nora, and all he would see was two men sharing a very small room, with a single bed, very late. Wesley would be bringing Sebastian as his guest to at least the Beckley Hunt Ball; probably best to avoid the chance of rumors spreading.

He went into his stateroom by himself, frowning at the empty bed in distaste. Well, it was temporary; he'd sneak into Sebastian's room after Dr. Wright finally left.

But when Wesley cracked his door a couple of hours later, Dr. Wright was still there.

Wake up, de Leon, this isn't your tropical paradise—

Sebastian's eyes flew open. For a moment, he had no idea where he was—on a mattress, in the dark, it was cold and his room was small and empty—

The bed shifted under him, the familiar comfort of a rolling ocean wave. The present came sweeping back to him: he was on a ship.

Sebastian's breath left him in a rush. His hands flew to his face, shaking where they pressed again sweat-drenched skin.

He was in a stateroom onboard the *Gaston*, sailing to Southampton. Alone, because he and Wesley had been watched. And he hadn't had a blood terror; this was just a nightmare, and he could move, and wasn't trapped. But the dream was still there, a memory as bright as if he were living it again.

Wake up, de Leon—

He clenched his jaw before a sound could escape. Had he been loud already, in the throes of the dream? Enough to wake other passengers? Had he panicked because his mind thought it was having another blood terror, the small space too reminiscent of the quarters he'd had when he'd been under blood magic in Germany—

He had to get some air.

He scrambled out from under the covers, sticking his feet into his shoes and pulling his overcoat over his T-shirt as he inched open the door.

The hall was empty and completely silent. Sebastian slipped along the corridor and out to the grand staircase's landing, which was deserted. A large clock on a pedestal read four a.m., though whether that was New York time, London time, or some other time in the middle of the sea, Sebastian didn't know.

He climbed three floors and stepped out onto the boat deck. It was freezing, the stinging wind cutting across the ship with knife edges. Sebastian pulled his coat more tightly closed and crossed over to the railing. He leaned on it, resting his head on his folded arms and taking deep breaths of cold, wet ocean air at the top of the ship.

Even as a non-paranormal, he was a disaster. Other people without magic could make it through a night in a bed alone and he couldn't even manage that—

A familiar voice broke through his thoughts. "I'm going to hold a grudge like you wouldn't believe against Dr. Wright for this."

"Wesley?" Sebastian startled, turning his head just as Wesley joined him at the railing, wearing his long green robe over his striped silk pajamas. "How are you here?"

"I ask myself that frequently these days." Wesley leaned on the railing. "I had been waiting for the doctor to finally leave so I could sneak over to your room. He was there a bloody long time. I dozed for a bit, then when I woke and opened the door, I saw you darting down the hall and I followed."

Sebastian furrowed his brow. "So you woke up again exactly when I woke up?"

"Seems like it," Wesley said. "I'd say that seems like quite a coincidence, but I was sleeping light and may have heard your door. Though I hope you'll notice *I* wasn't the one who went running out onto the icy boat deck. Although I did follow, so perhaps I haven't got the high ground here."

A surprised laugh left Sebastian, and despite the dark of the night, and the dream, and his thoughts, a smile curled on his lips.

He glanced each way down the deck, but they were completely alone, standing together at the railing in the freezing night, and so he turned his head to press his forehead into Wesley's shoulder. "I'm sorry."

"None of that." To his surprise, Wesley's hand touched his on the railing, and then slid over it until he had wrapped his hand around Sebastian's wrist, over the tattoo. "You know you never have to be sorry with me."

They stood like that together for a long moment, Sebastian finally able to push his thoughts away and focus on the physical sensations surrounding him—the velvet of Wesley's robe soft against his face, the pitch of the ship on the waves under his feet, the hum of the engines many decks below vibrating in his chest.

Wesley's voice floated on the wind above him. "Was it a blood terror? Or a regular nightmare? Not that nightmares aren't shit in their own right."

"Just a nightmare." Sebastian's voice was muffled by Wesley's coat. "But it was the same memories as the terrors, and it—it's not a place I want to be again."

Wesley's fingers tightened around his wrist. "Do you want to talk about it?"

Sebastian shook his head.

"All right," Wesley said. "But I will always be here, if you need to talk, if you think it could ever help. You know you can't shock me."

He slid his thumb under Sebastian's wrist so that it brushed along the tattoo. The gesture had felt different ever since the loss of the magic—but different didn't mean less or lacking. The sparks were just as bright, just as intimate. Possibly even more so, because every touch was a reminder that he hadn't lost Wesley.

He lifted his head from Wesley's coat to look into his eyes. "It's four a.m."

"I'm quite aware, yes," Wesley said, but he didn't sound mad, and there was something soft in the set of his mouth.

Sebastian made a face. "I think you were right."

"About what?"

"I really am a pain in the ass."

This time Wesley was the one to laugh, quiet and low. "Such a pain," he said, smile lingering. "But I didn't have nearly enough trouble in my life before you."

Below them and beyond them, the ocean was lost to a pitch-black darkness. But above their heads, the stars stretched out in endless points of light behind scattered wisps of clouds. "What if I'm like this forever?" Sebastian said, before he meant to. "I lost my magic, and the dreams still can't leave me alone?"

"I'm afraid people don't need magic to be haunted by their pasts," Wesley said.

"But how could it ever be fair to you if I can't sleep alone?"

"Fair?" Wesley repeated. "Life is never fair. If it were, it never would have given an angel like you to a devil like me." He brushed his thumb over the tattoo again, sending sparks across Sebastian's skin like the bright starlight above. "Everyone has their battles. If your past won't let you sleep alone, then we'll deal with that, and I will count myself as immensely fortunate that I am the one who gets to be at your side and fight your demons with you."

Sebastian's words stuck in his throat, overcome by the feeling in his chest—the sudden realization of his heart, which now knew, or maybe had known for a while, what he'd found in Wesley.

"I'm not going to be an arse and suggest you could somehow go back to sleep after terrible dreams," Wesley said. "There's a night staff; I bet with a large enough tip, one of them will go get us hot drinks. We can warm up by the fireplace in the drawing room and watch the sunrise. You love sunrises."

Sebastian swallowed thickly. "Yes," he said, with a small, rueful smile. "I do love them."

Chapter Eleven

The *Gaston* docked at the Port of Southampton on Thursday evening as forecast. Wesley and Sebastian went into the terminal building to wait for Arthur and Rory to disembark from second class. Lady Nora and Dr. Wright were nowhere to be seen amongst the other passengers; perhaps they'd had a car waiting and left straightaway for wherever they were going.

Sebastian sat with their trunks as Wesley went up to the counter, where sure enough, he had several telegrams. He briefly sorted through the stack from his family and solicitor, and then paused. He had a cable from Mateo de Leon, sent the day after they'd boarded the ship and labeled both *urgent* and *private*. He opened it first.

```
DO NOT LET SEBI TRY TO USE MAGIC AGAIN
STOP BUT DO NOT TELL HIM ABOUT THIS
MESSAGE STOP LETTER COMING TO EXPLAIN STOP
```

"What on earth," Wesley said, staring at the cable. Don't let Sebastian try to use magic? But don't tell him that order came from his brother?

There were, of course, two particularly alarming

things about the message. First, the sender was Mateo—formerly able to see the future of magic, before Sebastian had bound his magic. Mateo had once had a vision of Sebastian when he wasn't supposed to be able to, and that vision had allowed Wesley to save Sebastian's life. Under no circumstances would Wesley ever disregard or even doubt his messages.

Which lead to the second alarming aspect of the message: as far as Wesley knew, no one had told Mateo that Sebastian had tried to use magic in the Magnolia. They certainly had not told Mateo that Sebastian had tried using magic onboard the *Gaston*.

But Mateo had used the word *again* in his cable. He already knew.

There were goose bumps on Wesley's skin. "Your letter damn well better have an explanation," he finally muttered, tearing the cable into tiny pieces and putting them in the bin.

He made some calls, including to his footman, Ned, and his tailor, Mr. Lloyd, then made his way back to Sebastian. "Ned is arranging for accommodations tonight." And before Sebastian could ask why Wesley wasn't making plans to return to his own home, he added, "After all, why go all the way into London just to turn around and head west again for tomorrow evening?"

That was part of it, of course. But more than that, there was the question of what was going to happen when Wesley brought Sebastian to his home. His staff were accustomed to Wesley having men over, but those men had always slept in the guest room, which allowed everyone to pretend nothing more illicit than billiards ever happened.

But obviously Sebastian wasn't going to be sent to the guest room. Would Wesley's staff still be willing to look the other way when he obviously had a man in his room night after night?

He pushed those thoughts away to deal with after attending the Beckley Hunt Ball. That would be a big enough battle to get through.

Arthur and Rory finally joined them, and all four squeezed into a single car for the ride to the inn Ned had reserved. It wasn't a long ride, but Wesley was ready to be on solid ground. And he was frankly ready to get his hands on Sebastian, who was pressed up against his side in the cramped backseat as he talked to Rory. Maybe Sebastian hadn't had a blood terror last night, but he'd still had a nightmare the first time he'd tried to sleep without Wesley. It'd left Wesley feeling raw and on edge, almost territorial again, made him want to chase those demons away and remind Sebastian's mind and body that he was fully in the present.

The Swan & Swallow turned out to be a country inn of three stories, likely once someone's home, on ample grounds with tall hedges and a long drive. Lights were on in most of the windows and the front door opened as their car pulled up.

A gray-haired gentleman with a crisp black suit stepped out. "Lord Fine and party, I presume?"

More staff came out to handle their bags as they were shown into the inn and up a wide staircase by the man in the suit—Bertie, his name turned out to be. "The corner rooms are the largest, of course," Bertie said, as he opened a door to one of the rooms, revealing a sitting area. "But plenty of space and large beds in all the rooms. And of course, no expense has been spared in the appointments."

Once upon a time, Wesley would have cared about that, or at least about appearing to hold his accommodations to certain standards. At present, all Wesley actually cared about were walls, doors, and the blessed promise of no first-class passengers milling about.

"And we are the only ones in the inn, correct?" Wesley said, fixing Bertie with a stare.

Arthur was also leaning forward to hear the answer. But then, the beds in second class were likely even smaller than first, and he was even bigger and broader than Wesley; he might have also been ready to have more space for him and Rory.

"Absolutely, Lord Fine," Bertie said firmly. "It was made very clear that you had a trying voyage and are in need of space and privacy," which sounded like Ned had found a nice way to say that Wesley was a titled misanthrope who was prepared to pay handsomely to be left the fuck alone. "We'll have your luggage brought up and not a soul will set foot upstairs again unless requested. In the meantime, we've set a light supper in the dining room now. Will eight o'clock suit you for breakfast?"

The dining room was at the rear of the inn, with a large fireplace and a wall of tall, narrow windows that might overlook the garden in the daylight. There was a rectangular table in the middle of the room, which was set with trays of fruit, cheese, and sandwiches cut into small squares.

"I'm sending an update by cable to Jade," Arthur said, as they sat. "Though I don't like not having news from her or Gwen. If we don't have an update by morning, Rory and I might head south."

Rory made a face. He'd piled his plate high and was already through most of it—probably enjoying his first full meal since they left New York. "I'm gonna hope for news. I don't need to get on another ship."

Wesley felt a foot hook around his ankle under the table. Done differently, it could have been seductive, but Sebastian wasn't turning it into something more. Just another one of those affectionate gestures Sebastian seemed to do automatically.

What did Wesley do in this situation? Put his hand on Sebastian's knee? His thigh? Would that be wanted, or would Sebastian think that was escalating into something to take back to their bedroom? Escalating too quickly, perhaps? Not in front of Arthur and Rory?

Ugh, this was exactly why Wesley didn't engage in this kind of behavior. How was one supposed to know what to do? How did Sebastian always seem to know so easily?

And for fuck's sake, in this raw and territorial state, how was Wesley now supposed to think of anything but Sebastian's thigh, the way muscles would feel under his palm or the way Sebastian might shiver if Wesley let his fingers drift up—

Sebastian turned to look at him quizzically. "Everything okay?"

Great. Wesley had apparently made a sound, and not even a sexy one but a concerning one. "Just ready for bed."

Sebastian's lips curled up in a slightly wicked smile. "Tired?" he asked innocently, like his foot hadn't just slid up the back of Wesley's calf.

Arthur and Rory were focused on each other, Rory telling Arthur he had to try the cucumber sandwiches.

Wesley dropped his voice to something lower and quieter. "Tired of not having you to myself."

Sebastian leaned in. "Well, you know, I heard we're going to have a bigger bed tonight because this handsome, thoughtful viscount has reserved a whole inn for the four of us."

"Thoughtful and handsome? You're not talking about any viscounts I've met," Wesley said dryly.

"I'll have to introduce you to him, then," Sebastian said. "But I should warn you that he's already taken."

"Oh, he is?" Wesley's lips curled up, a warmth in his chest that was part desire, part something else he couldn't quite name. "Got himself a viscountess, does he?"

Sebastian grinned. His foot traced up the inside of Wesley's leg, sending a pleasant shiver down his spine, and that was it, they'd waited long enough.

Wesley stood up. "Well, you two have your keys and we have ours. Goodnight."

Arthur gave him an unimpressed look. "We should talk about tomorrow—"

"Breakfast is at eight. I don't want to see another person until then." Wesley grabbed Sebastian's sleeve. "Come on, hurry up."

Sebastian's grin had turned amused. "You just said you didn't want to see another person until breakfast—"

"You're not *people*. Let's go."

"Wes," Sebastian said, as they crested the stairs to the first floor and walked in step together down the hall. "I was thinking about the ball tomorrow, and—"

"No."

They stopped in front of the door to a corner room.

"You don't even know what I was going to say," Sebastian protested, as Wesley pulled the key from his pocket.

"Yes I do." Wesley unlocked the door. "You were going to say you think you don't need a tailcoat, that you can just wear your tuxedo, but I'm afraid you're quite mistaken."

Sebastian folded his arms.

"You'll be at a hunt ball posing as a count's son." Wesley opened the door and held it for Sebastian. "That requires tails. Not a dinner jacket."

"But—"

"And you cannot pout your way out of this one."

That got him a dirty look as Sebastian stepped into their room. "I'm not pouting."

"Now you're pouting *and* lying."

Wesley closed the door behind him. Tension seemed to literally leave his limbs as he turned the lock in the door, forming a barrier between the world outside and the warm, cozy world made up of just him and Sebastian. He'd never had something like this before, never known that the place one could feel most at home might not be a place at all, but with a person.

Their room was spacious, with a small seating area on one side and a large bed on the other, with its headboard against the wall. Windows filled the other two walls, but the curtains were thankfully already drawn and the radiator had the room warmed to a comfortable temperature.

Sebastian set his cap on the back of a wingback chair. "But I already have a tuxedo."

"And *I've* already called my tailor," Wesley said, balancing his own hat on the hat stand. "Mr. Lloyd will be here in the morning. There won't be time for something bespoke, but he'll see you properly dressed."

Wesley stepped into their sitting area, and Sebastian moved closer, most of the space between them disappearing. "You know I look ridiculous in the tailcoat and top hat, yes?"

Their height difference was always so much more noticeable up close: the way Sebastian had to tilt his head back so their eyes stayed aligned, the way his lips were just out of reach so that Wesley would have to bend in order to kiss him. "Balderdash. There is no possible way you will look anything but stunning."

"Not stunning," Sebastian insisted. "I look like a penguin."

His long-lashed eyes were deeper brown in the dim light, his hair in looser waves after a long day of travel. "Only if penguins were devilishly sexy."

"*You* look sexy in a tailcoat." Sebastian took Wesley's tie in hand, pulling it free from the waistcoat. "It suits you. I will not look so handsome the way you do."

"And you call me *shameless*." Wesley was reaching for him, unable to resist. "Flattering me as if you can get me to agree you don't need proper clothes for a ball."

"I would never," Sebastian said, with wide, innocent eyes. "You're much too smart to fall for flattery."

Wesley had to laugh. "You will be unbearably gorgeous, not that you have ever seemed to care." His hands found Sebastian's hips, his feet moving on their own. "I'm certain you could have the duke's entire circle eating out of your palm, but instead you're sulking over comfort. You're too wild for society's cages and gilding the bars can't change that."

Sebastian's body was pliant in his arms, letting Wesley steer him backward, to the bed. "I'm not what people consider wild."

"Because people don't understand. They only ever think wild is something to be feared." They hit the bed and tumbled down together, Sebastian on his back and Wesley on top of him.

"And yes, wolves are wild, but so are fawns," Wesley said, crawling over him. "And you're wild like a mustang on a beach, like your heart still beats in time with the wind and the waves. You don't care about a ball; you'd rather run free through the sand."

"You could run away with me," Sebastian said, as Wesley caught his hands and pinned them to the bed.

"Spoken like the fae trying to tempt a man away into the woods." Wesley bent his head, their noses nearly touching. "But this time, you're caught in my world, a world of traditions—and tailcoats. You're simply going to have to accept that, duck."

Sebastian groaned, but he was smiling. "You're such a bastard."

And then his eyes abruptly went wider. And just as suddenly, Wesley became aware of their position: Sebastian on his back, his hands held to the mattress on either side of his head as Wesley loomed over him. Wesley hadn't been paying attention, had been too busy talking and teasing to realize he'd pinned him in a position they hadn't been in since Sebastian had lost his magic.

The room had gone very quiet.

"All right there?" Wesley kept his voice a whisper. "Do you want me to move?"

Sebastian's tongue darted out to wet his lips. Held down as he was, with his wrists facing up, the black ink of the lion tattoo was stark against his skin and the bright white of the bed's duvet.

Then he shook his head. "Stay."

The word rippled over Wesley's skin like Sebastian had tattooed it onto him, a thrill down his spine that left his head spinning. He tightened his grip on Sebastian's hands and heard the quiet inhale. "Stay?" he repeated, making it a question, giving Sebastian room and time to change his mind.

Sebastian shivered. But he didn't tense, instead tilting his head to meet Wesley's eyes. "Stay," he whispered again.

Fuck. Wesley dropped onto him, finding Sebastian's mouth. Lips parted for his tongue, another gesture of trust and hard-earned surrender that went straight to Wesley's cock.

They kissed for long moments, Sebastian letting him set the pace, an intoxicating relinquishing of control that made it hard to think straight. Finally, Wesley moved to kiss his jaw. "For the record, I despised having an empty bed last night." Their fingers twined together as one of Wesley's legs slipped between Sebastian's. "Knowing you were down the hall but out of my reach."

He pressed his thigh down, finding Sebastian's cock a hard line against him. Sebastian's eyelashes fluttered, a noise catching in his throat. Wesley kissed down his neck, to the top of his collar. "At least I can make up for it now."

Sebastian's eyes were heavy-lidded as Wesley shifted to the side, plucking open his shirt buttons to get to the warm skin beneath. "I will never get enough of this side of you," he admitted, skating his hand over Sebastian's stomach to slip under the waistband of his trousers. "All mine to take apart however I like."

He wrapped his hand around Sebastian's cock, getting another full-body shiver. He slowly stroked up and down, hearing the lovely little noise that caught in Sebastian's throat every time he moved his hand. "And I can't decide if you're being sweet or wicked right now," Wesley said, "because you're letting me have you exactly how I want, but you know full well it drives me wild."

He tightened his hand, and Sebastian swore. "Wes," he whispered, and Wesley needed their clothes off, *now*.

In short order their suits were crumpled on the floor at the foot of the bed. Wesley pushed Sebastian over onto his stomach on the mattress and crawled over him. "I'm so enamored with your gorgeous face that I forget how good this view is."

Sebastian huffed a half laugh. "Shut up."

Wesley tsked. "That's not how nice boys talk."

"To you it is."

Another pulse of heat went through Wesley, the same urge he'd had in Manhattan, to have Sebastian pinned and panting under him. But then, he hadn't pushed, and the self-control had been more than worth it for this moment now, with Sebastian clear that he wanted this, wanted Wesley to take control. "I wanted you under me like this so badly the other day," he confessed, dropping his head to kiss Sebastian's shoulder.

Sebastian shifted under him, miles of soft skin and lean muscle that were all Wesley's to touch. "When?" Sebastian said, voice thick as he tried to look over his shoulder and didn't quite make it, flattened as he was to the bed.

"In New York." Wesley skimmed his hand along Sebastian's body, starting at his thigh to trace the curve of his arse and then up his side. "When you were being so impertinent in bed."

"All the way back in New York?" Sebastian's eyes were hazy golden brown, his lips slightly parted and shiny from Wesley's kisses. "And you waited?"

"Yes, and I would have waited an eternity if needed." Wesley lowered himself fully, his chest pressed to Sebastian's back. "I am never in a rush when it comes to you; I want you to crave this the way I crave you." He put his lips near Sebastian's ear. "Perhaps I ought to remind you."

Sebastian groaned, squirming under Wesley, whose cock was hard where it was pinned between their bodies, so that the smallest hint of movement sent sparks radiating through him.

"Oh, is that a *yes, Wesley, remind me that you can take all the time you want with me*?" He nipped at Sebastian's bare shoulder with just a hint of teeth. "How fortunate we have the whole night, the whole inn—and very welcome privacy."

Sebastian's eyes had gone half-lidded. "Arthur and Rory are taking one of rooms down the hall. You can invite them in if you miss them."

"And now you're being very fucking impertinent again," Wesley said, shifting his hips so that his hard cock pressed tight to the curve of Sebastian's arse.

"Only for you." Sebastian sounded a bit breathless.

Because you're mine, Wesley wanted to say. Instead, he rocked his hips again, torturing them both with pleasure and the promise of more to come. "I might say I'll hold you here all night," he said, more softly, "but you know I'll let you up any moment you want?"

"I do know." Sebastian slid his hand along the mattress, tucking it under Wesley's hand. "And I *don't* want."

That went straight to Wesley's head, and for all his talk of having an entire night, he had to have Sebastian now. Had to trail kisses over Sebastian's warm skin while his hands explored every inch they could reach. Had to search for every spot where his tongue made Sebastian whine and beg. Had to press his hard cock inside that tight body so the world became nothing but the two of them, together.

When Sebastian seemed to have lost his ability to form words in either language, Wesley rolled them onto their sides, Sebastian in his arms, his chest to Sebastian's back. And Christ, this was even better than Wesley's fantasy, a feast for someone who liked to touch as much as Wesley did.

"You're so perfectly at my mercy like this," he whispered into Sebastian's ear, as he pulled him even closer, ran his hand over his hip, then his stomach. "If I were a nice man, maybe I wouldn't enjoy that so much. But I'm not a nice man, and I could spend hours like this, making you mine."

Wesley wasn't exaggerating. It was almost impossible to believe anything could feel this good and he never wanted it to end. Sebastian made another noise in his throat, not an actual word but a good sound, if the way he was pressing back onto Wesley's cock was any indication.

"If I touch your cock, you're going to lose it, aren't

you?" Wesley asked. Sebastian whined, and he kissed his cheek. "I'll have to take my time with that too, then."

"Wes." Sebastian was craning his head back, reaching for Wesley. "Wes, please."

A jolt of pleasure went through Wesley, and he had to press his head to Sebastian's shoulder to keep himself in check. "Fuck, the way you *beg*."

Sebastian was trying to get to his lips, a hand threading its way into Wesley's hair. "Need you."

And that was it; Wesley couldn't torment either of them anymore. He wrapped his hand around Sebastian's cock, stroking him as he rocked into him, holding himself back from the edge just long enough to feel Sebastian come first. And feeling Sebastian stiffen and shudder in his arms, and around his cock, sent Wesley hurtling over the edge of his own release.

He came back to himself sprawled over Sebastian's back, pressing him tight to the mattress again. "So good, Wes." Sebastian's murmur was barely audible, slurred and muffled by the pillow. "Love you."

Wait. What?

Wesley lifted his head, needing to see Sebastian's face. But Sebastian's eyes were closed, his back rising and falling with slow, steady breaths under Wesley's chest.

Had he just said—?

No. No, surely not, Wesley had obviously misheard. For fuck's sake, Sebastian was half-asleep and Wesley was squashing the poor man into the bed; of course he wasn't going to be able to make out whatever Sebastian had actually said.

He rested his head against Sebastian's back.

In his most fanciful, private moments over the years,

Wesley had wanted to believe that maybe his own heart of stone would someday be able to love another person. Obviously it would be an utter miracle, but maybe he could be capable of love.

He'd been burned before, though, hoping he could learn to love someone but never finding it. Sebastian was so different in every way, but that was all the more reason to be cautious, to treat the thought of falling in love like a mirage: a distant hope, but something he didn't dare look at too closely else it vanish completely.

But the reciprocal of that, the idea that someone else could ever fall in love with *Wesley*—

That was such an outlandish fairy tale, so far beyond Wesley's wildest dreams, that the thought hadn't ever occurred to him. Life was unfair; people were unbearable; Wesley was unlovable. These were simply facts.

He stared unseeing into the dark, feeling the soft rise and fall of Sebastian's breath beneath him, hearing that heart beat steady and strong.

Facts.

Chapter Twelve

Wesley's driver, Marcus, arrived the next morning during breakfast, and he'd brought Wesley's tailor and his assistant. Sebastian still had a coffee cup in hand as he found himself steered back upstairs by Wesley.

"Mr. Lloyd has been advised you're the son of a Spanish count," Wesley said. "I think he's quite looking forward to outfitting you for tonight's ball."

"That makes one of us," Sebastian muttered.

"Behave," Wesley said, prodding him in the small of his back. "And you know, I rather like this cover story, actually."

Oh no. How long was Sebastian going to get stuck with this act? "What was wrong with telling people I was your business associate?"

"You're too bloody gorgeous for it," Wesley said bluntly. "You saw how Langford didn't believe it for a second. A count's son, though? People will be delighted to believe such a handsome man is an international aristocrat."

Sebastian rolled his eyes.

"Mind your manners," Wesley said. "Get into character now. Have you ever seen me roll my eyes?"

"*Yes,*" Sebastian said. "You do it all the time."

"Lies and slander," Wesley said, but he had a small smile. "I am aware you'd rather be on a beach, surrounded by twenty cats. But for tonight, play the part."

Sebastian sighed. "I *am* glad I get to go with you," he admitted. After the strangeness of Lady Nora and Dr. Wright on the ship, he wouldn't have wanted Wesley to be at this ball alone. "And it will be nice to see you in your element."

"No it won't," Wesley said bluntly. "You're going to see me being an absolute arsehole. I despise parties and can't stand any of the people we're seeing tonight. I would far rather be with you on your beach, cats be damned. But someone very wise once taught me that even when life is shit, there are things *in* life that make it worth it."

Sebastian grudgingly smiled.

"And so I will at least enjoy the sight of you in your tailcoat," Wesley said, "even if it does make you pout." His smile turned slightly sly. "Perhaps *especially* because it makes you pout."

"Did you decide to start being an asshole early?" Sebastian said dryly, which drew a soft laugh from Wesley.

They found Mr. Lloyd in one of the unused rooms, a white man of perhaps sixty who was about Sebastian's height and dressed in an impeccable gray suit with a blue tie. He was adjusting a full-length mirror, but turned as they entered. "Lord Fine. You're looking very well, sir." His gaze went to Sebastian. "Don Sebastian, I presume?"

Sebastian tried to smile.

The assistant, a blond man in his thirties, was unpacking a briefcase onto a table, a tape measure in his hand. Mr. Lloyd was subtly studying Sebastian, who tried not to squirm.

"What do you think?" Wesley said to Mr. Lloyd. "You can't imagine Don Sebastian's panic, being stranded in England with no tailcoat for tonight," and Sebastian managed not to roll his eyes again, but it was a close call. "Do you have something that will work for him?"

Mr. Lloyd nodded once, the gesture as crisp as his collar. "Your eyesight is as enviable as ever, my lord, and your description exceedingly accurate. I've brought a handful of options for Don Sebastian to try on, and we should be able to complete any necessary alterations by this afternoon."

There was a sudden knock on the door, then Arthur poked his head in. "Apologies, but I need to borrow the Viscount Fine rather urgently."

Wesley's eyebrow went up. "Excuse me."

They disappeared out the door, and Sebastian's gaze stole after them. Had Arthur finally heard from Jade or Gwen?

He tried not to fidget through several long minutes of being helped into various dress coats and having his measurements taken. "I do appreciate your time," he said to Mr. Lloyd, as the man adjusted his arm.

"It's my pleasure to assist." Mr. Lloyd made a small mark on the tape measure with chalk. "Our shop has served three generations of Viscounts Fine. Any friend of Lord Fine's is a welcome client."

Three generations. *My world is the world of traditions*, Wesley had said. A world of titles and rules. Sebastian did come from a wilder world, where magic trumped rules and danger lurked everywhere. Now, though, the danger to Sebastian's world might come from Wesley's world. And Sebastian would have to face it without magic.

Finally, the measurements seemed to be over. Mr. Lloyd's assistant was sorting through a small pile of white gloves when the door opened again.

"I beg your pardon, Mr. Lloyd," Wesley said, though his gaze was on Sebastian, "but it would seem that we have something of a situation. Do you have what you need from Don Sebastian?"

"Nearly," said Mr. Lloyd. "He hasn't picked a dress coat—"

"Whichever one you thought best," Sebastian said hastily.

"Very well." Mr. Lloyd lifted one of the coats off the bed, studying it. "We can have this ready for you by early afternoon."

"We may be out," Wesley said, glancing at Sebastian again. "But you can leave anything you wish in my room. Don Sebastian, if you could join us downstairs?"

"Thank you," Sebastian said to Mr. Lloyd, and hurried out after Wesley.

"What's going on?" Sebastian asked, in a low voice, as he fell into step next to Wesley, heading for the stairs.

"Miss Robbins and Mr. Zhang made port in Lisbon this morning and cabled immediately," Wesley said, matching his volume. "It seems your other friend, Mrs. Taylor, followed the trail of Mr. Hyde to Tangier. And she found his doctor at a resort—dead. The man appears to have been murdered on holiday, while Mr. Hyde himself was nowhere to be seen."

Sebastian's eyes widened. "But then where is Hyde? Did he murder his doctor and escape? Or is he still lost to Rory's magic and wandering somewhere in Morocco?"

"We have a lead, at least," Wesley said. "Hyde's doctor was affiliated with a second asylum, here in the West Country. That's where we're going now."

It was Sebastian's first time meeting Wesley's driver, Marcus, who turned out to be quiet man in his late thirties who'd served as a sergeant in Wesley's company. When their group of four came out of the inn, Marcus tilted his head. But if he found it odd that his employer was joined by three Americans, he didn't comment on it, and only said, mildly, "You said you needed to take the car, sir?"

"Yes, thank you," Wesley said. "The innkeeper has promised to arrange transportation back to London for you and Mr. Lloyd."

The car was parked on the drive, looking very familiar. Wesley and Marcus started walking toward it, and Sebastian followed. "Another Bentley Blue Label Tourer, yes?" he said, trying to sound casual. "Like the one I drove in Yorkshire? It's convenient I already know how to drive it, yes?"

"You're not subtle," Wesley told him, but he had a hint of a smile. "You can only drive on condition that you pay attention to your right turns this time." He hesitated, his gaze going back to his driver. "Marcus, you've met Mr. Kenzie and Mr. Brodigan before. This is Mr. de Leon."

"The man who gifted the staff the new painting of San Juan that Miss Elsie enjoys so much?" Marcus said, eying Sebastian. "I saw it hanging up in the basement the last time I spoke with Ned in his quarters. My compliments to the artist, sir, it's a very fine painting."

A paranormal painting that helped protect Wesley's Kensington home, but the staff wasn't aware of that part.

Wesley's tone was very formal as he said, "We have some obligations in the West Country, but Mr. de Leon may choose to return with me to Kensington afterward."

Sebastian kept his expression carefully blank. It would be nice to be with Wesley in his home. But Wesley had once said his staff was small these days—Marcus the driver, his footman, Ned, two maids, along with his cook, Mrs. Harris, and her eleven-year-old daughter, Elsie. Were they used to Wesley having men over already? But then, Wesley had also said he never shared a bed with lovers before Sebastian. So maybe if Sebastian was in his home, he would sleep in Wesley's guest room like all the others before him.

Sebastian swallowed.

"Consider me at your disposal then, Mr. de Leon." There was nothing but polite sincerity in Marcus's tone. "I'm certain the others will look forward to seeing you again."

Arthur and Rory joined them at the car, taking the bench seat in the back while Sebastian got behind the wheel with Wesley next to him in front. Soft droplets of rain dotted the Bentley's cloth roof as they made their way west, out of town and down a narrow highway.

"So of the original seven relics, there are two still missing, one of which is unlocked through the murder of a paranormal with three kinds of magic, which Mr. Hyde has," Wesley said, as they passed rolling hills in shades of green and brown under the gray sky. "Has there been an explanation for how Mr. Hyde was found and taken out of his asylum in the first place?"

"Rory and I did some digging this morning," Arthur said, "and we think perhaps no one accounted for academics."

"What do you mean?" Sebastian asked, as he slowed the car to wave at a grazing sheep.

"It's unfortunately not uncommon for paranormals to wind up committed," Arthur said. "Rory had the idea to ask the innkeeper last night to get us copies of recent medical journals. And sure enough, the asylum's head doctor published a study on his patients."

Sebastian groaned. "If you were watching the medical journals for signs of magic, a description of Hyde would definitely attract attention."

"Exactly," said Arthur. "And now he's vanished, and we don't know if he's still bound by Rory's psychometry or not."

"But we're gonna find out and we're gonna find *him*," Rory added.

Before he finds Arthur, or anyone else, he didn't have to add. Arthur would carry the claw marks from Hyde's interrogation forever. If he was loose, everyone was in danger.

The drive took nearly two hours, through villages and past farms. Finally, Wesley directed him down a gravel road. Sebastian could see a sprawling complex of buildings up ahead as he idled the car for a moment in front of an iron gate that was wide open.

Seward Mental Hospital, read the large sign in the middle of the gate. *Visiting hours from 9 a.m. to 11 a.m.*

Visiting hours? More of a hospital than a holding institution, then. "So Hyde's doctor also worked here?"

"Yes." From the backseat, Arthur sounded pensive. "Doesn't strike one as a particularly secure facility, does it? Patients could simply stroll out of the gate."

"Good thing Hyde was never here," Rory said.

There was a moment of silence.

Sebastian frowned. "Surely Hyde's doctor would not have moved him to a different hospital?"

"He better not have," Rory muttered. "But you better believe I'm gonna find out."

Sebastian brought the Bentley up the drive. Closer in, some of the buildings showed the compound's patchwork of centuries—walls of newer brick and wood, built off of older, more crumbly gray stone. To the right, a small cluster of bare-branched trees stood next to a pond with its surface frozen, and beyond that was a building that looked older than the others that might have once been a chapel.

The gravel drive ended in a small lot, where half a dozen other cars were already parked. Sebastian pulled in next to an Austin 7 and glanced over his shoulder at the backseat. "How do we do this?"

Arthur had an arm draped over the back of the benchseat, forming a protective wall around Rory, who looked on edge, his eyes shuttered behind his glasses. But then, Rory had once been stuck in his magic and committed to an asylum against his will. Sympathy flooded Sebastian's chest at the bad memories this must have been pulling up; hopefully they could get out of here quickly.

"I say I go into the lobby." Wesley was eying the main door. "We're past visiting hours but they've left the gate wide open. You said Mr. Hyde was a defector during the war? I can use that."

"I'll come with you," Arthur said. "But I'll let you do the talking; we want results fast, and you're so good at being a complete prick."

"Thank you, Arthur," Wesley said dryly.

"And what're we supposed to do while you're asking the questions?" Rory said tightly.

"You can wait here," Arthur said softly.

"No, I can't." Rory's jaw was clenched. "We want to know what happened, right? I'm the one who can see the history of this place. Maybe I can find out something about Hyde's doctor."

"Then I'm going to stay with you." Sebastian cut the engine. "Let's see what we can learn."

Chapter Thirteen

Wesley entered the asylum's lobby, Arthur behind him. It was a small, somewhat cramped space, with several empty chairs lining the walls and a large carpet on the floor. A clerk was sitting at a desk at the far end, and seeing them, he straightened up in confusion. "Gentlemen, may I help you?"

"I should bloody hope so," Wesley said curtly. "Do you think I put my life on the line for crown and country just to see the very traitors who endangered us all now receive better care than my former soldiers?"

"Sir?" the clerk said helplessly. He looked young, probably Brodigan's age, too young to have gone to war himself.

Wesley placed a hand on the man's desk. "I've been informed that a doctor at this very hospital provided the most advanced of treatments to a notorious defector to Germany. Care to explain yourself?"

"Defector?" The poor clerk looked completely lost. "I don't know anything about that. We're an asylum, sir, some of our patients might believe they did such a thing—"

Arthur leaned in. "My viscount friend here was a decorated captain on the front," he said, as if imparting a secret to the young man. "And I'm afraid he's quite upset at learning a man who switched sides during the war is now receiving care from your doctors."

"Viscount?" The man's gaze was darting between Arthur and Wesley. "Um. Perhaps you need my supervisor?"

"Perhaps we need *records*," Wesley said testily. "Pull them at once."

"Yes, sir," the man said meekly.

Arthur gave the man the details about Hyde and his doctor, and then the young man disappeared through a doorway. Arthur let out a long breath. "I hope Rory's holding up all right," he murmured.

"Brodigan is really quite formidable, you do know that?" Wesley said. "Sharp enough to think to check the medical journals for mentions of Hyde and he controls the sodding wind to boot."

"I know, I just worry," Arthur said. "Rory has had such bad experiences with asylums. I can tell he's on edge here and strong emotions don't always play well with magic."

There was a moment of silence, then Arthur and Wesley looked at each other.

"He did leave his ring in the car," Arthur said. "Didn't he?"

Sebastian and Rory made their way together along the side of the asylum. Ivy grew up the stone walls, and while it was likely very pretty in summer, in December it looked brittle as dead grass, only the empty stems.

"How big an object can you scry, Rory?" Sebastian asked, eyes peeled for nurses or security guards. Not that there was anyone to see; it was cold and still lightly raining, and no one else was out on the grounds. It rankled at Sebastian. Surely Hyde hadn't been transferred from the secure facility up north to this one?

Rory pointed just past one of the garden benches next to the frozen pond, to a nymph carved from white stone. "I can try scrying that statue. Maybe Hyde's doctor walked in the garden with his patients. But..."

"But what?"

Rory was reaching into his pocket. "I'll get better results if I take the ring out of its lead box."

His shoulders were still tense, his expression tight and unhappy. Sebastian cleared his throat. "And you're, um—feeling up to having the power of the wind right now?" he said, as nicely as he could. When he'd been bound to the brooch relic, it had been extra difficult to keep control of his magic when his emotions were high.

"I'm gonna be up to it," Rory said firmly. "We gotta know what happened."

He slid the bright gold ring relic onto his finger. The brown ivy stalks rustled ever so slightly in the breeze.

Sebastian bit his lip. Surely Rory knew what he was doing. It would be fine.

The clerk wasn't gone long before he returned to the lobby, a file in hand. Arthur and Wesley crossed back to the desk. "Now, I'm not supposed to share patient records," the clerk said, "but it would seem this man is no longer a patient here."

Well, shit. "No *longer* a patient here?" Arthur said, as Wesley stuck out his hand pointedly for the file. "So he *was* here? When did he leave?"

"Couple weeks ago." The clerk passed Wesley the file. "He was checked out by a relative."

"Relative?" Wesley repeated.

There was a sudden rumble overhead, a deep sound one felt in one's chest.

Wesley pinched the bridge of his nose.

"Was that—thunder?" The clerk frowned. "Well, that's something you don't hear very often around here, isn't it?"

"Excuse me." Arthur had gone a shade paler and was hastily backing up. "I think I need a moment of fresh air. A bit of a breeze, if you will."

He all but ran out the door, just as there was another clap of thunder, louder than before. It was accompanied by a clatter in the hall beyond the lobby, where a series of shouts went up. "One moment," the clerk said, turning and hurrying out into the hall.

Not likely. Wesley tucked the file into his coat and darted out the door after Arthur. As he opened the door, yet another rumble of thunder shook the grounds.

"Now, Brodigan? *Really?*" Wesley muttered, as he hurried to the car. Just as he reached the driver's door, the heavens opened up and the light drops of rain became sheets of water.

Wesley jumped into the car, getting behind the wheel just as the others came running up in a cluster, all of them already drenched. Rory looked particularly guilty, Arthur pressed tight to his side.

"Fleeing an asylum with three soggy Americans in tow—what has my life become?" Wesley set the folder on the seat, leaned out the side of the Bentley and raised his voice. "All of you, get in the car before the staff come out."

No one argued, and moments later they were back out on the country road. "Did you at least learn anything before your pet wind blew in a thunderstorm and soaked the place?" Wesley said, watching for potholes as rain pelted the Bentley's cloth roof.

"Yeah." Rory sounded like he was speaking through clenched teeth. "Hyde was at that hospital. I saw him in a wheelchair, by the statue in the garden."

Seeing the man who had tortured Arthur, even through scrying, might have been the trigger for Rory's loss of control. Wesley probably ought to give him a shred of grace. "Could you tell if your magical binding on him is holding?" he asked, trying to find a less judgmental tone.

"I think so," Rory said. "He didn't react to anything, not even when the nurse came up and said his relative was here. Whoever came for Hyde wasn't in the garden, though; the nurse wheeled him away."

Sebastian was paging through Hyde's file. "Says in here he was checked out by a relative to convalesce with family. Doesn't give the relative's name or an address."

"Who the hell could make off with a hospital patient and not even give a name?" Arthur said.

"A duke," Rory suggested darkly. "Rich assholes can do whatever they want. No offense, Fine."

"It'd be quite hypocritical to take offense when the staff just acquiesced to my demand for records I shouldn't have." Wesley made a left turn to the road Sebastian had driven down. "Lord Valemount quite possibly *could* claim whatever he liked and then demand anonymity in the records for protection."

Sebastian ran a hand through his hair. "We're going to that ball tonight. Valemount will be there; we'll see what we can learn."

"But if Rory's magic is holding, then we know Hyde

does, in fact, have three types of magic," Arthur said. "Is that what whoever's behind this wants from him?"

"That's the real question, isn't it?" Wesley said grimly, and drove on.

Chapter Fourteen

The downpour didn't let up, making the slow drive down the country roads even slower. They only made it back to their inn very late in the afternoon and Sebastian and Wesley had to scramble upstairs to change.

Wesley made quick work of getting into his dress coat and ensemble, doing up the many buttons of his shirt and adjusting the starched white waistcoat. On the nightstand were the two small boxes he'd asked to be delivered alongside his evening wear. He hesitated for a moment.

No, for fuck's sake, he wasn't going to chicken out of this, especially not when Sebastian was being dragged to a hunt ball of all places. Wesley wasn't going to choose the comfort of cowardice over the chance to make Sebastian smile.

He picked up the older of the two boxes and looked across the room. Sebastian was standing in front of the dresser mirror, getting his white bow tie in place around his high, stiff wingtip collar. His fingers were nimble and sure as he tied the bow tie as easily as if he wore them daily. Had there been a time when Sebastian had worn bow ties often, and gotten the practice? Or was he just skilled at learning and remembering movement, whether dancing or shooting or dressing? Why did Wesley not know which it was, yet?

Sebastian smoothed the finished bow tie, and Wesley felt the echo of those fingers along his own throat; after all, his body knew damn well how skilled Sebastian could be with his hands.

Sebastian glanced up then, and their eyes met in the mirror. His lips curled up in a fond sort of smile, like seeing Wesley had made him happy. "Did you have an opinion about my bow tie?"

"Just that I like it." Wesley tilted his head. "I was actually just thinking that there's so much I still don't know about you. You must be the most fascinating man I've ever met."

"Oh." Sebastian ducked his head. "I am not so fascinating, though—very simple, really. I like the ocean, and cats, and you."

"That last one is a rather rare quality, albeit not a particularly wise one." Wesley cleared his throat, the box feeling oddly heavy in his hand. "I, um." Christ, was he stumbling over this? Wesley forced himself to straighten. "I thought you might need more formal accessories for tonight, so I had Ned send an extra pair of—well. Here." He stuck out the box more abruptly than he'd meant. "Cufflinks."

Sebastian took the box, tilting his head as he opened the lid. "Are these—yours?"

"An inherited item, which I never wear, and I just thought, given that you needed a pair for tonight, and your affinity toward animals, and that it really was never my intention to drag you to a gala with hunting at its core—"

Wesley bit his tongue. For fuck's sake, he was babbling. Clearly Sebastian ought never to be allowed into formal wear; the sight had scrambled Wesley's ability to articulate.

Sebastian was lifting one of cufflinks out of the box, studying it closely. "Wait." His eyes lit up. "Are these little sheepies?"

"*Sheepies?*" Wesley pinched the bridge of his nose. "*No.* Those are rams. *Rams.* Like the fountain at Shepherd Hall. They were made for my great-great—you know, it doesn't matter. I inherited them but I've never worn them and if they're not to your liking—"

"I love them."

"You do?"

"Such a clever design, to hide the ram in there." Sebastian was smiling as he turned the cufflink, the light catching the gemstones along the edge. He glanced up at Wesley. "Didn't you tell me, when we were in your Yorkshire garden, that your mother's favorite animals on the farm next door were the lambs?"

He'd remembered that. There had been lambs in Wesley's life, once upon a time, innocence and gentleness, things he hadn't known again until he'd handcuffed Sebastian to his bed in London and discovered he'd caught a man who cared more for dogs and foxes than his own safety. *Yes*, Wesley went to say, only his throat had gone tighter. He nodded instead.

Sebastian held out his right arm. "Help me put them in?"

Wesley exhaled in relief. A task that needed doing—excellent, he could handle a task. Sebastian held still for him as Wesley aligned his cuff and fastened the cufflink into place. Then he stuck out his left arm, and

Wesley's fingers were wrapping around the lion tattoo on his inner wrist.

Without consciously planning to, Wesley let his thumb skate over the tattoo, the familiar lion now in the black ink. Sebastian's inhale was quiet, but unmistakable.

Don't let Sebastian try to use magic again, Mateo's cable had said. *But don't tell him about this message.* What did Mateo know that they didn't? When would his letter arrive?

Wesley's thumb kept moving, following the path of the lion. "Will you humor me and answer a question?"

"Of course."

"Back in New York, at the Magnolia, I asked if you could have accidentally created a relic when your magic disappeared. Why did you seem so sure you hadn't?"

Sebastian's gaze was also on the tattoo, following Wesley's thumb. "The relics required the siphon to make—and lots of planning. I don't think I could have made one by accident," he said. "If my magic had gone into an item, surely I would have felt the connection to the object? But there was nothing in there that felt like mine. I mean, except you, of course," he added, more playfully.

It sent a spark over Wesley, the thought of being Sebastian's. He let his thumb come to rest on the lion. "Does it bother you, that he lost his color?"

"No." Sebastian said it immediately, firm and resolute, like the answer had come straight from his bones. "I like him like this. The lion is my—how did you call it once? He's my battle scar. He doesn't remind me of what I lost—he reminds me of what I won."

He glanced up, smile growing, and touched Wesley's face with his free hand. "That's you, if you didn't know."

This time, Wesley heard his own quiet breath. *If you won me, take me with you, to your wild places wherever you go,* he wanted to say. *Let me stay with you, grow old with you, lives intertwined like the branches of two trees that can't be separated.*

"Stop trying to give me feelings, you absolute menace," Wesley muttered instead, and heard Sebastian's soft laugh. "May I give you a hand with your dress coat? It's going to be tight."

Sebastian nodded, and Wesley reluctantly let his wrist go to retrieve the tailcoat from the closet. Sebastian gamely stuck out his arms, and let Wesley help him into the jacket.

Wesley's gaze stayed glued to their reflection as he pulled the coat over Sebastian's shoulders. It went on as smoothly as silk over skin, following the graceful proportions of Sebastian's body while the line of the jacket's collar echoed the high cheekbones and definition of his jaw.

"Look at you." Wesley didn't recognize his own voice. In that moment, the acerbic bitterness and sharp edges were gone, replaced with something softer, maybe even a little dazed.

In the mirror, Sebastian made a face. "I look like a penguin."

"You really fucking don't," Wesley said, with feeling.

They needed to leave in the next few minutes; he didn't have time for any of the things he wanted to do with Sebastian, all of which involved some degree of getting him out of the clothes he'd just gotten into. But even if they couldn't fuck, surely this was a moment

Wesley could at least indulge in touch, or perhaps even kiss him—

"You're so sweet."

Sebastian followed that patently outrageous statement by turning and stretching up. And suddenly Wesley was watching his mirror image being kissed, Sebastian's lips soft and warm against his own as a hand found the back of his neck and pulled him down. And Christ, there was something about having a shorter lover shamelessly manhandle Wesley down to kissing height that had heat flaring through him.

Then Sebastian was pulling away. "I suppose we have to go," he said regretfully, his fingers lingering on the back of Wesley's neck and sending sparks across his skin. "Otherwise I am going to make you very late."

Wesley licked his just-kissed lips. "Right." He made himself straighten. He'd gone without sex, or frankly even touch, for months at a time. He could wait a few measly hours to have Sebastian to himself again.

Sebastian moved his hand off Wesley's neck and held up his wrist. The ram cufflink sparkled in the light while the black ink of the top of the lion tattoo peeked out from under the stark white shirt cuff. For fuck's sake, Wesley could have put a sign on him reading *Mine* and his damnable possessive streak probably would have found it more subtle.

"At least I get to wear your cufflinks tonight," Sebastian said happily.

Waiting was going to be torture.

Arthur drove the Bentley to the ball, Rory up front with him and Sebastian and Wesley in the back.

"Why is this place called Beckley Park when it's a

house?" Rory asked, as Arthur followed a Cowley onto a narrow country road. "Is it because the house is the size of a park?"

"Don't ask me to explain the English aristocracy," Arthur said, joining the line of cars approaching the lit manor house just ahead. "I haven't the faintest idea why they are the way they are."

"I heard that," Wesley said.

Rory glanced over his shoulder. "You ready to go onstage, Seb?"

"Sort of." Sebastian's wingtip collar was much higher and tighter around his throat than his preferred attached collars. He forced himself to keep his hands in his lap. Was this why Wesley carried a walking stick, to stop himself from fussing with his formal clothes? "I am not looking forward to holding my tongue around Lord Valemount's hunters."

"They're technically Lord Thornton's hunters," Wesley said. "Valemount's hunt is in Dartmoor, while this ball is for the Beckley Hunt here in Hampshire. But Thornton also belongs to our London shooting club and extended the invitation to all members. Not that I expect you to give a solitary fuck about that distinction," he added, his tone more sincere than snippy. "I'm sure you feel a fox should be left alone, whatever the county."

That *was* Sebastian's feeling on the matter. "So Lord Thornton is hosting, and Lord Valemount is attending. Anyone else I should watch for?"

"Depends on whether you're itching to meet my scant family members," said Wesley dryly. "My second cousin, Geoffrey, will be there. He's part of the London club and also Valemount's hunt."

"Ace and I oughta get at least a look at Valemount,"

Rory said. "Is there somewhere you can bring him where we can spy?"

"Assuming nothing has changed at Beckley Park since the last time I attended one of the marquess's events, there's a billiard room on the opposite end of the house from the ballroom, on the ground floor in the east wing," Wesley said. "If you two sneak onto the grounds and find the room, I should be able to convince Valemount to join me for a game."

"Make sure you open the curtains," Arthur said.

"Well, I didn't think you or Brodigan could see through walls," Wesley said testily.

"One of my cousins can do that," Sebastian said absently.

"I have a strong feeling our family gatherings are very different," Wesley muttered.

Not long later, Arthur was pulling the car up in front of a four-story country mansion of red brick with white trim, with rows of tall windows and graceful stairs up to open front doors. A doorman got the backseat door for them and they stepped out of the car to join the milling crowd.

"The Viscount Fine and guest," Wesley said to a man with a list.

"Of course, my lord." The man swept his arm toward the stairs. "Right this way."

"For the record," Wesley murmured as they climbed, so quiet Sebastian had to strain to hear him, "I don't want to go to a stupid fucking hunt ball, I want to whisk you somewhere private where I can hoard the sight of you in a tailcoat all to myself."

Sebastian matched his quiet volume. "If it was only the two of us, I would have already taken it off."

"*Not helping.*"

They stepped through the open doors and into an entrance hall decorated for Christmas, with a giant fir tree draped in ornaments and garlands adorning the tables. The staff took their top hats and overcoats, and then they were shown down a corridor to their left, past what looked like a library and into a large ballroom with chandeliers hanging from the lofty two-story ceiling and walls adorned with carved moldings and painted murals.

A man of about fifty in a scarlet jacket and stark white trousers was at the entrance, shaking the hands of every guest. Hunting coats. Great.

"That's Lord Thornton, the marquess." Wesley straightened up and said, more loudly, "Thornton, how are you?"

As Wesley made his greetings, Sebastian's gaze stole to the ballroom beyond. There were several men in matching outfits, the scarlet coats paired with white trousers and tall black boots. These must be the members of Thornton's hunt—

"Hello," said a deep, booming voice. "I don't think we've met."

Sebastian's line of sight was suddenly taken up by a broad-shouldered white man almost as big as Arthur, though his hair was chestnut brown instead of Arthur's striking raven-black. The man was dressed not in red, but in a black tailcoat and white tie, like Wesley and Sebastian himself.

"We have." Next to the man was a familiar young woman in a blue-and-gold sheath dress with a matching gold headpiece over her bob. "Aboard the *Gaston*," Lady Nora added, her expression unreadable as her gaze lingered on Sebastian. She extended her hand, her long gloves coming up over her elbows. "Don Sebastian. I'm sure my uncle here will also be pleased to meet you."

"Lady Nora." Sebastian took her hand. They weighed each other for a moment, gazes locked.

The large man next to her had her same brown hair and blue eyes—her uncle, she'd said, the new Duke of Valemount. The one who had asked her to travel with a doctor—though Lady Nora's companion Dr. Wright was nowhere to be seen. Had her uncle sent Dr. Wright with her as a spy—or worse, to murder poor Alasdair Findlay? Or could Nora herself have been in New York to work with Alasdair and the others, using a visit to her sister as cover?

Even if she wasn't part of the scheme, she was descended from both a paranormal duke who'd made the medallion relic with its hunting magic and Sebastian's own distant aunt, who'd made another relic. Did Nora know anything about that heritage? Or anything else she could tell them?

"I'm enchanted to see you again," Sebastian said, instead of voicing his tumultuous thoughts. "It's nice to be on land, but it was a lovely ship. I love to travel by sea—it is like stepping away into a private world for a bit, no?"

Lady Nora gave him a searching look. "It is," she finally said, as their hands released each other. "That's a lovely way to put it."

Valemount was looking curiously between them. Sebastian cleared his throat. "Sebastian, at your service, Lord Valemount. Just a friend of Lord Fine's."

"He's so bloody bashful, isn't he?" Wesley's voice broke in.

"Fine, old boy!" Valemount said heartily. "I thought you were in America?"

"Made it back just in time," Wesley said, shaking Valemount's hand. "Good to see you, Your Grace, and you again as well, Lady Nora."

"You're not half as reticent as my niece here, Fine," Valemount said. "So perhaps you'll indulge everyone and share more clues about your bashful friend here."

Nearby guests were surreptitiously leaning in, waiting for the answer. "Oh," said Sebastian self-consciously. He hadn't meant to attract attention. "I'm just—"

"Sebastian Miguel del Castillo." Wesley had given Sebastian's fake name in a loud whisper, as if he were imparting a secret that was sure to reach every eavesdropper. "His father is the nineteenth Count of Animales, a very old Spanish family."

Sebastian tried to smile. Well, with any luck, that had quashed the interest from the onlookers, and they'd go back to ignoring him—

"I'm sorry," said a new woman, stepping closer, "but did you say a count's son?"

"*Eldest* son, by any chance?" a second woman asked.

A third woman leaned in. "And how long will you be in England?"

As more questions rolled in, Nora tilted her head. "Well, look at that," she said to Sebastian, with the tiniest smile. "I knew you'd make the party more interesting."

Chapter Fifteen

Sebastian lost sight of Wesley almost immediately. He tried to move farther into the ballroom, but was first swept up by a group of older women wanting to know his age and if he was married, then by a pair of young women asking if he watched the pictures and knew Rudolph Valentino, then by a group of men demanding Sebastian settle the question of whether Zorro was based on a true story. After that there was dancing, and quite a bit of time had passed when he finally broke away.

Even then there were voices behind him, whispers that still reached his ears.

"Do you think he owns property on the Spanish coast?"

"Have you heard what they say about Latin men, that they're randy all the time?"

"He doesn't speak English very well. But with a face like that, who needs him to talk?"

Sebastian raised his eyes heavenward, then took a breath through his nose, grabbed two wide-brimmed coupes of champagne off a passing waiter's tray, and began to weave through the crowd. Hopefully he looked like he was looking for someone and no one would stop him.

Because yes, he'd very much like to find Wesley, but if he couldn't, he might down both of these glasses himself.

But he did spot Wesley, over near a wall speaking to a man in his mid-thirties. He looked a lot like Wesley, with the same light brown hair, angular jaw and straight, thin nose, and standing the same height. Was this Wesley's second cousin, Geoffrey? Should Sebastian go over there, or would Wesley prefer if he stayed away?

He hesitated too long, and someone bumped into him from behind. He nearly stumbled but turned it into a stride, catching himself before the champagne spilled, and as he looked up Wesley's gaze was on him, his expression walled off so Sebastian couldn't tell what he was thinking.

"Don Sebastian." Wesley had raised his voice enough to carry. "Would you care to meet my cousin?"

The man who looked like Wesley was eying Sebastian with open scrutiny, like he was a horse at the race and Geoffrey was weighing whether he was worth a bet. "It would be an honor to meet your family," Sebastian said sincerely, offering champagne to Wesley, who accepted it. He turned to Geoffrey. "I'm—"

"I'll take that other drink," Geoffrey interrupted. "Geoffrey Collins. You're the one they're talking about, the Spanish count's son?"

No champagne for Sebastian, apparently. Probably for the best, considering how easily he'd still managed to get drunk on the ship, but he still handed the second drink over to Geoffrey a bit grudgingly. "I'm really not worth talking about," Sebastian said ruefully, "but I'm pleased to meet you, Mr. Collins. Lord Fine has spoken well of you."

Geoffrey snorted. "You're a terrible liar," he said, as he brought the champagne to his lips.

Sebastian's eyes widened. "What do you—"

"There's no way Wesley spoke well of me." Geoffrey sipped his champagne. "I don't think I've ever heard him speak well of anyone."

"Don Sebastian is a kind and cultured man who deserves to be addressed with respect," Wesley said flatly. "And now I've spoken well of someone in your presence."

"What's this about Fine speaking well of others?" Lord Valemount's loud voice boomed from behind Sebastian's shoulder. "I should think we'd want Fine to speak well of us. A man with aim like that oughtn't be crossed."

Geoffrey laughed. "You're right enough there," he said, as Valemount and Lord Thornton in his red coat joined them.

"Don Sebastian, wasn't it? Have you seen Fine shoot?" Sebastian was suddenly the recipient of Lord Valemount's full attention as the man pretended to cock and fire a gun. "Fine's aim is almost magical."

Coincidental choice of words? Or was the duke implying something? Sebastian carefully didn't look at Wesley. "We practiced trap shooting aboard the *Gaston*. He is the best shot I've ever seen."

"That he is, that he is," Valemount said agreeably. "And how are you finding our English winter, *Señor*? Cold and wet enough for you?"

Thornton made a disapproving cluck. "I'm sure the young man could do with a bit of cold; it's good for the constitution. Soft weather makes for soft men."

Before Sebastian could figure out how he could possibly respond to that kind of backhanded comment,

Valemount waved it off. "Balderdash. The Valemount line has Spanish blood, you know."

"It does?" Sebastian said, trying to sound surprised.

"Oh yes," Valemount said. "It goes back many generations but the first Duke of Valemount married a Spanish countess." He gestured at Wesley and Geoffrey. "They're cousins; perhaps you're secretly cousins with the Valemounts too!"

He said it with a laugh, like it was an outrageous idea. Sebastian forced a smile.

"Thornton!" A few yards away, another man in a red coat was waving at their group. "Beagles versus bassets, come settle the argument."

Lord Thornton perked up. "Excuse me," he said, turning.

As the marquess left their group, Wesley turned to Valemount. "How are things, the past months?" he asked, which seemed like a tactful way to say, *Been involved in any clandestine attempts to wipe magic off the face of the earth, perchance?*

"Keeping busy." Valemount cocked his head. "And what of you, Fine? Never took you as the adventuring type, then next I hear you're gallivanting across Europe and America. Making new friends," he said, with a nod at Sebastian, "and coming to parties."

"Hardly," Wesley said. "I'm just waiting for an excuse to leave this ballroom for something I can smoke or shoot."

"Christ, yes, I could use a smoke myself," Valemount said. "I haven't any use for dancing or gossip; I say we sneak off to Thornton's gun room. We can at least have a look, and then shoot billiards, if not the guns."

"Lead the way." Wesley set his glass down, still mostly full. "Don Sebastian, would you care to—"

"Don Sebastian!"

"There you are!"

Two women Sebastian hadn't met yet had suddenly materialized out of the crowd. "You simply must come dance again," the taller woman said, as she took Sebastian's arm. "I love a waltz."

"Or what about bridge?" said the shorter woman, taking his other arm. "And there will be the Christmas play starting too, and the party games—you can't miss any of that."

Wesley, Valemount, and Geoffrey faded from sight as Sebastian was pulled back into the crowd.

"Take the most handsome man you've ever met and dress him to the nines," Wesley muttered under his breath, as he followed Valemount down the hall. *"Surely that's a bloody great idea, Wesley. That could never backfire on you, Wesley."*

"What was that?" Valemount asked.

"Nothing." Wesley pushed away his reprehensible possessive grumblings and focused on the man next to him. Geoffrey had gone to the gambling tables, leaving Wesley alone with Valemount, and he needed to make the most of this opportunity.

"How did the season treat you?" he asked, gaze on Valemount out of the corner of his eye as they walked.

"Barely had time to make my own opening meet," Valemount said, shaking his head. "Damn busy autumn. I've cursed Alfred more than I did when he was alive—which, let me tell you, is a feat—though I suppose you know a thing or two about elder brothers leaving you a mess to clean up."

"I suppose." The duke—Louis Fairfield, at the time—had been sent home from the war early on, but Wesley had been on the battlefield when he'd learned of the deaths of his father and elder brother, which had left him unexpectedly a viscount. There hadn't been much cursing, only numbness.

"But then, you've been busy too, apparently," Lord Valemount continued. "Picked up a Spaniard friend—son of a count, you said? How far can his line be traced?"

"Fifteenth century," Wesley said, quite truthfully.

"Scandalous time in Spain," Lord Valemount said, which truly wasn't how Wesley would have chosen to describe the Spanish Inquisition. "His accent is a bit unusual."

"Childhood in a colony," Wesley said.

Valemount nodded slowly. "And is he staying with you in England?"

"If he likes." Why was Valemount asking all of these questions? Was there a chance he knew Sebastian's true identity and was toying with Wesley, or was he simply curious?

Lord Valemount pursed his lips. "Handsome fellow, at any rate. Seems popular with the ladies."

"Don't I know it," Wesley muttered.

They passed the dining room and entered the back corner of the ground floor, where the marquess had his gun and billiard rooms. There was a sharp crack of billiard balls knocking into each other, followed by a man's curse.

"Sounds like we weren't the first to have this idea." Valemount walked past the gun room and stepped into the billiard room instead. "Well, well, well. Not surprising to find you two here."

In the billiard room, Lord Ryland, a baron with a country estate not far from Wesley's in Yorkshire, was smoking a cigar with a pool cue in his other hand. Sir Reginald, a baronet notorious for enjoying gambling without skill, stood at the billiard table, glaring red-faced at the white ball.

Valemount clapped his hands together. "Gentlemen, you've started without us."

"Oh, I don't know about that," Ryland said dryly. "I'm not sure you could call whatever Reginald's been attempting *billiards*."

"Don't you have more screeching progeny to create?" Sir Reginald said irritably, which, given that Ryland had ten children under the age of twenty, was possibly fair. "Fine, what are you doing here? I thought you were in America."

The billiards room had a large marble fireplace on one wall, surrounded by mounted animal heads and flanked by a taxidermied bear on its hind legs, which Sebastian would have had some choice feelings about. Just beyond, the wall was lined with windows with their curtains tightly drawn. "Our ship docked last night," Wesley said, surreptitiously moving past Valemount, as if he wished to study the trophies.

A footman in servant's livery quietly stepped into the room, a box of cigars in his hand, and offered the box first to Valemount, then to Wesley. Wesley grabbed a cigar at random. "It's a bit stuffy in here," he said to the footman.

"I can open a window, my lord," the footman offered.

"You want a window open?" Sir Reginald said. "On this ghastly night?"

"The country air is good for all of us," Ryland said, as the footman opened the curtain on the nearest window.

The glass was black with night, reflecting the room back like a mirror. Wesley kept his expression carefully neutral. Hopefully Arthur and Brodigan were out there and could get a look inside.

"Speaking of country air." Valemount took a drag from his cigar. "Fine reminded me that I'm well behind Thornton in hunts this year and it's already December. Are we game for one in Dartmoor?"

Wesley's eyebrows went up.

"Brilliant," Sir Reginald said. "I'd join you tomorrow."

A chance to visit the Valemount ancestral country home, knowing the first duke had certainly been a paranormal, couldn't be passed up. But—

"To Dartmoor tomorrow, then!" Valemount gestured at Wesley with his cigar. "I can see what you're thinking, Fine," he said, though Wesley very much doubted it. "The hounds will get the fox, it's true, but there'll be plenty for you to shoot."

"I haven't gotten out on a hunt for weeks and Charlotte adores Nora. We'll come." Ryland put the cigar between his teeth as he stepped up to the table. "You're a cracking good shot, aren't you, Fine? I'd like to see that."

Wesley inhaled from the cigar. "Well—"

"I'm certain Geoffrey will join us, and you can't let your cousin show you up," Valemount said. "And bring your friend Don Sebastian. I bet he's never seen the hounds go mad for a scent. He'll love it!"

Oh no. No no no, Sebastian was *not* going to love this, Sebastian was going to throw a *bloody fit*. "He's—er—a bit of soft touch for the animals, actually—"

"Soft for animals?" Sir Reginald blinked, like Wesley had said something incomprehensible. *"Why?"*

"No matter," Valemount said, waving it away. "We'll bring him round. This will be a treat."

This was going to a fucking disaster.

Chapter Sixteen

Sebastian finally broke away from the dancing and party games, flushed from exertion in his many layers of dress clothes and wanting fresh air. He slipped across the ballroom, past the crowd milling around the bar, women in sparkling gowns and headpieces, the men a checkerboard of black tailcoats and crimson hunting coats.

From the ballroom he ducked into the hall, heading for a quiet nook with a large window. He stood for a moment, resting his temple against the cold glass, letting his eyes adjust to the darkness of the garden beyond.

From behind him, voices were coming down the hall, a man and a woman.

"I didn't know you were on the same ship home as my cousin. You said you were in Canada? Is there anywhere you haven't been?"

"Of course. It's a very big world, Mr. Collins. One can travel to every port and still have only seen a fraction of it."

Was that Lady Nora, and Wesley's cousin Geoffrey walking the hall together? Geoffrey sounded awkward but not grouchy—in fact, he sounded just like Wesley did when he was making a genuine effort to be nice but wasn't sure he wasn't doing it right.

As their voices faded down the hall, Sebastian ran a finger through the condensation on the window, leaving a clear streak of black glass behind. Was there more to Lady Nora's North American travels—more that involved relics, and magic, perhaps?

The loss of his own magic hit him as hard as it had on the ship. If only he still had his magic. Then they wouldn't be stuck dancing figuratively around awkward questions, or literally dancing at balls, to try and determine if the Duke of Valemount or his niece were paranormals. Sebastian would have known long ago if Lady Nora had any kind of magic of her own.

Before he could stop himself, he was seeking inside himself for his magic, almost tasting the spark that had been part of him most of his life. Maybe this time, when he reached for it, he'd find it waiting—

"There you are."

Sebastian blinked. "Wesley?" he said, as the urge to reach for his magic disappeared like smoke in the wind. "How did you find me here?"

Wesley had a small furrow between his brows. "You'd been dancing quite a while; I just got the sense I ought to find you. Are you holding up all right? Or are the other guests still treating you like an exotic animal to gawk at?"

Sebastian snorted. "You heard some of the comments?"

"They're driving me mad, the things they're whispering about you," Wesley said flatly. "Proof that one can be wealthy and privileged and still insular and narrow-minded, though I suppose that's just as true in America and probably everywhere else." He sighed. "And I suppose we need to get back before we're missed."

As they fell into step together, Wesley seemed to not quite be looking at him. "I, ah. I should tell you something."

"What's that?" Sebastian said, as they entered the ballroom. On the opposite side of the room, Valemount was talking to Thornton in his red coat, while Lady Nora had a drink in hand and was chatting with another woman as they headed in the direction of the ladies' drawing room.

Geoffrey was at the nearby bar, but his gaze had alighted on Wesley and Sebastian as they entered, and now he strode his way toward them. "I've just heard the news." Geoffrey nodded at Wesley as he sipped his drink. "Did you tell your friend here? Damn brilliant, isn't it?"

"I wouldn't say that," Sebastian heard Wesley mutter. More loudly, Wesley said, "Don Sebastian, I've been charged by the duke to relay his invitation."

Sebastian furrowed his brow. "What kind of invitation?"

Geoffrey scoffed. "What do you mean, *what kind of invitation?* Isn't it obvious?" He waved around them. "We're at a ball celebrating Thornton's hunts; of course Valemount wants to show the old boy up. Don't you have foxes in Spain?"

Oh *no*. Sebastian cut his eyes to Wesley.

Wesley wasn't exactly squirming, but he didn't look particularly comfortable as he said, "That's the invitation, yes." He met Sebastian's eyes. "We'd be at the Valemount ancestral manor for at least three days. The family line has held the property since the fifteenth century; I thought you might be interested in having a look."

"A look at *what*?" Sebastian said. "Some poor fox torn to shreds by dogs?"

"Oh, it's a sight," Geoffrey said. "Wesley here isn't particularly fond of it, but that's because he'd rather show off with a gun. But if you want to see *real* sport, the hunt is—"

"I realize this wasn't in your plan for England," Wesley said, a little more hastily. "But I think we need to make the most of this opportunity."

No, Sebastian wanted to say. *No, I'll solve this with magic, and we can leave the foxes alone.*

But he didn't have magic. And someone out there had wanted there to be no magic at all, and Sebastian could never let that happen.

A chance to investigate at Valemount's manor could not be missed.

But *why* did it have to be a hunt?

Wesley kept his society face in place as he said his goodbyes. Sebastian had gone nearly silent, only speaking when necessary to keep their cover.

You're being a child about this.

It's just a damn fox—a glorified rodent, a pest and a nuisance.

Christ, can't you move past this already?

Those were the kind of things Wesley would have said only months ago, even to a lover. But he didn't say any of it now. It wasn't *just a fox* to Sebastian and he was genuinely upset. Yes, Sebastian had a ridiculously soft heart, but somewhere along the line, Wesley had stopped seeing that as a character flaw and it had instead become a valued rarity.

They stood together at the top of the stairs, waiting for Arthur to bring the Bentley around. Sebastian still hadn't spoken, and his gaze seemed to be on one of the ram cufflinks.

"Um." *Come on, Wesley, think of something.*

But what could he say? He'd promised Sebastian there would be no fox hunts, and now he'd broken his promise.

Arthur pulled up in front of Beckley Park a few minutes later, and Wesley and Sebastian climbed into the backseat.

As soon as they were heading down the driveway, Rory turned to look over his shoulder. "Valemount was the big one in the billiards room, yeah?" When Wesley nodded, he said, "Is he a dick? He looks like a dick."

"Thank you, Brodigan, for describing His Grace in such choice terms," Wesley said dryly.

"Anyone who might've let Hyde loose is a dick, I promise you," Rory said. "You get any sense of whether Valemount's behind all this? Could he be the so-called relative who took Hyde outta that asylum?"

"If Valemount kidnapped a paranormal, it's certainly an interesting choice to invite us to his home." Wesley relayed the news to Arthur and Rory about their invitation to Valemount's fox hunt.

"Well, that's not suspicious at all," Arthur said sarcastically. "The duke coming up with an excuse to invite you to his home?"

"Us and a whole party," Wesley pointed out. "They can't all be in on it, can they? My cousin is coming, along with a baronet. Thornton is coming too, and hell, Ryland is bringing his wife."

"What do you think, Seb?" Rory asked.

Sebastian hadn't spoken yet on the ride. After a long moment, he said, "I don't know what's going on. And I think we have to go to this hunt to find out."

I'm sorry, Wesley wanted to say. *I swore there would be no hunt and now I'm a liar.* But those were paltry words only meant to ease his own conscience while not fixing the actual problem, and he and Sebastian weren't alone anyway. Wesley swallowed it all down.

"Well, Rory and I are coming too, at any rate," Arthur said firmly. "You said the Valemount estate is near a village, correct? We can find lodgings there. We'll follow behind your train tomorrow in the car."

"It's a long drive," Wesley said.

"Respectfully, Wes," Arthur said patiently, "what you consider a *long drive* as an Englishman and what I consider a *long drive* as an American are not the same thing. We'll be fine."

A short while later, they were pulling back up at the inn. Arthur parked the Bentley, and the four of them went into the inn's lobby.

"I'm going to talk to the innkeeper," Sebastian said to Wesley, before they reached the stairs.

Wesley hesitated. Was Sebastian about to ask for another key to one of the rooms upstairs? Did he want to sleep alone tonight—because he was angry with Wesley?

Wesley could hardly blame him. "Sure," he said, and turned and went upstairs.

In the room, he stripped off his tailcoat and dressed in his pajamas. He wasn't particularly tired, but he turned off the main lights, leaving the bedside lamp on. He got into the bed, put on his reading glasses and picked up his book. He held it open in his lap, but his gaze was on the door that almost certainly wasn't going to open.

For fuck's sake. He'd slept alone for thirty-two years. If Sebastian wanted his space, Wesley would handle that. He forced his eyes to the page.

The door suddenly swung open.

Wesley blinked.

Sebastian walked into the sitting area just past the bed, already shrugging the dress coat off his shoulders. "I told the innkeeper we're heading to Dartmoor tomorrow." He was undoing first one cufflink, then the other as he spoke.

"Oh." Wesley watched as Sebastian carefully set the ram cufflinks back in their box. "So that's the only reason you stayed in the lobby to talk to the innkeeper?"

"Yes." Sebastian's waistcoat had come off next, and he'd moved on to unbuttoning his dress shirt. The man could shed formal wear faster than anyone else Wesley had known. "Why?"

Because I thought you might not want to talk to me, or even see me tonight. Wesley shook his head instead of saying it. "No reason."

Sebastian draped his dress shirt over the back of the chair with his jacket and waistcoat and then disappeared into their room's private bath.

He'd come back. Did that mean he was willing to talk to Wesley about Valemount's hunt? Or had he returned to argue, or worse, simply grab his clothes and then leave again?

Wesley set his unread book and glasses on the nightstand and turned off the bedside lamp. He stared up at the ceiling, listening to the water run in the bathroom sink.

Acutely, painfully aware that he hadn't the first fucking clue how to navigate an actual relationship.

Sebastian came back out, turning off the last lamp on the dresser and sending the room into darkness. A moment later, the mattress dipped.

And then Sebastian was sliding under the blankets and curling up at Wesley's side. "I cannot believe we have to go to a fucking fox hunt."

"I'm sorry." The words that had been on the tip of his tongue finally spilled from his lips. "I *am* sorry, duck. I promised you this wouldn't happen, but now here we are."

"It's not your fault."

"Of course it is. You were at a hunt ball with my entire hunting club—"

"But you didn't mean for this to happen." Sebastian rested his head on Wesley's heart. "Even if you hunt yourself, you would never have purposefully dragged me to one. You are kinder than that."

Wesley stared into the soft dark, the shapes of the furniture just visible. What on earth did he do with an angel like Sebastian, who thought so incomprehensibly well of him? Where did he get such faith in the goodness of a devil like Wesley—now, of all times? And how could Wesley ever hope to keep him when he couldn't even keep a promise?

His fingers itched for Sebastian's skin, more powerful than a cigarette craving, the urge to prove to himself that Sebastian was real, or maybe to say through touch what he could never seem to put into words. He forced himself to keep his arm on the bed. He already had Sebastian against him, and he still wanted to touch him *more*? For fuck's sake, how greedy was he?

"I have come to think that kind hearts shouldn't have to learn to be cruel," he said, instead of indulging himself. "Not that I expect anyone else on this earth would believe me capable of such a mindset."

"Because you don't have enough people who know *you*." Sebastian made a disgusted noise. "People are fucking terrible sometimes."

"Christ." A huffed laugh escaped Wesley. "None of that, you sound too much like me."

"No, see, we have always been on the same page about this. Why do you think I like animals so much?"

That got another laugh out of Wesley. "Are you saying animals are better than people?"

"Sometimes," Sebastian said, with feeling. "You will see, when you go home to Crumpet and Flan."

When Wesley went home, he wanted Sebastian to be with him. He still hadn't figured out how to broach Sebastian sleeping with him with his staff. But there, in the warm and cozy bed, with Sebastian's head a perfect weight on his chest, Wesley let himself have one moment of believing that maybe, somehow, it would all work out, that he could have that perfect fantasy of having Sebastian wherever life took them, be it America or Spain or the Caribbean or his own London home. Maybe he could even learn how to have a relationship, how to satisfy his endless craving for touch through affection.

Or maybe Wesley should just admit he was thinking of fairy tales now.

Sebastian tilted his head up, and there was a light

kiss on Wesley's jaw. "Sorry if you thought I was angry with you. Sometimes I can't find words in any language, but I wouldn't give you the icy shoulder."

A tiny smile softened Wesley's lips. "*Cold* shoulder." And Christ, of course Sebastian wouldn't have done that. Did Wesley still not know *him* at all, not understand that the soft heart that didn't want to hurt foxes didn't want to hurt Wesley either? When was his first instinct going to be to have faith in Sebastian?

The skin of his jaw still tingled with the echo of Sebastian's lips. Well, he could damn well start now, with the belief that he could admit something deeply vulnerable and trust Sebastian would never laugh at him.

"Sebastian," he started hesitantly, "may I ask you a fairly embarrassing question?"

Sebastian tilted his head back, so he was looking up at Wesley. "Of course."

Wesley wet his lips. "How, um. How do you know what to do?"

"When?"

"When you're—you know. The kissing and the touching."

Sebastian furrowed his brow. "You are already good at both of those."

"That's not—"

"Like, you are *so* good—"

"Very flattering, but not what I meant." Wesley cleared his throat. "When we're *not* having sex. How do you know what to do?"

Christ, who asked a question like this? Surely every human being on earth was born instinctively knowing these unwritten rules, and Wesley was simply broken?

But Sebastian wasn't laughing. "Oh." He rolled off

Wesley's chest but stayed close, his head now pillowed on Wesley's arm as he lay on his back on the mattress in a mirror of Wesley's pose. His air was thoughtful, like he was giving the question serious consideration. "I don't think it's all that different from sex, actually."

"They're *quite* different, I assure you. Or else I've been getting sex terribly wrong."

Sebastian gave a quiet laugh. "No, I mean—you touch me how you think I will like, don't you? And you pay attention to how I react? It's all the same things."

Wesley frowned. "No, sorry, I can't accept that explanation. Nothing is ever that easy."

"You're right, you caught me," Sebastian said wryly. "I'm pretending to be considerate about you, but the truth is that mostly I just touch you how I want."

"Oh please, that answer is even worse," Wesley said. "If I always touched you how I want, I would never take my hands off you."

Sebastian laughed again, soft and low. "So then don't take your hands off me. Well, in public, yes, you probably have to. But in private, no."

"It's not that simple." Wesley turned his head toward Sebastian. "What if I did something you didn't like?"

"Then I would tell you, and you would stop." Sebastian shrugged, and Wesley felt the movement through the arm he'd claimed as a pillow. "Some people don't like to be touched. I like it a lot. Every relationship is different and you figure it out together."

Sebastian *liked* being touched. And here Wesley had been enjoying Sebastian's affection while offering none of his own. Had Wesley been so self-obsessed, so worried about looking foolish, that he hadn't been giving Sebastian what he needed? That was an unpleasant, chilling thought. Or did Sebastian like *some* affection, but would quickly get sick of Wesley's incessant craving for touch?

Wesley eyed the outline of his profile, what he could see in the dark. "I'm probably making this harder than it needs to be," he confessed. "But everything having to do with people is always so difficult."

"Well." Sebastian rolled onto his side, so he was facing Wesley. "You did say I wasn't *people*. So maybe with us, it really can be easy, yes?"

Easy.

Wesley rolled to his side as well, so that they were nearly nose to nose on the same pillow, Sebastian's head still on his arm. He reached out with the hand not pinned under Sebastian and trailed his fingers up Sebastian's arm, the way he usually only let himself do in the afterglow, or when Sebastian was asleep.

"I really think you're not prepared for how much I want to touch you," Wesley said, and his voice was a little hoarse.

"Wes, I spent three years as a prisoner of blood magic," Sebastian said, just as hoarse. "Every time you touch me, it quiets another bad memory and reminds me I'm free. I don't think you could ever touch me *enough*."

"Christ, come here." Wesley closed the distance between them and kissed him, his free hand going to the back of Sebastian's head to thread fingers through his hair.

There was a word for the feeling coursing through Wesley, warm as a distant tropical sun. He'd once believed his heart was too hard to ever let someone else in. But here he was, with part of his heart irrevocably belonging to Sebastian now, even if Wesley still wasn't brave enough to think the word that went with this feeling, let alone say it.

He pushed Sebastian over onto his back. "I know I just asked how to touch you outside of sex," Wesley whispered, "but I might put you straight through this mattress now."

Sebastian put both arms around Wesley's neck and pulled him down into a kiss.

Chapter Seventeen

"I was thinking," Wesley said, trying for a casual tone as they dressed the next morning, as if it was no big deal to invite Sebastian to his home, "that we likely don't need all of our things in Dartmoor. Perhaps we should send whatever luggage remains to Kensington?"

Sebastian looked up from where he was tying his tie in the dresser mirror. "To your house?"

"That was my thought," Wesley said. "That is, if you wished to—"

"That's perfect." Sebastian was heading for the door. "The inn's cook has a little herb garden. Let me go see if she grows catnip."

"Catnip—"

"I will send it to your cook's daughter, Miss Elsie, for her to play with the cats. She can plant it in your back garden if she wants."

"In *my* garden—"

The door had already closed behind him.

Well, it gave Wesley a moment, at least. He picked up the telephone receiver and rang down to the front desk. "Have I received a delivery this morning?"

"Just arrived, sir," said Bertie.

Wesley quickly went downstairs. He had several

things waiting from Ned, including his hunting coat and revolver, but also a stack of mail—with Mateo's letter. Wesley took everything into the small reading room and immediately opened the letter.

Dear Fine:

This will have to be short: you and Sebi left onboard the *Gaston* yesterday, and I need to mail this in time to reach you as soon as possible after you arrive in England.

Sebi's binding on my magic is holding, but as I told you, I still get flashes of visions, especially in dreams. I've had one of him.

There is a reason his magic is gone: he must not have it when he faces what's coming. I can't say more than that. Just know that many lives are at stake—including yours.

Don't let him try to use it. And don't tell him or anyone else about this. And thanks for the record. I play it constantly.

P.S. You're going to have so many cats visiting your garden after that catnip grows.

"For fuck's sake," Wesley said, re-reading the letter. "Sebastian can't have magic when he faces what's coming—what in ten vague hells does that mean? What's coming *when*? Today? Next year? Ugh." He raised his eyes heavenward. "Mateo de Leon, I know you can't hear me, but next time you tell me the future, put in useful details like a sensible man."

He read it a third time and then tore it in half and tossed it in the fire, watching to be sure it was in ashes before heading back upstairs to finish preparing for the trip.

Finally, catnip had been acquired and Wesley's second trunk packed with his and Sebastian's things, the lot of it on its way to Kensington. Arthur had found an available room in the village closest to Valemount's estate, and he and Rory were still planning to follow in Wesley's Bentley. Wesley drew him a map of what he knew of the area, including the Valemount ancestral home, Valemount Hall, and its grounds.

Arthur then walked him outside and they stood on the inn's steps, light raindrops falling on their hats. The day was very gray and quite cold, and Sebastian was hiding inside the inn with Rory until the car was ready to leave.

"I had a cable from Jade," Arthur said under his breath, as staff packed a hired car with Wesley and Sebastian's trunks for Dartmoor. "They're heading from Lisbon to Paris now, instead of Tangier, to meet Gwen and Ellis, then all of them up to London from there. She said to expect them in three days."

"Right after our hunt, then." Wesley nodded. "With any luck, we'll have enough information to plan our next steps."

He didn't mention Mateo's letter. Arthur had been around magic much longer than Wesley, and might have more ideas about the meaning of that cryptic message, but Mateo had explicitly said not to tell anyone, and Wesley would follow his request.

Finally, the car was ready, and Sebastian joined him. They rode to the train station, and from there began their connections of trains through the West Country. They had to switch at multiple stations, and by the time they were on the main line to Exeter, it was late enough for tea. They sat at a table in the first-class dining car, the window framing the darkening countryside as it rushed by, rolling hills just visible in the fading light. As they waited for service, Wesley fit his monocle into place and unfolded his paper while Sebastian looked out the train window. "Mira, Wes, there are ponies in that field."

"It's December; it's already dark. You can't see any ponies."

"It's twilight, you can still see them," Sebastian insisted.

"If you say so." Wesley turned a page. "In my newspaper I can see a front-page story about banking."

Sebastian subtly kicked him under the table. "I wonder if we'll see a giant glowing dog in Dartmoor."

"Of course you've read *The Hound of the Baskervilles*," Wesley muttered. "It has a dog right there in the title."

"You've read it too."

"Excuse me?" Wesley said, looking up. "Why would I read fiction when one can spend one's time engaging with facts?"

"Because you like logic and solving mysteries," Sebastian said, and he wasn't wrong. "I bet you've read every Sherlock Holmes story."

Wesley wasn't admitting to anything. He dropped his gaze back to his paper. "If we do see a murderous phosphorescent hound, just promise me you won't try to pet it."

Sebastian's gaze had gone back out the window. "At least a glowing dog might be proof of Valemount magic," he said, more quietly. "It's so frustrating not to be able to tell who has magic, when it used to be so easy to use my magic to find out."

There is a reason his magic is gone. Gone—for how long? Another day? *Forever?* Wesley's next letter to Mateo was going to have some choice words about vague fortune-telling nonsense.

Sebastian's gaze was still on the window, handsome face partially reflected in the glass. "I almost tried again last night."

Wesley nearly fumbled his paper. "You almost tried using your magic again last night?"

"Yeah." Sebastian huffed a short sigh. "Stupid, right? I know it's gone. I guess old habits don't die without a fight."

"It's *die hard.*"

"Old habits don't die hard?"

"No, they do, I meant—never mind, I like your idioms better anyway." Wesley set his paper on the seat next to him. "I'm not going to pretend I have any idea what you're going through," he said softly. "But we're a pair of very clever gents. We'll find another way to figure it out, one that *doesn't require magic,*" he added, just a little more firmly than he'd meant.

Sebastian glanced at him. "If you say so," he said, with the smallest hint of a smile.

It was evening when they were picked up at the village train station in a gleaming white Hispano-Suiza H6 tourer that had Sebastian's eyes lighting up.

"What a show-off the duke is," Wesley said under his breath, as they drove along a particularly bumpy stretch of country road. "Sending the Spanish car when horses would make more sense on this landscape."

"The H6 set a world record at Brooklands last year."

Sebastian ran a hand along the top of the door. "I wonder if I can sneak into Valemount's garage and drive it."

They traversed several miles through moors and park, not that Wesley could make out much of the landscape in the dark beyond impressions of scattered dwellings and low, fog-wrapped hills. Once they turned onto the road that crossed the Valemount estate, the quality of the pavement improved significantly at least, but it was still more than three miles to Valemount Hall itself.

The manor was easy to spot, even in the distance; it had been refitted with electricity at some point and its white stone and pilasters were lit like a beacon in the night. Three long rows of tall, rectangular windows stretched up to a prominent entablature, and the entire house was surrounded by gardens. As they approached the house, Wesley caught sight of the kennels and stables, set apart from the main house a short distance from what might have been the garages.

"Look." Sebastian was pointing out at the gardens, which ended at a tor topped with a two-story house built in an echo of the manor's style. Lights were on in the upper floor.

"Guest house," Wesley said. "I wonder if that's where we're staying."

When they pulled up at the manor, however, they were greeted by Valemount's butler, Horace Lester, who explained they'd be staying upstairs.

"I'm afraid the guest house is undergoing renovations, my lord. It was built on the ruins of the original fifteenth-century hall and the foundation needs regular maintenance," Lester said, with a small bow, as a pair of footmen came out of the house to collect their bags.

"But we have rooms for you ready in the east wing. If you'll follow me?"

They were led first not to their rooms, but to a small, elegant dining room with a large table, although Wesley and Sebastian were the only ones seated at it.

"Lord Valemount extends you his full hospitality," said Lester, as they were brought a late supper of cold beef and asparagus. "He's been detained in the village and apologizes for not being here to welcome you himself, but he'll be here tomorrow."

"Are we the only ones here?" Wesley said, exchanging a glance with Sebastian. That certainly did not bode well.

But Lester immediately shook his head. "No, sir. Lord and Lady Ryland arrived this afternoon, as did Sir Reginald. They have rooms on the same floor as both of you. They all retired after supper, however, to rest after their journeys. We're expecting several more guests in the morning, including Lord and Lady Thornton and most of the Valemount Hunt."

After the meal, they were taken up the curving, red-carpeted main stairs and into the east wing, where Sebastian was given the Bluebell Room and Wesley the Heather Room next door.

"Lester, a moment," Wesley said, in his most imperious voice. Sebastian had been walking into the Bluebell Room, but paused.

"Yes sir, Lord Fine?" Lester said.

"I am a man who deeply values his privacy," Wesley said. "You must tell the staff that they are not to disturb me in my room, is that understood?"

"Yes sir," Lester said, with a politely blank expression that perfectly hid whether he found the order or tone of voice insufferable.

Wesley went into his room. He gave it time, preparing for bed but listening to the footsteps in the hall. When all had been silent for a good thirty minutes, he ducked out of his room and into Sebastian's.

Sebastian was already in the bed, just a lump under the covers on the side farthest from the door with the blankets pulled up over his head. He'd lit the candle on the nightstand, which filled the room with the softest light.

Wesley crossed the room and slipped under the covers on the empty side. He stretched out his arms, reaching for Sebastian and finding him curled on his side facing the other direction.

Sebastian's sleepy voice came from under the blankets. "Wesley?"

"Well, it's not Valemount." Wesley entwined his arm around Sebastian.

"*Wes.*" Sebastian gave a soft, relieved sort of sigh, already shifting closer to Wesley. "But you can't be in here—"

"Don't tell me what to do." Wesley pulled Sebastian against him. "Sir Reginald is likely drunk off Valemount's liquors and sleeping like a brick. The Rylands will be too busy with each other to give a solitary fuck what we're doing—they have ten children for a reason." He rested his head against Sebastian's. "You've ruined me for sleeping alone. I can only think of all the touch I'm missing."

Rain had begun, pattering against the window as Sebastian ran his hand down Wesley's arm, entwining their fingers. "Okay," he said, his voice quiet but happy. "You know I like you here."

His hair was soft against Wesley's face, the sound of their mingled breaths layered in his ears over the gentle rain. Wesley would need to sleep light, listening for footsteps, but it was a small price to pay for this closeness. He closed his eyes.

He woke only once in the night, because Sebastian was murmuring in Spanish. "Cuídalo mucho. Protégelo."

Wesley cracked an eye. "Duck? Are you awake?"

Sebastian didn't answer, only rolling over to rest his head on Wesley's chest, right over his heart.

Sebastian stirred when Wesley snuck back to his room in the darkness just before dawn, but dozed off again, coming awake an hour later for breakfast. He dressed in his country tweeds, mind on the night before. He had the vague impression of a dream, of the moors and music, of stone ruins, perhaps, but whatever it had been had vanished with the morning light.

A footman took Sebastian downstairs to the morning room. Wesley was already there, speaking with a couple who looked to be in their late forties, a white man around Sebastian's height with brown hair and eyes, and a white woman with blond hair in a neat bob.

"Don Sebastian, good morning," Wesley said, perfectly proper, and not at all like they'd spent the night together. "Have you met Lord and Lady Ryland yet?"

Introductions were made and conversation was easy over breakfast. Sebastian liked hearing stories of children's antics, and the Rylands had ten times the usual amount to share. Their children were apparently on their way to the coast with their grandparents, and the Rylands would join them after tomorrow's hunt—the one Sebastian was trying hard to pretend wasn't going to happen.

Sir Reginald stumbled in late, grouchy and hungover. Wesley and Sebastian left him to his own breakfast, heading down the hall. The house was a flurry of activity, servants bustling about, preparing for the duke's return and the arrival of at least a dozen more guests.

"I realize the weather isn't much to your liking," Wesley said, as they hastily stepped into a small study and out of the path of three maids heading for another wing. "But what would you say to a walk on the moor? It's cold, but it's not raining, at least. We might see birds, or rabbits, or some of the famous Dartmoor Ponies. Ponies in the daylight even," he added meaningfully.

Sebastian wasn't going to say no to that.

They got their overcoats and hats. The kitchen staff was willing to make them up a lunch basket, which they took with them as they hiked across the moor, a landscape of rocky hills broken up occasionally by hearty bushes and small clusters of trees. The morning fog gave way to cool gray skies as they wandered up hills and into ravines, and passed more than one ancient stone wall, crumbling in places but still standing. At one point, Wesley pointed out a kestrel high in the heavy clouds that promised more rain to come.

For lunch, they climbed to the top of the highest tor, high enough to give them a view of the manor and its grounds. "Are you going to be completely insufferable if I admit to having read *Hound of the Baskervilles*?" Wesley was looking over the side of the tor into the ravine below.

"I knew it." Sebastian's gaze had fallen on the guest house, and was lingering. "What did the butler say about the guest house, again?"

"That it was built on the ruins of the original fifteenth-century manor, and the foundation needs maintenance." Wesley took a seat on a stretch of stone wall at the tor's edge, facing the manor and grounds. "Though it looks fine enough from here."

"No ladders or scaffolds," Sebastian observed, joining him on the wall. "It looks in good repair."

"Unlike those ruins over there." Wesley pointed beyond the guest house to the east, to a small building of crumbling stones beyond the edge of the manor's gardens. "You can tell from up here that it was once a chapel."

Sebastian squinted at the ruins Wesley was pointing out. "I think you're right. It's still got the arches and part of the roof."

"And more tellingly, the graveyard," Wesley said. "There's a mausoleum that's newer, eighteenth century maybe, but those chapel ruins could be as old as the original manor. Perhaps some of the graves are too." He tilted his head. "I wonder if Alfred Fairfield, the previous Duke of Valemount, is buried in the mausoleum."

Sebastian gazed out at the gray dots of gravestones against the brown December moor. "He was Lady Nora's father, yes? What happened to him?"

"Went to Kenya on a group safari about two years ago, never came back," Wesley said. "Apparently he'd gone out alone tracking game, but dropped his gun with the safety disengaged and it went off. Shot him right in the ribs."

Sebastian pursed his lips. "How do you know what happened if he was alone?"

"I rather like it when you're suspicious," Wesley said approvingly. "I suppose we can't say for certain, but there were several others on the hunt who substantiated the story. Some of them are on *this* hunt: Louis Fairfield; Lord Thornton; my cousin Geoffrey, even."

"And they saw the body?"

Wesley paused. "I suppose I never asked Geoffrey point-blank if he saw Alfred Fairfield's body," he admitted. "It's hardly the sort of question one thinks to ask without a reason. But there was an article in the paper about it, at the time, and I remember a doctor was quoted saying the wound was clearly inflicted by the dropped gun."

"A *doctor*," Sebastian repeated. "And after this doctor declared the previous duke accidentally shot himself, then his brother, Louis Fairfield—who was on this safari—became the new duke?"

"That he did," Wesley said, more slowly, exchanging a look with Sebastian.

Chapter Eighteen

After lunch on the moor, they took their time returning, swinging far wide of the manor itself to visit the garages, then the kennels and the stables. There were plenty more animals to talk to, including an elderly dappled mare who liked nose rubs. Given a choice, Sebastian would have stayed out with the animals all night.

By late afternoon, however, the gray clouds that had looked like rain delivered on their promise, chasing Wesley and Sebastian back to the manor. Sebastian dried off, then changed from tweeds to black tie for dinner.

He'd just finished tying his bow tie when someone knocked politely at his door.

"Don Sebastian? It's Horace Lester, sir."

Sebastian opened the door to reveal Valemount's butler, who gave a small bow. "I beg your pardon, but His Grace would like to see you for a moment."

"Oh." Sebastian paused. Neither he nor Wesley had seen the duke since they arrived at the manor the previous night. Apparently he'd returned. "Did he say why?"

"Yes, sir," Lester said. "His Grace understands you weren't expecting to join a hunt during your time in England and may lack your own kit. He requested I bring you to the gun room so he can offer whatever you need."

"Oh," Sebastian said again, much more awkwardly. "No, no thank you, I don't need—"

"He insists," said Lester.

Sebastian gritted his teeth. "Okay," he said, and reluctantly followed.

Lester led him down the stairs to the ground floor, and into another wing. From there, they traversed a long hall with tall windows draped in crimson red. Finally, Lester took him into a small room paneled in dark wood.

Valemount himself was standing in one corner, already dressed for dinner in black tie. He was bent over a writing desk with a tense set to his shoulders, and didn't look up as they entered. "Lester." Valemount's tone was sharp. "I told you to bring Don Sebastian."

"I did, sir." Lester's polite tone couldn't quite mask his confusion. "He's here with me."

Valemount jerked his head up. His brow furrowed. "Don Sebastian." He glanced down at the desk, then back at Sebastian. "Ah. Well. Thank you for coming."

Sebastian tried to smile, ignoring the weapon racks on the walls. It was one thing to improve his aim shooting clay pigeons in the middle of the Atlantic with Wesley; he had no intention of ever aiming one of these things at a real animal. "Your Grace is very considerate," he said, as Lester left them, "but I do not need anything for tomorrow."

Valemount's gaze flicked between Sebastian and the desk again. "Nonsense," he said brusquely. "If you're here, you're going to be ready to hunt. Our family has been exceptional hunters for as long as we've been Valemounts."

That was probably true, considering the original Duke of Valemount, in the fifteenth century, had possessed tracking magic that he'd put in the medallion relic. "But I am not much of the hunter myself," Sebastian said. "Animals are a delight when they're alive."

Valemount snorted. "My niece has already tried to get me to come around to that point of view." He was still looking at the desk, his shoulders tight and his movements almost fidgety. "I'm afraid you'll have no more luck bringing me around than she did. Seeing the world through someone else's eyes isn't what it's cracked up to be," he finished, almost to himself.

"Hunting was what killed your brother, though, no?" Sebastian said, before he'd meant to.

That got Valemount to look fully at him. "You heard about that."

Sebastian could see the surface of the desk now. Valemount wasn't working on a letter; he had a revolver on the desktop, his hand resting over the grip. "I did," Sebastian said. "And I'm sorry for your loss."

"Damn fool way to go. Alfred should have known to keep the safety on." Valemount continued to stare at him. His fingers were curled around the revolver, his hand big enough to cover most of the gun's grip.

"I saw the mausoleum today, on our walk," Sebastian said, watching Valemount carefully. "I would pay my respects, if you approve."

"Alfred's not buried there," Valemount said, his expression very blank.

"Why not?" Sebastian had to ask.

"We were on safari. It's not something to say in polite society, but the truth is, that by the time we found him, the hyenas had ensured the body was in no shape to bring home." His gaze darted to the revolver again. "I suppose sometimes you're hunting lions, but all you find are jackals."

Valemount suddenly shook himself. "Forgive me, I'm intolerably jittery today," he said, more warmly. "The Valemount line are hunters, yes, but we're also descendants from a Spanish countess ourselves, and your presence honors us, Don Sebastian. If you'd rather not have a weapon, then I won't insist."

"Thank you," Sebastian said, trying not to sound surprised at the sudden shift in tone.

"I'm sure they're missing you at dinner already," Valemount said. "Go on ahead without me; I'll be there shortly."

He gave no indication of why he wasn't following, and Sebastian could feel his gaze on his back as he left the gun room.

Sebastian wasn't answering knocks on his door, so Wesley went downstairs on his own, where he was shown by a footman to the ground-floor Great Hall and given a drink. Despite the last-second decision to host a hunt, Valemount had more than a dozen other guests already in the hall, including both the Marquess and Marchioness of Thornton, who were speaking with Sir Reginald and Lord and Lady Ryland. Geoffrey had also arrived from London at some point during the day, standing in a circle with several men and what appeared to be a couple of their wives.

"Cousin," Geoffrey said, beckoning Wesley over, "come meet the Valemount Hunt."

By the time introductions had been made, Lady Nora had arrived, dressed in a loose turquoise sheath with intricate beadwork. Sebastian had also joined the guests, distracting as ever in his tailcoat. The two of them were in conversation over by the wall, and Lady Nora actually seemed slightly animated as she spoke to Sebastian. Had she decided she liked him? But then, Sebastian's sweetness and earnest nature had proven attractive to even the most curmudgeonly of the aristocracy. Wesley should know.

Finally, Valemount himself joined them, giving no clue as to where he'd been all day but greeting everyone heartily. Then they were all taken to the dining room with its long table set with silver. The rugs were a vivid crimson under the gilded ceiling and crystal chandelier, and the walls the same shade of crimson, hung with gold-framed art. It was a bit too much like being inside someone's arteries for Wesley's taste, but Sebastian was probably delighted about the two lit fireplaces.

The duke was at the table's head and the rest of them seated somewhat by rank. Wesley found himself between Sebastian on his right and Geoffrey on his left, with Nora directly across from him between Sir Reginald and the Baroness of Ryland. The women seemed genuinely fond of each other, with Nora asking after all ten children by name and Lady Ryland doting on Nora like an aunt. Perhaps the baroness had been close with Nora's mother, the late Duchess of Valemount.

As with most big tables, there was little chance of hearing or speaking with anyone outside of one's neighbors, which meant Wesley would need to find another way to talk to Valemount.

Sebastian leaned forward. "You will keep telling us

about your travels around the Mediterranean, yes?" he said to Nora. He turned to Wesley. "She was telling me about a river steamer she sailed down the Nile—or it is actually up the Nile, you reminded me, as it flows into the Mediterranean?"

A tiny smile lifted Nora's lips, but Sir Reginald said, "Or we could talk about tomorrow's hunt, perhaps?"

Nora's smile vanished as Sebastian narrowed his eyes. "Is it really necessary to hunt the fox?" Sebastian said. "They are charming little creatures, no?"

"That's exactly how I feel," said Nora, and next to her, Lady Ryland patted her hand in a reassuring sort of way.

"Foxes are nuisances," Geoffrey said, in what he probably imagined was a reasonable and logical tone but drew twin glares from Nora and Sebastian. Unfortunately, being terrible with people seemed to be a common trait among men of the Fine lineage. "They overrun the hutches and eat the chickens."

Sir Reginald nodded emphatically. "The hunt is necessary pest control."

"But using the dogs to chase and slaughter seems cruel," Sebastian said.

"I agree," said Nora. "There are more humane ways to protect the livestock."

"I suppose we could have Wesley here shoot them all," Geoffrey said dubiously.

"Geoffrey, do not bring me into this," Wesley said testily. "I'm going to sit here and eat my oysters."

"You're quite the shot yourself," Sir Reginald said to Geoffrey.

"Farsight runs in the family." Geoffrey cut into a caviar canapé with his fork. "Lord Valemount is a cracking shot too, and his collection of antique firearms might be the country's best."

"I saw them," Sebastian muttered.

Wesley glanced at him.

"Just before dinner," Sebastian added, meeting Wesley's gaze. "Lord Valemount had sent for me to offer a firearm for tomorrow."

Wesley raised an eyebrow. That was interesting. "If you wanted a firearm, I could have provided you one."

"But I don't," Sebastian said wryly. "I thanked His Grace for his consideration but declined."

"Declined? Are you mad?" Geoffrey said. "I'd give my right arm to use some of those guns."

"You don't know how to shoot without your right arm," Wesley said.

Geoffrey gave him an unimpressed look, then turned back to Sebastian. "Does your family collect antiques?"

"Yes," Sebastian said, which was quite true, albeit omitting the detail that most of them were enchanted. "But my favorites are the art, not the weapons."

"Did you hear that?" Nora said, addressing Lady Ryland on her left. "A man at my uncle's table who doesn't like fox hunts and admits he likes art? Be still my heart."

Geoffrey glanced between Sebastian and Lady Nora, a frown forming.

"My dear, you must show Don Sebastian the Greeks." Lady Ryland gestured down the table, where Lord Thornton and his wife were speaking with Valemount. "I don't believe Lady Thornton has ever seen the gallery. If you offer a tour, I'm sure she'll join, and perhaps some of the others as well."

A tour of the art and possibly antiques owned by a

duke descended from a paranormal? That sounded quite useful. But before Wesley could comment, Sir Reginald said, "I'm looking forward to cards. Fine, are you any good at poker? His Grace has promised me a redeeming round after the tables at the Beckley Hunt didn't go my way. We'll grab all the fellows for it—Collins, you're in too, aren't you?"

"Not tonight," Geoffrey said. "I'll join the art tour."

Wesley side-eyed him. "Really?"

"I like art," Geoffrey said testily.

"Since when?" said Wesley.

"Since tonight," Geoffrey said, through clenched teeth.

"That's settled, then," Nora said, looking pleased. "The gamblers can have their fun after dinner, and we'll have our tour."

The rain picked up strength during dinner, a steady drumbeat against the windows behind their thick red drapes. The table finished their dessert course, and then Wesley disappeared with Valemount and several other men down a hall into another wing.

Sebastian instead joined Geoffrey to follow Nora, who had gathered Lady Ryland, the Marchioness of Thornton, and some of the other hunters' wives. Nora led their group up the curving main stairs to the second floor, heading in the opposite direction of the guest wing and finally opening an ornate door to another room with a gilded ceiling done in crimson and gold like the dining room. It was long, like a large hall, with double doors open at the far end, and the walls were hung with paintings on both sides.

Geoffrey stepped to the side to study the contents of

a glass case while the other women spread out through the gallery with appreciative murmurs. Nora, however, stayed with Sebastian. He couldn't be sure, but she seemed to have thawed slightly toward him. He wanted to ask Nora for more information about Dr. Wright, her companion from the ship, but held his tongue. They'd have three days here; if he wanted her to be honest with him, he needed to deserve her trust.

There was, of course, the chance that Nora herself was part of the plot to destroy magic that had entangled Langford and Alasdair. But the more time Sebastian spent in her company, the more he dismissed that idea. He found himself liking her, obviously not the way he liked Wesley, but the way he liked Jade, or Gwen, or his cousin Isabel.

"This collection was commissioned by my great-grandmother," Nora said, in a quieter voice, as they approached the first painting. "And while I'm sure my uncle would prefer to show you the sword our great-grandfather was gifted by the king—"

"Is that this sword?" Geoffrey said, a bit too loud, as he pointed at the glass case.

"Yes. *But*," Nora said, stressing the word, "Uncle Louis isn't here, so Don Sebastian is going to visit with the Greeks." She gestured at the first painting, of a powerfully built man in war dress. "Though unsurprisingly, this one is my uncle's favorite."

Sebastian took in the details, from the spear and shield to the headdress. "Is this Ares? Such a detailed interpretation. If you look behind him, you can even see the temple on the hill."

Nora tilted her head. "So you are indeed an art fan?"

"My cousin Isabel is a painter." Sebastian would

skip the detail about her ability to create paranormal paintings that could stop magic. "She insisted I learn to appreciate the work that goes into creating beautiful things."

"How sweet," Nora said, sounding sincere. They stood quietly for a moment, looking at the painting.

"This sword's very nice too," Geoffrey called.

Sebastian heard Nora's tiny sigh.

They moved to the next painting, of an enormous muscular man locked in combat with a giant lion. "And here we have, unsurprisingly, my uncle's second favorite," Nora said.

"Hercules?" Sebastian asked, pointing.

"Yes." Nora cleared her throat. "I'm sorry if this is a forward question but—is that a tattoo?"

"Oh." Belatedly, Sebastian realized his sleeve had risen when he'd raised his arm. "Not a forward question; it's right here where everyone can see it. It's my cousin's artwork."

Nora looked intrigued. "You come from interesting family."

Sebastian and Nora came from the same family, if you went back to the fifteenth century, but he only nodded. "I am very lucky to have them."

Nora smiled. "Enough of my uncle's choices; come see *my* favorite of the paintings."

As they walked past Geoffrey and the glass case, Sebastian faked a cough. Geoffrey looked up, and Sebastian meaningfully jerked his head. "Don't you want to come see Lady Nora's favorite painting?" he said pointedly.

"Oh!" Geoffrey said. "Yes, yes, I do," he added, hurrying to catch up with them.

Nora led them to the end of the hall and stopped in front of a larger painting. It was a forest scene, a woman in the foreground with robes flowing loose around her knees and a quiver across her chest. In the background, several women played in a stream. "Artemis!" Geoffrey said, sounding proud of himself for recognizing her. "I'm surprised she's your favorite, Lady Nora, if you don't like hunting."

"It is perhaps ironic," Nora admitted, "but she's so beautiful and free. Who wouldn't want to run off with her?"

"Not if I have to shoot things with arrows," Sebastian said ruefully.

Nora shot him a grin. "Perhaps you can run off with Aphrodite, then. She's just here—no hunting, only hedonism."

Sebastian glanced at the next painting, a woman in the ocean, long tresses strategically covering her nakedness. "Very beautiful," he admitted. "She favors the Botticelli work."

Nora swept her hand toward the open doors at the far end of the room. "If you have any interest in artwork from that time, we have portraits of the first Duke of Valemount and his wife."

The three of them stepped into the gallery. Again, the walls were lined with art, but Lady Nora was leading the way to the far end. "Here he was," she said, indicating a painting on wood, of a white man with an ear-length brown bob under a wide-brimmed red hat, dressed in a gold-embroidered doublet and black cape. The display tag on the wall beside the portrait had at least nine names. "And that was his wife, a Spanish countess before she became the duchess."

And just like that, Sebastian was staring at a painting of his own distant aunt.

"Mariana de Leon." Nora was still gazing at the portraits. "Such a beauty, wasn't she? Such style." The corners of her lips turned up. "Actually, I fancy she might look a bit like you."

Sebastian eyed his aunt. The countess wore several pieces of jewelry—including a distinctive wrist cuff, set with jewels, that Sebastian had seen drawn in his family's books. Had the countess transferred her magic into the cuff already, when this portrait was painted? Was he looking at the relic that had held her ability to cast curses?

"Lady Nora," the Marchioness of Thornton called, from the gallery behind them. "You must come tell us more about Aphrodite!"

Nora glanced back toward the gallery, shaking her head fondly. "Excuse me," she said. "Unless you care for more art history?"

"I will catch up with you two," Sebastian promised. He gave her what he hoped was a disarming smile. "Your Spanish ancestor intrigues me."

As Nora's and Geoffrey's steps retreated behind him, Sebastian stepped closer to the portrait of the duke. And there it was, hanging from a gold chain around his neck in the painting: the medallion that had eventually held the duke's tracking magic.

Had both of them been painted with their relics? Then what had happened to the relics, after Sebastian's inquisitor ancestor came after them? Had their altercation happened here, at the site of the Valemounts' ancestral home? Was this where Sebastian's own family curse had been cast?

Sebastian's gaze stole back to his distant aunt, the inquisitor's sister. Lord Valemount's words about his brother echoed in his mind.

Damn fool way to go. Alfred should have known to keep the safety on.

Wesley had said the prior Duke of Valemount's death had been substantiated by a doctor. Surely it was too much of a stretch to think that doctor could have been Dr. Wright? But Lord Valemount was close enough to Dr. Wright to send him to America with Nora. A doctor could have substantiated the story behind Alfred Fairfield's death, could have helped facilitate the transfer of Hyde to a less secure facility, could have snuck into a New York mental hospital and poisoned Alasdair. Lord Valemount had been missing the prior night and through the day. Could he have been with Dr. Wright that day?

There was one place on the grounds where no guests were currently allowed. And if you wanted to hide a guest, a guest house was a good place for it.

Sebastian glanced over his shoulder. The women were in the gallery, gushing with each other about the art, while Geoffrey was focused on Nora. Lord Valemount himself was occupied, playing cards with Wesley and the other men.

No one was paying any attention to Sebastian.

As quietly as he could, he slipped out the door of the gallery.

Chapter Nineteen

Valemount's billiard room was even more ornate than the one at Thornton's country manor, Beckley Park, had been. It was decorated in hunting trophies and in addition to the billiards table also sported a large round card table surrounded by velvet chairs.

Some of the other guests had been invited, and they'd ended up with a group of eight men that included Wesley and Valemount, but also Thornton, Lord Ryland, Sir Reginald and three other members of the hunt. As they took their seats, three footmen appeared, one carrying cards and poker chips, one with a silver tray of crystal tumblers and three bottles, and the third with a box of cigars. When he reached Wesley's seat, Wesley made a show of looking the cigars over and then chose one at random.

Sir Reginald picked up his drink the instant it was poured. "Suppose it's no surprise the Spaniard went with the ladies." The man had already had several drinks with dinner. At a table like this, the stakes would be outrageously high; it didn't bode well for his wallet.

"You'll notice Geoffrey also joined them," Wesley said dryly. "So if you're trying to imply something unsavory about Latin men's desire for women, you ought to extend it to our countrymen as well."

Sir Reginald's expression soured. Good.

"Don Sebastian told me he's not much of a hunter." Valemount picked up the deck of cards. "Perhaps he's not much for poker, either."

Sebastian had said Valemount called him to the gun room, to offer a hunting weapon. Had that truly been his entire motive? But what else might he have wanted with Sebastian?

"The ladies seem happy to have Don Sebastian's company, at any rate," Lord Ryland remarked drolly, as the footmen finished attending them and disappeared back out the doors on silent feet.

"It's the most I've ever seen Nora willingly speak to a man." Valemount's gaze went to Wesley. "You said your Spanish friend is in England on holiday? By himself, it seems—no wife at home, then?"

A particularly uncivilized emotion began to curl in Wesley's gut. "What an interesting question." He struck a match on his thumbnail, and the flame burst into life in blue and red. "Don Sebastian is a bachelor, yes."

"And has he said anything to you about my niece?" Valemount pressed. "She's got a rather dour disposition, but he seems like the kind of chap who tolerates that sort of thing."

"It'd be difficult for him to bear my company otherwise," Wesley said coolly.

"You think Lady Nora likes him?" Sir Reginald asked.

"Oh, I don't give a good goddamn what she likes," Valemount said bluntly. "She's my last unmarried niece and I'd wager her off at this table if I could. Here I've been trying to solve the problem of what to do with her when lo and behold, Fine here brings me an answer—send her to Spain."

That drew laughs from the other men at the table. "Brilliant," Thornton said. "How do I do that with my wife?"

Wesley brought the cigar to his lips, gaze on Valemount. Did the duke suspect Sebastian's true identity? Or was Nora the real reason Valemount had put together an impromptu hunt and invited them both? "You think to match Lady Nora and Don Sebastian, then?"

Valemount spread his hands. "Think of it as international diplomacy."

Sir Reginald snorted. "They could launch a diplomatic mission to save the foxes together."

Valemount laughed again, as did all the other men around the table. Except for Wesley, who lit the tip of the cigar and inhaled the smoke that was just as poisonous as his cigarettes but cost fifty times as much.

"And what say you, Fine?" Valemount had a sly sort of smile. "Will you offer up your Spaniard for my diplomacy?"

Wesley blew out smoke. "He was planning to return to London with me."

Valemount waved that away. "Leave him behind," he said, like Wesley's wants, or even Sebastian's own, were no matter at all. "Think what a striking couple Don Sebastian and Nora would make—no nice man would stand in their way."

Possibly not. Wesley, however, was not, and would never be, a *nice man*.

"Think on it, at least." Valemount bridged the deck.

"Shall I deal, gentlemen? Lord Fine, don't tell me you're as good at cards as you are with a gun."

Wesley picked up his whiskey, an amber-gold brown in the dim light, like Sebastian's eyes. "Funny you should mention that," he said, tilting the glass. "In fact, only days ago I was bested by a twenty-one-year-old American antiquarian."

There was another chuckle around the table, this time with a derisive edge. Sebastian would have let them laugh because he was strong enough not to care if other men thought he was weak.

Wesley let them laugh because battles were easier when one disarmed one's opponents first.

"Really?" Valemount said, as he began to deal.

"I'm afraid so," Wesley said truthfully. "Terribly embarrassing, honestly; I was so confident I could win, and then, in his own words, he took me straight to the cleaners."

"And is that how your games usually go?" Thornton asked, eying Wesley over his drink.

Of course it wasn't how Wesley's games usually went. Rory was fucking psychometric. Take magic out of the equation, and Wesley generally obliterated his opponents at cards. Or billiards. Or revenge.

"Well." Wesley set his whiskey down, unsipped. "I don't typically lose to *antiquarians*."

The other men laughed again. Wesley used their distraction to subtly push his whiskey to the side.

"At least you've got deep pockets," Sir Reginald said, rubbing his hands together like Wesley had brought him Christmas.

Valemount began to deal. "Get your bets ready, gents."

As cards landed in front of him, Wesley tapped the

ash off his cigar and put it back to his lips. Valemount wanted a suitor for his niece and thought he could help himself to Sebastian.

The fucking audacity.

Sebastian got his coat and a flashlight from the staff, claiming he was just stepping out for a smoke. The footman directed him to a door on the ground floor that opened to a portico and then the gardens beyond.

It was perhaps a quarter mile's walk to the bottom of the garden and then back up the next hill to the guest house. Sebastian buttoned his coat tight as he strolled through tall hedges and past manicured shrubs. The heavier rain had eased to a misty fog, but the air was cold, and the moon and stars were blocked by the clouds just visible against the night sky.

The guest house itself seemed even bigger up close, larger and more impressive than any home most people would ever own. Unlike the prior night, when they'd arrived, all of the windows were dark now, giving it a foreboding, unwelcoming countenance. Sebastian cautiously climbed the front steps on light feet; if the foundation really was undergoing repairs, he needed to be careful where he stepped. But there was no evidence of ongoing repairs anywhere; no evidence of anyone at all inside.

He tried the front door, which opened easily. When you lived miles from the nearest village—or even the road—with a whole staff to man your grounds, perhaps you didn't worry too much about intruders. Sebastian stepped inside the front hall, under the chandelier suspended from the vaulted two-story ceiling. His flashlight beam illuminated rich carpets leading into other rooms to both his right and his left, and in front of him, a carved staircase gracefully curving up to the second floor. It was silent inside, but not dusty. Empty, but not abandoned.

Sebastian ducked into every room on the first floor, shining his flashlight around the floors and walls, but there was no evidence that anyone had stayed there recently—no books off the shelves in the library, no cushions out of place on the settee; no drapes open on the windows. He went up the stairs instead, which opened into a long hall lined with bedrooms. He went into each one in turn, not sure exactly what he was looking for but finding nothing out of the ordinary.

Finally, at the room at the very end of the hall, Sebastian's flashlight found something out of place: a black glove on the floor, just barely visible against the dark floor where it poked out from under the bed. He bent and picked it up, turning it over in his hands. It seemed to be a typical thick glove, like anyone might wear to keep their hands warm in winter—except it had no fingertips, as if they'd been cut off.

Suddenly, from downstairs, he heard a voice.

"Don Sebastian? Did you come in here?"

What on earth was *Geoffrey* doing in the guest house? Sebastian hastily crammed the glove into his overcoat pocket and hurried back to the stairs. "Mr. Collins?" he called, as he took the first steps down.

"Man, what are you *doing*?" Geoffrey said, sounding very much like Wesley when he was irritated. "You can't be in here."

Sebastian winced. "I know, but I was being mindful of the foundation—"

"That's not the issue," Geoffrey said testily. "That's

just a lie Valemount told to keep us all out. Apparently some distant cousin of his was staying in here, ill as anything. That's the real reason we're in the main house."

Sebastian frowned. "*Was* staying in here?"

"He's been moved to a hospital," Geoffrey said. "I only found out because I nearly wandered in here myself out of habit; I usually stay in the guest house on these hunts. But I ran into the man's doctor, who had to explain the real situation to me."

"A doctor?" Sebastian said in shock. "What was his name?"

"How would I know?" In the edge of the flashlight beam, Geoffrey looked a lot like Wesley then too, as he eyed Sebastian curiously. "Why are you down here anyway? Wesley said you've got that Mediterranean blood and hate the cold."

"I wanted to see the gardens at night," Sebastian lied. "Why are *you* here?"

"I saw you leave the gallery and the footman said you'd gone out," Geoffrey said.

"So you *followed* me?" Sebastian said.

"I knew you wouldn't know about Valemount's cousin," Geoffrey said, "and I don't know if they've properly sanitized the house with all of us here."

Sebastian folded his arms. "That's not much of a reason."

"Yes it is," Geoffrey said curtly. "Look, how many friends do you think Wesley has? Can you imagine how he'd react if you caught scarlet fever and he found out I'd let it happen?"

He gestured at the door. "Come on, you've been in

here too long already. I bet we've both been missed at the manor by now."

Sebastian subtly slipped his hand into his overcoat pocket. "I'll follow you," he said, as he curled his fingers around the glove.

Back in the main house, Sebastian followed Geoffrey into another wing, through twisting corridors until they came to a solid door. As Geoffrey opened the door, Valemount's angry voice spilled out from the room.

"Goddamn you, Fine." Valemount was bright red, as the other men looked on, wide-eyed. "The H6 is my fucking favorite."

Wesley had one finger on the single chip in the center of the table and was calmly pulling it toward himself. "Perhaps you shouldn't have wagered it, then."

Valemount threw up his hands, his gaze going to the door. "Geoffrey, thank Christ," he said snappishly. "Come collect your cousin before I lose the bloody house."

Sebastian looked questioningly at Wesley, who held up the chip. "I believe you mentioned something about wanting a chance to drive the H6?"

Sebastian's eyes widened. Surely Wesley wasn't implying—

"Well, that's me done for the night." Wesley looked around the table. "Unless any of you gents wanted to play another round?"

Not a single one of the other seven men were meeting Wesley's eyes.

"I think I'll retire," Sir Reginald said.

"Me as well," Lord Ryland said quickly.

"Breakfast will be served at seven, then to the kennels." Valemount's tone was still very dark. "We loose the hounds at eight sharp."

Sebastian's stomach turned over.

The men filed out of the room, talking too loudly to each other as they all traversed down the halls and up the curving main staircase to the second floor. Sebastian was trying to think of an excuse to get Wesley alone when Wesley said, loud and clear, "Don Sebastian. Could we speak for a moment?"

The other men exchanged knowing looks. What did they think Wesley wanted to talk to him about?

Well, Wesley would know what he was doing. Sebastian followed Wesley into his guest room as the other men continued down the hall. Sebastian firmly shut the door behind him and leaned on it, blowing out a long hard breath. "I have things to tell you," he said quietly.

"I have things to tell *you*," Wesley echoed. "But first—"

He was suddenly on Sebastian, pressing him to the door, swallowing Sebastian's noise of surprise with a kiss. Sebastian's mouth parted automatically, eyelashes fluttering closed.

"I was wrong," Wesley said against his lips, bringing Sebastian's hands up above his head. "Fuck tailcoats, and tradition while we're at it. Let's run away together to the wildest places we can find."

Sebastian bit his lip, hard, to hold in a groan, as Wesley kissed his inner wrist, where the shirt cuff had been forced up and his tattoo revealed. "Did you really win Valemount's *car*?"

"He wants to fob his niece off on you," Wesley said, his lips against the lion.

Sebastian's eyes popped open. "He what?"

"Marry you and Lady Nora, without a thought for what either of you might want. Or what *I* might want, which admittedly he doesn't know that I have a stake in this, but I still did not take it with grace," Wesley said. "So yes. I took that pretty Hispano-Suiza that picked us up. And one of his lesser London properties. And a side printing business. The car is for you, by the way. You'll look delectable behind the wheel."

Sebastian had to laugh. "*Wesley.*"

"I will not apologize or return any of it." Wesley brought their faces back together. "Imagine Valemount thinking he could take you from me," he said, his breath ghosting against Sebastian's lips. "Frankly I let him off too easy."

Sebastian kissed him, heart pounding from Wesley's words and the breathless rush of having Wesley on him. He would have dropped to his knees, but the sound of voices cut through the door, Lord and Lady Ryland laughing with each other across the hall.

Wesley pulled back, and they looked up into each other's eyes for a moment.

"What did you wish to tell me?" Wesley finally said, letting Sebastian's wrists go with obvious reluctance.

They moved deeper into the room together, Sebastian filling Wesley in on his evening.

"Geoffrey followed you?" Wesley said, frowning.

Sebastian shrugged helplessly. "He seemed to think you'd be mad if he let a friend of yours catch scarlet fever."

"Well," Wesley said grudgingly, "he's not *wrong*. I just wouldn't have imagined he'd care whether I was angry or not." He stood by the end of the bed, still frowning. "And Geoffrey said there was a distant

Valemount cousin with scarlet fever down at the guest house? When that dangerous paranormal, Mr. Hyde, was taken from his asylum supposedly by his relative?"

Sebastian pulled the glove from his pocket and held it out. "I took this from one of the bedrooms."

Wesley accepted it, examining the glove. "The fingertips are missing."

"Hyde has claws he can't retract," Sebastian said quietly. "It's part of the magic left in him from our time under blood magic together."

"Christ," Wesley muttered. "But if Hyde was in the guest house, where is he now? Was Valemount moving him, and that's why the duke has been missing until this evening? I wonder if Brodigan could learn anything if he scried this glove."

"Or Rory might not see anything at all," Sebastian pointed out. "Like on the ship."

"We won't know unless he tries." Wesley pursed his lips. "I think we can use Valemount's scheming to our advantage. We'll tell him you want to stay behind during the hunt tomorrow to visit with Lady Nora. I'm sure you'd rather not join a fox hunt anyway."

"It's almost worse to stay behind," Sebastian muttered. "Knowing what's going to happen to the poor thing and being too cowardly to face it."

"It's not cowardice, it's strategy," Wesley said. "We have a missing paranormal who is, by your accounts, quite dangerous. We have a plot against magic that may or may not be related to Lord Valemount. If you stay behind, perhaps you can get Arthur and Brodigan here to investigate while Valemount is busy on the hunt."

"I wish we had some of the others here too, with their

magic." *I wish I had my magic*, Sebastian didn't say. *I would make sure it protected you.*

"There is no need for magic," Wesley said, almost too firmly. "We can use our eyes, and our minds, to look for connections and—" He abruptly cut himself off.

"What?" Sebastian said curiously.

"Just a wild thought." Wesley's gaze was on the glove again. "You said Geoffrey was told the story today by a doctor, which could have been Lady Nora's mysterious Dr. Wright."

"I think we have to assume it's possible," Sebastian said.

"And would you agree that it was difficult to place Dr. Wright's age, or even make out his facial features behind that thick beard and glasses?"

"Yes," Sebastian said. "Why?"

"I'm just realizing," Wesley said, "that we've never actually seen Valemount and Dr. Wright together."

Sebastian's eyes widened. "You don't think—"

There were voices in the hall again, louder than before—the Marquess and Marchioness of Thornton, perhaps. Then someone knocked on Wesley's door. "Fine?" Sir Reginald's voice came through the door. "Fine, aren't you done talking to the Spaniard yet?" There was a hiccup. "I want to ask you some poker questions, open up."

"I can't stay," Sebastian said, under his breath. "Maybe we got away with it last night, but there are too many others tonight, including your own cousin. I need to go back to my room."

"And what about me?" Wesley said, just as quietly, as he wrapped a hand around one of the canopy bed's posts. "I'm supposed to leave you to your demons and what the night might bring?"

"It's not cowardice," Sebastian repeated ruefully. "It's strategy." He sighed. "We can't sleep together here, Wes. We don't have a choice."

The knocking came again. "Fine." Sir Reginald sounded quite tipsy still. "I'm tired of losing at gambling, man. I want to talk to you."

Wesley gritted his teeth. "One moment," he said to Sebastian.

He crossed toward his trunk, kneeling to open the lid. He rummaged in the trunk for a second, and then was straightening with something green and folded in his arms. "Here." Wesley held it out. "Indulge me and at least take this."

Sebastian recognized it immediately: the full-length velvet robe monogrammed with Wesley's initials, the one Sebastian had swiped for himself a couple of times. He took it with unsteady hands, looking up at Wesley as he held the robe tightly to himself. "Why give me this?"

"Obviously this is not to be considered a concession that it fits you." Wesley had a tiny wry smile. "But it will keep you warm if you sleep in it. And maybe if you wake in the night, you'll feel it around you and it will help you remember where you are."

Sebastian swallowed. *This is why I'm in love with you*, he wanted to say. "This is really kind, Wes," he said instead, and he was only a little hoarse.

"Please. I just whipped a man at poker and took his prized vehicle because he had the nerve to think he could set my lover up with his niece," Wesley said. "Kind I am not—"

Sebastian threw his free arm around Wesley's neck,

clutching the robe while bringing their lips together, and catching Wesley's soft, surprised noise with a kiss.

"This is really kind," Sebastian said again, against his mouth.

"Okay," Wesley said helplessly.

There was another, more insistent knock. "Fine?" Sir Reginald called. "What are you doing in there?"

Wesley licked his lips. "Off you get," he whispered. "Or I'm not going to be able to let you go."

Sebastian wanted to kiss him again, but he didn't trust himself to stop either. Instead he nodded, hiding the robe in his overcoat as he stepped out the door and past Sir Reginald, heading into his own room.

After Sebastian left, Wesley got rid of Sir Reginald with a brusque *My best gambling tip for you is to fucking give it up.* Then he dressed in his pajamas and lay down on the bed, staring up at the canopy.

I'm sure you'd rather not join a fox hunt anyway.

It's almost worse to stay behind. Knowing what's going to happen to the poor thing and being too cowardly to face it.

Wesley could perfectly recall the slump to Sebastian's shoulders, the dejected expression, that had gone with those words. Sebastian was one of the bravest, toughest men Wesley had ever met, had survived three years of torturous blood magic that would make every hunter in that manor cry with fright. And instead of boasting, he was distraught over the fate of some pest of a fox.

And it was Wesley's fault Sebastian was here, entirely Wesley's fault Sebastian was sad.

It's not your fault.

Sebastian's voice replayed in Wesley's head, the conversation they'd had two days ago at the inn.

Of course it is. You were at a hunt ball with my entire hunting club—

But you didn't mean for this to happen. Even if you hunt yourself, you would never have purposefully dragged me to one. You are kinder than that.

Except it *was* his fault. It was Sebastian who was too kind, who was *always* too kind with those rose-colored glasses when it came to Wesley—

More of Sebastian's words came back to him, this time from across an ocean and a cold night in Manhattan.

It must be the rose-colored glasses. After all, how would I know anything about bad men?

Wesley frowned. Christ, hadn't he just been recalling what Sebastian had survived, his bravery and toughness? Was Wesley still as bad as all the other men in this manor, mistaking a soft heart for a weak one?

It can't go both ways, Sebastian had said that night in Manhattan. *You say I know evil better than Langford. But I'm saying that he's wrong about you, and you won't listen to me.*

Wesley stared unseeing at the canopy, thoughts tumbling together. He knew damn well Sebastian wasn't sheltered or naïve, wasn't deluding himself that all flowers were free of thorns. No, Sebastian didn't wear rose-colored glasses; he knew the difference between barbed wire and a rose.

And somehow, he believed Wesley was the latter.

I have come to think that kind hearts shouldn't have

to learn to be cruel. Not that I expect anyone else on this earth would believe me capable of such a mindset.

Because you don't have enough people who know you.

Wesley swallowed. For years he'd known most people thought of him as the worst person they'd ever met. And Wesley had believed they were right.

But Sebastian knew him better than anyone else, and he believed Wesley was *kind*. Here Sebastian was, dragged to a fox hunt, yet he didn't blame Wesley; he knew Wesley would never have done it on purpose, understood that nothing short of the fate of the magical world could have gotten them here.

How could Wesley have ever explained how precious Sebastian's faith was? What it meant to have found a person who looked into his heart and saw good, who made Wesley see the good in himself, when no one else, not even Wesley, had believed in it?

Fuck passively wishing that a capricious life might somehow deign to give him his fairy tale future with Sebastian. Wesley was going to *make* it happen if he had to fight another war to keep him.

And he would start tonight, by trying to make Sebastian happy.

He doused the light and let himself fall into a light sleep, distantly aware of the occasional noise in the hall, other guests talking in low tones or making midnight trips to the bathroom.

Finally, at three a.m., he let himself come fully awake. He dressed in the dark, in warm wools for outdoors with his heavy overcoat in his arms and, most importantly, his gloves.

As quietly as he could, he eased his door open and snuck down the hall.

First stop was the kitchens. Some poor young woman was awake, setting loaves of dough to rise at one end of the room, but it was easy enough to ask her to grab him a brandy to help him sleep. When she'd disappeared, Wesley ducked into the larder and helped himself to several choice cuts of meat.

From the kitchens, he found a servants' door to the outside. The moor was silent as he walked on light feet from the house down to the kennels he and Sebastian had visited.

He could hear the warning growls of the hounds as he approached. Their kennel was chained closed for the night, but their barks would be loud. Before they could sound an alarm and wake the master, he began tossing the steaks over the fence and into their yard, and the growls quickly turned to slobbery chomping instead.

The hounds master had a small shed just past the kennels. Wesley slipped inside. Lighting a match, he studied the shelves until he found the label for what he was looking for.

Scent rags.

He pulled out the basket and nearly gagged. Christ, it smelled like the rags were soaked in—well, exactly what they were soaked in.

Fox piss.

Perfect for training the foxhounds to scent and trail a fox—and, with any luck, also perfect for confusing said hounds when they couldn't find the real fox in a mess of scent.

Wesley gingerly picked up a rag in one gloved hand and held it up in disgust.

Ugh. He'd have to use them all for the best chance. Really rub them in too, on the stumps and empty trunks and rocks that'd he passed on his walk with Sebastian today.

Fox piss. Christ.

The things he did for Sebastian.

Chapter Twenty

Wearing Wesley's robe did help. Sebastian made it through the night, not waking until the gray sunlight of winter dawn filled his room, the green robe still pulled tight and cozy around him. He touched the monogram on the chest. Wesley was never getting this back. Sebastian would have a new one made for him, but this one was his now, and Wesley could just tell himself that *no good deed goes unpunished*.

In the pale light, Sebastian could see his tattoo, the black ink partially covered by the robe's thick cuff.

Does it bother you, that he lost his color? Wesley had asked.

No. I like him like this, Sebastian had said.

Staring at the lion now, against the green of the robe Wesley had given him, Sebastian realized that wasn't quite the truth.

He *loved* the lion like this.

What a gift he was, a scar from the battle that had saved someone as courageous and kind as Wesley. Sebastian was going to ask Isabel for another tattoo, in just the black ink, to match.

He dressed and headed down the stairs. A footman was standing at the bottom of the staircase, and deferentially led Sebastian to the morning room. He could hear Wesley's voice as they approached.

"...simply makes sense to have him stay here," Wesley was saying, "if you think Lady Nora wouldn't mind."

"I think she'd be delighted," Lord Valemount's voice boomed back. "And you think he'll agree?"

"I feel certain of it," Wesley said, head turning as Sebastian entered. "But here's Don Sebastian himself, and we can ask." He tilted his head. "The other women were planning an outing to the village today, but it would seem Lady Nora isn't feeling well. I suggested to the duke that perhaps you would be willing to skip the morning's hunt and remain at the manor in case she needs anything."

"Oh." Sebastian tried to school his face into an expression of surprise, like he wasn't expecting an excuse for him to stay behind. "Should we call for her doctor?" he said pointedly. "We met Dr. Wright aboard the *Gaston* with Lady Nora."

"Oh, no need for Dr. Wright, I shouldn't think," Valemount said, a little too quickly. "He's probably making rounds in the village. If you'll stay behind, Don Sebastian, I'm sure Nora would appreciate it."

Wesley and Sebastian exchanged a meaningful look. "Yes, of course," Sebastian said. "I probably made it obvious last night that I am not much of the hunter myself."

"To say the least," Sir Reginald said, exchanging a smirk with another hunter.

After breakfast, the entrance hall was a flurry of men in scarlet coats and women dressed for town arranging their days. In the chaos of the crowd, Sebastian snuck away to the ground-floor study near the ballroom, and sure enough, there was a candlestick phone on the desk. He kept an eye on the doorway and an ear attuned for footsteps as he asked the operator to put him through to Arthur and Rory's inn.

"I am staying behind from the hunt," Sebastian said quietly, when Arthur got on the line. "They are all leaving now."

"We'll head your way then," Arthur said. "The drive to Valemount Hall is about three miles across the estate from the road, you said? We'll find a place to stash the car and walk the last bit."

"You can avoid the hunt?" Sebastian said.

"Our resident animal lover might not know this," Arthur said, in a nice tone, "but fox hunts are *loud*. The dogs bay, the men shoot at birds, some asshole usually plays a trumpet—it's an entire circus. We should be able to keep our distance and find another path through the moor, but if we are caught, we'll just pretend we were exploring the park and accidentally crossed onto the property. Wesley is smart enough to play along. Where should we meet you?"

"There is a guest house on the hill near the manor." Sebastian explained what had happened the night before. "I have the glove for Rory to scry, but maybe we should go back to the guest house too and search some more. Or I can do that before you get here—"

"Christ, no, wait for us," Arthur said sharply. "If you go anywhere by yourself and anything happens to you, Wesley will want Rory and I drawn and quartered, and I'm not sure if being a viscount actually gives him the authority to do that in England but let's not find out. Is there anywhere less visible than a guest house on top of a hill?"

Sebastian pursed his lips. "The stables and kennels should be empty while the hunt is out, yes? Maybe just a horse or two left behind."

"Perfect," Arthur said. "We should be able to find the stables easily enough. Meet us there."

After hanging up the phone, Sebastian found the housekeeper and asked after Nora.

"She says she's quite ill, I'm afraid," the housekeeper said. "Refuses to leave her rooms or have anyone come in."

"I'm so sorry to hear that," Sebastian said, and meant it. "Are you sure you don't want me to call her doctor?"

"You're sweet to offer," the housekeeper said, "but Lady Nora doesn't want to see Dr. Hughes either."

"I thought her doctor's name was Dr. Wright," Sebastian said.

"Wright?" The housekeeper frowned. "Dr. Hughes has always been the family doctor. I've never met a Dr. Wright."

"I see," Sebastian said slowly. "I must have misheard."

He went back into the entrance hall, which was very quiet now with only a pair of maids polishing the silver. He slipped past them, then ducked down a different hall by the dining room for a quick detour through the kitchen, where a young woman was slicing loaves of bread.

"Excuse me," Sebastian said politely. "But I was hoping you might have some extra carrots or oats?"

She smiled, dusting flour off her hands. "Visiting

the horses, eh? As long as you're not looking for meat, I think I can find you something."

"What happened to the meat?" Sebastian asked, as she walked through an archway.

Her voice drifted out of the larder. "Your guess is as good as mine. Seems to have disappeared." She emerged a moment later with three carrots and a turnip. "If I may be so bold, the next time your friend Lord Fine can't sleep, warm milk is more help than brandy."

"Oh. I, um, I'll let him know." Sebastian could not fathom Wesley ever agreeing to drink warm milk, but he also hadn't realized he'd been awake in the middle of the night. He'd have to ask Wesley about it.

From the kitchen, he found the garden door and stepped outside, heading west to the stables. As he neared the low, long building, the scent of hay and horse floated on the air. He cautiously approached, a story ready on his tongue about wanting to see the animals.

"Sebastian."

He heard his name first, then saw Rory and Arthur coming around the side of the building. The elderly dappled mare Sebastian had met before poked her head over a half door, watching them with interest.

Sebastian let out a breath and hurried down the building's side. "Stables appear empty, but who knows for how long," Arthur said, as the three of them met in front of the mare, who started sniffing interestedly at Sebastian's hair.

"I'll keep a lookout," Arthur went on, "while Rory scries and—why do you have a carrot?"

Sebastian held it in place as the mare ate it straight from his hand. "I got it from the kitchen before I came down."

"*Before* you came down?" Arthur repeated. "You were on your way to help Rory and I infiltrate a duke's estate and decided to stop for carrots first?"

Sebastian ran a hand over the back of the mare's neck, stroking her straw-colored mane. "She didn't get to go out with the others. Shouldn't she at least get a snack?"

Arthur raised an eyebrow. "Out of pure morbid curiosity, what does Wesley have to say about your priorities?"

"Yeah," said Rory. "Where's my snack?"

Arthur pinched the bridge of his nose. "That wasn't—never mind. You did also bring something for Rory to scry?"

Sebastian fed the mare the end of the carrot, as he pulled the glove from his overcoat pocket. "This," he said, holding it out to Rory. "I took it from a bedroom in the guest house last night."

Rory took the glove, frowning. "No fingertips," he said, exchanging a meaningful look with Arthur.

"Tell me again about your encounter with Wesley's cousin," Arthur said, as Rory held the glove and closed his eyes. "Don't you think it's odd that he followed you?"

"Yes," Sebastian said. "But he came right out and told me that is what he'd done. He was not acting like a man who thought he had something to hide."

"I suppose *shame* isn't a concept Wesley puts much stock in either." Arthur gently touched Rory's shoulder. "Don't you go too deep into history there."

"Don't worry; I can't." Rory opened his eyes with a frustrated huff. "I can't see the past of this thing either.

What the hell is going on with these Valemounts and doctors that I can't see history?"

"I don't know, but it has to be something magical," Sebastian said. "And we think there's a chance Lord Valemount *is* Dr. Wright."

He explained Valemount's absence the day before, Wesley's train of thought, and the housekeeper's confusion. Rory let out a low whistle. "But why would the duke have bothered with a disguise onboard the ship?"

"If Valemount was masterminding the destruction of magic by combining two relics, we did foil his plot," Arthur pointed out. "Perhaps Valemount came to find out what happened to Langford, Alasdair, and Sir Ellery, but he didn't want anyone to know he'd been in New York."

"Especially if he murdered Alasdair while he was there," Sebastian said grimly. "But surely Lady Nora would have known on the ship that her doctor was really her uncle? I don't think she knows about magic, and even if she did, I don't want to believe she would be involved in murder."

"Maybe she's keeping his secret for other reasons." Rory pursed his lips. "You said Valemount was gone all day yesterday. What if he was moving Hyde again?"

"Or Hyde's *body*." Sebastian and Rory both turned to look at Arthur, who seemed deep in thought. "You said the key to unlocking this medallion relic with hunting magic is the death of a paranormal with three kinds of magic," Arthur said. "And Hyde fits that bill."

"Shit," Sebastian muttered. The mare nosed at him again, and he offered up the last carrot, mind racing.

"This estate's huge," Rory said. "No end to places you could bury a body."

"But there's a graveyard to the east, by the mausoleum and the ruins of the chapel." Sebastian blew out a long breath. "Maybe we should go look for new graves."

"Where is this damn fox?" Valemount said, as they marched down yet another sloping hillside dotted with scattered rocks.

"The dogs keep running off," Sir Reginald observed with a frown. "But then—nothing."

Wesley kept his mouth shut.

They'd been out wandering the moor for nearly two hours. He'd watched the landscape like a hawk, but he hadn't seen so much as a flash of orange indicating an actual fox, and so far his false trails had held the hounds' attention.

"There are birds, at least." Geoffrey pointed at a grouping of taller hills ahead, covered in clusters of hardy bushes and short trees. Another ancient, crumbling stone wall jutted out halfway up one of the hills. "I bet we could find some pheasants hiding among the rocks."

"Worth a look," Wesley said. And if he could get some separation from the others, he could check that no idiot foxes were hiding up ahead and about to meet an untimely demise at the hands of Valemount's hounds.

The dogs scattered as they reached the bottom of the new hills, their noses to the ground. As Valemount and the others turned right and started hiking up, Wesley quietly went left, around the hill's base. He had his revolver in hand, but his gaze was on the ground.

"Hello, foxes," he called under his breath, as he watched for telltale burrows. "There better not be any of you about. Please tell me your tiny, furry brains understand the basic concept of *runaway* and you're not foolishly hanging around these hills, waiting to be found by a bunch of dogs and armed men."

Still alone, he turned and began to hike up the backside of the hill. About halfway up was a decent-sized tree, its leafless branches stretching above Wesley's head and a large hole in its trunk.

"Any foxes hiding in here?" Wesley subtly kicked at the trunk, the noise reverberating. "Yes? No?"

He waited long moments, but nothing came scurrying out.

Wesley raised an eyebrow, eyeing the tree. "Well, wouldn't this be a damn first?" he mused. "Something actually going right—"

Two sharp cracks split the air, almost in tandem, exactly as Wesley's knees gave out. He pitched forward, his legs and arms completely useless, only barely managing to hit the ground on his side and avoid smashing his face. He crashed into the mud, skidding downhill, unable to stop.

There was no fucking mistaking it this time: he'd just been hit by a wave of the familiar watery and useless limbs of Sebastian's magic.

A moment later, his limbs were in his control again. Wesley shoved up to his hands and knees in a puddle of mud and looked up the hill, toward the tree where he'd been standing only seconds ago.

A branch that had been at the same height as Wesley's head was now missing half the limb.

Gunshots filled the air then, accompanied by a ruckus of noise—men's shouts, dogs' barks, birds' squawks.

Wesley took a deep breath, reaching for his army

training and pushing any panic down into the box where it couldn't interfere with his rational thoughts.

Another man might have thought he'd only heard a single crack, and that had been the snapping branch.

But Wesley had heard two cracks.

And he knew a goddamn gunshot when he heard one.

"Fine!" Valemount was coming around the rocks, accompanied by Thornton, Ryland, Sir Reginald and Geoffrey. "Fine," Valemount said again. "What happened, man?"

All of them were armed, as were the other men still scattered within the rocks. Any of them could have fired at a pheasant just now, the bullet simply going wide toward Wesley's tree.

Conceivably an accident.

Or conveniently *looking* like an accident.

"I tripped," Wesley lied. "Like a damned fool."

"Rotten luck." Ryland was gingerly picking his way down the side of the rock. "Mud's slippery here. Can you stand?"

Valemount was also coming Wesley's way, his footing more sure than Ryland's. Two of the hounds were prancing around Valemount, tails wagging. "These hills are tricky as anything. Ground's uneven and can give without warning."

"Wesley." Geoffrey moved ahead of Valemount. "Are you hurt?"

Wesley got to his feet. His heart was pounding, and his chest was tingling oddly, but he kept his tone bland. "Nothing to be concerned about, unless you're planning to launder my clothes," he said, brushing uselessly at the mud now painted on his hunting coat.

Valemount stepped up to the tree, studying the broken branch. "Typical of winter. The trees ice and the heavy branches break too easily. And then there's the mud, which gets soft as quicksand; a man's got to step careful."

It had been raining, a few degrees too warm to ice. And Wesley *had* been stepping carefully. It had been unquestioningly Sebastian's magic that had taken him down to the ground.

"I say," Ryland suddenly said. "Is something glowing on your gun?"

"What?" Valemount said sharply. He glanced down. "Don't be ridiculous, man," he said, immediately tucking his gun into the holster. "I've got an heirloom mounted in the grip; you saw the light reflecting off it."

Wesley's gaze went back to the tree. Geoffrey was kneeling next to the now-broken branch on the ground, the one Wesley had been standing by when the gunshot went off. The branch that had snapped exactly at Wesley's height—the way it might have done if Sebastian's magic had taken him down at exactly the right moment and the bullet meant for Wesley's head had hit the tree instead.

Wesley shoved down his feelings, keeping his expression carefully blank. "Did anyone manage to shoot anything?"

"We got a few birds," Lord Ryland said. "Geoffrey, mostly. He's a very good shot."

Geoffrey was still kneeling on the ground next to the tree, one hand now balled into a fist. Geoffrey had followed Sebastian the night before with a frankly flimsy excuse. He was next in line for the Viscount Fine title, but surely—*surely*—he didn't want it that badly?

Wesley's eyes met his cousin's. Geoffrey's expression was perfectly blank. "Runs in the family," he said, never taking his eyes off Wesley.

Chapter Twenty-One

Sebastian led Arthur and Rory past the guest house on its hill and through the gardens, keeping behind the tallest rows of hedges. They'd just come to the garden's edge in a thick copse of trees when Rory went very still.

"I can feel it," he whispered.

Arthur touched his arm in concern. "Feel what?"

Rory shivered and rubbed at the arm without Arthur's hand, like he'd caught a sudden chill. "Magic."

Arthur looked questioningly at Sebastian, who shook his head. He couldn't feel a thing. "Where is it coming from?" Sebastian asked Rory.

Rory gestured in front of them. Sebastian could just make out the rounded top of the mausoleum in the distance and the crumbling stone walls of the chapel ruins. "Something up there."

"Could it be the source of whatever is blocking your psychometry?" Arthur said.

"Don't know," Rory said honestly. "This feels like— like when you walk up to the Dragon House, and it's got all that guardian magic in place that makes your skin buzz." He shook his head. "I don't think my psychometry is gonna work on these grounds. I don't even know if I can call in the wind here."

"But the Valemount line is descended from *two* paranormals," Sebastian said. "Why do we keep running into blocks against magic?"

"Well, you do have an ancestor from that same line that hunted magic for the Spanish Inquisition," Arthur pointed out. "At any rate, if there's a new grave, we'll still be able to see it with our eyes. I say we—"

In the distance, there was an unmistakable howl.

Rory swore. "That's the hunt back, isn't it?"

"You two have to go now," Sebastian said. "Go back to your inn. Wesley and I will find a way to come back out here and search, then we'll call you."

Arthur and Rory exchanged some kind of look that seemed to hold a lot of meaning, although what they were communicating to each other, Sebastian had no idea.

But then Arthur said, "Then you meet up with Wesley. And the two of you stick together, all right?"

Sebastian nodded, and then Arthur and Rory were disappearing ahead, into the trees.

Sebastian took a breath and stepped out, ready to pretend he'd been strolling the gardens.

As soon as they were through the front doors of Valemount Hall, Wesley cleared his throat. "You'll excuse me while I find something not covered in mud, yes?"

"What's that?" Valemount made a distracted motion with his hand. His gaze was on his gun, where it was holstered on his hip. "Of course, of course."

"Don't tell me you're injured from a little spill," Sir Reginald said dryly.

"Not at all." A slight lie, as Wesley had certainly

scraped and bruised a few limbs on his fall. But he was alive, which very clearly hadn't been someone's intent.

He strode up the stairs, but had only just stepped into his own room when there was a knock on the door. He muttered a curse. "Whoever you are, I don't want visitors—"

But he opened the door to reveal Sebastian, his lip caught between his teeth, his warm brown eyes big and worried. "Wes," he said. "They said you fell—are you okay?"

The contrast between the others' mocking and Sebastian's genuine concern was so obvious that Wesley was once again struck by how much his life had changed since meeting Sebastian. Someone gave a damn about his well-being.

Wesley shook the emotions away. He grabbed Sebastian by the wrist and pulled him inside, before anyone overheard them.

"You're covered in mud," Sebastian said, as Wesley shut the door behind them and locked it for good measure.

"That tends to be what happens when one tumbles down a wet moor hill," Wesley said.

"So you tripped?" Sebastian asked.

Wesley hesitated. But no, he knew what he'd felt on the moor. There was no question. Sebastian might not want to hear it, but Wesley was going to be honest. "Your magic knocked me down."

"My magic?" Sebastian blinked. "*Pero mira*, Wes—"

"No, do not *pero mira* me," Wesley said, holding up a finger. "I know your magic. I know the feel of it in my aura and my limbs, know your magic's touch the way I know the touch of your hands. I would recognize your lips in the dark and I am telling you, Sebastian, it was your magic I felt on the moor." He leaned forward. "And I suspect it saved my life."

Sebastian's eyes widened.

"Someone took a shot in my direction," Wesley said. "Your magic sent me to the ground just in time and the bullet hit the tree where I'd been standing."

"Wait." Sebastian stepped forward, hands catching Wesley's upper arms. "Someone *shot* at you?"

"Yes, and if I had any doubts about what I'd felt, that would clear them right up," Wesley said. "Your magic feels like you, it comes from you, and it has always saved me when I needed it."

"But who *shot at you*?" Sebastian said.

"I don't know," Wesley said. "I have suspicions, of course, but when you get right down to it, it could have been any of the men. We were all carrying firearms. And there was no one with me to rule out, because I had taken another path to—ah." He hastily cut himself off. "Because I had taken another path."

Sebastian raised his eyebrow. "What were you about to say?"

"Nothing."

"Not *nothing*."

"It was," Wesley insisted. "Nothing important."

"It has to be important." Sebastian was moving closer. "Because you're *blushing*."

"Um."

Sebastian was close enough Wesley could have pulled him into his arms. "Why were you alone on a different path?"

"Um." Wesley wet his lips. "I just. Checking. Something."

"Checking what?"

"A, um. A trail. A thing. A thing on the trail."

"Something on the trail?" Sebastian pursed his lips. "But what about the dogs? And the others? I thought all of you were following a fox."

"Right. Yes, well, that is typically how a fox hunt would go." Wesley wet his lips again. "It's possible that I might, perhaps, have engaged in just the smallest touch of sabotage."

"Sabotage?" Sebastian was somehow even closer, looking up into Wesley's eyes. "Wes. Are you trying to say that you sabotaged…the fox hunt?"

Christ, Wesley could feel his cheeks growing hotter; this was completely unacceptable. "Look, I know that you think the stupid little pests are cute and charming and you hate the whole idea of fox hunts, and you were so sad about the whole thing and obviously I won't stand for anything making you sad—"

"You sabotaged the fox hunt." Sebastian was breaking into a smile, his eyes bright, his expression wondrous. "For me?"

"Well, I didn't do it for Geoffrey." Ugh, how did people bear their face feeling this hot? "Yes, I snuck out this morning and set false trails for the dogs on the moor, and yes, of course it was for you, and if you haven't figured out by now that I'd do bloody anything in the world to make you happy then—"

Sebastian's lips landed on his, his arms going around Wesley's neck to pull him in and Wesley was suddenly being kissed within an inch of his life. "Wesley," Sebastian said again, "I love you so much—"

"You *what*," Wesley said helplessly, but Sebastian

toppled him down to the bed and his words were lost to the kiss that hadn't stopped.

This was not some incomprehensible half-asleep words muttered into a pillow. This was crisp and clear and unmistakable.

Sebastian loved him.

Sebastian loved him.

Wesley's mind simply couldn't process the onslaught of thoughts and feelings that threatened to swamp him. Love was a fiction that was always going to be out of Wesley's reach—

I love you so much.

Wesley's body abruptly took over, because maybe his mind couldn't comprehend the words but every muscle and inch of his skin knew how it felt about being loved. And all at once Wesley didn't care that he was covered in mud, or that he was getting the bed and Sebastian covered in the same mud, or that there might still be danger or that they had an entire mystery on their hands. He was kissing Sebastian in return, rolling him over onto his back and pressing him down into the mattress.

"Thank you," Sebastian said against his mouth. "Wes, I can't believe—wait, wait wait wait, someone *shot at you*." He pulled his lips away. "Someone tried to *kill* you?"

"Possibly," Wesley said impatiently. "But we can talk about that later—"

"No we can't." Sebastian was squirming out from under him and sitting up. "Tell me everything that happened."

Wesley sighed but relayed the events of the hunt.

Sebastian's eyes had gone wide again. "And you really think it was my magic that knocked you over?"

"I know it was," Wesley said, getting to his feet.

"But Wes, I don't have any magic anymore. I couldn't feel anything now, with Rory and Arthur."

Wesley paced as he listened to Sebastian describe Rory's inability to scry the glove, Arthur's suggestion that Hyde could be dead, and the sensation of magic as they'd gotten closer to the graveyard. When he'd finished, Wesley frowned. "Where are Arthur and Brodigan now?"

"I told them to go back to their inn," Sebastian said.

"Oh, is that what they said they were going to do?" Wesley steepled his fingers. "Tell me: do you actually believe Arthur listened and acted in self-preservation, like a sensible man?" He gestured to the room's large window, which overlooked the gardens. "Or do you think it more likely he and Brodigan are still lurking out there somewhere on this estate, prepared to do something brave but completely foolhardy? Which one sounds like the Arthur you've met—"

There was a polite knock on the door. "Lord Fine? Don Sebastian?"

Wesley and Sebastian exchanged a look. "Lady Nora," Sebastian said.

Wesley pursed his lips but went to the door. He opened it to reveal Nora, standing alone and wringing her hands. "My apologies," she said. "But I was hoping to have a quick word with Don Sebastian. I'll give him right back," she said to Wesley.

She certainly didn't *look* ill. "Of course," Wesley said, even if his jaw was slightly clenched. He didn't exactly want to let Sebastian out of his sight.

"Thank you," Nora said graciously, stepping back from the door to wait.

"Pero mira, Wes," Sebastian said pointedly, under his breath, "perhaps you should not be alone after someone tried to shoot you—"

"What kind of fool do you take me for?" Wesley said, just as quietly. "She asked for you, not us, and she might not be willing to talk if I'm there. Ask her what she knows about Dr. Wright."

"But—"

"No one could fire a gun in the middle of the upstairs hall without alerting half the manor," Wesley said. "Go on. I'll stay in here with my bloody door locked until you return."

Sebastian frowned, but finally went out the door, his frown changing into one of his unfairly charming smiles as he offered Lady Nora his arm.

As they disappeared down the hall, Wesley firmly shut the door. This was fine; everything was fine. Nora wasn't going to proposition Sebastian, or even if she was, it didn't matter, because Sebastian loved *him*.

Christ. Sebastian *loved* him—

There was another knock on Wesley's door, much louder and more demanding than Nora's had been.

"Lord Fine? It's Dr. Wright. Lord Valemount has asked me to come see to you after your fall."

Wesley scoffed out loud. Oh please. How gullible did Valemount think he was? "Thank you, Dr. Wright," Wesley said, with a hint of mockery, "but your services are not required at this time."

Then Lord Valemount's voice came from behind the door. "Dammit, man, don't be a stubborn fool. I can't have my guests breaking limbs and whatnot. Open the damn door."

Was Valemount actually standing at Wesley's door,

doing two different voices? That truly was beyond the pale and Wesley was going to catch him in the act.

Wesley turned around and cracked open the door.

He paused.

There were unmistakably two men standing there: Lord Valemount, and Dr. Wright, from the ship.

Wesley's gaze darted from Valemount, to Dr. Wright, and then back to Valemount. "Oh," he finally said.

Dr. Wright gave him a very tight smile. "Now we get to see how *you* like someone barging in."

"What?" Wesley said inelegantly.

But Dr. Wright had already shoved his way in, with more strength than Wesley had expected. A moment later, an uncapped bottle was right under Wesley's nose, a pungent ether-like odor in his nostrils.

"What the hell—" he started to say.

But his vision was going black around the edges.

And then the world was dark.

Chapter Twenty-Two

Sebastian followed Lady Nora down the hall and into a different hall, and finally into a small study along the back side of the manor. "Close the door, if you please," she said, as she stepped toward the study's tall, narrow windows.

He did, pulling it shut behind him. "Are you feeling better?"

"Please. I'm obviously not sick. I needed to do some investigating." Nora was staring out the glass, at the gardens and manor grounds. "I saw you."

Sebastian froze, still by the door. Seen him what? With *Wesley*? "Lady Nora—"

"With the two strangers, one tall and one short, heading through the gardens toward the mausoleum." She looked over her shoulder then, at him. "I haven't told anyone yet," she said, her serious gaze on him. "But I know those two are not among the guests. And I think you owe me an explanation of what you were doing and why they were here."

Sebastian bit his lip. "We were searching for someone," he finally admitted.

"I see," Nora said lightly. "And did you find this *someone*?"

Sebastian weighed his next words carefully. They still didn't know her motives, or her relationship with Dr. Wright, whoever the doctor truly was. But they needed an ally and Sebastian's gut continued to think he could trust her.

"No. But we think we know where we'll find him." Sebastian swallowed. "In a grave."

Nora's eyes widened. Her gaze flitted over his face, like she was weighing his expression. "You're serious?" She frowned. "Who?"

"A man from my past, a murderer and a torturer that I knew in very unpleasant circumstances," Sebastian said. "But we think he may have been murdered himself, and that his murder could mean something even worse to come."

"My word." Nora looked shocked. "But who—wait."

Her eyes narrowed. Then she abruptly strode forward, and Sebastian had to hurriedly sidestep out of her way as she went up to the door behind him and grabbed the handle.

She yanked it open, revealing Geoffrey, whose eyes went almost comically wide.

"Mr. Collins." Nora stepped back, her own eyes still narrowed. "Do you make a habit of listening at keyholes?"

Geoffrey raised his chin. "Apologies," he said brusquely. "But sometimes needs must."

"Really?" Nora said flatly. "And what necessitated spying on a private conversation?"

"The need for some bloody answers." Geoffrey glanced down the hall, then back at Nora and Sebastian. "May I come in?"

Nora huffed, but stepped back, letting Geoffrey

enter and shutting the door behind him. He still wore his hunting coat, and Sebastian could see his revolver clearly holstered on his hip.

"He's armed," Sebastian said quietly, to Nora.

"Armed *and* a damn good shot." Geoffrey pointed at him. "Are you working with Lord Valemount?"

"*Me?*" Sebastian said. "Why would I be working with Valemount?"

"I'm sure I don't know," Geoffrey said, "but he took a shot at Wesley this morning."

"He what?" Nora said in shock, as Sebastian stared at Geoffrey.

"Your uncle tried to murder my cousin this very morning, on our hunt." Geoffrey stuck out his fist, then opened his fingers to reveal a bullet casing, resting in the palm of his hand. "I found this in the exact spot Wesley had been standing," he said. "Valemount thought none of us were looking, but I saw him aim straight for Wesley's head. I thought Wesley was *dead*."

Nora had paled. "There must be some mistake."

"No mistake," Geoffrey said darkly. "I don't know how Wesley managed to fall at exactly the right moment, but Lord Valemount tried to kill him and I will swear to that in any court of law."

Nora covered her mouth. "What on earth is going on?" she said, as if to herself.

They didn't have time to guess. "Come on." Sebastian was already moving toward the door. "We have to go back to Wesley."

The world slowly began to creep back in for Wesley, his head pounding, as nauseated and woozy as if he'd drunk three bottles of whiskey. He could hear voices as if from a distance. Two men, it sounded like, their voices edged with the echo of hard walls and floors with no carpet to soften them.

"He's stirring," one voice said.

"Finally." The other voice was suddenly much closer. "It might interest you to know, Lord Fine, that one perk of pretending to be a doctor is one can fill one's bag with all kinds of interesting items and no one thinks anything of it."

Wesley managed to crack his eyes, and found his vision filled with Dr. Wright.

"Ethyl chloride," Dr. Wright said. "A useful anesthetic, of course, but also quite potent when inhaled."

Quite potent was an understatement. Wesley felt like he'd been flattened by a lorry, but he wasn't going to give either of them the satisfaction of showing it. "What do you want?" he said, through clenched teeth.

It was dim, wherever they were, and what light there was was mostly yellowish, like a lantern's. It was enough to see Dr. Wright as he looked over his shoulder. "Damn miracle you didn't kill him too soon."

"It was your bloody order for me to take the shot," Lord Valemount said, as he stepped into view at Dr. Wright's side.

"Well, obviously he can't have the H6," Dr. Wright said. "But never mind. He'll be dead soon enough."

Well, *that* didn't bode well. And why the devil was a doctor giving orders to a duke?

He tried to shift, and found his arms were bound behind him, his ankles tied or chained together as well. He seemed to be on a flat surface, hard as stone and cold enough to seep through his clothes, and the air was unpleasantly stale with the dampness of earth. He tried to clear his throat. "You haven't said what you want."

Dr. Wright and Lord Valemount paused their bickering and looked down at him. A sliver of scant light came in from beyond their heads, illuminating a ceiling in ill repair, crumbling and buttressed with thick wood planks. The wall beyond was riddled with recessed cubbies, each holding a coffin. Was he underground, then? In a family crypt, perhaps, chained on top of some decaying Valemount's sarcophagus?

Lord Valemount raised his arm, and Wesley was suddenly staring at the barrel of a revolver. But then Valemount turned the gun so that Wesley could see the grip. Set into the wood was a circular medallion, and it was glowing as if lit with lamplight.

"We have several questions for you, Fine," Valemount said darkly. "But the first one is—how do you have de Leon magic?"

Wesley tore his gaze off the medallion and up to Valemount's face.

"That shock looks real enough," Dr. Wright said, gaze on Wesley's face. "I think he actually didn't know."

Sebastian's magic. It was with *him*. Fuck, of course it was—had it been with him all this time?

"De Leon must know about the relics," Valemount said to Dr. Wright. "Then the coward hid his magic in this hapless idiot." He gestured to the glowing medallion set in the grip again. "That's why the medallion didn't light up when I had it near de Leon before dinner last night, but here's the magic now, in Fine, plain as day."

Wesley opened his mouth, a thousand possible lies on his tongue—

"Don't waste our time pretending not to know what that means." Valemount tapped the medallion. "The original Duke of Valemount was a consummate hunter who even had his own tracking magic. That magic is in this relic, and I control it now. It's like a hound—if I give it a scent, the magic can track it."

Wesley's head was clearing, the anesthetic wearing off and adrenaline taking its place. But even with a clearer head, none of this was making sense. "How would you have de Leon magic to track?"

"Because of me." Dr. Wright took off his glasses, tossing them carelessly to the side. "And my distant uncle's curse that runs in my veins."

Sebastian led the way to Wesley's room, but found it empty as well. He frowned at the vacant space.

"Where did he go?" Geoffrey was also frowning.

"Somewhere else in the house, perhaps?" Nora offered.

Sebastian and Geoffrey both shook their heads. "Lord Fine is very smart, and he does not act rashly, ever," Sebastian said. "He knew someone had tried to kill him. He said he would wait here."

"Except he's not here now," Geoffrey pointed out.

Sebastian ran a hand through his hair. "There are people everywhere," he said. "Staff and guests on every floor. *Someone* must have seen where he went."

"Let's just hope he's not with Valemount," Geoffrey said grimly.

Nora winced. "I can't believe Uncle Louis would shoot at Lord Fine. I don't understand why."

Sebastian took her hand. "Lady Nora," he said beseechingly, "I apologize, but I must ask you an awkward question. Dr. Wright, that we met on the ship—he is not really your doctor, is he?"

Nora winced. "No," she said quietly. "He's not."

"And is he actually your uncle?" Sebastian asked carefully.

"You're asking if Dr. Wright is Uncle Louis?" Nora huffed a kind of laugh with a rough edge. "No. He's not my *uncle*." She winced again. "I swore to keep their secret. I was so happy at the news, I would have agreed to anything—I trusted they had a good reason for the lie, but I don't want anyone to get hurt—"

"Tell me this then," Sebastian said, worry for Wesley turning his stomach into knots. "If someone were to have taken Lord Fine from the house, how could they have gotten out unseen?"

Nora pointed down the hall. "The second-floor library has a priest hole hidden behind the northernmost bookshelf. There's a secret catch at the back of the second shelf that conceals the stairs. Obviously Valemounts aren't hiding Catholic priests from Tudor raids anymore, but we still have the network of tunnels under the manor. They split off and come up at various places throughout the estate, but the main shaft leads to the family crypt under the chapel ruins. But surely—"

"I'm going there." Sebastian squeezed her hand. "The two men you saw me with might still be on this estate—might have gone to the graveyard by the chapel. They are my friends and if you trust me, you can trust them. Go to them and tell them what you told me, yes? And then meet me by the chapel."

"I'm coming with you—" Geoffrey started.

Sebastian shook his head. He couldn't let Wesley's cousin or Lady Nora be put at risk, not if magic was involved. "Stay with Lady Nora." Wesley's revolver was still sitting on the dresser where Wesley had set it not an hour ago. Sebastian snatched it up. "Keep each other safe, and find my friends, please," he said. "I'm going to find Wesley."

Chapter Twenty-Three

Wesley's heart had picked up speed. "What does that mean," he said to Dr. Wright, "*your distant uncle's curse that runs in your veins?*"

Dr. Wright had already removed his glasses. Now, he grabbed the edge of his beard and tugged. "This thing itches like mad."

A moment later, the beard was dangling from his hand, and Wesley was looking at a man he'd met a handful of times several years ago: the prior Duke of Valemount, who'd been lost in a hunting accident on safari.

"You're Lord Valemount." Wesley's eyes had gone wide. He looked between his two captors. "But then—but why—"

"But then why have I pretended to be dead these last two years while my younger brother stepped into the role of the duke?" Dr. Wright—no, Alfred Fairfield, the actual Duke of Valemount, scoffed. "Do you know how hard it is to act with any secrecy when you're a duke? I couldn't get a bloody thing done until I got Louis here to take up the mantle for a bit."

Wesley could see a resemblance between them now, the same thick chestnut brown hair and blue eyes, just like Lady Nora. But Louis, the younger brother, was taller, with broader shoulders and a sharper jawline.

"Why would you need secrecy?" Wesley said. "And what *curse*?"

The only family Wesley knew of that was cursed were the de Leons. But then, the Valemounts were descended from the sister—did the Valemount line somehow share Sebastian's family curse as well as the blood?

"The original Duke of Valemount married a Spanish countess with magic of her own," said Alfred. "But her brother was a tool of the Spanish Inquisition and came looking for them. This inquisitor used their shared blood to take control of her relic and curse the duke's bloodline so that none of their descendants could ever use magic."

He snorted, a deeply bitter sound. "We can't use it, and it won't work on us. Our entire line might as well have blood made of lead."

That was why Rory couldn't scry any of their possessions. Wesley looked between the real Duke of Valemount, Alfred, and the brother, Louis, again, because something wasn't adding up. "But you said you control a relic," he said to Louis. "How could you control something with magic if you're cursed to be unable to use magic?"

"Blood will out, as they say." Louis turned the revolver back and forth. "I don't share the curse."

Why would that be? If it was a blood curse, like Sebastian's, passed down through the paternal line just like the title—oh. "Because you don't share a *father*," Wesley said, in realization. "And of course your father could not be known as a cuckold, so your parents hid that you're a bastard."

"I would have gone my entire life not knowing the

truth either," Louis said, sounding as bitter as Alfred now, "if it wasn't for magic."

"Magic is a gift," Wesley said tightly.

"It's a curse," Louis said, just as tight. "I have farsight—but not like you, where it's useful. No, I have magical farsight that lets me see through the eyes of others when I touch their possession—and it works without my consent or control." He gave a frustrated huff. "I went years without knowing I had magic, because the Valemount curse means my magic won't work on their possessions. But then war came and, well. As I said: it's a curse. Everyone knows I was sent home from the front; they don't know I came home raving."

"It was *war*," Wesley said. "No one with a speck of empathy should judge you for wounds of the mind, not just the body, regardless of whether you have magic. And now you're here, with your half brother, who wants to destroy magic—"

"Good," Louis said viciously. "I want it gone. Magic has brought nothing but misery to me, while enriching so many others who never deserved it."

"Why should Louis have suffered? Why should *I* be cursed while a family like the de Leons thrive?" Alfred said. "It isn't fair."

"You're a fucking *duke*," Wesley snapped. "Are you really complaining something isn't fair?"

"Watch your bloody mouth," Alfred said, as Louis pressed the revolver against Wesley's chest. "You're only alive because your death is about to be useful."

Alfred held out his arm, his layers of sleeves riding up to show the golden cuff encircling his wrist. "This was Mariana de Leon's relic, all those generations ago," he said, running a finger over it reverently. "Her power to curse, trapped in here, growing and strengthening over the centuries. I brought it to that paranormal who heard magic, weeks ago, and thanks to him I know how to free it."

"Alasdair Findlay." Wesley gritted his teeth. "You convinced him to join your plot to destroy magic, only to murder him after? Did you sneak into his hospital room as Dr. Wright?"

"I couldn't let him share my secrets with all of you, could I?" Alfred ran a finger over the cuff reverently. "The inquisitor tried to hide the truth from his descendants—that it takes the death of de Leon magic to unlock the curse cuff. The same magic that's now buried in *you*."

Wesley drew a breath through his nose.

"And so you see, you have a part to play in all of this," Alfred said, as Louis's revolver dug into Wesley's chest, over his heart. "The curse magic in this cuff has been growing for centuries. And when I unlock it, I think its new strength will disintegrate the curse on my blood and free me. I think I'll be able to use magic, as is my birthright, and wield this cuff relic to cast curses. Then Louis will use his hunting relic to find paranormals, and I'll destroy them."

Louis cocked the revolver as Alfred drew a silver dagger. "I wonder if I can curse magic itself," Alfred said, almost dreamily. "I'm about to find out, aren't I? Because the magic in you isn't yours, but your death will kill it, all the same—"

Something surged through Wesley, a rush in his ears and chest like a tidal wave sweeping out with him at the center. Louis cried out and recoiled, dropping the revolver. A deafening echo split the air, leaving Wesley's ears ringing as Louis shrieked even louder, clapping a hand to his shoulder.

"You idiot." Alfred grabbed Louis by the collar. "You shot *yourself*? Was the damn safety already off?"

"Well, this feels ironic," Wesley muttered.

"The gun *burned* me," Louis snarled. Red was welling under his palm where he held it tight to his shoulder. "I couldn't hold it any more than I could hold a fire poker."

Alfred brandished the dagger at Wesley. "What did you do?" he said, pressing the blade to Wesley's throat as Louis struggled to retrieve the revolver, one hand still clutched to his bleeding shoulder.

"I don't know," Wesley said tightly, refusing to flinch as the dagger pricked his skin. "But I know Sebastian's magic. And it will never let you kill me."

Alfred's eyes narrowed, but Louis barked, "Alfred!"

Wesley glanced over to see Louis holding up the gun. The golden medallion set into the revolver's wooden grip had dimmed; it was no longer glowing.

Louis looked to Alfred in shock. "Where has the magic gone?"

Sebastian found the priest hole exactly as Nora described, and followed the hidden staircase down to the small room with its single light. From there, the underground tunnel trailed off into utter darkness. Sebastian didn't hesitate; he stumbled forward as fast as he dared, straight into the black. His left hand he kept against the dirt wall for guidance, and in his right hand, he clutched Wesley's revolver.

He passed several openings in the wall, the other tunnels that spread out under the estate grounds, he'd guess. But Nora had said the main shaft led to the crypt, and so he kept pushing forward, straight ahead.

After maybe a quarter of a mile, the faintest light began to glimmer up ahead. Sebastian slowed his steps but only slightly, moving as silently as he could through the tunnel. A few steps more, and he could just make out voices as well.

"—couldn't let him share my secrets—"

"—disintegrate the curse on my blood and free me—"

"—not your magic, but your death will kill it, all the same—"

No.

"*Wesley.*" The whisper was torn out of Sebastian, fear surging through him and driving him forward even faster. Whatever they planned, he had to stop it—

Noise exploded up ahead, a man's shrieks, a gunshot that shook the tunnel walls. Sebastian's hand scrabbled along the dirt wall, mud raking up under his nails as he dropped his own gun and hit his knees, his heart stopping.

They hadn't—

"I don't know. But I know Sebastian's magic. And it will never let you kill me."

Sebastian's breath left him in a rush at the relief of hearing Wesley's voice. He snatched the revolver back up and shoved up from the wet ground like a sprinter off the mark. Wesley was alive, but he wasn't alone, and someone had fired a gun. He could still hear a man's bellows, growing louder as he ran down the tunnel toward the light.

Alfred stared for a moment at the dimmed medallion. Then he grabbed the gun from Louis, whirling around to aim it at Wesley. "Call the magic back."

"Why don't you help your brother, *Dr. Wright*?" Wesley snapped, yanking futilely again at the cuffs on his arms. "He's losing quite a lot of blood."

Louis now clutched a handkerchief to his wound, but it was already soaked a deep red. He stumbled a couple of steps backward and sat heavily on the sarcophagus opposite Wesley's, his face a sallow and unhealthy green.

Alfred glanced over his shoulder at Louis. "Chin up, old boy," he said to Louis. "Just a nick, isn't it?"

"Are you fucking serious?" Wesley yanked at his cuffs again. "You brother is *shot*—"

"I didn't come this close to removing my curse and having revenge on paranormals just to be deterred by a bit of blood." Alfred jammed the gun under Wesley's chin. "Call the magic back."

"It's not one of your *dogs*," Wesley said through clenched teeth. "I don't know how to call it back even if I wished to."

Alfred pressed harder, forcing Wesley's chin up with the gun. "Don't lie to me."

"Who's lying?" Wesley met Alfred's eyes without flinching. "I can't control Sebastian's magic. And I don't have a drop of my own magic in me. You'll gain nothing from my death."

"Not *nothing*," Alfred said. "I can at least have the H6 back—"

"Let him go."

Sebastian's voice cut through the crypt, tight with controlled rage.

Wesley took a measured breath, carefully boxing his emotions to look at later, as his gaze went to the end of the crypt. And there was Sebastian, panting hard, sweaty hair sticking up wildly and mud on his flushed face as he stood beneath a crumbling arch.

"I don't think I will," Alfred said menacingly, his gun still digging into Wesley. "Hands up, Don Sebastian—or should I say, *Señor de Leon*?"

Sebastian grudgingly raised his hands as his eyes darted over Wesley like he was assessing for injuries. Then his gaze flicked to the other side of the room, where Louis had slid down on his sarcophagus, his eyes glassier. A furrow appeared between Sebastian's eyebrows. "Lord Valemount is hurt."

"Louis isn't actually Lord Valemount," Wesley said. "The prick with the gun aimed at my brain is Alfred Fairfield, and he's the real Duke of Valemount. Takes a bit of explaining, but I promise they're both arseholes."

The furrow hadn't left Sebastian's forehead. "Louis might be going into shock. He needs help."

"You hear that?" Wesley said to Alfred. "Sebastian was an army medic; I daresay he knows shock when he sees it."

"Lower your gun already," Sebastian snapped, concerned gaze still on Louis, "so I can treat your brother."

Alfred's eyes had gone very narrow. But he didn't remove the gun from under Wesley's chin. "If Señor de Leon here came for you, I feel that he might be the sort of chap to bargain, don't you? His life for yours?"

Sebastian's gaze darted back to Alfred. "You're endangering your own brother—"

"Yes," Alfred said, without concern, "but I daresay I'm endangering Lord Fine more."

Sebastian set his jaw. A moment later, Wesley recognized his own revolver, now in Sebastian's hand and aimed at Alfred. "You're not the only one who's armed," Sebastian said.

Alfred laughed. "Oh please," he said derisively. "You couldn't bear to hurt a damn fox. Your hands are shaking like a coward's now; you're not going to shoot me."

Wesley saw Sebastian's chest rise and fall with a hard breath. "Your gun—in the grip," Sebastian said, his gaze on Alfred's weapon. "I know what that medallion is. It belonged to the original Duke of Valemount—the relic he made for his tracking magic." He frowned. "Why is it glowing?"

Oh no.

Wesley could see Alfred come to the realization at the exact same moment. "Sebastian, get *down*," Wesley barked. "Your magic is here and he wants to destroy it—"

Alfred jammed the revolver up under Wesley's chin, and Wesley felt, more than heard, Alfred's finger pulling the trigger—

"No!"

Sebastian's shout echoed around the crypt. And then Wesley's limbs were suddenly hit with that wave of familiar magic, his entire body going heavy as lead.

Alfred swore like he'd touched fire, the revolver clattering to the stone floor and going off again in another ear-splitting blast. Wesley winced, body flinching involuntarily as Sebastian staggered into the arch with his hands over his ears.

Then Alfred was lunging for Sebastian. Sebastian put up his hands but Alfred was bigger, slamming him into the crypt wall so hard that Wesley's revolver flew out of Sebastian's hand.

"What did you do?" Alfred demanded.

Sebastian's shoulders were heaving, his cheeks flushed with color. "Magic," he said, a look of wonder in his very wide eyes.

Alfred's nostrils flared.

"*My* magic," Sebastian said, raising his chin, still breathing hard. "Enervation. It's trying to weaken the medallion relic. I don't know if we'll win, but my magic will stop you from shooting until you've run out of bullets."

"Fucking paranormals." Alfred shoved him again, knocking Sebastian's head against the stone wall and then jamming his forearm up against Sebastian's throat.

"Valemount." Wesley yanked at his cuff again and felt metal bite into his wrist. "If you don't get your fucking hands off him—"

Somewhere above their heads was the sudden pounding of feet and shouts in familiar voices.

"Don Sebastian!"

"Wesley!"

Alfred pressed his forearm harder into Sebastian's neck. "Who the hell is that?"

"I didn't come alone," Sebastian said hoarsely, through a clenched jaw.

Alfred bared his teeth.

"Lord Fine!"

"Sebastian!"

"You can kill me if you want," Sebastian said, his voice strained, maybe from the pressure on his throat, "but my friends will stop you before you hurt anyone else."

Alfred abruptly shoved Sebastian to the side, straight into another sarcophagus. He grabbed Sebastian's revolver from the floor and sprinted away, under the arch and into the darkness Sebastian had come from.

"Shit." These bloody chains. Wesley yanked uselessly at them again. "Sebastian. Are you all right?"

"I'm all right." Sebastian was stumbling across the stones, in a crawl on hands and knees. "Are you—"

"I'm copa-fucking-cetic," Wesley snapped. "Never mind me. Is Louis alive?"

Sebastian was already at Louis's side. He'd slid off the sarcophagus at some point during the fight, sprawled now on the crypt stones, his skin wet with sweat and his eyes glassy. "I have not forgiven you for shooting at Wesley," Sebastian said, low and tight, "but I'm not going to let you die. Can you lie on your back? If we can elevate your legs and put more pressure on this wound—"

"You have more mercy for me than my own damn brother." Louis's voice was a harsh croak. "I'll live. It's Alfred you need to stop."

One hand was still clutched against his bloody shoulder, but with the other he reached into the red hunting coat and pulled out a small key. "Here." He held it weakly toward Sebastian with a trembling hand. "For Fine," he said, as Sebastian took the key and scrambled up to his feet. "But you must go after Alfred. There's no time."

"Sebastian, wait," Wesley said sharply, as Sebastian bent over him and reached for the handcuffed wrists in the small of his back. "It could be a trap—"

"No trap," Louis said. "I have pretended to be the Duke of Valemount for two years, have done everything Alfred asked for in his revenge. Now he thinks he can throw me to the wolves to save himself, but he is mistaken."

He addressed Sebastian again. "Alfred is a coward; if he believes himself outnumbered, he'll head for his cars and flee. But he won't stop hunting for de Leon magic to kill for the cuff relic," he added. "Whether that's you or your family."

Wesley heard Sebastian swallow.

Voices came again from overhead.

"Sebastian? Wesley?"

"We're coming!"

"You want the third tunnel on your left: follow it straight to the garage," Louis said to Sebastian. "And take my gun. The medallion will stay lit for your magic and give you light."

There was a soft snick, and then Wesley's arms were finally free. "Thank Christ," he said, shaking his arms out. "Sebastian—"

"Here." Sebastian pressed the handcuff key into Wesley's hand. "It's just your ankles now. I assume a dangerous rogue like yourself can handle it from here."

"You did not just say that." Wesley tried to sit up, but his ankles jerked at the chains. "Sebastian, wait for me—"

"You heard him." Sebastian was scooping Louis's revolver off the stones. "If he gets away, he might go after my family. There's no time."

"Sebastian," Wesley said warningly, "you are exactly what Valemount needs to unlock that relic, don't you dare go alone—"

But Sebastian had already disappeared, his footsteps echoing into the distance.

The medallion gave off just enough light to see by as Sebastian sprinted down the tunnel, his heart pounding, every inch of him buzzing like he'd drunk twenty coffees, or like a stampede of horses storming his veins.

He didn't have time to be grateful or welcome the wild horses back; he had to hope he could somehow catch and stop Alfred.

He kept his eye on the left wall, passing first one, then two, and then finally turning down the third tunnel on the left, as Louis had said. He pushed himself, gravel and stones clacking against each other under his feet as he ran under what he'd guess were the gardens and toward the kennels, stables, and garage.

Finally, the tunnel began to slant upward, until he finally emerged in the tight confines of a closet. He pushed at the wall in front of him and it opened, revealing a small shed full of shelves. He burst out of the shed and found himself just beyond the kennels.

A flurry of barks and howls started up. Sebastian didn't stop for the dogs, heading straight for the garage. And then, up ahead, he heard the sound of a powerful engine starting up. He sprinted into the open door of the garage just in time to see Alfred climb into the running H6. "Get out of the car!"

And Sebastian's magic leapt from him, sweeping out through the garage, ready to flatten everything in its path like the rushing tide.

Except Alfred only slammed the car door. "Give up," he snapped. "It makes no difference if you're a paranormal; my curse makes all magic useless against me."

Because Sebastian finally had magic again, but he couldn't stop Alfred from driving. He brought Louis's revolver up, trying to keep it steady. "I don't need magic to shoot."

His voice came out with a waver. Alfred scoffed. "I'll just as happily kill you like this," he said, as he revved the engine.

Then he hit the gas, and the H6 came barreling straight out of the garage. Sebastian threw himself off the drive and into the grass, feeling the rush of wind as the H6 flew by.

Sebastian rolled onto his back and brought the revolver up, tightening his fingers on the trigger.

Wesley's voice whispered in his head, a memory from a ship's deck in the middle of the ocean. *Square your shoulders. Focus on where you want the bullet to go.*

Sebastian took a breath. And then he fired.

The bullet went true, exactly where he wanted it—

Right into the left rear tire of the H6.

There was a loud squealing scrape as the H6 veered to the side. Sebastian fired another shot, aiming for the other tire. This time the bullet went wide, but the H6 was already careering off the drive and across the moor as Alfred struggled to keep control.

Sebastian ran after the car, gun at his side.

The H6 finally spun to a stop, but Alfred was climbing out. "You shit." He had Wesley's revolver in hand and was coming straight for Sebastian. "I see you're simply determined to die."

Sebastian tried to bring the gun up, but Alfred sent him reeling with a vicious shove that sent the gun careening off into the moor. Sebastian tried to dodge the next blow, but the moor was slippery with mud. As he stumbled, Alfred kicked at Sebastian's leg, which crumpled under him so that he hit the ground in a painful heap.

Alfred stepped over him, Wesley's revolver in his hand. "A quick death is more than you deserve." On Alfred's wrist, the golden cuff flashed bright in the gray light. "But at least I can use your death to unlock this relic. And then I'll have all the time I want to curse your paranormal friends and family. Perhaps I'll even curse Lord Fine."

Alfred brought the gun up. "I'm sure your friends are still coming for you. But they're going to be too late. Too bad you didn't shoot me when you had the chance—"

A crack rang out, something zipping between Sebastian and Alfred faster than an angry bee.

Sebastian's eyes widened. Alfred touched the brim of his hat, his finger slipping into the new hole exactly the size of a bullet.

Wesley's voice came from a distance. "Back away from Sebastian."

Sebastian jerked his head toward the sound. Wesley was by the kennel, a new revolver in his hand and aimed directly at Alfred. Behind him, Arthur and Rory were also hurrying across the moor toward them.

"Maybe he won't shoot but I assure you I will," Wesley said darkly. "Gun on the ground. Hands in the air. This is your only warning."

Sebastian held his breath as Alfred's gaze darted from Wesley, to Arthur, to Rory, and then back to Sebastian. And then, finally, after a long moment, Alfred raised his hands and stepped back.

Sebastian's breath left him in a rush of relief. A moment later, Arthur and Rory were grabbing Alfred as Sebastian sat up, just as Wesley came to him.

"Hey," Sebastian said adoringly, with a soft smile.

"Don't try to be cute. You're in so much trouble." Wesley bent down and stuck out his hand to Sebastian. "I told you to wait for me."

"If I'd waited, Valemount would be halfway to the

village by now," Sebastian pointed out, as he let Wesley pull him to his feet. "And *you* got kidnapped when you were supposed to stay in your room with the door locked."

"You're adorable, thinking logic could work on me right now." Despite his words, Wesley's fingers were gentle as he brushed some of the mud off Sebastian's face. "Did you shoot the H6's tire out?"

Sebastian smiled, a little sheepish. "I had a good teacher." He squeezed Wesley's hand. "Are you okay? What happened in the chapel—where did you get another gun—"

"The gun is Geoffrey's," Wesley said. "The others appeared just as I got my legs free. Arthur and Rory did find Mr. Hyde's grave in the graveyard; it seems Alfred and Louis Fairfield used Hyde's death to bind the medallion relic to Louis. The three of us ran across the moor while Geoffrey and Nora stayed behind to get Louis back to the manor and send for a doctor. As for what happened in the chapel before all of that, well…"

He reached for Sebastian's other hand and turned it over. Sebastian's eyes widened; on the inside of his wrist, the tattoo was a brilliant swirl of color that seemed to pulse with life. And *now* the rush of emotion couldn't be held at bay, seeing the bright glow of his magic in his eyes, feeling the familiar stampede rushing in his veins. His magic was really back.

Wesley brushed his thumb over the tattoo, and Sebastian caught his breath, the touch ricocheting across every inch of his body.

"Would you look at that," Wesley said, with a tiny smile. "Maybe sometimes hope does win."

Chapter Twenty-Four

Between the four of them, they had the cuff relic confiscated and Alfred secured just as the police arrived.

"We were called by a Mr. Collins," the head constable said to Wesley. "He said there was an attempted murder today and there's a fresh corpse buried in the Valemount graveyard. What a right mess."

"That's one way to put it," Wesley muttered.

With Alfred loaded into the police lorry, they went back up to the manor. "I will make sure both the medallion and the cuff relics are locked up in my family vaults," Sebastian said, as they walked through the gardens with Arthur and Rory not far behind. "We should check on your cousin and Lady Nora. And we should make sure a doctor arrived for Louis, although I am still angry with him."

Wesley raised an eyebrow. "*You're* angry?"

"He tried to shoot you, Wes, of course I'm—shit."

Without warning, Wesley's knees turned to liquid, sending him stumbling forward.

"Wesley!" Arms quickly came around Wesley from behind, catching him before he hit the ground. "Sorry, sorry," Sebastian said, pulling Wesley upright. "The magic got away from me."

Wesley snorted, the last of the watery sensation leaving his limbs. Perhaps another man would have been annoyed at the realization that he was probably going to fall several times over the next few days, but the thought made Wesley smile. "I think the odds are fairly certain that this won't be the only time you lose control."

"I'll be fine," Sebastian insisted.

"You just said you're still angry."

"I mean, I *am*, but—"

"You're the one who told me it's harder for paranormals to keep control of their magic when emotions are high." Wesley let his fingers brush against Sebastian's wrist, the one with the tattoo. A platonic enough gesture for public, but still letting himself have that touch. "And you *are* a paranormal again. There's no question."

A tiny smile curled on Sebastian's lips. "I guess I am."

"Exactly," said Wesley. "So do you really think you ought to walk into the manor and knock the whole house to their knees?"

"I won't," Sebastian insisted. "It will be fine—oops." He grabbed Wesley by the arm, just barely keeping him on his feet as another rush of magic swept the garden path. "You know what? Maybe I will not go anywhere near Louis. Maybe I will just go up to my room and change into clothes without mud. Alone."

"Good thought," Wesley said, letting his fingers indulge in another quick brush against Sebastian's wrist.

Inside the manor, Wesley found Geoffrey and Nora in the ground-floor library. Nora was pacing and shaking her head. "Uncle Louis is stable and resting." She sighed. "I'm not sure what I'm going to do about him. Or about Father. And I don't have the faintest idea how my sisters are going to handle this when they find out."

Nora and Geoffrey had missed all the magic, so that secret was safe. But Nora and her sisters would certainly have plenty else to deal with. "So you did know, this entire time, that Dr. Wright was really your father?" Wesley asked.

"Of course I did," she said. "But only for a few weeks. I really was in Canada visiting my sister. Father came to me as I was preparing to come home. Said there had been an attempt on his life two years ago, and Uncle Louis was pretending to be the duke so Father could investigate. He asked me to assist with the doctor cover story on the ship home. I was just so happy that he wasn't actually dead; what cause did I have to doubt them?"

"None," Geoffrey said firmly. He was standing rather close to Nora. "I think you've been absolutely admirable throughout the whole ordeal. As brave as Artemis herself."

"Really?" Nora paused in her pacing and eyed Geoffrey. "You know, it's going to be a very trying time, dealing with all of this," she finally said. "Some of my sisters have very strong opinions about reputation. I could use some company I can trust…if you'd like to stay?"

"Oh," Geoffrey said, looking rather surprised. "Yes, actually. I'd be happy to."

A maid stuck her head into the library. "Begging your pardon, Lady Nora, but all four of your sisters have telegrammed. Two of them are already on their way and Lady Euphemia is on the phone now."

"Oh dear." Nora sighed again. "Gentlemen, if you'll excuse me?"

Wesley watched Nora follow the maid out of the library. "I still don't understand why you followed Sebastian to the guest house," he said to Geoffrey. "I mean, you're right that I would have been livid if you had knowingly let Sebastian wander into a house infected with scarlet fever. But since when do you care if I'm cross?"

"Oh, I don't," Geoffrey said. "But Don Sebastian had been such a decent fellow in the art gallery, giving me a chance to talk to Lady Nora. It really would have been poor of me to let him catch scarlet fever. But obviously I couldn't say *that*; Don Sebastian would think I didn't know how to talk to women."

"God forbid he got that impression." Wesley tilted his head, considering Geoffrey. "You know, there was a moment, out on the hunt, where I was worried that you'd been the one to take the shot at me. After all, that would make you Lord Fine now."

"That is incredibly insulting, Wesley," Geoffrey said, sounding genuinely affronted. "We're *family*."

Wesley gave a tiny shrug. "Yes, well—"

"And also," added Geoffrey, still testy, "*I* wouldn't have missed."

Wesley pinched the bridge of his nose.

After Wesley had come to a suitable arrangement with Geoffrey and finally changed out of his muddy hunting coat and cleaned up from the moor, he joined Sebastian, along with Rory and Arthur, in the manor's gardens.

"Geoffrey has agreed to handle everything and keep all of your names out of it," said Wesley.

"Out of the goodness of his heart?" Rory said skeptically.

"Partly," said Wesley. "And partly because I bribed him with the Bentley. I have a second one in Yorkshire that can come to Kensington; today I want to take the H6. After all, I did win it."

"The staff has already put the new rear tire on it." Sebastian had also changed out of his muddy suit. He was still nearly glowing with energy—or more likely, with the magic still storming through him, the stampede of wild horses finally finding their way home. "It's ready to go."

"Shall we get out of here then?" Wesley said. "Sebastian, are you going to attempt some kind of flimsy subterfuge to get the keys?"

But Sebastian immediately shook his head. "Arthur should drive."

They all looked at him, and he flushed. "As Wes has noticed, my magic is a little hard to hang on to right now," he said sheepishly. "Arthur has Rory's magic in his aura that saves him from being knocked down by mine. I don't want to risk an accident myself—or accidentally causing an accident, if Wesley is behind the wheel."

"So your magic is really back?" Arthur asked.

Sebastian held out his wrist, showing a familiar swirl of colors returned to his tattoo. "Yes," he said, and Wesley could hear the happiness in his voice.

Rory squinted at the colors. "No more lion?"

"Oh, he's still there," Wesley said, eyes on the rampant lion hidden in Sebastian's tattoo, always all Wesley's, whatever form he took.

Not long later, they were on the road and heading east. The rain became light snow as they drove, flakes landing on the H6's windshield. By the time they'd made it back to London's outskirts and then into Kensington, it was well into evening. Wesley's footman, Ned, was already coming down the front steps as they pulled the H6 up to the curb.

"My lord." He had a big smile as he opened Wesley's door, seemingly unbothered by the significant amounts of barking clearly coming from next door. "Delighted to see you."

"Why do I hear *two* dogs?" Wesley said suspiciously, as he stepped to the curb.

"Because Lady Pennington got her Maltese, Powerpuff, a friend," Ned said, as he held the door open for Sebastian to exit. "A darling little spaniel. They're playing in the garden."

Sebastian had gone doe-eyed. "That's so sweet."

Wesley sighed. "Just tell me there's dinner."

"Yes sir," said Ned, as Arthur and Rory joined them on the curb. "Your other friends have just arrived, and you've brought Mr. Kenzie, Mr. Brodigan, and Mr. de Leon too? Miss Elsie will be delighted. Mrs. Harrick's made a late dinner; she's showing off her skills tonight."

"My other friends?" Wesley said, blinking.

But as he walked into his home, he realized he could hear Jade's and Zhang's familiar laughter, and new voices he didn't recognize.

"Oh, they've all made it!" Arthur said. "Wesley, come on, you have to meet Gwen and Ellis. If you think you and Sebastian have a complicated past with us, you've got nothing on these two. They adore Sebastian, though, so you'll probably love them."

Wesley huffed a laugh. "Be right there."

Arthur and Rory hurried toward the dining room. Sebastian had disappeared when they got out of the car, probably sneaking in through the basement, which left Wesley alone with his footman. "Ah, Ned." Wesley cleared his throat. "About sleeping arrangements—"

"I'm glad you brought that up, sir," Ned said seriously. "You see, we have a bit of a problem."

"We do?" Wesley braced himself. "What's that?"

"Well, sir," Ned began, "Your friends Miss Robbins and Mr. Zhang have said they're staying with the Taylors, but Mr. Kenzie and Mr. Brodigan will need rooms here. And I'm afraid the basement room isn't available."

Wesley blinked. "Not...available?"

"No sir," Ned said. "The cats are in there."

"The *cats*?"

"Yes sir," said Ned. "And so you see, we're not going to be able to put Mr. Kenzie or Mr. Brodigan down there. I'm afraid they're going to have to share the guest room."

Wesley opened his mouth, then closed it.

"You see the other problem of course, my lord," Ned said. "With Mr. Kenzie and Mr. Brodigan in the guest room, and no basement room, Mr. de Leon is going to have to sleep in your room."

"Oh," Wesley said, and blinked again.

"We've gone over it already, the whole staff, and I'm afraid there's no other solution," Ned said primly. "You'll all just have to share."

A young voice piped up. "You look nice when you smile, sir. You should be happy more."

Wesley looked over to see Miss Elsie beaming at him while holding a fluffy orange-and-white cat. Sebastian appeared behind her, another orange-and-white cat in his arms. It had its tiny paws on his shoulder and was rubbing its face into Sebastian's cheek. No amount of torture would have gotten Wesley to call the sight *cute*, but Sebastian had big sappy eyes for both animals, and even Wesley would admit it was nice to see him so happy.

"What a smart and kind thought," Sebastian said to Elsie, which caused her to go beet red. She set her cat on the table, stammered something back at him, and raced away down the hall.

"I think she still fancies you," Ned said to Sebastian.

"Can't fault her taste," Wesley muttered. Louder, he said, "What is this, a zoo? Cat, get off that table immediately."

"Her name isn't *Cat*, it's Flan." Sebastian held up the cat in his arms. "This one is Crumpet."

"I'm not concerned with their names, I'm concerned with their *presence*." Wesley pointed at Flan. "You're supposed to stay in the basement. Apparently even have your own room down there," he said, keeping a straight face.

Sebastian grinned. He let Crumpet leap down to the floor, and Ned shooed them toward the stairs.

"I should change for dinner," Wesley said.

"If you want," Sebastian said. "We will all understand and wait for you. But I promise no one will care how you're dressed. We're your friends; you can join us exactly as you are."

For fuck's sake. Wesley *was* smiling. "I'm famished," he admitted. "Let's just eat."

Wesley let Sebastian go into the dining room first, following close behind. Sebastian was almost instantly enveloped in hugs from the woman with witch-sight, Gwen Taylor, and her husband, Ellis.

But a moment later, Gwen was turning to Wesley.

"Oh good," she said immediately, holding out a hand. "Your aura is completely intact."

Wesley felt a tension he hadn't realized he was carrying leave him. "It is?"

She was touching the air around him, almost like a doctor examining a patient. "Whatever happened with that wretched pomander relic in October, you're completely healed." She tilted her head. "Although..."

"Although?" Wesley sputtered. "What do you mean, although?"

She shook her head. "Just a funny coincidence." She touched the air, directly over his heart. "There's one spot, right here, where I can't see anything. Not a tear, you understand, just a place that my magic can't see."

Wesley put a hand over his chest. "But what does that mean?" he said, a bit unsteadily. He tried to scoff. "Does it mean I have no heart? You'd hardly be the first to claim that."

Gwen made a thoughtful face. "You could decide that was the reason, if you liked. But there is another possible explanation." She tilted her head. "You see, my magic has never been able to see Sebastian's magic. His mix of Isabel's magic and his own enervation that gives the lion its colors blocks my witch-sight too."

She looked up, and she was smiling. "So perhaps you have no heart. Or perhaps there are still traces of Sebastian's magic blocking mine, because your heart is where it took shelter until it was safe to return to Sebastian."

Christ. Wesley could not possibly let himself think about that—he would have feelings and they would never stop. "I had a letter from Mateo de Leon," he said quickly. "He'd had flashes of visions of Sebastian's magic. He seemed to think it needed to stay away for a reason. And of course it helped us stop the Dukes of Valemount and saved my life. But how did Sebastian's magic know to stay away?"

"I can only speculate, you understand," Gwen said. "But Sebastian used his magic to bind his brother's magic. It might be that, through their connection, a touch of Mateo's foresight lingered in Sebastian's magic."

"Can that happen?" Wesley asked.

Gwen shrugged. "Magic, you know. It's such a hard concept to explain, like friendship. Or love."

Wesley's gaze stole to Sebastian, who was laughing with Arthur and Ellis. "Yes," he said slowly. "I suppose so."

It was surreal—perhaps even *magical*—to have dinner in his own home at a full table, to hear laughter and stories layered over Stella Robbins's record on the gramophone and most of all, to *enjoy* it. Wesley might like his privacy and solitude, and that would never change, but this did have its appeal, having people in his life who felt not like peers, but like *friends*.

Finally, when Jade was hiding yawns and Rory nodding off into his sponge cake, they called it a night, plans being made for the next day. Arthur and Rory had already disappeared into the guest room as Wesley led Sebastian up the stairs. "I can't believe my staff is blaming the cats for you sleeping in my room."

"They want to see you happy," Sebastian said, as they walked down the hall. "Do they put on a big Christmas here?"

Wesley shook his head. "They have their own families. I give all the staff the holiday, so Christmas is just me, and my smokes, and my whiskey."

Sebastian paused outside Wesley's door. "We could stay in England for a bit, and then what would you say to Christmas in Spain?"

Wesley raised his eyebrows.

"It's just a little celebration," Sebastian said, with a hint of a smile. "Two weeks and about thirty de Leons showering you with food and attention."

"Thirty de Leons." Wesley's eyebrow went up. "And how many dogs and cats?"

"*Lots*," Sebastian said, sounding like that was a Christmas present all in itself.

Wesley huffed a half laugh. "And you're certain you want to bring a very male viscount home for Christmas?"

"My family is big and some of them are a bit eccentric," Sebastian said. "There will probably be many guests much stranger than you. And Isa is going to bring Molly; we can say we're Bohemians like them."

"Bohemians? I think I'd rather openly admit I love your cock," Wesley said in horror, which made Sebastian snort. "Brodigan might be jealous if I'm the one who goes to the Mediterranean."

"I was going to invite him too," Sebastian admitted. "And the others. But I promise you can complain about all the people and pets as much as you want."

A real laugh escaped Wesley. "I think I'm offended by how well you know me." He pushed open the door to his room. "Is your entire family paranormal? *Eccentric* paranormals?"

"Pretty much," Sebastian admitted. "It can get pretty wild, as you would say."

Being swept away into Sebastian's wild world of magic—Wesley could think of nothing he wanted more.

"I'll happily follow you to Spain, or anywhere you'd like to go—provided we can start with my room. Right now."

"Does it look different if you're not wearing handcuffs?" Sebastian said, as Wesley grabbed him by the sleeve and tugged him into the bedroom.

Wesley firmly shut the door behind them. "Come here and find out—"

His knees promptly went weak, and he pitched forward, right into Sebastian's arms. "Oops," Sebastian said, too innocently.

"You arsehole," Wesley said, though he could feel himself smiling again. "You did that on purpose, just to show off that you have magic again."

Sebastian grinned. "Maybe," he said. "Or maybe I just—whoops, no, that time actually *was* an accident," he said, as he scrambled to catch Wesley before he hit the floor.

They fell together on Wesley's bed, a tangle of limbs and magic and laughter. Outside the bedroom window, the snow was falling as he rolled Sebastian onto his back. "You can use that magic all you want," Wesley said, crawling over him. "Doesn't change that you like it here, under me—"

His arms and legs gave out, and a startled *oof* left him as he fell flat on top of Sebastian.

"I can use it all I want, hmm?" Sebastian said, pushing Wesley over onto the mattress.

Wesley's limbs were tingly and heavy as lead, his eyes half-lidded with the effort of keeping them open, and the return of the sensation was as welcome as the smile on Sebastian's face. "You think you're so cute."

Sebastian lowered himself so their bodies were

aligned as he stretched out directly on top of Wesley. "I think I have you right where I want you."

"For a moment, perhaps," Wesley said, limbs alight with magic and the bliss of Sebastian's warmth against him. "But you see, I know you too. And I know you don't have enough control of your magic yet to keep this up."

Sebastian narrowed his eyes. "Yes I do."

Wesley scoffed. "Maybe by tomorrow you will. But tonight? Considering the amount of control you need to exert to keep your magic just on me? You really don't."

"I *do*," Sebastian insisted. "I can keep you here, at my mercy, as long as I—shit."

The heavy sensation in Wesley's limbs promptly doubled. There was a clatter somewhere in the house, the sound of dishes falling and someone cursing.

The magic abruptly disappeared, and Wesley instantly rolled them over. "Oh no," Wesley said, deadpan, as he pinned Sebastian to the bed. "What happened, duck? Don't tell me you…lost control of your magic?"

"Don't be smug," Sebastian said, as he squirmed under Wesley.

Wesley pinned him more firmly to the bed. "And which of my staff did you knock down with that little slip?"

Sebastian winced. "I think it was Ned."

Wesley tsked. "And are you going to keep trying to control your magic while my poor staff tries to work?"

"No," Sebastian muttered.

Wesley leaned in, lips close to his ear. "So I guess you're just going to be at *my* mercy now."

Sebastian's eyes seemed to darken, his tongue darting to wet his lips. Wesley settled on top of him, pulling his wrists up to pin them to the mattress on either side of his head. "We are most certainly skipping the handcuffs, though; I'm not quite mad enough to chain either of us up when your control is questionable."

"But however will we entertain ourselves without handcuffs?" Sebastian said wryly.

"Oh, don't worry," Wesley said, leaning in for a kiss. "I keep more than just handcuffs in my nightstand."

"Wait, what?"

Wesley found his lips, slipping his tongue into Sebastian's mouth, kissing him long and slow until Sebastian was soft and pliant under him. When he finally pulled back, Sebastian's cheeks were flushed and his gaze hazy. Wesley shifted to place lingering kisses below his ear and over his throat, keeping his hold on his wrists.

Sebastian's breath was coming faster. "Wes, you can't draw things out tonight; I really will keep losing control of my magic."

A shiver of desire went through Wesley. "I love how you say that as if it could possibly turn me *off*."

Sebastian half laughed, half groaned. "I'm serious."

"So am I." Wesley kissed his jaw. "I changed my mind; my staff will just have to adjust, because I want to see if I can make you send the whole house to the floor by the time I'm done with you."

Sebastian groaned again and turned to catch Wesley's lips in another kiss. Clothes needed to come off, Wesley's hands desperate for warm skin, the endless touch he craved and Sebastian had promised was welcome.

But his gaze was drawn up the bed, where Wesley was still pinning Sebastian's wrists to the mattress as he had only days prior. Except this time, the lion was a bright blaze of color dancing on Sebastian's wrists: Sebastian's magic, which had trusted Wesley enough to show him the lion before they'd even kissed—had trusted Wesley enough to take shelter with him these past weeks. The brilliant colors were like a glimpse inside Sebastian, into the bright, kind heart that had somehow inexplicably decided it wanted Wesley.

Wesley couldn't resist stretching up to press his lips to the tattoo.

Sebastian's inhale echoed around the room. "Still mine," Wesley said, against his wrist.

"Always yours," Sebastian whispered.

I love you so much, Sebastian had said, back at Valemount Hall.

And the realization hit Wesley harder than the magic, and he was finally brave enough to think the word.

He loved Sebastian too.

"Ah." His tongue suddenly seemed too big for his mouth. "Sebastian. We didn't talk about that thing. You remember. That thing you said. Back at Valemount Hall, before the kidnapping bit? The thing?"

"Oh." Sebastian's cheeks colored. "You mean the thing I said after I found out you sabotaged the fox hunt? That thing?"

"Yes," Wesley said. "When you said…the thing."

Sebastian's cheeks were still flushed, but he raised his chin and met Wesley's eyes. "I remember." He swallowed. "You don't have to say it back, not tonight, not ever," he said quickly. "But I meant it."

"Oh." It was Wesley's turn to feel his face heat. "Well. I mean. I, um. I just—that thing you said. Well. Yes. Likewise."

Likewise? *Really?* That was Wesley's big romantic declaration?

But Sebastian had broken into the sweetest smile Wesley might have ever seen. "Okay," he said happily, and then he was kissing Wesley.

Because this was Sebastian, and he understood what Wesley was saying when Wesley was bad at words, and he saw Wesley's heart, and when Wesley had hated everyone, and hated himself most of all, Sebastian had come along and changed everything.

Epilogue

January 1926
San Juan

Wesley stood alone on the tiled rooftop patio, under the awning's shade. In front of him, the ocean stretched out endlessly to the horizon until it met the rich blue of the deepening evening sky. Down below, turquoise waves were rolling up on cream-colored sand, their gentle roaring in his ears, the warm breeze ruffling his hair.

Wesley watched the beach for a long moment, the scent of salt in his breaths. "Well, I'll be damned," he finally muttered. "It really is that color."

"Wes."

He looked over to see Sebastian coming out of the house, a drink in each hand. He looked deeply relaxed, with rolled-up sleeves and the collar of his white linen shirt open to show tanned skin beneath. "Tomorrow is going to be a full day, with the wedding." Sebastian held out one of the glasses. "But tonight we have time for drinks."

In the golden-hued light of a tropical evening, the vivid colors of the magical lion tattoo on his inner wrist nearly glowed. Wesley absently brushed his hand over his own heart, then took the blessedly cold drink. "It's about time Miss Robbins and Mr. Zhang got hitched. It was nice of you to invite everyone here for the wedding."

"It was my pleasure," Sebastian said, with feeling. "All of it."

Wesley sipped his drink, a new flavor as bright on his tongue as liquid sunshine. Mango, perhaps? "Geoffrey sent a cable. Seems both Alfred and Louis Fairfield will stand trial for Hyde's murder, although given they're from a duke's line, I have my doubts on how much justice they'll actually see."

"We have their relics, though, and have found all seven relics now," Sebastian said. "We will keep our eyes on the Valemount line. And not just us: Jade is starting a paranormal ladies' society with Gwen. Maybe they are not *you*," he added, with a teasing smile, "but I would not want to cross them."

"Fair enough," Wesley admitted, with his own rueful smile.

Down below on the beach, a large knot of friends and family had gathered to bask in the tropical evening: Jade and Gwen laughing with Isabel and Molly; Jade's brother, Benson, diving in the waves with Ellis and Zhang; Stella looking particularly glamorous lounging on her beach chair with Benson's family and her girlfriend, Sasha, as Sasha's brother, Pavel, strolled hand-in-hand along the shoreline with Zhang's cousin, Ling. Even Rory's aunt, a Mrs. McIntyre, was there, sharing celebratory drinks with two American tourists and watching with a fond smile as Arthur seemed to be trying to show Rory how to throw an American football, with Mateo patiently waiting to make a catch. Mateo would have to board his ship back to New York the day after tomorrow to make his train to Ohio and back to university, but for the moment he had a broad smile.

"Can your brother see if this is our future?" Wesley said.

"I want it to be," Sebastian said, almost shyly. "Puerto Rico, England, Spain, New York—it doesn't matter where. My favorite place in the world is wherever you are."

Wesley set his drink on the small table and pulled Sebastian into his arms. "Mine too."

Sebastian smiled, and then they were kissing as the ocean rolled endlessly on.

* * * * *

Acknowledgments

So grateful for the incredible people who help these books go from dream to reality:

To C—I could never write a romance hero half as amazing as you;

To my family and friends—I am deeply blessed to have your love and support;

To my readers—thank you for being bright lights in dark times, and for bringing your enthusiasm and joy to these characters;

To my author crew—I don't know how I'd survive publishing without you;

To my brilliant editor, Mackenzie Walton, who can make a book shine;

To my agent, Laura Zats, and to Stephanie Doig and the art, marketing, and production teams at Harlequin;

And to T, my pride and joy, who brings such brilliant sunshine to my life.

About the Author

Allie Therin is the bicultural author of the internationally acclaimed debut series Magic in Manhattan. She also is, or has been, a bookseller, an attorney, a parks & rec assistant, a boom operator, and a barista for one (embarrassing) day. A longtime fan of romance, mystery, and speculative fiction, she now strives to bring that same delight to her readers. Allie grew up in a tiny Pacific Northwest town with more bears than people, although the bears sadly would not practice Spanish with her.

Allie loves to hear from readers! Find all the ways to connect with her at her website, allietherin.com.

In a thrilling alternate-universe Seattle, empaths are disappearing—and it's up to grumpy Reece and his mysterious protector, Grayson, to investigate...

Read on for an excerpt from Liar City *by Allie Therin, the first in her Sugar & Vice series. Liar City is a gritty urban fantasy romance trilogy, with the happily-ever-after coming in book 3.*

Chapter One

The question everyone asks, of course, is what do we know about the empath mutation? We know the correlating empathic abilities threaten our privacy and the sanctity of our minds. We know the empaths cannot be allowed to freely use this empathy, because no amount of so-called pacifism gives them the right to use their abilities to discover emotions we do not consent to share.

But there is a far more important question they ought to be asking: what **don't** *we know about the empaths?*

—C. Stone, *confidential funding memo to the Empath Initiative*

Reece supposed if he'd been a *look on the bright side* kind of empath, he might have had a platitude ready, something pithy about how insomnia's single perk was being awake no matter what time someone called.

But platitudes and perks and so-called *bright sides* were for people who could still lie to themselves, and no one had been able to lie to Reece since March. So when his chirpy ringtone shattered the silence of the diner, he instead jerked in surprise and dropped his cup, which crashed to the Formica table and sent orange juice flooding right off the edge onto his jeans.

He cursed and scrambled out of the booth. Under the hard stare of the lone waitress, he snatched the phone up in gloved hands and fumbled to silence it. Ducking his head so he wouldn't have to meet her suspicious eyes, he squinted at the screen.

Unknown caller.

"Great," he muttered. This was obviously going to be good news, an unknown caller at four a.m. on a Tuesday. He put the phone to his ear. "Who is this?"

"We've never been properly introduced."

The man on the other side of the phone had a deep voice and a sugar-sweet Southern accent, and that was the extent of what Reece could read. Even before March, he'd despised how electronics stripped a voice, replacing a symphony with a cheap music box. Now it grated on him to no end to have to flounder blindly with a stranger. "How did you get this number?"

"Seattle's only got two empaths. I'd wager everyone has your number."

Reece narrowed his eyes. "Not my new one. And that wasn't an answer."

His thigh was already growing cold and sticky. He balanced the phone in the crook of his neck as he grabbed a cheap napkin from the dispenser and scrubbed at his jeans. The napkin shredded against the fabric without soaking up any juice.

There was a noise in the caller's background, a rushing sound, as the man said, "Maybe Detective St. James gave it to me."

Please. Jamey would eat her own badge first. "Maybe you be straight with me or I hang up."

"Aren't you awful prickly for an empath?"

"I don't like phone calls." Were those cars Reece was hearing? A highway, perhaps?

The deep drawl rolled through the phone like a lazy river. "I'm Evan Grayson."

The hairs on the back of Reece's neck rose. He knew that name from somewhere, like the echo of a dream that had vanished in the daylight. "Should I care?"

"You—"

"More importantly: are you driving right now?"

There was a pause.

"I knew it," said Reece. "You shouldn't talk on the phone when you're behind the wheel. It's dangerous for you and everyone else on the road."

"That's not more important than my name."

"Yes it is. Cell phones cause one out of every four car crashes in the US."

"You've got no idea who I am," Grayson said, "and the empath priorities of a Care Bear."

"Just doing my part to keep the streets safer. Somebody should and it's obviously not going to be you." Reece sat back down on the dry side of the booth. He was still being watched by the waitress, but then, she'd had eyes on him since he came in. More specifically, she'd had eyes on his gloves, and it wasn't the stare of someone wanting a phone number from the short, skinny guy covered in juice. He lowered his voice. "So, Evan Grayson, what do you want?"

"Are you sitting down?"

"Dancing, actually. I can't contain my joy that I'm party to your four a.m. reckless endangerment—"

"Tell me you're sitting."

Sittin'. Reece glanced out the droplet-streaked window at the dark street beyond, where a liquor store's neon signs illuminated the flecks of sleet in the falling rain. Even stripped by the phone, the out-of-place accent was a shot of unexpected warmth against the freezing November night, and Reece's defenses were apparently cold traitors because he found himself answering instead of hanging up. "Yes, I'm sitting."

"There's been a murder."

Reece fumbled the phone. He seized it in both hands before it could fall. He clutched it too tightly, clenching his teeth.

Grayson's voice floated up from the speaker, tinny and distant. "Did you drop your phone?"

Reece put it back to his ear. "No," he lied.

"Now you know why you needed to sit. I'm used to empath pacifism. Most of y'all don't even like that word."

Reece took a hard breath. Blew it out. He couldn't make out a single emotion in that drawl and had no idea if he was being mocked. "So why tell me about it?" he said tightly, trying to shove away encroaching thoughts of human cruelty, of pain and suffering beyond his help.

"Because this murder is gonna be the biggest case of Detective St. James' career and she's got nothing."

Reece's stomach dropped. "Nothing?"

"No leads. No theories. No clues. The city's not gonna take her failure well. You might know what an unhappy press is like."

He swallowed hard. He knew exactly how unforgiving the press could be, and the thought that the news might drag Jamey through that same mud—but no, she wasn't a fool who ran her mouth like him, and there was no better person to solve a major crime. "If there's something to find, she'll find it."

"Unless finding it would take an ability she doesn't have. An ability only a handful of folks with delicate ears have. Pretty sure you know where I'm going with this."

"What I *know*," Reece said, free hand balling into a gloved fist, "is that Jamey would call me if she needed an empath."

"For a petty theft? Sure. Grand larceny, even, assuming no one got scratched. But the way I hear it, Detective St. James would take a bullet before she called her precious baby brother to a homicide."

Reece tightened his jaw. "I would help her with anything."

"That's why I called. She's at the Orca's Gate Marina."

And Grayson hung up.

Reece stared at his phone in disbelief, then slapped it down on the table with a huff. He didn't know Evan Grayson from the president. He could be a bully wanting to ridicule the empath aversion to violence. He could be another anti-empathy activist who'd dreamed up a new conspiracy. He could be simply *lying*; thanks to the phone, Reece wouldn't know.

He bit at one gloved thumb and worried it between his teeth. He'd noticed Jamey's car was gone at three a.m. when he'd given up on falling back asleep and gotten off her couch for a drive. But he hadn't thought anything of it. Jamey didn't need much sleep and sometimes she was out at night. It didn't mean she was on a case. It didn't mean Grayson was telling the truth. And it certainly didn't mean his sister could use his help.

He found himself dialing her number anyway.

Four rings, then voicemail. He dropped his phone to the table again and buried his face in his hands, his pulse too loud in his ears. Was he really considering going to the scene of a—

He cut off the thought before the word formed, but he was already on his feet. If there was even a chance Jamey needed him, he would be there.

As he approached the register at the end of the bar counter, the waitress came over with dragging steps and stopped a few feet away. She pointed at his hands. "You never took off your gloves."

His fingers automatically flexed inside the stiff material. "Of course I didn't—"

"I thought you were just cold when you came in. But you're an empath, aren't you?"

Great, another place to cross off his list of insomnia haunts. "I'm also a Pisces, but no one ever asks about that." Under her relentless stare, he reached for his wallet, pointing back to the booth with his other hand. "If you have a rag, I can—"

She recoiled. "How did you know I was pissed about having to clean up?"

"There's juice everywhere, anyone would be—"

"Are you reading my mind?"

"Emotions aren't—"

"I thought the gloves keep us safe from empathy!"

Reece bit his lip, then said, "They do."

He knew it would be a lie before he said it. And sure enough, the sound rang sour in his ears, like hearing himself sing off-key.

The gloves did block his empathy, that part was true, but it would take only a second to yank them off and get bare hands on her bare skin. Only a second for the touch of his hands to shred every mask and expose her true emotions to him, clear as words on a page, whether she wanted to share them or not.

And she was still safe. He'd never read her without consent. No empath would. It was a lie to say the *gloves* kept people safe because what kept people safe was the empaths themselves.

But he wanted to drive the fear from her eyes, so he chose the lie she and the rest of the public needed to believe.

No one knows the gloves can't stop you from hearing those lies now—

Reece quickly shoved the thought away. He put half of his meager cash on the counter, enough to cover the juice, tax, tip and extra for the cleanup. "Sorry about the mess." At least it wasn't another lie.

He pulled his hood over his dark hair as he pushed out the doors of the diner, the bell jingling too brightly behind him as he darted through the sleet to his car.

It was closing on five a.m. by the time Reece arrived at the marina north of the city, and his clothes were still damp with rain and juice despite blasting the heat the entire drive. He slowed his car as he approached the turn-in, his pulse speeding up. There was a police perimeter set up at the entrance, and what looked like most of the force in the parking lot beyond, whirling red and blue lights bright against the night's tenacious darkness. Mixed in with the cruisers was an ambulance, a black Explorer—and the unmarked navy blue Charger the Seattle Police Department had given Jamey.

Reece gritted his teeth. He'd wanted Grayson to be wrong.

He pulled up to the barricade and an officer in a

puffy coat tapped on the driver's window, which was luckily the one that still worked. The previous owner had not been kind to the car, but that's why it had been in Reece's budget. He managed to roll the window halfway down with only a grunt of effort.

The officer shone his flashlight into the car, making Reece's eyes water. "This is a crime scene. You should be in bed, kid."

Cold rain peppered Reece's face as he held up his consultant ID card, a recent gift from the SPD's public relations front man, Liam Lee.

Your big mouth might make me less work if the press knows you're officially part of the team, Liam had said, when he'd created the card for him.

Your big sister is worth putting up with her wreck of a brother, more like, but Reece would grudgingly admit the card came in useful.

"Oh!" The officer glanced at the card, but he was more interested in the gloves. "You're the detective's brother. I've heard about you. Did she call you in?"

"Why else would I have come?" Reece said, because *no* was the wrong answer.

The officer jerked his head toward the chaos beyond. "Go on in. I'll tell her you're here."

Reece drove down to the lot and parked his Smart car next to Jamey's navy blue Charger. He killed the engine but sat in the car, fingers clenched tight around the steering wheel. The tiny space seemed claustrophobic and overheated as he tried to pretend his rapid breaths weren't loud enough to drown out the rain dotting his roof.

This Grayson guy had been right about where Jamey was. Based on the slew of officers on scene, he was likely also right about why. And as much as Reece wanted to turn around and drive anywhere else, Grayson might also be right about Jamey needing his help.

He stared at the whirling red and blue lights as he tried to slow his breathing. The police would let him help, even on a case like this. *Especially* on a case like this. No matter how much buzz the empathy bans were getting, they weren't in place yet, and most law enforcement were still happy to exploit empathy if it got the results they wanted.

A shock of freezing wet air swirled in as the driver's door of his Smart car was yanked open.

"What are you doing here?"

Jamey had found him, her tall figure bundled in a thick coat and a hat tugged over her dark curls. There were stress lines at the corners of her deep brown eyes, but the sight of her was still steadying enough to slow Reece's heart to something close to normal.

He tried for a smile and managed a grimace. "Possibly having a panic attack?"

She huffed and moved to shield his open door from the worst of the rain. "You don't want to be here."

"I really don't."

"How did you find this place?" She wrinkled her nose. "And why do you smell like oranges?"

Ugh, her nose was too good. "I got a call that you needed my help."

She frowned. "Who?"

"Some guy with this outrageous Southern accent. Said his name was Evan Grayson."

Jamey blanched.

Reece's heartbeat promptly rocketed right back up. "Funny," he said, gaze locked on the fear on her face, "he seemed to think I should know his name too. Who—"

"Out of the car." Reece started to twist out of his seat, but Jamey, as always, was faster. She grabbed him by the arm and extracted him with one easy tug. "Let's go."

"Go where?" he asked, as she steered him through the rain and the parking lot, past a barrier set up around a Ford Transit with a smashed headlight and toward a plastic tent stamped *Property of Seattle Police Department*.

"Somewhere I can keep an eye on you."

"Who's Evan Grayson?"

Jamey shook her head. "Not right now," she said. "This is a homicide scene and you're three seconds from a panic attack. We're not talking about Grayson too."

"But how could Grayson make it worse?"

"Not *now*. You're already a mess."

"When am I ever anything else?" he muttered bitterly.

"Stop," she said. "I know better than anyone that your compassion's a strength."

She tugged his arm. He sighed and tried to make his legs move faster.

The tent was at the end of the parking lot, right before the edge of the tarmac and a sharp drop-off to the ocean beyond. Past the tent was an arched sign that read *Orca's Gate Marina*, adorned with a smiling killer whale that seemed inappropriately cheerful, given the circumstances. Beneath the sign, a well-lit wooden ramp led to a collection of pristine yachts and private sailboats moored at the docks.

When they reached the tent, Jamey abruptly paused,

one hand on the plastic flap. "Put your hands in your pockets."

Hide his gloves? He drew back. "Since when do I embarrass you?"

She gave him a funny look. "Since never?"

He folded his arms over his chest, but that had been unfair of him. She'd looked out for him his whole life. Whatever her reason, it would never be shame.

The icy rain dampened his hair as she bent to his eye level. "I know what you think—that if you show you're willing to hide, it will make people more nervous about empaths," she said. "But just this once. Trust me."

He sighed. "You know I do."

She was studying his face. "You were sleeping when I left. I guess that didn't last much longer."

"I look that bad, huh?"

"Don't be a jerk," she said. "I do notice your insomnia."

"Yeah, well, nightmares will do that to you."

"They'll stop soon." Her promise was twisted into discordance and he cringed. Her shoulders dropped an inch. "Sorry," she said. "I wish I really believed that. You used to sleep like a baby."

He blew out a breath. "You used to be able to lie to me. A lot's changed."

She gestured pointedly around the marina. "I would like to have changed you running mindlessly toward anywhere there are people in pain or you think you can help. This is the last place you should be right now."

There was a strained edge to her voice, a tense set to her shoulders. He tried for a lighter tone, even if only for a moment. "Careful with that concern. People will wonder which one of us is the empath."

She made a face. "No they won't. The touchy-feely shtick is your thing, just like I don't call you for a spot at the gym."

"I don't even know what that means."

"Exactly."

As she pushed the plastic tent flap aside, he jammed his hands deep in the pockets of his hoodie and said, "Grayson's name put fear on your face."

She hesitated. "It was—"

"Don't tell me it was my imagination. I'm an empath. It's never my imagination." He kept his gaze on her. "Nothing scares you. Why does Grayson?"

He watched subtle emotions dance across her face as she tried to decide what to tell him. Finally, she said, "Because I think this is his kind of crime."

The hairs on the back of Reece's neck rose. "You're afraid Grayson might be behind this?"

"No." She ducked into the tent, her words barely reaching his ears. "I'm afraid he might show up."

Chapter Two

...while acknowledging SB 1437 would impose the strictest limits on empathy yet, bill sponsor Senator Hathaway said, "We simply cannot have empaths in government jobs. If one can know another's emotions, it would be too easy to manipulate them, and we have only the empaths' word for it that they would never. Our citizens must be able to trust that their elected officials operate with autonomy."

When asked for her response to critics who point out the bill will impact even nonpolitical agencies, Hathaway replied, "To those who call the act fearmongering or overreach, I say it is only the start of the protections we need."

—excerpt from the Emerald City Tribune, *"Proposed bill would limit empath involvement in government, politics"*

Inside the police tent, a space heater ran on a generator, and while it didn't make things warm, it was better than outside. More than a dozen officers were packed into the tent, mostly clustered around a folding table set with cardboard carafes of coffee. Two officers were hunched over a second folding table, concentrating on a laptop.

Several heads turned in Reece and Jamey's direction as they entered, but most saw Jamey and went right back to their business. The few interested looks that persisted were on her, not Reece, and people being interested in Jamey certainly wasn't new.

She pulled Reece against the plastic wall at the far side of the tent, officers shifting to give them a patch of space. "Stay here and keep a low profile until—"

"Low profile?" Reece matched her whisper. "If you need an empath's help—"

"We can't have it." And before Reece could ask why the hell not, she said, "I'm getting you out of Seattle."

Reece's eyes widened. "I think you better tell me who Evan Grayson—"

But she touched a finger to her lips, so he clamped his mouth shut. A moment later, he heard the voice too.

"—of course, of course." A sleepy-eyed police officer, probably in his early thirties like Jamey, was pushing out from the crowd, a phone glued to the side of his face. His gaze zeroed in on Jamey. "Detective St. James would be happy to go back to the yacht—"

"Little busy here, Taylor," said Jamey.

"—and I'm sure she can answer your questions," Officer Taylor said into the phone. "I'm looking for her right now." Taylor covered the phone with one hand and mouthed *please*. "I'll drive the kid home," he whispered, jerking his head toward Reece. "How'd he wander into this mess?"

"I'm *twenty-six*," Reece said. "She's just tall."

"He's my brother," said Jamey.

Taylor's gaze darted between Jamey's light brown

skin and Reece's paleness. "Half brother," Reece clarified, like he usually had to.

Taylor jammed his hand tighter over the phone's speaker. "Your *empath* half brother?" he hissed at Jamey. "*Here?* I am all for it, but if Parson finds out, aren't you gonna get sacked?"

"What?" Reece said sharply.

"I'm trying to get him out of here," Jamey said, ignoring Reece. "If it was up to me, I'd hide all the empaths in the Pacific Northwest."

"What a mess," Taylor bit out. "You know the FBI prick is already asking about the senator's anti-empathy bill? And he's trying to get Stensby to stop working on the list of pulp mills you wanted—"

"No, we *need* that," she said. "The van's tires reeked of sulfur."

"I believe you," Taylor said quietly, "but that prick doesn't because the rest of us can't smell it."

"Maybe the rest of you should—smell harder," Reece interjected, with a quick glance at Jamey. She was usually so careful about hiding things like that. If this case was bad enough to have her slipping up—

Maybe he wouldn't think about that.

There was conflict in Jamey's eyes as she looked from Reece to the wooden ramp that led to the moored yachts. "Fine, I'll talk to Agent Nolan, but quick," she said to Taylor. "*Please* stay with Reece."

"I don't need a babysitter!" Reece snapped, as Taylor flashed her a thumbs-up.

But she'd already disappeared.

Reece sighed. He looked over at his new companion, who was now thumbing through the phone. He opened his mouth, but before he could ask Taylor why Reece showing up could get Jamey fired, his own phone vibrated in his pocket.

With a frown, Reece pulled it out.

Stay where your sister tells you

Don't wander off

Goose bumps broke out over his skin. Like with the call, there was no phone number to see, but it had to be Grayson—Reece could count on one hand the number of people with his new number and have fingers left over.

But why would Grayson send a text like that? Reece was here to help Jamey. Where would he possibly wander off to at a *crime scene*?

He jammed the phone back into his pocket. He glanced at Taylor again, at his open, guileless face. High time *someone* gave him some information tonight. "So." He bit his lip. "Some case, huh?"

"No kidding," Taylor agreed. "Stensby wanted to call you and Jamey shut him down. I thought we weren't going to even talk about bringing an empath here, but I guess the case is crazy enough to make her risk it."

Reece coughed awkwardly. "Guess so."

"Stensby said Jamey won't call you at all anymore if anyone is so much as bruised. The last few months, the rule's been no violence, or else no empath consultant."

Reece tried to shrug it off. "It's been complicated." *Hey, I'm not even lying.*

"Ah." Taylor nodded knowingly. "Girlfriend." At Reece's scoff, he shrugged. "Boyfriend?"

"There's no one," said Reece. "Who wants an empath around?"

"I do," said Taylor, which wasn't a lie and which Reece found reassuring right up until Taylor added, "And none of the officers are going to rat you out for showing up. A senator murdered on a billionaire CEO's yacht—this story's going to be big enough. Can you imagine what the press would say if they knew we'd added an empath to this horror show?"

Horror show. Cold sweat broke out on Reece's brow. He curled his fists tightly in his pocket and tried to focus on Jamey. Grayson had said she needed his help. The dead didn't have feelings; they wouldn't need an empath for those already lost. "Any leads?"

"Just the witness we can't reach."

"Can't reach?"

Pity softened Taylor's eyes. "Hard to talk when you're catatonic."

Oh.

"The theory is he actually saw the killer. But there's no reaching him, unless—" Sudden hope lit Taylor's face. "Is that why you're here?"

Don't wander off, Grayson's text had said.

But this wasn't *wandering off*. Grayson didn't know about the witness—or maybe the witness was how Reece could help. And whoever Grayson was, he didn't get to tell Reece what to do.

Reece adopted the most casual voice he had. "Remind me: where was the witness?"

It was easy enough to ask Taylor to grab him a cup of coffee, then slip out of the tent without anyone noticing. Reece pulled his hood up again against the rain and tried to dodge the worst of the ice-edged puddles as he scurried across the dark parking lot to the ambulance tucked in among the cruisers.

He knocked on the vehicle's door, and an EMT with a blue uniform and bloodshot eyes poked her head out. He held up his hands, making the gloves obvious. "Can I see the witness?"

Relief crossed her face, and she moved to let him enter, warmth washing over him as he climbed the two steps up into the cramped ambulance interior.

His gaze went straight to the middle-aged man on the gurney, propped in a sitting position and wired to unfamiliar machines. The man was staring blankly into space, a small spot of red blooming on the gauze beneath his nose. At least the poor man didn't seem to be in any pain.

"He's still catatonic?" Reece asked, as he pulled his damp hood back.

The EMT nodded. "I thought there was no way we were getting an empath on scene. Who called you in?"

"Detective St. James is my sister." Not actually an answer, but it was good enough to smooth the concern from the EMT's face. He gestured at the man. "Do we know his name?"

"Vincent Braker, marine mechanic who services motors in the dry dock here at the marina. His time card puts him off-shift at eleven. We think he hit the bar down the street then came back for his car."

"People shouldn't do that," Reece said, before he could stop himself. "Drunk driving kills thousands every year."

She shot him an unimpressed look. "Is this really the time?"

He winced. "Sorry." He gestured at himself with gloved hands. "Empath. Sometimes my feelings just kind of come out of my mouth before I can stop them."

"Aren't you guys supposed to be all sweetness and rainbows and pacifism?"

"*Pacifist* and *polite* aren't actually synonyms," he said weakly. "And I'm really sorry he's hurt. What happened to him?"

The EMT ran a finger down her chart. "Well, his blood alcohol level was .07, so that part of the story checks out."

The EMT's forehead was wrinkled, like she was worried about more than Braker's drinking. "What part doesn't check out?" he asked.

She hesitated. "Nothing."

Lie. "It's a little more than nothing, isn't it?"

The EMT startled, her gaze going to his gloves again, and he could have kicked himself. People were jumpy enough with what they knew empaths could do. No one needed to know an empath was walking around capable of *more*.

But then the EMT relaxed. "Of course I can tell *you*. Detective St. James was the one to ask for the tests. She said to keep it private, but if she knew you were coming, she must have intended you to know."

"She must have," Reece said, a little weakly.

"His catecholamines are way above normal." His confusion must have shown on his face, because she clarified, "Adrenal hormones. He's got blood work like I'd expect from the Hulk—well, if the Hulk was catatonic."

Why would Jamey have wanted to test a catatonic man's adrenal hormones? Reece took a seat on the bench opposite Braker and stuck the tip of his gloved thumb between his teeth. "If he's catatonic, what makes everyone think he's a witness?"

"He's the one on the 911 call." He glanced at her, confused again, but she nodded. "On the call, he says he thought he heard screaming, then suddenly starts screaming himself and the call is cut. We were first response and found him curled in a ball on the dock." She gestured at the gurney. "Already gone."

Reece's chest twisted.

"I don't know much about empaths." She snorted. "Guess no one really does, though, right? That's why you have to wear those gloves, why Stone Solutions has all those ads." She mimicked a man's deep voice. *"Stone Solutions, Defending American Minds."*

"I've seen the commercials," Reece said flatly.

"I guess you would have," the EMT said awkwardly. "All I meant was, can you help him?"

"In theory," Reece said.

He hadn't done a read of his own on anyone since March, since the one he emphatically *did not think about*. But empathy might be able to help now, and he'd do it if it could save Braker.

Except getting through Braker's catatonic state would take surgical precision, the kind Reece had never learned. And since March his empathy felt about as controlled as an angry bear on a fraying leash. "Maybe we should call a stronger empath. Cora Falcon, at the Seattle Veterans Medical Complex, is—"

"We tried her already. She's not answering her phone."

He frowned. That was unlike Cora. "Did you try

the hospital? She works first shift, maybe she got there early."

"We tried that too. I know it'd be controversial, getting an empath involved in this murder, but—" The EMT let out a frustrated huff. "Nothing we try helps."

Reece couldn't care about controversy, not when more red was blooming on the gauze beneath Braker's nose. "Why haven't you moved him to the ER?"

"We were about to and then we got the orders."

"Orders?"

"Staff already on-site can care for him but no new doctors." She gestured at Braker again. "And no hospital."

That didn't make sense. "Who could give an order like that? *Why* would you give an order like that?"

"I have no idea," she admitted.

Reece was in no state to use empathy—hadn't been in months. But Braker was in a worse state that he was. "He can't consent to my read," Reece pointed out, but he was already moving to sit on the edge of Braker's gurney. "And evidence obtained with empathy is inadmissible in court. The defense might move for everything he says to be thrown out because an empath woke him up."

"I don't care about legal hypotheticals," she said impatiently. "I care about his life."

Reece did too. He stared at the man's blank eyes, his too-slow blinks. "I don't know if I can help him."

"No reason not to try, though, right? Procedural and privacy issues aside, they said in basic that empathy itself is safe as snuggles."

Reece huffed a half laugh at the ridiculous metaphor. "It is. Empathy can't hurt anyone."

Lie.

He stilled.

Lie?

Reece touched gloved fingers to his lips. How? Lies were *intentional*; the speaker had to believe they were lying. He'd been telling the truth.

"See?" she said. "If it can't hurt, you should try."

"I, uh. Right." He tried to push his confusion to the side. There was a catatonic man who needed help, and there was no part of Reece that actually believed empathy could hurt anyone. "I—"

In his pocket, his phone vibrated again.

Oh no. No, Reece wasn't going to look at that—except he'd snuck away to the ambulance, and his stupid guilty empath conscience was already pulling the phone out of his pocket.

Another text, from an unknown number, and this one made Reece's heart stutter.

Don't touch the witness

Chapter Three

Austin; Phoenix; Los Angeles; San Francisco. Four crime scenes; four dead empaths. Four stories skipped by all news outlets; four police reports redacted to the point of uselessness.
This is some bullshit.
—Detective Briony St. James' personal notes

The wooden dock shifted under Jamey's feet as she strode quickly past rows of rain-slick moored yachts pearlescent against the blackness of the choppy sea.

Reece was right; she rarely felt fear and she wasn't a fan of it now. But she could appreciate the way it put the world in knife-sharp focus. She'd need that focus if even half the rumors about Evan Grayson were true.

If he really was the Dead Man.

Half the force would argue the Dead Man was fake, nothing more than another empathy conspiracy theory. Jamey couldn't blame them. Who believed in shadow agents, rumored to appear anytime crimes involved empaths? It sounded ridiculous.

Except Jamey had followed the rumors since their first whispers, a couple years ago. And now the senator behind the toughest anti-empathy bill ever drafted was dead, and who was on Reece's phone within hours? It didn't matter that Jamey had kept her suspicions out of tonight's reports and run distractions. Grayson was real and Grayson knew about Senator Hathaway's murder and Grayson had *called her brother.*

Ten to one he was already on his way to Seattle, and she had to get Reece out of here.

The yacht with the bodies, *The Bulwark*, loomed up ahead but a man she didn't recognize was coming straight toward her, in his late thirties, perhaps, with brown hair, pale skin, and narrowed eyes. "Detective! A word."

His voice was obnoxiously loud in the thin, cold air. She reluctantly stopped on the dock. "What kind of word, Officer…"

"Agent," he snapped. "Special Agent Nolan. We have a crisis."

"Triple homicide, yes," she agreed. "It's terrible."

"Terrible doesn't cover it, St. James. This isn't some random hobo. This is Senator Hannah Hathaway, dead from fuck knows what, on Cedrick Stone's yacht, in the town where American Minds Intact is headquartered. And not one single hippie at this crime scene seems able to put down the weed long enough to grasp what that means."

Random hobo? She'd definitely found Taylor's FBI prick. "What does weed have to do with anything?"

"I have to assume you and everyone else is smoking it. Why else would you take an officer off the highest-profile murder investigation in years to compile a list of pulp mills?"

The mud caked into the Ford Transit's tires had reeked of sulfur and wet wood, and she didn't have time to waste before following that lead. "I have a sensitive nose. I thought I smelled something."

"What, are you fucking pregnant or something? We have IDs on the two thugs murdered with the senator. They were obviously hired to kill Hathaway and they weren't from any pulp mills. It's a hit, we should be looking for the money trail."

Two bodies had been found with Hathaway. One of them had been a former wrestler and notorious muscle-for-hire with a long rap sheet. His neck had strangulation marks, deep enough to be made by an offensive lineman—but narrow and small, the right size to match a petite sixty-five-year-old senator who would have struggled to carry a full bag of groceries.

Jamey had a hard time believing the answers were going to be as straightforward as a hired hit.

"Who's *we*?" she said, instead of voicing her other thoughts. "The *highest-profile* murder investigation in years should mean FBI agents swarming this yacht like flies, ready for a big jurisdiction fight. Where are the rest of you?"

A muscle in Nolan's jaw twitched. "I don't know."

"You don't *know*?"

"I'm here from DC for a cruise. I know Lieutenant Parson, I got suckered into this because he called me personally. The FBI has a Seattle office; I was told more agents were on their way, but…" He gestured around the yacht.

Rare unease shivered down Jamey's spine. "But they're not here."

"That's not the only problem," Nolan said, his lip curling. "Now there's the security footage."

The marina itself normally ran security cameras throughout the parking lot. Those cameras had been shut off just after midnight, and the marina's staff were clueless as to how it had happened.

But the gas station across the street had a camera that caught the edge of the marina's exit. She'd watched the night's footage twice herself: a partial view, the edges of the bumper and body molding as a red car with wide tires came barreling out of the exit so fast it had fishtailed.

Then, twenty minutes later, thin and bald tires under a green bumper, driving out of the marina at a leisurely pace.

They'd already put out an APB on the second car, which was thought to be Vincent Braker's green Hyundai—although obviously their catatonic witness wasn't the one behind the wheel.

Forensics was still working to identify the make and model of the red car as soon as possible. The driver could be another witness—or in serious trouble.

"What happened to the security footage?"

"You tell me, Detective," he said, lip still curled. "Because all of a sudden, every file we got from the gas station is gone."

"Gone?"

"Technical issues," Nolan said, making air quotes around the words. "Your officers are still trying to recover the files. How hard can it be?"

Files vanishing before they could identify the car or the driver.

How very convenient that FBI agents would fail to show and technical issues block their investigation right when Evan Grayson got involved.

"The mayor called again," Nolan said. "American Minds Intact found out about the murder, and now we have the loudest opponents of empathy in the damn country claiming the senator was killed because of her anti-empathy agenda."

Jamey barely managed not to wince.

"This case is a shit show," he said. "I'd almost expect the Dead Man to show up, if I believed in ghosts."

He strode past her, continuing up the dock toward the tent and the parking lot, disappearing at the top of the ramp.

Ghosts.

Jamey had a folder in her desk at headquarters, kept in the locked lower drawer. It was full of cases she'd been collecting over the past two years. The most recent one was from the summer, another multiple homicide but with an empath among its victims. She'd requested records directly from San Francisco PD. The report had been barely two pages long, with no photos of the crime scene available and the empath's cause of death listed as drugs.

As if anyone who knew an empath would believe that.

There had been no arrests associated with those murders, and despite the shock of multiple deaths, it hadn't made national or even local news. It'd made the anti-empathy blogs, though, gleeful speculation that the mythical Dead Man had appeared to quiet the press and bring everyone to justice.

There were rumors about what Grayson considered justice too, and it didn't involve due process.

Reece needed to be long gone before Grayson got here.

Reece stared at the text on his phone, mind churning.

Don't touch the witness

How the hell did Grayson know what he was doing?

Before he could come up with an answer, his phone went off again.

Get out of there

Run

Reece shot to his feet, nearly dropping his phone with fumbling hands. The EMT was staring at him like he'd lost his mind, which might not be far from the truth. He looked helplessly toward the ambulance door. "I, um, I have to—"

The EMT's expression crumpled. "You're not leaving, are you? Look at him, he needs you."

There was more blood on the gauze under Braker's nose now. "Mr. Braker," the EMT said, pleading eyes on Reece. "We've got someone here to help you."

Was Reece really going to abandon this man to his catatonia because of some texts? Because of some inexplicable lies? No string of words mattered as much as this man's life.

Reece jammed his phone back in his pocket and perched on the edge of the gurney. He shoved down all of his nerves about the read; Braker hadn't given any signs of pain, but even if he did, Reece would take it in and deal with it.

It wouldn't be like March.

"Can you hear me at all, Mr. Braker?" The catatonic man wouldn't see them, but Reece held up his gloved hands anyway. "I'm an empath."

Braker jerked upright and screamed.

Shock sent Reece tumbling off the gurney and crashing to the floor. *"Help him."*

But the EMT was already in motion, elbow-deep in one of the overhead bins.

Reece rolled onto hands and knees and looked up just in time to see her grab a syringe. He flinched, covering his face as she went for Braker's neck.

The screaming stopped.

"Figures the empath isn't a fan of needles." The EMT was loud in the sudden silence. "You can look now."

Reece reluctantly peeked through his fingers. Braker was slumped on the gurney, eyes closed, chest slowly rising and falling. "What did you do?"

"Sedative," she said. "What did *you* do?"

There was a suspicion in her voice that hadn't been there a moment ago. Reece shook his head. "Nothing. I don't understand—"

The ambulance door swung open without a knock or a warning, revealing a tall man with a hard mouth and wide eyes. "I thought I heard screaming—" His gaze landed on Reece and outrage blossomed. "Who the hell let this kid in here?"

"I did, Agent Nolan," the EMT said. "He's an empath."

"Empath?" Nolan's gaze darted to the gloves, then to Reece's face. "How did you find this scene?"

Reece cleared his throat. "It's complicated."

"Oh, it's not complicated," the EMT said, perky and helpful. "He's Detective St. James' brother."

That was the wrong thing to say, Reece instantly knew. Nolan's confusion hardened into anger. "Brother." He moved closer to Reece. "And is there a reason Detective St. James didn't tell the FBI she's got an empath brother?"

Shit. "Why should she?" he said defensively. "She's also got a ficus and too many shoes and I bet she didn't mention those either."

Nolan's lips pressed flat. "Putting aside that I found her brother, not her ficus, cozying up to our only witness, it's because the murder victim is Senator Hathaway."

Shit shit *shit*. Every empath in the country knew who that was, because Senator Hathaway had put forward the harshest anti-empathy bill ever drafted. Cora had railed against it yesterday because it would ban empaths from government work and she'd have to leave the veterans' hospital.

No wonder Reece wasn't supposed to be here.

Nolan's eyes were still narrowed. "I'd like to know what an empath thinks he's doing at the scene of Hathaway's death."

"Trying to *help*," Reece said, ignoring Nolan's eye roll. "I don't care about her job or her agenda. I'd be sorry for anyone this happened to."

"You sorry for that guy too?" Nolan jerked his head at Braker. "And you thought your sister and your bleeding heart gave you the right to trespass on our investigation?"

"He was going to try to bring the witness out of catatonia," said the EMT.

Nolan stilled. "Empaths can do that?" He looked between Braker and Reece, the scorn slipping from his face. "Can *you* do that?"

Reece watched Braker's chest slowly rise and fall. "I don't know."

Nolan jerked his head at Reece's hands. "You still have your gloves on. Did you actually touch him?"

"No," Reece admitted. "But—"

"But nothing," said Nolan. "We need to know what he saw. Get your hands on this guy."

Reece looked at the EMT, but despite her lingering distrust, she nodded. "He's right. You didn't actually try."

Because Braker had *screamed*. Reece hesitated.

"I need to talk to him," Nolan said, as he bent over to examine Braker's face. "He's catatonic, for crying out loud, it's not like you can make him worse—" Nolan froze. "What the hell is that?"

Reece stared, his stomach curdling.

A thin trail of blood, like a tear, was trickling out from the corner of Braker's eye.

Reece staggered up to his feet. The EMT was already at Braker's side, on her radio, but Reece could only stare, disbelieving, at Braker's face.

No.

No, bleeding eyes were things that happened in nightmares, not real life.

Reece moved toward Braker but Nolan grabbed him by the hood, yanking him back. "What's happening to him?" Nolan demanded. "Was it something you did?"

"How could it be?" Reece snapped. "An empath couldn't hurt him if we wanted to!"

Lie.

Reece drew in a sharp breath. "Empathy can't hurt him." *Lie*. "I can't hurt him." *Lie*. His hand went to his mouth.

How was he lying? What the hell part of him could possibly believe that wasn't the truth?

The EMT was shining a light in Braker's eyes and muttering quick words into her headset, calling for backup. Nolan still had Reece's hood in his fist. "If you didn't do it," he said tightly, "can you fix it?"

Reece's gaze stayed fixed on Braker's bleeding eyes. Maybe Reece was the problem. Maybe part of him thought his empathy wasn't controlled enough for catatonia—that he was still too fractured since March.

And if his empathy could somehow hurt this poor man—

He rapidly shook his head *no*. "And don't ask me to try."

Nolan dropped Reece's hood, his hand going to the small of his own back, where Jamey kept her handcuffs. "Listen, kid—"

The EMT shoved between them, scrambling for something in the cabinets. Reece seized his chance. He darted for the stairs and leaped for the door.

If empathy could hurt Braker, Reece was going to put his out of reach.

As Jamey was running up the dock, Taylor was coming down, paper cup in hand. She skidded to a stop. "Who screamed?"

Taylor blinked. "I didn't hear anything."

She strained her ears but the screaming had stopped. There was nothing to hear but officers in the parking lot and the soft lapping of waves against yachts. Taylor was looking at her questioningly. Taylor—and only Taylor. "Where's Reece?"

"I was coming to ask you that." Taylor held up the paper cup. "I got his coffee."

"Coffee." Jamey took a breath through her nose. "Did he ask you to get that for him?"

"Yeah, he did," said Taylor. "And then he disappeared. I looked everywhere, but he's not in the tent, he's not in the parking lot—"

"Tell me you didn't tell him about the witness."

Taylor's eyebrows drew together. "He didn't already know?"

Jamey scrambled past him. Taylor chased at her heels, coffee cup still in his hand. "Jamey—"

Distantly, she heard the ambulance door smack the side of vehicle, sneakers on concrete, and then, most tellingly, the soft purr of a fuel-efficient engine.

And as she crested the top of the ramp and looked to the marina exit, there was nothing left to see but a pair of vanishing Smart car taillights.

And the turn signal. Of course.

She was nearly to her own car when Nolan came tumbling down from the ambulance. "Detective!"

She spun on her heel and met Nolan head-on. "What happened?"

"Your *empath brother*—" He stressed the words. "—fled a crime scene. The EMT says he told Braker he was an empath and our only witness started screaming bloody murder. No pun intended."

Jamey looked to the marina entrance where Reece's car had just disappeared. "He ran from someone who was screaming?"

"No," Nolan said pointedly. "He stuck around until Braker started bleeding from the goddamn *eyeballs*."

Shit.

"He's two seconds away from an arrest," said Nolan.

Jamey tried to push down her concerns enough to

deal with Nolan. "For what? You said he got close. Did he actually touch the witness?"

"Just because there was no contact—"

"No contact means no empathy, no Fifth Amendment violation, and forget assault or battery—empaths are incapable of even self-defense," Jamey said. "All flight, no fight."

Behind her, Taylor was sipping from the coffee as his gaze went back and forth between them.

"Don't worry," said Nolan. "I've got a bone to pick with you too. Did it slip your mind to tell me that one of Seattle's two empaths happens to be your brother?"

"Reece can't help with violent crime."

She turned away but Nolan got back in front of her. "Why the fuck not? Maybe you're sweating your DA throwing a fit, but the empathy laws can be interpreted a little more loosely than you might be used to. Your brother just pulls the witness out from catatonia, then leaves. He doesn't read the witness's emotions, we don't write it down, our evidence stays nice and admissible, see?"

"This isn't about trials and fruit of the poisonous tree," she said, because maybe Nolan was cavalier about bending the law, but she wasn't, and that wasn't the problem anyway. "We have to keep the empaths away from this investigation."

Nolan went a deep shade of red. "You don't have the authority to make that call."

"And *you* don't have the authority to force Reece to use empathy. He's still a person and he's still got rights, no matter how much Senator Hathaway wanted to change that."

Nolan went even deeper red. "So you'd rather let a

murderer run loose in Seattle than inconvenience your brother?" His lip curled. "Don't be surprised when the press quotes me saying you're a disgrace to the force."

On Jamey's priority list, her own reputation fell somewhere below finding jeans with a decent inseam. She'd lost her chance to catch up to Reece by car, so she turned away from Nolan and quickened her steps toward the tent.

Taylor scrambled after her. "For the record," she told him, as she slowed enough he could catch up beside her, "Reece won't touch caffeine." Between the empathy and the anxiety, he said his blood pressure didn't need any help rising. She plucked the half-full coffee out of Taylor' hands and took a long sip. "And you owe me one for losing him."

"Worth it to see you go head-to-head with Agent Jackass."

"Great, because I need a favor." She passed him back the cup. "Off the record." Taylor paused, tilting his head. "Can you get a fake driver's license made in a couple hours?" she said. "A good one?"

"You thinking of doing undercover work?"

"Not for me."

"But then—oh!" he said, understanding flashing on his face. "You thinking of hiding Reece from the empath controversy on this case? Probably a good idea; the press would lose their shit if we had an empath working Hathaway's murder. And, well." He coughed. "Considering what happened the last time Reece talked to the press…"

Ugh, even Taylor knew about that. But while having Reece on the case would be a public relations nightmare in more ways than one, having him on Evan Grayson's radar was worse. "There's a lot to hide him from."

"I'll see what I can do," Taylor promised.

Speaking of the press. Jamey stopped just outside the tent, pulling out her phone and turning to shield the screen as she sent a text. It wasn't strictly against the rules for an SPD detective to date their public relations manager, but it didn't mean they were advertising it to the force.

Did you mean it when you said your dad's charter was mine anytime?

Liam probably wouldn't be able to reply yet—they had a dead senator, his phone was probably ringing off the hook with reporters and politicians and conspiracy theorists—

But his answer came almost instantly.

Always

And despite her worries, Jamey felt the tiniest pang of hope. Maybe she really could put Reece out of Grayson's reach.

A second text came in from Liam: please tell me Reece isn't working this case.

Over my dead body, she sent back.

That would take approximately three SWAT teams, so good enough for me

She snorted. She'd call him in a minute. She sent Reece a text he'd see when he parked, and checked for flights from Seattle to Juneau. There was still a seat on an eleven-thirty direct. Perfect.

She heard the rumble of engines as she bought the ticket, and her gaze went back to the marina's entrance just in time to see the first local news van pull up.

"Circus is starting," Taylor said.

"And there goes Nolan." She pointed to the FBI agent, who was trudging up toward the barrier. "How long 'til he tells them I'm a disgrace to the force?"

Taylor snorted. "Guy's a prick. The same people who freak out over empathy and privacy don't think twice about letting their phones and internet browsers record every detail of their lives. Everyone sane knows empaths can't hurt anyone."

Jamey's gaze stole down to the marina, to the bobbing yacht with its bloody bodies. "Right," she said slowly. "What you said."

Don't miss Liar City *by Allie Therin,*
available wherever books are sold.
www.Harlequin.com

Copyright © 2022 by Allie Therin